# Lost
## Are Found

What is lost to us, is not lost to God. In God, the lost are found.

*A Prairie Heritage, Book 6*

# VIKKI KESTELL

*Faith-Filled*
*Fiction™*

www.faith-filledfiction.com | www.vikkikestell.com

# Lost Are Found

**A Prairie Heritage, Book 6**
©2014 Vikki Kestell
All Rights Reserved
Also Available in eBook Format

## BOOKS BY VIKKI KESTELL

A PRAIRIE HERITAGE
Book 1: *A Rose Blooms Twice*, **free eBook, most online retailers**
Book 3: *Joy on This Mountain*
Book 4: *The Captive Within*
Book 5: *Stolen*
Book 6: *Lost Are Found*
Book 7: *All God's Promises*
Book 8: *The Heart of Joy—A Short Story* (eBook only)

GIRLS FROM THE MOUNTAIN
Book 1: *Tabitha*
Book 2: *Tory*

NANOSTEALTH
Book 1: *Stealthy Steps*
Book 2: *Stealth Power*
Book 3: *Stealth Retribution*

# Lost Are Found

**A Prairie Heritage, Book 6**
by Vikki Kestell
*Also Available in eBook Format from Most Online Retailers*

Joy Thoresen Michaels has lost the two most precious people in her life: her husband and her only child. She cannot receive her husband back from the dead, but she has hope for her son—hope that he will be recovered:

> "I spoke a moment ago about my prairie heritage—the enduring faith my papa and mama lived as an example for me. It is because of their faith that I have such hope for Edmund even though he is, today, lost to us.
>
> "You see, what is lost to us is not—is not—lost to God! I remember Papa saying this very thing: In God, the lost are found. Our Lord sees the entire world—and nothing in all of his creation is hidden to him! I am comforted to know that wherever Edmund is, God is there with him."

Four families bind themselves in a solemn pledge: They vow to never stop searching for Edmund and to never stop trusting that God will restore him to them, whether in this life or the next.

Lost Are Found, the conclusion of this spiritually rich series, chronicles how God answers those who utterly trust in him, no matter the circumstances—and no matter how long the wait.

# DEDICATION

I dedicate this book to those parents
who know the pain of losing a child.
God, our Father, knows your pain.
He lost a child, too.

# ACKNOWLEDGEMENTS

Many thanks to my esteemed proofreaders,
**Cheryl Adkins, Greg McCann,** and **Jan England**.
I am honored to work with
such dedicated and talented individuals.
I love and value each of you.

# TO MY READERS

This book is a work of fiction,
what I term "Faith-Filled Fiction™,"
intended to demonstrate how
people of God should and can respond
to difficult and dangerous situations
with courage and conviction.
The characters and events that appear in this book
are not based on any known persons or historical facts;
the challenges described are, however,
very real, both historically and contemporarily.
I give God all the glory.

# AWESOME GOD

# ℘ROLOGUE

## APRIL 1911

The trees above their heads rustled in a warm breeze; new-green leaves and a scattering of clouds shaded the mourners gathered near the freshly dug grave. Next to the grave, a simple coffin rested upon a stanchion.

Joy stood before the mourners, as tall and with as much decorum as she could muster.

"My husband, Grant Michaels, faithfully served his Savior all the years that I knew him. I don't believe I have ever known a man as devoted to the Lord and his family as he was, unless it was my father, Jan Thoresen.

"To lose Grant . . . *again*, will pain me the rest of my days on this earth, but . . . but you may be surprised to hear that it will not pain me as much as it did four years ago when his ship went down at sea.

"I confess to you that the woman I was when I lost Grant the first time is not the woman I am today. My faith in my heavenly Father has changed in these last years. Grant and I both grew in our faith and, although our love for each other was deep and abiding, our love for our God was greater, as it should be."

She paused and looked off in the distance as though remembering something. "I should say, too, that I have had a good example of how to deal with loss and suffering. I have watched my mother bear with dignity her own grief and loneliness. She has set her heart to live a life of service to the Lord and to others. How can I not but follow her example?"

Joy swallowed and waited until her voice was hers to control again.

"My mother has, several times in the past two years, mentioned something I thought rather curious. She has alluded to her "prairie heritage." I didn't understand her—I didn't realize what it meant. I think now I do.

"Some thirty years ago, during the darkest time in her life, she came west, searching for solace. In a tiny country church out on the prairie, she found Jesus and made him her Lord and Savior, and she found consolation in a simple farming life lived for God.

"Farmers may seem plain and unsophisticated, but the hardships of the prairie require honest work, spines of steel, and faith that cannot be shaken. This is the heritage she found out on the prairie, *this faith that cannot be shaken*, and this is the heritage she and my father passed to me as I was growing up and the heritage I hope to pass on.

"We are here to say goodbye to my beloved husband and to testify how he lived for Christ. We will see him again in the Resurrection. I am confident in this and look forward to That Day. His testimony will live on in all of us—and in our son.

"Which is why, while we are here together, I will also speak of our little boy. My arms long to hold him. I have wept until I have no tears left. I tell you, my heart is broken, but I will also proclaim to you that *my faith is not*.

"Where is Edmund? Where is our baby? I ask this question every hour of every day.

"I do not believe he is . . . dead, but I could be wrong. If I am wrong, then *I know* with certainty that he has merely gone home to join his papa, ahead of the rest of us. I say *home*, because life upon this earth is not our real home, you know. Here we are merely sojourners and pilgrims. We are merely passing through.

"But because I sense in my heart that Edmund *is* alive, I will not forget to pray for him. I have set my heart to remember him in prayer daily and to believe that, even though he is apart from me, *God will make himself known to Edmund* and, on That Day, the day when we see Jesus face-to-face and every injustice is revealed and recompensed, we will see each other again and all this grief will vanish away.

"I spoke a moment ago about my prairie heritage—the enduring faith my papa and mama lived as an example for me. It is because of their faith that I have such hope for Edmund even though he is, today, lost to us.

"You see, what is lost to us is not—*is not*—lost to God! I remember Papa saying this very thing: *In God, the lost are found*. Our Lord sees the entire world—and nothing in all of his creation is hidden to him! I am comforted to know that wherever Edmund is, *God is there with him*.

"How do I feel about the man who took our son? I confess that I am tempted to hate him and to curse him, but . . . I cannot call myself a Christian if I do.

"And so, here and now, I declare that I forgive Dean Morgan for every wrong he has done me. I leave his life and our vindication in God's hands. I believe that the just and righteous God I serve *will make all things right in the end.*

"I will not hate and I will not be afraid; I will not allow my mind's eye to wound me with fearful imaginings. And I will not lose hope.

"This is how I stand before you today; this is how I will live: with faith that cannot be shaken. From now until I draw my last breath, I will believe that, if I cannot hold Edmund in *my* arms, my heavenly Father will hold him in *his* arms—until he brings us all safely home to himself.

"Like my papa, I declare, *that in God, the lost are found.*"

A ripple of *amens* followed Joy as she stepped toward the grave. Tears washing her face, she kissed her hand and placed it on the coffin, letting it linger. Then she straightened and, composing her face, she turned away.

Edmund O'Dell was next to walk to and stand beside the coffin. As he did so, he was remembering the most remarkable conversation of his life.

*My friend, I don't have many months left to me—No, no. Why do you deny this? It serves no good purpose. Nothing can be done to help me, and death comes to us all in due time, doesn't it? My departure will be my entrance into eternal joy, and I am glad beyond measure that you, too, have received the Savior's gift. Someday you and I will meet again, in the glorious presence of God the Father and his Son!*

*Now, because I am dying, Edmund O'Dell, my dearest friend, I must talk plainly: I know you once had feelings for Joy. Please do not protest. I knew this the first time I saw you look at her—while you still thought her a widow.*

*I do not mention this in condemnation! Rather, I say this to one of the most honorable men I have had the privilege of knowing. I have never feared you, Mr. O'Dell, because I know your worthy heart, just as I know that Joy's heart belongs to me. No, you did not dishonor me, and I say this to your credit, realizing the struggle you endured.*

*Why did I write and ask you to come to Denver? Before it is too late, I wish you to make me a solemn promise. I wish you to promise me that when I am gone you will watch over Joy and our son.*

*In time, if it is God's will and when Joy's grief allows her to love again, I hope you will marry her and raise my son—my son to whom I gave your name.*

*I cannot think of any man I would wish to be a father to my son besides you! I say, "if it is God's will," because he will lead and guide you in this. I am content that, if you pray and follow his direction, all will be well.*

*I am asking a difficult thing of you, my friend, I know—but it is so strong in my heart, and I sense death closing in on me. I cannot let what time I have left slip away without speaking to you and asking for your sincere word.*

*Will you give me your word on this?*

O'Dell, too, rested his hand on the casket for a moment. "I will miss you, Grant, and I will miss your example of godly manhood. As long as I live, I will not stop searching for Edmund. When I find him, I will cherish him as my own. I will not relinquish my promises to you."

# $\mathcal{C}$HAPTER 1

*And all these,*
*having obtained a good testimony through faith,*
*did not receive the promise,*
*God having provided something better for us,*
*that they should not be made perfect apart from us.*
*(Hebrews 11:39, 40, NKJV)*

*The Lord is not slack concerning his promise,*
*as some men count slackness;*
*but is longsuffering to us-ward,*
*not willing that any should perish,*
*but that all should come to repentance.*
*(2 Peter 3:9, KJV)*

We live in a fallen, sinful, unjust world that will one day come to a fiery end. To put it plainly, life can be hard and filled with unanswered questions—even for those with faith.

We will not see perfect justice on earth before and until The Righteous Judge returns. But we can *know* The Righteous Judge who will make all things right when he returns.

*We can know him now . . . and knowing him makes all the difference.*
—Vikki

## FALL 1990

Kari Hillyer perched on the very edge of their bed, still and watchful, trying hard to keep her weary back straight and rigid. Her hair, a soft brown shot with a thread of gold, hung down that weary back all the way to her waist.

She made an effort to ignore the wisp tickling her cheek, but she was tired.

So tired.

*Every man in my life has either left or betrayed me*, she brooded. *And, guess what? Today isn't any different.*

Then she blinked as she realized that she wasn't as crushed as she'd thought she'd be . . . right now, as her husband announced that he was discarding her.

*I've already been crushed to the bone over the last seven years.* This she knew.

"Kari, pay attention; this is pretty important." David Hillyer's temper, never far from the surface, was heating. "This *is* our marriage I'm talking about."

He rubbed his eyes with forefinger and thumb as though destroying her was, after all, *very* hard work.

"I'm listening," Kari whispered. She did not look at him although David usually demanded direct eye contact when he was "communicating" with her. She tucked the offending curl behind her ear and made another effort to straighten her posture.

"What I said was that I will take the house. You can't afford the mortgage payments on what you'll be making, so it seems best to me that I keep it." He shrugged. "I've paid for it, after all."

He paid for the house?

*Their home?*

Kari's thoughts flew over the years they'd lived in the rambling stucco house nestled in the foothills of Albuquerque's Sandia Mountains. Feeling like a stranger peeping through a window at someone else's life, she dispassionately weighed David's statement against the many bright promises he had made when they had first seen this house.

"We'll turn this place into a showcase, Kari. You just wait and see!" he'd boasted. "Ample money and some dedicated effort should do the trick."

But how had he expected "a showcase" to magically appear when he was never available to do any of the work? Or when he had argued against and refused to let her spend any money on repairs or upgrades? In fact, David hadn't allowed her to buy anything without his permission in years.

She recalled the hopes she'd nourished, the yard she'd painstakingly landscaped herself, and the walls she'd textured, painted, or papered—all on the stringent budget that only David controlled.

*Just like he controls me.*

Despite David's iron hand on their bank account, Kari had found ways to make their home a place of simple beauty: She'd forgone buying clothes for herself to eke out a few dollars for wallpaper, and she'd trimmed her own hair, spending money she could have spent with a beautician on house paint instead.

And she'd reveled in the joys of everyday tasks—the carpets she'd vacuumed, bathrooms she'd cleaned, and countless meals she'd fixed— *because it was their home.* The first real home she'd ever known.

Now *their home* was nothing more than another dream dashed to dust. Just one more disappointment in a long line of the same.

She sighed over the necessity of giving it all up, of relinquishing her fragile hopes . . . this time for good. Kari looked up from where she sat on the edge of their bed.

"No." It was all she could muster.

David frowned. "What do you mean, 'no'?"

She forced herself to face him directly. "I mean . . . no, you won't be able to keep the house either, David."

David's face tightened. "What the devil does that mean?"

"Well, it means . . . New Mexico being a community property state . . . we will need to sell the house and split the equity."

Kari figured she wouldn't have to wait much longer—she'd provided the spark, and David's temper would ignite momentarily. But not quite yet. No, she pretty well knew what had to play out first. She shivered a little, foreseeing what was coming.

"And I . . . I'll need some money to start over."

Oh, *why* had she added that? How she hated sounding so—so *weak* and dependent. *Pathetic!*

"Kari." David gentled his voice. In the manner of a parent patiently explaining a great disappointment to his child, he shook his head, even managing to look regretful.

"Kari, this might be difficult for you to hear right now, but do you recall the prenuptial agreement we signed? We discussed this quite painstakingly before we married, do you remember? The agreement stipulates that if we divorced within ten years, whatever each of us contributed financially to the marriage would determine how the property was divided."

Kari's memory was working perfectly. She'd left her job as a librarian at The University of New Mexico—where David taught and they had met—less than a year after their wedding, right after they had bought this house. David had insisted that she make a home for them—and for the babies they'd be having soon.

Except, of course, David had changed his mind about the babies.

"Just let me get a bit more put aside before we try to have a baby, okay?" was how his change of heart had started.

Then it was, "If I'm appointed Department Chair, they'll expect me to put in a lot more hours the first semester. It won't be a good time to be worrying about a pregnancy."

The coveted position at UNM had come through, and the first semester had turned into a year and then the year into three years before he'd "confessed" that he'd never thought of himself as "good parenting material."

The dreams had started dying then. Now, at thirty-eight years of age, Kari had to admit to herself that she was too old to find someone new and have children. She had to face the harsh truth that her hopes of having a family and a home—*a real, enduring home*—were over.

Done.

Shattered.

She would be alone soon.

Again.

*What a fool I've been. I never should have quit my job!*

Kari sat staring at her husband and, as much as she knew she needed to harden her heart toward him, she couldn't help but see him right then as she had when they'd first met and married. Tall and wonderfully good looking, David could glance at her, and Kari would heat inside with longing.

*We were a striking couple once,* she reminded herself. She was tall and slender and, against his chest, the long strands of her light brown hair had shimmered with golden highlights, the perfect complement to his darker looks.

*He was everything I needed! Everything I wanted!* she mourned. *We were going to have a good life together!*

Especially after her disastrous first marriage.

Both David and Kari had been married previously. Kari's first husband had been mysteriously unable to stay employed, and they'd struggled for three years until she'd stumbled on the evidence of his many lies and his longstanding drug problem.

According to David, *his* first wife had been blatantly and shamelessly unfaithful, something he declared he would never again tolerate—which was what had prompted his insistence on a prenuptial agreement.

Kari had understood his reasoning at the time, *especially the adultery clause*. But now . . .

"Yes, David, I remember," she answered softly.

"Well, then. My lawyer can work out the numbers. You're entitled to a small percentage of the equity—not a lot, since you didn't contribute much—and I'll cash you out, but I don't plan on selling this house. Not now that we have it fixed up right."

*We? We have it fixed up right?* Kari swallowed down the anger churning in her stomach.

David lifted his right hand, one finger pointing upwards—a gesture that signaled that he had already moved on to another, more important topic and was impatient to drop the present one. It was the same gesture he used to manage discussion in his classes or departmental meetings.

*I didn't contribute much? I quit my job to make a home for us! I turned this drab shell of a house into a place of beauty and comfort! I cooked and cleaned! I—*

Kari took a calming breath; she couldn't go there—and she didn't need to. She squared her shoulders, unconscious of doing so.

"David, do you remember the adultery clause in the prenuptial agreement?"

*Ah.*

She noted the color leave his face and saw his jaw clench, followed by a hasty attempt to cover his shock.

"Come on, Kari, I think I know you better than that," he bluffed. "You'd be the last person in the world to commit adultery."

He laughed a little to cover his unease, but his right hand was hanging uncharacteristically still at his side. His 'tell.' "So, what? Are you about to confess some torrid affair to me?"

"No," Kari murmured. "I'm about to confront you with yours."

They stared at each other for a long, charged moment. Kari willed herself not to look away first.

Finally, David snorted in derision. "Yeah, right."

He started to turn away but whirled back, the anger she'd anticipated barely in check. "As usual, you're being totally ridiculous—and it won't work, Kari. My God! I should have left you last year."

"You mean last year when you were having an affair with Jules Rivera? Or last year when you dropped her to seduce Gil Trask's wife?"

David mouth twisted and he shook his head viciously. "Oh, no, Kari. This won't work on me." He jabbed his finger close to her face. "I won't listen to you slander me like this. And if you talk this kind of trash to anyone outside of this room, you'll live to regret it." He turned away and moved toward the door.

"You know, I'm not concerned with Jules Rivera or Molly Trask anymore," Kari replied, her words contemptuous. "Beth Housden is your current 'flame,' isn't she?"

Kari took advantage of David's facing away from her to stand, her legs wobbling, and edge away.

But when he spun back, instead of hurling the filthy insults she'd expected, he studied her hard for several thundering beats of her heart.

"I don't know how you concocted these interesting stories, Kari, but your strategy is ingenious. Too bad for you that your accusations are baseless. Not that you would have benefited from that morality clause even if you could prove your lies. I believe I had my attorney write the clause to apply only to unfaithfulness on *the wife's* part."

"My attorney believes it can be enforced on either party." Kari was breathing hard now.

"*Your* attorney?" She'd surprised David again.

"Yes. The one I retained three months ago—when I found you'd sold off 850 shares of our stock. At $67 a share, that was a nice little chunk of change."

"I reinvested the money elsewhere," he retorted, but his gaze wavered.

"Oh, yes. I know. A sapphire and diamond necklace—from an estate sale through Beauchamp and Company—was part of your 'reinvestment,' I believe." Kari sniffed, her derision out in the open now.

She was ready when the flat of his palm connected with her face. She even managed to stay standing despite the ringing in her ears.

"You—!" He cursed her vilely, ending with, "I promise you'll get *nothing* from me, do you hear me? *Nothing.*" His face was suffused with anger and he spat the last word.

"Well, I don't need anything *from* you," Kari hissed, "because this house, everything in it, your investments, and even your retirement are *mine*, thanks to your own actions and your tidy little *morality* clause. My attorney says I can take it all—*everything*—and walk away from you, shaking your dirt off my feet on the way out the door."

David laughed, his mirth ragged. Harsh. "This is great, Kari. You're playing the part very well. It'll be interesting to watch you try to pull this off. Not only will you be unable to prove any of this, but I'll countersue and keep you in court so long that, even if your lawyer works on contingency, he'll give you up long before it's over. I'll empty the checking account and cut you off from the credit cards before the bank closes today. You won't even have grocery money by the end of the week."

Kari, her breathing uneven, didn't answer. She walked on shaky legs to her dresser, pulled open the top drawer, and removed a thick manila folder.

"These are all copies. The originals are with my lawyer. The investigator I hired in December of last year is very good and very thorough. Even the photo quality is good, don't you think?" She spread the folder's contents on the bed.

David gaped at color eight-by-tens of himself and Beth Housden— outside her apartment door, inside his car, seated in several restaurants: kissing, petting, smirking. In several photos Beth wore a very nice sapphire and diamond necklace. From Beauchamp and Company.

Kari was panting and growing light-headed. She edged toward the door of their bedroom. "I told my lawyer that we would take it easy on you, that I just wanted out with my fair share. I still feel that way, but I can be persuaded to change my mind."

David's dark, smoldering eyes burned her.

"By the way," she added, "I paid my lawyer a $10,000 retainer. Maybe a *little* over the top, but you never can tell how long these things will drag out—*right*?

"How did I pay him? I cashed in a few of 'your' CDs. *All of them, actually.* And did you know? There's quite a penalty when you cash them out before maturity! I opened my own account at the credit union with the remaining money. Just in case you wanted to play hard ball."

She reached for the door jamb to steady herself. "Oh, right. And my lawyer has already moved to freeze all of your other assets including the *joint* bank accounts and your retirement. You can't sell any more of your stock now, my darling, and I doubt if Beth Housden will want you long after she sees what you're left with."

Kari was struggling to suck in air and, despite her determination, tiny black spots danced before her eyes. *O God, I'm panicking. No, please! I can't! Not here! Stop it. STOP IT RIGHT NOW!*

She forced herself to keep breathing even as her vision darkened around the edges. "One teensy thing more, David. My lawyer will have this lovely bruise on my cheek photographed tomorrow morning when it's looking its very best. I'm sure the judge will want to see it when I request a restraining order against you."

She hugged the bedroom door, gutting out her anxiety attack. "And now I would like you to leave. I'll be living here until the divorce is final and the house sells. I want you, your clothes, and your personal items out. *Now.*"

David swore violently and bore down on her, fists lifted to strike. He jerked back when a short, stocky man with silvering hair appeared behind Kari in the bedroom doorway.

"Who the devil are you?" David demanded.

The man nudged Kari aside and nodded at the folder on the bed. "Anthony Esquibel, private investigator. I see you've been admiring my work."

He pulled an Asp—a short, telescoping baton—from his back pocket and, with a flick of his wrist, extended it. "I believe you've been asked to leave. I'll give you ten minutes to get your clothes together and make your exit—during which time you will mind that foul mouth of yours."

David gaped at him and Esquibel slapped the baton once on the door to get his attention. "Listen up. Kari's gonna have around-the-clock security here until the restraining order is in place and all the locks are changed. Any questions?" He glanced at his watch. "No? The clock has nine minutes and twenty seconds on it."

David didn't move.

Esquibel whipped the baton against the doorframe, splintering its wood with a resounding crack. "Nine minutes, fifteen seconds."

"Son of a—!" David screamed.

"Yes, you are. Now, get moving. With or without your clothes you *will* be out in another . . . eight minutes and fifty-five seconds."

Kari's soon-to-be ex-husband left the house with five seconds to spare. She sank down on the living room couch feeling emptier than she could ever recall feeling.

"You okay?" Esquibel asked quietly.

"Thanks to you."

"How 'bout some ice for your cheek? That eye looks a bit puffy."

"Yeah, well, don't we want it to look really ripe for the picture tomorrow?"

"I don't think ice will detract from its photogenic quality."

"That good, huh?" Kari leaned her head back against the cushions.

"Believe me, I've seen worse." Esquibel wandered through the living room and back. He hesitated and then asked, "Kari, has David ever really . . . I mean *really* hit you before? Like, beat on you repeatedly? Have you had any broken bones, been to the E.R.?

"I probably should have gone once or twice, but I got over it." She crossed her arms and rubbed them.

"Look, you hired me to do a job for you, I get that, but some of my clients kinda grow into friends. I start to care for them. A few of them have gone through worse than this; some of them less, but they all feel the same after it's over. Pretty much like, well, *poop*, if you get me."

"Yeah?" Kari laughed at his reticence, but she felt resentment simmering in her gut. "Like I said. I'll get over it."

"Uh-huh. Well, see? That's the deceptive part of this. They *didn't* just 'get over it'. Which is why, *mija*, you being one of those clients I consider a friend, like I just mentioned, I want to make a very strong suggestion to you." Esquibel reached into his shirt pocket and retrieved a card. "Take this."

"What? A social worker? A shrink?" Kari's anger was burning hotter and, as much as Anthony didn't deserve it, he was going to be on the receiving end of it shortly.

"Nah. This woman is another friend of mine. She has sort of a gift for helping women put the blame where it belongs and get back on track again after something like this."

He sat down across from Kari and gently took her hand, placing the card in her palm. "I think you've just done the bravest, most difficult thing you've ever had to do in your life, and you've done it with strength and dignity."

When she didn't respond, he insisted, "Kari, look at me for just a second." Kari might have believed she was masking her feelings, but he'd seen them too many times to be fooled.

"The past few months have been . . . difficult, but in the next few days and weeks you're going to go through something far worse."

Her face twisted. "Are you kidding me? How can anything be worse than," she gestured haphazardly, "than all this?"

"It will be worse because now you have deal with the future, with *who you are* after all *this*. Please trust me on that count." He closed her hand over the card. "I'm going to tell this woman that you'll be calling her. If she doesn't hear from you, I'm going to give her your number. Are you okay with that? Kari?"

The doorbell rang.

Esquibel sighed. "That'll be Gabe. He'll be here, in the house, until seven in the morning. Peter will relieve him and will be changing out the locks. I'll be by to escort you to Baldonado's office at ten. We should have the restraining order in place by tomorrow evening." Esquibel tipped her chin toward him, and she grimaced.

"Always a dad at heart, right?" she quipped. Then she crumbled.

Esquibel let her sob on his shoulder. "Yeah, that's me. Always *el papá*. And like a good *papa*, I don't like *matónes* beating up on my girls. Let's see if we can put this behind you, okay, Kari? Let me help?"

Kari only cried briefly. She'd wept so much in the past six months that her crying jags were short, over in a few minutes. "Okay," she sniffed, yet she doubted if any of this would ever be "behind her."

"Right. Let's let Gabe in and get you buttoned down for the evening. Don't forget—we have a car to buy for you this week, too. You must be able to get around."

Kari only nodded.

"Hey, Babe." Esquibel kissed his wife before wearily dropping into his La-Z-Boy.

"Is she all right, Antonio? Did everything go okay?" Gloria Esquibel used the remote to mute the television.

"Y'know, I recognize that this is only supposed to be a job, but after a night like this, I'm really tempted to go back to the firehouse."

"Sure you are. At your age? And after all the months we've prayed this through? You're just exhausted. Did she do well tonight?"

"She did great. Probably the first time she's ever gotten the best of that . . . *Ay!* The more I deal with low-lifes, the harder it is to keep my mouth clean." He raised his right hand to heaven. "God, please help me, I'm asking you."

"Well, if you get out of line, I can always run a bar of Dial soap around in your mouth—isn't that what your mama—God rest her!—used to do to you boys?"

Esquibel grinned. "She certainly did. The summer I was fifteen she must have shoved this one bar of soap into my mouth a dozen times. And not open my mouth when she told me to? Oh, my! I would never have dreamed of refusing such an order.

"I believed that God's lightning would strike me dead if I so much as raised my voice to her. But for some reason, as soon as I was out of her presence, I would go right back to swearing—until spitting soapsuds got real old."

He frowned. "And I don't know *how* she always knew!"

"Your mama raised good boys. Fine men," Gloria answered. "So did you give Ruth's card to Kari?"

"Yeah. I'll let Ruth know to expect her call."

"Then let me get you some dinner, *Corazón*. Your sister and I made *tamales* today. You will feel better after a good meal. Then we will pray for Kari, and God will continue to move on her behalf. Hasn't he already? And he says that if he begins a good work, he will see it through to the end, no?"

Esquibel took her hand and pressed it to his lips as she got to her feet. "Ah, how I love you, old woman. You will always be my jewel, Gloria."

"Who are you calling old, *abuelo*?"

Esquibel grinned. He was feeling better already.

# CHAPTER 2

With Anthony's help, Kari stumbled through the next few weeks in a dazed stupor, scarcely conscious of what she was doing or what went on around her. When she came to herself one morning, a plain used car—a white, late-model Reliant—sat in her driveway, and she had new locks on her doors, a restraining order against David, and a court date to commence divorce proceedings.

She also had an appointment to meet with Ruth Graff.

Kari stared at herself in the bathroom mirror. Instead of her daily hikes in the foothills above their house, she'd holed up, spending hours dwelling on her pain, only leaving the security of her home when necessity forced her.

Now the image reflected by the mirror was disheveled. She couldn't remember when she'd last showered and washed her hair. Her usually bouncy locks hung in lank strings. Her eyes were ringed with shadows. And she'd lost more weight.

She studied her protruding ribs with distaste. *You look like a third-world refugee, Kari. Disgusting.*

She sighed and turned her attention to the appointment card in her hand: Thursday, 4 p.m. *That would be today.*

She had, with reluctance, agreed to meet with Anthony's friend, Ruth, and Anthony had said he would make the appointment for her. He'd stopped by yesterday and pressed the card into her palm.

"Promise me you will go," he'd urged in his fatherly manner. And Kari had promised.

She sighed again, then turned the shower on, stripped off her filthy clothes, and stepped into the welcoming heat.

"Hi, Kari; I'm Ruth."

Kari stared at the hand extended toward her. The therapist or counselor or whatever she called herself was maybe in her late fifties, plump and pleasingly rounded. Her shock of silver-streaked hair was tied in a loose ponytail and she grinned, her black eyes crinkling and her cheeks dimpling as her mouth curved.

Her greeting didn't come off, Kari decided, as one of those false, put-on things, but as a pleasant, authentic welcome.

22

Kari took Ruth's hand and the woman drew her toward a chair. "Here—sit here. It's the best chair in the place. What do you think of that view? Lovely, isn't it?"

Kari glanced where Ruth pointed: The window framed Sandia Crest, and the late afternoon sun was painting the mountain a brilliant magenta.

"It's perfect," Kari admitted, sinking into the offered chair. *Like the view out our back door.*

"Things of beauty help us realize that life isn't over," Ruth murmured, "even when life has beaten us up pretty good."

Kari looked up and Ruth's smile had faded. In its place was calm compassion and acceptance.

"Us? Has life beaten *you* up 'pretty good'?" Kari couldn't help the sarcasm that crept into her words.

"Oh, yes. I spent two weeks in the hospital the last time my ex-husband beat me up. And that was just the *last* time he beat me."

She pointed to the left side of her head. "That was fifteen years ago, but I still wear my hair in a ponytail or chignon to hide a bald patch I have right here. My husband hit me with a bottle—six times, I think—cutting up a couple of inches of scalp. The ponytail covers the spot where my hair wouldn't grow back.

"The doctors say it's possible that I lost that piece of scalp when he beat my head against the window until it shattered, but I don't remember any of that. The next thing I knew was when I woke up in the hospital a couple of days later."

Kari stared in horror as the older woman delivered those lines without self-pity or anger. She didn't know what to say in response.

Ruth took a seat opposite Kari and filled in the silence. "Kari, you've just come through some similar difficulties, I believe. I want you to know that I am here to listen to you and to accept you just as you are as you work through the aftermath."

"The aftermath? It's over now."

"Yes, but . . . abuse, whether it is verbal or physical, has well-documented aftereffects. We can talk about abuse and how it affects a person so that you will be able to recognize those feelings if you have them."

Ruth's mouth smiled although her eyes did not. "I've experienced the aftermath of abuse myself, so I'm not likely to spout senseless platitudes about something I'm unfamiliar with. I just want you to know, first of all, that you are not alone."

Kari's mouth twisted. *Not alone? Right. I've been alone my whole life.*

But Ruth either didn't see her reaction or chose not to respond to it. She just kept chatting, occasionally asking for simple responses from Kari. An hour later, Kari realized that she and Ruth had covered a lot of ground.

"So, what do you think, Kari? Can we do this again?" Ruth asked, flashing that engaging, eye-crinkling grin.

Kari shrugged. She didn't want to admit it, but she did feel a little better, a little less isolated. "All right."

"Well, I'm glad. And I've enjoyed getting to know you a bit. How about next week at the same time?"

Kari nodded; Ruth scribbled on and then handed her another appointment card. Then Ruth sat back and studied Kari.

She saw a tall woman in her late thirties—a little thin for her height—unaware of how striking she was and unconscious of her appeal. Even in jeans, wrinkled t-shirt, and scuffed ropers, her honey-colored hair hanging free down her back, Kari Hillyer was oblivious to the effect she had on others—particularly the effect her eyes had. They were a startling blue, a deep, penetrating blue. But her eyes were also haunted. Damaged.

*She is broken,* Ruth observed. *And not, I wager, by only this failed marriage and her husband's abuse and infidelity. Something much more . . . elemental has been wounded.*

"Kari, I'm a counselor, and I specialize in helping battered women, but I want to be up-front with you about my counseling approach."

Kari looked at Ruth with suspicion. "Which is?"

"The thing is, I'm a counselor, but I'm also a Christian. I don't separate my faith from my function as a counselor because I believe that many of our struggles are spiritual in nature and can be addressed from a spiritual perspective.

"When I observe a spiritual truth during a session, I will present it to you. You are free to listen and think about it or you are free to tell me to go fly a kite—I will never, of course, try to cram my faith down your throat. Please *do* tell me to go fly a kite if ever I come on too strong."

Kari turned Ruth's words over in her mind, recalling her first year in foster care. *Maybe at one time I believed that God was good and that Jesus loved me,* she reflected, *because I have memories of praying . . .*

*I remember begging God to bring Daddy and Mommy back. I remember crying and pleading with God to rescue me from the awful loneliness. After a while when God didn't answer my prayers, I asked him to just kill me so that I could go wherever Daddy and Mommy were. He didn't answer that prayer, either.*

Kari closed her eyes. *I don't know where my childhood belief in God came from, but all those unanswered prayers—and the hopelessness of my messy life—have taught me the futility of religion.*

Ruth leaned forward. "Kari, I want you to know, ahead of time, that I will frequently bring spiritual facets into our conversations. Can you accept that?"

"I suppose. But you'd better be prepared to fly a lot of kites," Kari sniffed. She kept her thoughts on God to herself.

Ruth chuckled. "Fair enough. Until next week then."

As Kari stood, Ruth reached out her hand again. When Kari took it, Ruth gently tugged her into a light embrace.

Kari was surprised and a little flustered, but Ruth just squeezed her and gave her back a few light pats. "It's going to be all right, Kari," Ruth whispered.

It was as though an artery burst somewhere deep in Kari's heart, spurting grief and hopelessness. Without intending to, she found herself sobbing on Ruth's shoulder.

Ruth gently rubbed Kari's back while she cried and, once, smoothed her hair. "Don't you worry, Kari," she murmured. "God will get you through this and get you to a better place. I know he will."

At the mention of God Kari's tears dried up as though a spigot had been cranked off.

*God? God will get me through this?* Kari frowned. *If he's so "great" and so "almighty," isn't all this his fault in the first place?*

Kari met with Ruth regularly over the following weeks. The most valuable thing Kari began to recognize during their sessions had to do with *why*—why she had, not once but *twice*, chosen poor marriage partners, and *why* she had tolerated their lies, infidelities, and abuse as long as she had.

"It seems that your 'picker' is broken, Kari, and so you choose the wrong type of spouse. Why don't you tell me about your family, and we'll try to figure out why you do that?" Ruth asked during their third session.

"My family?" Kari shivered.

"Yes; tell me about your parents, growing up, siblings, and so on," Ruth coaxed.

"Well, my parents died when I was six," Kari answered, "and I have no siblings." A familiar stab of pain accompanied that simple statement.

"I am so sorry," Ruth whispered. "How did they die?"

"I was told it was a car crash," Kari answered. "I don't remember it happening. In fact, I don't really remember anything before they died."

"Nothing?" Ruth was surprised.

"Not really. When I try to remember, it's like I have my eyes closed. I can't see anything. I remember what Mommy and Daddy were like—what they smelled like and felt like and sometimes I remember their voices, but . . . but I can't see them. I don't recall where we lived or much of anything else."

"Considering the age you were when they passed, that is unusual, Kari." *And concerning,* Ruth added, to herself.

Kari shrugged. "They are buried here in Albuquerque, but I—they—had no relatives, so I was first put into foster care. Later, when I was nine, I was adopted by a couple, Nell and Bill Friedman. They fought all the time and got a divorce when I was twelve."

Ruth's lips parted and she frowned. "What happened after they divorced?"

Now it was Kari's turn to frown. "Well, for a while I lived with Nell's mom while Nell tried to get a job and a place for us to live."

"I notice that you don't call Nell and Bill 'Mom' and 'Dad' or Nell's mom 'Grandma.'"

It wasn't a question, so Kari simply nodded and thought about it. "Even though they legally adopted me, I don't think I ever got close to them. As far as I was concerned, I already had a mom and dad, but . . . they were gone. And I remember Nell and Bill arguing and bickering every day, from the first day I was with them until they split. The situation wasn't very conducive to affection."

Kari described how, later, she moved from place to place with Nell, some places better than others, some much worse. She talked about the men Nell allowed to live with them and how, when Kari was seventeen, Nell came down with TB.

"The state sent Nell to a sanitarium and sent me back to foster care. Bill didn't want me—he was remarried—and that was all right with me. I got out of foster care when I turned eighteen.

"I heard Nell died a year later. I'd worked in the library my senior year in high school, so I started taking a few classes at the junior college and then at the university, working my way along in the library sciences."

"You mentioned that sometimes Nell allowed men to live with you. Did they ever . . ."

"Ever try anything? Once, but I told Nell and she threw the guy out. No, I was not molested or sexually abused."

Ruth started to ask another question but noticed that Kari had lapsed into silence, staring into space. Ruth waited for a full five minutes before interrupting Kari's reverie.

"Kari."

Kari turned unseeing eyes toward Ruth.

"Kari, what are you thinking about?" Ruth asked.

Kari blinked and looked down at her hands; they were twisted into the fabric of her shirt. "I . . . I was thinking about the nightmares."

Ruth sat up straight and peered at Kari. "You haven't said anything about nightmares."

"No, I don't suppose I have."

"Can you tell me about them?" Ruth probed, her voice gentle.

"I think they started . . . when I was in foster care," Kari whispered.

"In foster care. The first time or the second time?"

"The first time. It seems like I've had them my entire life, really."

"What can you tell me about them?"

"I can tell you they really bothered Bill! He hated when I would wake up screaming," Kari said in a dreamy tone. "So I started waking myself up when it came. Or I'd stop myself from having it."

"When *it* came? *It*?" Ruth leaned toward Kari.

"The dream."

"You had the same dream? The same nightmare?"

"Oh, yes. It's always the same place but I can't remember much about it. It's . . . frustrating." Kari's words trickled to a stop.

"Hmm. Maybe we should talk more about the nightmares later," Ruth suggested, sensing that Kari was closing up, "but how about if right now I make an observation and you tell me what you think?"

"Okay," Kari said, shrugging.

"All right. Here it is: You've never had a home, Kari."

Kari snorted. "Big revelation, Ruth."

"Think about what that means for a minute? Maybe think about what has motivated you in life? In marriage?"

Kari pondered what Ruth said. "I think at this point I've given up on having a home. It's one of the things that most discourages me . . . looking ahead."

"It discourages you because you have given up on marriage?"

"Because I'm too old to start over, to get married, to have kids. I turn thirty-nine next month. Forty feels like it is lurking around the corner, waiting to pounce on me."

"Forty is a sobering milestone." Ruth's smile was wan. "Fifty isn't any better, trust me. But back to what has motivated you. Can you articulate what you looked forward to when you, say, married David? What drove you? What did you look forward to?"

Kari frowned. She didn't like talking about David, but . . . "We were both working when we got married. Then we bought our house. I'd never owned a house before! And David wanted me to quit working so that I could be a homemaker, so we could start a family. We planned to have a baby right away . . . and I was so happy . . ."

"Because you were making a home? A family?"

"Oh, yes. It was like a dream come true. I thought it was going to be perfect . . . *for the first time*, perfect."

Ruth didn't say anything. Kari finally looked at her. "That's it, right? Why I put up with all of his . . . bad behavior?"

"It is certainly part of it, Kari, but I think it likely that there is more. I think you have what I term 'a thorn of rejection' buried in your heart. Rejection is a tricky thing. If it becomes part of your identity, it can make a person a little passive-aggressive."

Kari wasn't buying it. "What do you mean?"

"What I mean is, rejection can color all of a person's interactions. When a person feels rejected, they often beat everyone to the punch by sabotaging themselves.

"To put it into your context, I think—and this is my observation— that in *your* mind your sense of rejection justified David's abuse. Yes, you were afraid he would leave you—but at the same time you made sure he would."

"What?" Kari was outraged. "How dare you put David's actions on *me*! I—"

"Kari, I didn't say you were responsible for his infidelities or his abuse. Nor did I say that they were excusable.

"What I *am* saying is that you, by being afraid of being rejected and by being passive toward his abuse, waved a big, yellow flag that shouted, *Go right ahead and treat me like dirt, because I'm too afraid you will leave to give you any grief about it!*"

Kari sat still, stung by Ruth's words but electrified by them at the same time. "You're saying . . . I expected him to be unfaithful and controlling?"

Ruth nodded. "When, in our innermost beings, we don't feel that we have value, we project that sense of worthlessness to others. In subtle ways—and perhaps not-so-subtle ways—we advertise our lack of worth. If that other person is selfish, he or she will treat you as the worthless person you consider yourself to be."

Ruth changed directions. "Tell me more about what you were thinking when you married David."

Kari sighed and thought. "Well, I wanted . . . I *needed* a home so bad. Permanence. A place, a husband, children . . . who would always be there and would never leave me, never . . . abandon me. David promised all of that."

Ruth nodded. "Can you talk about the word abandon and how it makes you feel?"

Kari started shaking her head. "'Abandon' means being alone. It is always there, always there. *No one wants me* and I'm always alone, *always . . .*"

Kari was trembling and tears clogged her throat. "No one stays with me! They all leave! Why can't I keep them from leaving!" Her shaking increased and then she couldn't breathe.

It took Ruth a moment to realize that Kari was experiencing a panic attack. When she did, she jumped to Kari's side and wrapped her arms around her.

"It's all right, Kari. I'm here; I'm not leaving," Ruth crooned. "You are all right. Just take steady breaths until it goes. Even if you pass out, I will still hold you. You will wake up all right. Steady breaths, now. Steady breaths."

Ten minutes later, an exhausted Kari lay limp against Ruth. The panic had passed, leaving her wrung out.

"How often does this happen, Kari?" Ruth inquired.

A weary Kari shook her head. "Whenever the nightmares come, either while I'm sleeping or when I wake myself up. When I started waking myself up to stop the dream and stop myself from screaming—that's when the attacks started. Sometimes they happen during the day. When I think too much about certain things."

Kari gathered herself and sat back in her chair, her chin dropping to her chest. Ruth resumed her seat also. She watched Kari and waited.

"What should I do?" Kari whispered. "How do I fix this?"

Ruth nodded but thought for several minutes.

"Kari, this is where I would like to bring in a spiritual truth. I want to read something to you from the Bible. It's about Jesus." Ruth tugged a well-used book from her desk drawer and thumbed through it. "Here it is.

*He is despised and rejected of men;*
*a man of sorrows,*
*and acquainted with grief:*
*and we hid as it were our faces from him;*
*he was despised, and we esteemed him not."*

Kari wrinkled her nose. "They said that about Jesus? But I thought he was, you know, supposed to be revered and worshipped. And stuff."

Ruth's eyes were sad. "And little children are supposed to be loved and cherished and *never abandoned or rejected*, Kari. What they did to Jesus was wrong and should never have happened. Just like what happened to you was wrong and should never have happened."

She turned back to her Bible. "This is how the next line reads.

*Surely he hath borne our griefs,*
*and carried our sorrows"*

She closed her Bible. "I just want to say, Kari, that when wrong things happen—things that should *not* happen—Jesus understands. When we feel rejected, he understands, because those he loved rejected him. When we feel abandoned, he understands, because when he needed his friends and family the very most, they all left him.

"Don't be afraid to take your pain to Jesus, Kari. He already carried your griefs and sorrow. You can take them to him and let them go."

That night Kari closed her eyes and thought again about what Ruth had read to her. It didn't make sense and she was still so very angry, but some tiny piece of what Ruth had read seemed to resonate inside. Kari rejected Ruth's religious overtures, but that one tiny piece hung on anyway.

Beginning in mid-January, Kari's attorney, Jorge Baldonado, pursued her divorce with the precision of a surgeon and the ferocity of a pit bull.

In court, he presented the incontrovertible evidence of David's infidelities and financial maneuverings to cheat Kari out of her share of their property. He was both eloquent and concise—and he was ruthless. Kari watched in breathless awe.

David's attorney, on the other hand, one Richard Forster, presented no case other than attempting to badger, belittle, and discredit Kari at every opportunity. David sat through that part of the proceedings pursing his lips, a tight, smug smile playing about his mouth.

Later in Ruth's office, Kari had raged and fumed, "I wanted to bash his smug face, Ruth. I wanted to see the look on his face *then!*"

Fortunately, Baldonado had coached Kari so that she was able to respond to Forster's accusatory questions in calm, succinct sentences. At every juncture she thwarted Forster by keeping cool and maintaining what Jorge called "the innocence of angels." When Kari stepped down from testifying, a vein was throbbing in the middle of David's forehead. She flashed a smirk his way and watched him redden with suppressed ire.

Then Baldonado turned his ferocity on David and David paled and stammered under his onslaught.

Forster whined to the judge, "Mr. Baldonado is badgering and intimidating my client."

The judge, looking over his glasses, replied in a dry voice, "Perhaps you should have better prepared your client, counselor."

Kari sighed in satisfaction.

In his concluding remarks, Kari's attorney asked the judge for a fair and equitable division of Kari and David's assets. He did not ask the judge to enforce the adultery clause in the prenuptial agreement.

Then it was over. The judge finalized Kari and David's divorce, and Kari received sixty-five percent of all of their assets—the extra fifteen percent in recognition of the stocks David had sold off without her knowledge or permission and the other assets David had not declared.

Baldonado had demonstrated to the court's satisfaction that David had disposed of joint property in an attempt to hide the funds during the divorce proceedings. Kari, though, had declared the proceeds from the CDs she'd sold. The judge included them in their shared assets, not holding them against her.

Kari walked out of the court, thanked her attorney, and went straight to an appointment with Ruth. By then Kari had been seeing Ruth for five months and had come to trust Ruth as a friend and confidant.

"It was glorious, Ruth, on so many levels," Kari admitted. "I know I'm not supposed to gloat, but . . . well, it felt good to win for a change instead of being beaten down."

Ruth shook her head but smiled in understanding. "I'll let you get away with the gloating today, but not after today. No gloating next week, okay? So. Next steps?"

"The judge said I can list the house with a realtor now. A court representative will oversee the disbursement of the proceeds from the sale."

"And then?"

Kari shrugged. "Get a job, of course. I've been looking, but no luck so far."

"Will you keep David's name? Hillyer?"

Kari shrugged. "What would I go back to? Friedman? I have enough to deal with without adding to a worsening identity crisis."

Saddened, Ruth nodded. "I take your point." *O Lord, please help this woman!* she prayed.

A month later the house sold—or it was at least under contract. The realtor warned Kari that the buyers were waiting for the sale of their home to close before they could finalize and close on Kari and David's house.

"This is not a contingency sale," she assured Kari. "Their house is sold. It is now just a matter of timing, for their sale to close and then fund your sale."

The realtor projected the entire process to take up to ninety days; Kari estimated perhaps another thirty before the court authorized the funds from the sale to be disbursed to Kari and David. In the meantime, David was only obligated to pay a quarter of the mortgage on their house and none of the utilities since Kari benefited from living there.

David, under Anthony Esquibel's watchful eye, came and claimed the rest of his personal belongings. Then Kari went through what remained in the house, sorting what she would keep and what she would sell, and giving away the rest. She was ready to move, but could not until the sale closed and paid out.

As the days passed, Kari watched in horror as her bank account dwindled. Baldonado had used all of the retainer and more.

Would she have enough to live on until she received her share of the sale of the house? Would she have enough to get into an apartment when the sale closed?

*I have got to get a job—like, yesterday!* she fretted.

Before and during the divorce proceedings, she had applied to every job she qualified for and was invited to four interviews—but she was yet to receive a job offer, even though she was bilingual, nearly fluent in Spanish, a definite advantage. Visions of having to vacate the house but having nowhere to go haunted her.

*I'll have to take a job at McDonald's or Taco Bell soon,* she fretted, *and it still won't be enough.*

Time dragged on and, for a while, Kari took care of herself again. She resumed her daily hikes and managed her eating and personal care. But in spite of her weekly meetings with Ruth, Kari felt herself sinking. She could tie the moment things really began to go south to the session where Ruth had explained what she called "the plan of salvation."

Kari sneered just thinking about it.

"I recognize the feeling you are describing, Kari," Ruth had said softly. "We all have a God-sized void in our hearts. I had the same emptiness you are expressing. Jesus came to fill that void. He asks us to admit that we need him, that we have fallen far short of God's standards. Rather than condemn us, he asks us to surrender our lives to him so that he can fill the void and heal our hearts."

Kari had stared at Ruth with ill-disguised contempt. "I haven't said so up until now, Ruth, but you really should know: I have an intense dislike of all things religious. So, when I want you to preach to me, I'll let you know. Until then, please keep your religious claptrap to yourself."

Kari's words had gushed out with more vehemence than she had intended, and Ruth had drawn back, stung. "I apologize for offending you, Kari," Ruth had answered, carefully wetting her lips. "Shall we call it a day, then?"

Kari's mouth turned down farther. *Ruth doesn't understand,* she reasoned. *She has a family! She has kids, even grandkids! She's never been alone like I am. Never. No, she doesn't understand.*

The thing was, Kari couldn't stop thinking about Ruth's words—about the "God-sized void in her heart" Ruth had described.

*But it's not God I need to fill that void,* Kari insisted. So why did it feel like she was trying to convince herself?

# CHAPTER 3

## APRIL 1991

It was supposed to be spring, but spring in New Mexico is nothing if not fickle and unforgiving. Cold air slipped into the state overnight and the gusting wind had a harsh bite to it. Midmorning Kari wrapped herself in a ragged afghan and trudged to the mailbox.

She pulled fliers, newspaper ads, junk mail, and "real" mail from the box. The box was stuffed full—she hadn't picked up the mail in four days. Back in the house she dropped the afghan carelessly on the sofa and wandered into the kitchen. She dumped the pile of mail on the island and sifted through it, sighing over envelopes containing rejection letters from prospective employers and groaning over the bills—lots of them, including one from Esquibel Investigative Services.

*I haven't paid Ruth lately. I haven't even paid Anthony and Gloria, after all they have done for me!* Her self-respect plummeted yet another notch.

Kari swallowed, thinking about her latest application to an open position in the UNM library system where she had worked before she and David married. Kari hadn't yet been asked to interview. She wondered if David—out of spite—had somehow influenced the hiring manager against her. And even if she got a job at UNM, the idea of working on the same campus and possibly running into him made her shiver.

*I've been out of the job market too long. Maybe I just have to keep applying for lower paying jobs with Albuquerque Public Schools,* she thought, *and to any receptionist position I find.*

Sinking down onto a stool at the kitchen island, Kari tried to ward off the cloud of discouragement that swirled around her.

It—the discouragement—was like quicksand, tugging at her, just as it had since spending Christmas by herself. It pulled at her, sucking her closer to despair, toward a crevasse with no bottom. The darkness in the crevasse called to her, dared her to step into its fathomless fissures . . . and then what?

A few casual friends, mostly old coworkers, had insisted that she "get out there again." "Come out dancing, Kari," they had urged.

They had invited her out to The Midnight Rodeo to immerse herself in country-western dance. "It's all the rage," they told her. "Just come out to some free lessons and have a little fun."

But Kari didn't want to "get out there again" or put herself back "on the market." *Haven't I made enough mistakes already?* she disparaged herself.

But the voices inside would not stop. They goaded her without mercy.

*What will you do with the rest of your worthless life? Oh, yeah— what life?* they taunted. *You've managed to fail at everything: Two marriages, no children, no family, no job! No one to even spend the holidays with. You're worthless! Better to die and free the world of your useless existence,* they urged.

And she heard familiar, tormenting whispers repeating, "We don't want *her*! We don't want *her*!"

That phrase, "We don't want *her*!" was well known to Kari; she had heard those words all her life. Somewhere in the recesses of her mind they persisted—always soft and subtle and sly, as though she wasn't supposed to hear them whispering, "We don't want *her*! We don't want *her*!"

She always did, though.

The familiar phrase made her apprehensive, as though she should—she *needed*—to *do something* or *stop something*. Only she could never remember *what*.

Today as the phrase repeated itself, anxiety tightened her throat, the harbinger of an impending panic attack. Kari focused on the mail and forced herself to systematically sort it—any physical or mental exercise to distract herself and ward off the dread.

She slapped junk mail into a pile to be ripped up and trashed. She laid bills aside in another stack, fingering the last envelope to be sorted. It was addressed to her, the return address unfamiliar: *Brunell & Brunell, Attorneys at Law.*

*Probably another bill collection notice,* was her first jaded impression. She tossed the envelope on top of the junk mail and then paused. Picking up the envelope by one corner, she scrutinized it. Against her better judgment, she slit it open.

"What?" Her eyes narrowed as she skimmed through the one-page letter. She got to the end and returned to the top, re-reading slowly.

*Dear Ms. Hillyer,*

*Our firm represents the estate of Peter N. Granger, lately of New Orleans, Louisiana. Mr. Granger passed away in 1964 at the age of ninety-two, leaving all he owned to his nephew, Michael D. Granger.*

*Unfortunately, Mr. Granger was estranged from his nephew at the time of his death, and we had been unable to locate Mr. Michael Granger until, in this last year, we uncovered notice of his untimely death in 1958 at the age of forty-seven. We discovered in the same notice that at the time of Michael Granger's death he had a daughter. Since our discovery last year, we have been actively searching for Michael Granger's daughter.*

*If you are KariAnn Alicia Hillyer, born in 1952 to Michael D. Granger and Bethany M. Granger, and legally adopted by William and Eleanor Friedman in 1961, would you kindly contact our offices at your earliest convenience?*

*Brunell & Brunell has been managing Mr. Peter Granger's estate for many years now and we are most anxious to settle it.*
*Cordially,*
*C. Beauregard Brunell, Managing Partner*
*Brunell & Brunell, Attorneys at Law*

Kari stared at the letter until she caught herself gnawing on the inside of her cheek. *This has to be a joke or a scam*, she reasoned. *I mean, what kind of nut names their child 'C. Beauregard,' for heaven's sake?*

And no one had called her KariAnn in decades. She never used the second half of her name nor did anyone else. Only Daddy and Mommy had.

Peter Granger. The name seemed to jingle a bell; she squeezed her eyes shut and tried to remember—always a problematic exercise. Even on a good day her earliest memories were cloudy and troubling, fraught with the threat of a panic attack.

*KariAnn?* Kari could hear her mother call her, could hear her father, laughing and playful, tease her by name. *KariAnn!* he sing-songed.

*Oh, Daddy!* her heart mourned. *Mommy!*

The emotions she'd been holding at bay swept over her, a tide that could not be stemmed or turned. Kari slipped to the cold tile of the kitchen floor and rocked back and forth, her keening wails heard only by the echoing house.

She reached for the arms held out to her in her dreams and the aching in her breast swelled: *Daddy! Daddy!*

It was always the same; today was no different. As she lifted her arms to her father and just as Daddy's hands were about to touch hers, he was torn away, severed from her by *The Black*, the panic-inducing curtain that came crashing down on her clouded mind.

*The Black* filled her and the well-known voice whispered, "We don't want *her*! We don't want *her*!"

The swelling in Kari's chest was going to crush her and burst her heart. She couldn't breathe! A great roaring filled her head. She had to let *The Black* take her.


When Kari awoke she wiped her face with her hand and, groaning, she struggled to her feet. She didn't know how long she had sprawled on the kitchen floor, but she was aching and chilled to the bone.

The worst part of the nightmares and panic attacks came afterwards—like now—when she awoke with that lingering sense that something vital, something *irreplaceable*, had been ripped away at the last moment. No matter what she did, she could never grasp the threads of what she had almost—*almost!*—remembered.

Hours had passed. The mail was still sorted into tidy stacks on the counter. The wind still howled, but the sun was far down in the west, splashing the Sandias with glorious pink.

Kari hesitated and then took up the strange letter again. *Was my father this same Michael Granger? Could I be the daughter they are looking for? What does all this mean?*

The name Peter Granger tugged at the back of her mind: Kari thought she heard her mother's voice murmuring the name *Uncle Peter*, and she had the faintest impression of her father's brows pulling together, competing sadness and anger flitting across his face.

And then there was nothing more. She glanced at the letter.

*In 1958 I was six years old. The timeline seems right. Daddy was forty-seven?* Kari had no photographs and little information about her parents. Other than newspaper clippings of the car crash that killed them, she had been unable to find anything further as she grew older.

For the first time, Kari realized that her father had been middle-aged when he died, meaning he had been forty-one—just two years older than Kari's age now—when she had been born. About her mother she knew even less. Nothing more than her name.

*They left me alone in the world*, her heart sobbed.

That was the pain Kari lived with: *Alone. Alone in the world. Not a soul I can call family.*

Swallowing, Kari studied the return address on the letter: *Brunell & Brunell, Attorneys at Law. 761 Collier Avenue, Suite 100, New Orleans, Louisiana.*

"I can't afford a long-distance call on a phone bill I already can't pay." She dug in a drawer and found a reasonably clean notepad and a single crinkled envelope. Pushing through her muddled thinking, she tore off a sheet of paper and managed to scrawl a response.

*Dear Mr. Brunell,*

*I am KariAnn Alicia Hillyer. I was born on May 28, 1952. My father may have been the Michael Granger you mention in your letter.*

*However, please advise me regarding Peter Granger. My father died when I was six and, to my knowledge, I have no relatives.*
*Cordially,*
*Kari A. Hillyer*

At the last second, she jotted her telephone number under her name. Her hand shook as she smoothed and addressed the envelope. Resolutely, she wrapped herself in the same tattered afghan and walked the stamped letter to the mailbox. She slipped it inside, pushing up the red arm that told the postman she had outgoing mail.

When she returned to the house, the phone was ringing. She picked it up. "Hello?"

"Kari? It's Ruth."

Kari cringed. She had to be such a disappointment to Ruth—and Ruth was sure to sense and want to know about her latest panic attack.

"Hi Ruth."

"Hi, yourself! I'm just calling to ask if we are on for tomorrow." Ruth's words held no reproach, even though Kari had skipped her last appointment with Ruth.

And the one before that.

*Without calling to cancel,* Kari realized, feeling guilty.

"Uh, sure. Four o'clock, right?"

"Yes. Well, good then. I look forward to seeing you." Ruth sounded on the verge of saying goodbye but she paused. "So, how is the packing going? Anything new happen we can talk about tomorrow?"

Kari had picked up the letter from Brunell & Brunell just as Ruth asked if she had anything new to talk about. "No. Well, yes. Maybe. Um, I got this letter. It's rather . . . unusual."

"Oh?"

"I'll bring it with me tomorrow and let you read it." Kari was immediately glad of the letter. *It will give us something to talk about other than me,* she thought, relieved.

Kari had grown to like Ruth—love her, even—but the woman was persistent in bringing all of their conversations back to two topics: *God* and the "roots" of Kari's worsening depression. Ruth's knack for asking penetrating questions regarding Kari's past had made the sessions hard for Kari, and she was weary.

*Maybe with this letter I can deflect some of Ruth's probing attention elsewhere,* Kari planned.

Ruth read the letter a second time, in much the same way Kari had done, her usually dimpled mouth pursed in consideration.

"And you don't know who this Peter Granger is? Was?"

Kari shook her head. "I have a sort of hazy memory of my mother saying the words 'Uncle Peter,' but nothing more."

*Nothing more, that is, except my father's reaction,* she added silently. *I would hardly know how to describe it. Troubled? Pained? Angry? I don't know. It was a long time ago. And it hurts too much to talk about Daddy.*

"And you answered this letter?"

"Yeah. Silly, huh? I mean, it's got to be some sort of a scam, right? And if it isn't and I'm actually who they're looking for, then I've probably inherited a *spoon collection*—you know, one spoon for all fifty states plus Niagara Falls, Disney World, and Graceland? Or a ship in a bottle, right? I really need *that*."

Kari chuckled and Ruth laughed with her, that carefree, open, and happy laugh that Kari liked so well. They both grinned and Kari was, after all, glad she had come today.

"Well, I just choose to believe that God has something wonderful for you in this. The Bible says that every good and perfect gift comes down from above," Ruth smiled. "In some way, some how, this will be a good thing for you."

*There it is again—the God thing.* The smile dropped from Kari's mouth and she shook her head.

"If you say so."

Undaunted, Ruth asked, "Will you call me the minute you get their response? I'm so curious! Aren't you?"

The fact was, Kari *was* a tiny bit curious—but she was also defensive. "I guess so," she shrugged. "Guess I'm more the 'waiting for the other shoe to drop' sort of person. With my luck, I might have inherited a big old house but, *guess what*? The taxes haven't been paid in thirty years! Like that."

"Balderdash! Go ahead and have a little fun imagining something grand, why don't you? Don't be afraid to believe for something *good*."

"*Good?*" Again Kari's response was harsher than she'd intended. "Sorry, but 'good' isn't what the universe usually doles out to me."

As it turned out, Brunell & Brunell did not write in response to her letter: They telephoned.

On Monday, as Kari hauled her meager groceries for the next two weeks into the house, the phone was ringing. A little breathless, Kari answered. "Hello?"

"Ms. Hillyer?"

"Yes. Who's calling, please?" Kari opened the fridge and started unloading her perishables.

"The law offices of Brunell & Brunell, Miss Dawes speaking. Please hold for Mr. Brunell."

Kari stopped stuffing lettuce and apples into the refrigerator when a male voice came on the line. His deep, southern lilt resonated with Kari, and then she realized how near the man's accent was to her father's.

"Ms. Hillyer, C. Beauregard Brunell at your service. We are in receipt of your prompt response to our letter—for which we thank you. I apologize for imposing upon you, but would you have a few minutes to speak with me at this time?"

Kari shoved a half gallon of milk into the refrigerator, pulled on the hinged door, and used her hip to make sure it swung closed.

Kari scanned the remaining groceries—cans and dry goods sitting on the counter. She sank onto one of the kitchen bar stools. "Um, yes; I guess now would be fine."

"Ms. Hillyer, I cannot tell you how delighted we are to have found you! After all this time, too. We are most anxious to close what is our longest standing estate probate—*twenty-seven years*."

The kitchen clock ticked as Kari mulled over his words. "I would think that the courts would have ordered the estate sold off by now," she thought aloud. "Isn't that how it works?"

"Ah. In most cases, yes; however, the terms of Mr. Granger's will were quite specific, and his estate such that it has sustained itself over the years. Mr. Granger was first my father's client and then my client after Father passed until Mr. Granger himself passed in 1964.

"Mr. Granger was so insistent upon finding Mr. Michael Granger and bestowing this estate upon him, that he set the terms of his will in such a way that only Mr. Michael Granger or his heirs could inherit and the estate could not be disposed of otherwise for a lengthy period."

Kari's thoughts were whirling. "So . . . not just a spoon collection?"

"I beg pardon?" Brunell's intonation reflected his confusion.

Kari laughed a little. "I'm sorry. I've been telling myself that the, ah, *estate* consists of a spoon collection. You know, Statue of Liberty, Seattle Space Needle, Mount Rushmore?"

Brunell laughed with her. "Ah, yes! I see your thinking—how very amusing!"

Then he was silent and Kari wondered if the long distance connection had been broken.

"Mr. Brunell? Are you still there?"

"Yes. I apologize." His tone had softened and Kari strained to hear him. She waited another few seconds before he again spoke.

"Ms. Hillyer, are you able to get away at this time?"

Kari pulled the receiver from her ear and gawked at it. "What do you mean, 'get away'"?

"My dear lady, the other senior partners and I feel that we should administer the details of Mr. Granger's will to you in person. We would like to fly you to New Orleans at your earliest convenience to meet with us."

Kari gaped again. "Is this a joke? Do you think I am so foolish as to go gallivanting across the country on the word of a stranger? And I can scarcely fill my gas tank let alone buy *a plane ticket*."

Kari was about to slam the receiver onto the wall phone; instead she took a deep breath, her hand in midair. She decided to wait for the con artist on the other end to hang up.

Instead, the line came alive again as the attorney chose his words with care. "I assure you, *most* solemnly, Ms. Hillyer, that this is no prank, nor do we have any but the highest interests of you, our client, in mind. What I am proposing would be paid for entirely by our firm."

Before Kari could offer another objection, he went on. "But recognizing your *quite* reasonable reluctance to take us in good faith— after all, from your perspective we are perfect strangers.

"I propose that Brunell & Brunell provide proper *bona fides* to you. I will direct the outside accounting firm we use to draw up a notarized letter attesting to our law practice's reputation and send it to you by registered mail."

Dazed, Kari hung up the phone. She was more confused than she had been before the call. Then she called Ruth and repeated the entire conversation.

The *bona fides*, as Brunell had termed them, arrived six days later by U.S. Post Office registered mail, signature required. Kari signed for and then opened and studied the notarized letter attesting that Hegelund and Cooperage, CPAs, had been the accounting firm of Brunell & Brunell for thirty-seven years. The letter declared Brunell & Brunell "a firm of the highest moral and ethical character" with "a reputation of unsullied excellence in the great state of Louisiana."

"I think they went overboard, don't you?" Kari queried Ruth.

"It's a bit on the flowery side, I admit. But it certainly meshes up with the research you did."

Kari hadn't waited for Hegelund and Cooperage's letter to arrive. She had gone directly to UNM's law library and had sent out queries through the electronic database search tool, *LexisNexis*, used primarily by journalists and lawyers.

It had taken but a few minutes to get her first return. Eventually Kari had printed full briefs written by Brunell & Brunell and rulings of cases in which they were cited.

Kari had shown them to Ruth with raised brows. "I guess they are on the level."

"So you'll go?" Ruth now asked.

"Why don't *you* go? You're more excited about this than me," Kari groused.

"Oh, no, Kari. This will be *your* adventure," Ruth grinned, "but I'll tell you something. I have been praying for you over this whole inheritance thing and, like I told you before, truly believe that something *good* is going to come of all this. Something wonderful and good—from God himself."

Kari glared at Ruth. "It's always *God* with you, isn't it, Ruth? Well, is this where I get to tell you to go fly a kite?"

Ruth's impish grin only widened. "If you come back from New Orleans and something wonderful hasn't happened, then I'll treat you to lunch at Little Anita's on Juan Tabo and afterwards we'll go to Loma Del Rey Park where you can watch me fly that kite."

"Little Anita's, huh?" Kari pursed her lips trying to stay mad, but against Ruth's infectious enthusiasm she couldn't manage it. "I could use a little 'green chile therapy.' All right. Deal."

She moistened her lips with her tongue. "I have a bigger problem if they really want me to come to New Orleans right away."

"What's that?"

"I need to get out of the house and then clean it from top to bottom, but . . . I don't have enough money right now to get into an apartment—especially while I'm paying most of the mortgage."

Ruth "hmmmed" and thought for a moment. "Do you have enough to rent a storage unit?"

Kari thought about it. "You mean, move out and put my furniture and stuff into a unit? I could do that . . . but then I wouldn't have a place to stay. I'd need to stay somewhere for at least a few weeks. Maybe longer than a month."

"I'm sure we could find somewhere for you until the court releases your money. In fact—" Ruth tapped her chin. "The Esquibels have a spare room, and you know they care about you."

Kari shook her head. "Oh, Ruth. I wouldn't feel comfortable—" The shadow of her unpaid bill to Esquibel Investigative Services loomed large over her—as did her unpaid counseling bills.

"It's only a few weeks, Kari."

Kari's voice dropped to a whisper. "Ruth, I still owe Anthony money . . . and you, too."

"Well, do you plan to pay your bills when the house money comes through?"

"Of course!"

"Then tell him that. I have a feeling Anthony knew you would be strapped for cash after you got your divorce. Just talk to him. Like you are talking to me right now."

Kari nodded. "All right. I will. And thank you for being patient with me."

Ruth patted her hand and then grinned. "Well, then! Will you call Mr. Brunell or wait for him to call you?"

Again, Kari did not need to make that decision. C. Beauregard Brunell called the following morning at 9:15 a.m. sharp.

"Ms. Hillyer? A good day to you! Are you in possession of the *bona fides* from our accounting firm?"

Reluctantly, Kari allowed the word "yes" to slip out. When she hung up twenty minutes later, all the arrangements had been made: Mr. Brunell's secretary would have Rio Grande Travel, an Albuquerque agency, deliver the tickets to Kari's home.

Kari would fly out of the Albuquerque Sunport a week from the coming Monday. Mr. Brunell himself would meet her when she landed at the New Orleans International Airport and personally escort her to her hotel.

"In the morning, after you have breakfasted and refreshed yourself, my son, Mr. Oskar Brunell, will call for you at the hotel and escort you to our offices to meet with our three senior partners."

Kari's head was whirling. *Call for me? Escort me?* Mr. Brunell's Old South hospitality was charming—and overwhelming.

*And why do I need to meet with three senior partners?* she wondered. In the pit of Kari's stomach, she was beginning to suspect that the inheritance left by Peter Granger to Michael Granger or his offspring could be no mean or common thing.

And Ruth's words danced in her ears all day. *I've been praying for you and I truly believe that something good is going to come of all this. Something wonderful and good from God himself.*

"Not a spoon collection, then."

Kari made herself breathe deeply as she reviewed the arrangements. "Definitely more than a spoon collection."


Kari was caught up in a flurry of activity over the next week. She finished packing up the house and held her garage sale—adding a few welcome dollars to her account at the credit union. Still, she watched the balance in the account dip dangerously low after she paid the utilities and two months' rent on a storage shed.

But how she would move everything to the storage unit was beyond her. *I can take most of it a carload at a time,* she figured. *It might take twenty trips, but I can do it.* The furniture, though, she would have to hire done and she had precious little left to pay for that.

To her amazed surprise, Anthony rounded up a few friends and, with two pickup trucks, moved everything she owned, except two packed suitcases and an overnight bag, into the storage unit. Kari was even more amazed—and deeply touched—when Ruth and Gloria showed up with buckets, supplies, and a rented carpet cleaner and began cleaning the house with her.

A few hours later Anthony handed Kari the key to the storage unit. "It all fit in the unit just fine, Kari, and we left everything nice and tidy. Your little file cabinet is right at the front. You can get into it without too much trouble if you need to."

Kari thought briefly of what was in the cabinet: her birth certificate, adoption papers, employment and job search records, letters of recommendation, tax returns, her divorce papers, and a mostly empty scrapbook containing the paltry news clippings reporting her parents' accident. Copies of her parents' death certificates.

Anthony looked over the now-clean house and patted her on the arm. "We'll go on home. You come and get settled in when you are ready, okay?"

Her friends left and Kari spent an hour walking around the house and around the yard, knowing she was saying goodbye. *I will never come back here,* she told herself, and she cried bitter tears over what was lost.

That night Kari slept in Anthony and Gloria's spare bedroom. She was exhausted, emotionally and physically, but she felt safe, even if she felt empty at the same time.

Tomorrow was Sunday; she would leave for New Orleans the following day. She would pack one suitcase and her overnight bag for the few days she expected to be there.

# CHAPTER 4

Blinking in the bright afternoon light of the New Orleans arrivals terminal, Kari recognized C. Beauregard Brunell before he recognized her: He was tall, lean, silver-haired, and dressed impeccably in an "old southern gentleman" manner—just as she had imagined him. The silver in his hair extended to his impressive mustache and goatee. Drooping pale blue eyes twinkled from under white brows as he clasped Kari's hand and bowed over it.

"Ms. Hillyer, 'tis a pure pleasure to make your acquaintance," he drawled.

Kari's heart swelled as his soft, soothing accent fell on her ears. Memories of her parents' voices carried the same inflections.

*How is it that all this time I hadn't realized they were from Louisiana?* she reproached herself. In almost the same thought she reminded herself, *But, in truth, what do I know about them? So very little. So precious little.*

Suddenly, whatever information the attorneys of Brunell & Brunell could give her about her father and his family loomed dearer and more desirable than any tangible inheritance.

C. Beauregard had taken her hand and kept hold of it, studying her for a long moment, a soft light glimmering in his drooping eyes. But all he said was, "Shall we see if your luggage has arrived, Ms. Hillyer?"

They waited in comfortable silence for the airline to offload the flight's luggage. C. Beauregard collected her suitcase and tucked her arm into his, escorting her to a waiting vehicle. Kari's mouth dropped open when she saw the sleek black town car, its tinted windows, and uniformed driver. She slid into the car's cavernous back seat while the driver stowed her bags in the trunk.

"We'll take Miss Kari to her hotel now, Rufus," C. Beauregard instructed the driver.

As they pulled away from the curb, he inquired, "Ms. Hillyer, my wife and I would be delighted to have you join us for dinner this evening—may I collect you, say, at five-thirty? You have a busy schedule tomorrow so we won't keep you late, but we don't wish you to dine alone on your first evening in town."

"Thank you. You're very kind," Kari answered, struck again by his sweet manner.

The car stopped under the tall portico of *The Grand Marquis*, a stately old hotel. C. Beauregard escorted her to the front desk while Rufus brought in her bags.

"Your reservation is in order," the front desk man assured her. He issued her a heavy room key. "Room 690. Please call the front desk if you need anything. Anything at all. And we hope you enjoy your stay at *The Grand Marquis*, Ms. Hillyer."

"Thank you; I'm sure I will." Kari stared around the foyer and shivered with delight. *Positively dripping with old-world elegance,* she exulted.

After Rufus turned her bags over to a bellman, Kari and C. Beauregard stepped into an elevator reminiscent of a black-and-white Humphrey Bogart/Katherine Hepburn movie. The elevator may have retained its classic façade, yet it whisked her to the sixth floor with modern speed and efficiency.

The bellman led the way. At the door of her room, C. Beauregard bid her goodbye. "Until this evening."

When C. Beauregard arrived to take her to dinner, they rode in his personal car, a silver Mercedes driven by a chauffeur who opened the rear door for Kari with a deferential tip of his charcoal grey hat. He offered the same tip of his hat when they disembarked in the curving drive of a white, three-story Colonial, complete with pillars and matching covered porches on the first and second floors spanning the front of the house.

A magnificent old magnolia overspread the lawn. Its deep-green, glossy leaves were the perfect backdrop for the masses of blooms perfuming the air. Kari drank deeply of their scent as C. Beauregard escorted her up the wide semicircular steps to the front door.

"Ms. Hillyer, may I present my dear wife, Lorene? My darling, this is Ms. Hillyer."

Lorene surprised Kari when she embraced her and kissed first one cheek and then the other. Kari was left with the warm scent of powder and perfume and the caress of a softly wrinkled cheek.

"So lovely to meet you, Ms. Hillyer. I have heard so much about you. We're delighted to have you in our home." Lorene took Kari by the arm and led her into a large sitting room. Kari could see, through open double doors, a dining table set for dinner.

Dinner was pleasant, and Kari was completely charmed by Lorene Brunell, who, with few words, managed to make her guest feel important and valued.

Lorene kept the conversation light, easy, and yet fun. Almost immediately, Kari was at her ease.

*How can she be so gracious and caring without being sickeningly sweet at the same time? What an art!* Kari was sure Lorene embodied legendary Southern graciousness.

"Do call me Lorene," the woman requested with a smile.

"And please call me Clover," C. Beauregard asked, that twinkle in his rheumy eyes. "All my friends do."

"Clover!" Kari was astonished. *And I wondered what kind of nut named their kid 'C. Beauregard!'*

"It's a Southern thing, my dear," Lorene purred, perfectly understanding Kari's bemusement. When she said "thing" it came out the softest, silkiest "thayng" Kari could conceive.

"I confess that I have always been loath to place 'Clover Brunell' on my business cards or our letterhead," Clover chuckled. "B'sides, when a caller asks to speak with C. Beauregard or Clover, my staff can tell immediately if the caller knows me personally or not."

The three of them laughed, and because Kari was having such a good time, she relaxed further. *Tomorrow won't be too bad,* she assured herself.

"I'm eighty-one years old and semiretired now," Clover mentioned during dinner. "But I still keep my oar in at Brunell & Brunell, make sure we're staying the course, particularly as regards Peter Granger's estate."

Kari was astonished. "Goodness! You certainly do not look to be eighty-one!"

"Ah, but sometimes these bones will not let me forget it, Ms. Hillyer, I assure you."

"Nor will *I* allow you to forget it," Lorene reminded him. She turned to Kari. "We just cannot seem to grasp that we can't do any longer all we used to do with such ease. So we mind each other's blind spots—he mine and I his."

Later that evening Kari explored the suite in which Clover had deposited her. The three rooms were sumptuous with that old-world ambiance—a sitting room, a large bathroom, and a separate bedroom, all appointed in fine, classic style: heavy furniture upholstered in costly fabrics; wall hangings, knick-knacks, and other *objets d'art*. The suite was pleasing in a manner Kari intuitively knew was only possible with impeccable taste coupled with significant expense.

She wandered into the cavernous bathroom and eyed the sunken bathtub hungrily. Kari inserted the plug, turned the handles, and a stream of hot water began filling the tub. She studied the variety of bath salts arranged on the tub's surround and poured a wealth of lavender under the tap, gratified by the soft scent that arose from the filling tub.

Minutes later she eased herself into the steaming water and sank into its embrace with a sigh of pleasure. After soaking for half an hour, she dragged herself from the cooling bath water, wrapped her languid body in the largest bath towel she had ever seen, and stumbled into the bedroom.

She had thought she would have difficulty sleeping in a strange bed, especially with the morning's meeting on her mind. But when Kari slid between the silken sheets she fell at once into a deep, dreamless sleep.

The following morning, Kari was ready when the front desk rang her room. "Ms. Hillyer, your car is waiting," the desk manager drawled before hanging up.

"My car is waiting," she muttered, *sotto voce*. "So hoity-toity, aren't we?"

She had wanted to don comfortable clothes—jeans, t-shirt, and boots. Instead, figuring the occasion called for a bit more formality, she slipped on a light dress, one of three her attorney had picked out for the divorce proceedings. She wound her long hair up into a reasonable facsimile of a French knot, added pale lip color, slipped on open-toed sandals, and called it good.

Through the lobby windows Kari spied a long, sleek town car awaiting her at the curb, the same car that had picked her up from the airport. A much younger version of C. Beauregard Brunell greeted her as she approached the hotel doors.

"Ms. Hillyer? Oskar Brunell at your service. May I escort you to our offices?"

A woman with flawless caramel-colored skin and sleek black hair waited for her just inside the wide entrance doors. "Miss Hillyer? I am Miss Dawes, executive assistant to the senior partners. We have spoken on the phone."

Kari might have been imagining it, but it seemed that Miss Dawes ran a quick but appraising eye over her.

Kari stared at the classic and tasteful lines of Miss Dawes' suit and at her expensive shoes and stockings and realized that her own attire was far too informal by Miss Dawes' standards.

*Oh, dear. What will Clover think of me?* Kari wondered. *I'm so underdressed!*

Sweeping another critical glance over Kari, Miss Dawes added in a soft voice, "You may take her back, Mr. Oskar. They are ready for her."

Miss Dawes went ahead of them through a large, open, rotunda-like work area. Not just Miss Dawes, but the receptionist and the many lawyers and assistants working within the rotunda all cast their curious, appraising eyes on Kari.

When Miss Dawes reached her own office, she busied herself at her desk. Oskar turned right and led Kari down an impressive hallway beyond Miss Dawes' office, past several empty offices, and opened the door to a conference room.

Kari faltered. The room was impressive—a solid mahogany table stretched the length of the room—a room whose walls were papered in ivory watered silk and hung with the imposing portraits of (Kari presumed) former and current Brunell & Brunell partners. Kari was feeling more self-conscious with each step.

As Oskar swept her into the room, the four men who had been seated at the table stood to their feet and nodded courteously. They, too, seemed to be evaluating her.

"Ms. Hillyer! You are looking rested and fresh this morning." Clover smiled, his drooping pale blue eyes welcoming. Kari looked into his honest face and was comforted. Oskar slipped out while she was not looking.

"May I introduce you?" He waited for Kari to nod; she did, stealing glances at the other three individuals waiting beside their chairs. One man was silver-haired; the second may have been at one time, but he was now mostly bald. Clover and these two men were of a similar age.

"Ms. Hillyer, may I present Mr. Jeffers Brunell, my brother, and Mr. Clive Brunell, my cousin? We three are the senior partners of Brunell & Brunell. Jeffers, Clive, this is Ms. Hillyer."

Kari shook the gentle hands of the two aged men and then cut her eyes toward the fourth person in the room. He was much younger, perhaps in his late forties. His skin and hair gleamed a deep ebony. He nodded and smiled as Kari's eyes swept over him.

"And Ms. Hillyer, last but certainly not least, may I present Mr. Owen Washington? He is our lead investigator."

Clover gestured with a pleased smile toward the black man, "Mr. Washington is to be credited with finding you—at last! Mr. Washington, Ms. Hillyer."

Owen Washington's hand was warm and his clasp firm. "A pure pleasure, Ms. Hillyer," he murmured in the melodic tones Kari was finding to be so universal of New Orleans.

Clover held a chair for Kari at the head of the table and seated her. The four men took their seats, two on each side, and turned their attention toward her. Kari swallowed—*hard*—and tried to remain calm.

Clover was seated on Kari's right. He poured a glass of water for her from a cut glass decanter sitting on a sparkling silver tray and placed it within her reach.

"Now, Miss KariAnn—may we call you Miss KariAnn?"

Kari nodded. "Just, er, Miss Kari, please. I . . . I've never used KariAnn." *Only Mommy and Daddy have ever called me KariAnn*, she did not add. "I much prefer Miss Kari to Ms. Hillyer."

"Very well, then, Miss Kari, let us start with what we can tell you regarding Mr. Granger and his association with our family and our firm, shall we? The history of Mr. Granger's estate will be of interest to you, I believe."

Clover shuffled a few papers before he began. "Our records indicate that Mr. Granger came to New Orleans a decade after the turn of the century—1911, to be exact. He immediately purchased a home for himself, his brother's widow, Alicia, and her son, Michael. Your father was, at that time, a newborn."

Kari's eyes widened. *My middle name is Alicia!* She willed herself not to become emotional. "I know so very little—nothing, really—about my father. Are you sure this is him? Are you sure this is *my* father?" Her voice squeaked at the end.

With a genteel flourish of his hand, Clover deferred to Owen Washington, seated to his right.

"We are quite confident that he is your father, Miss Kari," Washington replied. He consulted his notes. "Michael and Bethany Granger passed away on October 8, 1958, as the result of a vehicular accident. The accident occurred on eastbound Route 66, about halfway between Gallup and Grants, New Mexico, while Mr. and Mrs. Granger were pulled off to the side of the road, presumably because of car difficulties.

"We have obtained copies of the police report on the accident and the intake forms with New Mexico social services. They both clearly identify you, and we have determined that this is the same Michael Granger who was nephew to Peter Granger."

Kari nodded and stared at the table in front of her. After a moment Clover cleared his throat. "Miss Kari, may I continue?"

"Yes," Kari whispered.

Clover cleared his throat again. "Mr. Peter Granger—I'll refer to him as Mr. Peter as we go forward—established himself as a reputable financial advisor in our fair city. He did very well for himself, very well indeed, even through the market crash of 1929 and the turbulent decades following.

"When he withdrew from the market prior to the crash, he recommended that his clients do likewise. He then advised them to eliminate all debt and to invest directly in real estate, gold, silver, and other precious metals. I won't go into his other advice over the following difficult years, but the few of his clients who followed his direction survived and many did well."

Clover smiled. "Our father—that is, Mr. Jeffers' and my father— and our father's brother, Mr. Clive's father, were clients of his. Because of Mr. Peter's timely advice, our family survived the Great Depression and prospered in the years following. Mr. Peter later— much later—became a client of our law firm."

Clover spoke earnestly. "Our family could have lost everything when the markets crashed, Miss Kari. Our debt of gratitude to him is one of the reasons we, as a family, have taken such care with his estate. Another reason has to do with the nature of Mr. Peter's will. I will cover that as we progress."

He consulted his notes. "Although Mr. Peter was known to be scrupulous in his business dealings, Father recounted that Mr. Peter was not an easy man to interact with other than on a business level. Oh, his manners were perfect and he mixed with the socially elite with ease, but it was all quite superficial.

"He was aloof, perhaps even guarded, in his personal life. He grew a reputation in the city for being utterly cold-blooded in his dealings when the situation required.

"His clients loved him for his accuracy in the markets and his ruthlessness when it came to protecting their accounts, but they took care to never 'get on his bad side,' was the term I believe Father used. It seems that he formed no personal connections or friendships of significance that we know of.

"As far as our records show and family history tells us, Mr. Peter had a satisfactory home life. While he could be cold and impersonal, the singular exception to this regarded his nephew, your father."

Kari looked at Clover now and hung on his every word.

"Father told us that Mr. Peter doted on Mr. Michael, and they were often seen together in public as the boy grew. When Mr. Michael was still in the stroller, Mr. Peter took to taking him for long walks through their neighborhood. Later, when Mr. Michael was in elementary school, Mr. Peter was known to drive him to classes and pick him up daily. The only affection Father ever observed in Mr. Peter was toward that child."

Clover made a note on his pad and nodded to himself. "Sadly, I must now speak of the estrangement that later occurred between Mr. Peter and Mr. Michael. But perhaps you would care for a short recess?"

Kari blinked and looked at Clover. "Please don't stop! I am learning so much about my . . . family." She choked as she said the word and cut off a sob before it could escape.

Clover nodded, his expression grave and considerate. "It is a great deal to take in, my dear. Please tell us if you need a moment to compose yourself at any time."

Kari nodded.

"The Grangers' home life continued in the fashion I described. Mr. Peter's sister-in-law, Alicia, never remarried, and she seemed content to raise her son and care for Mr. Peter's needs. However, in 1926, when Mr. Michael was about fifteen, Miss Alicia became ill. Cancer, I believe it was. She passed away in 1927 when Mr. Michael was sixteen.

"It appears that Alicia Granger was the glue that held their little family together. When she passed away, Mr. Michael had a very difficult time. According to what has been passed down to us, Mr. Peter was not the most empathetic individual, even for a doting surrogate father. He was unable to sympathize with the boy on an emotional level or help him through his grief and loss."

Clover cleared his throat. "A short while before the illness of his mother was diagnosed, Mr. Michael made a new friend, a boy nearly a year older than him. He visited a church with this young friend of his and experienced a spiritual conversion. In short, he became a Christian."

Kari's mouth dropped open. "A *Christian*?"

Clover, something inscrutable flashing across his face, only responded, "Yes, ma'am, a Christian. A very devout follower of Christ."

*My father was a Christian? One of those religious fanatics that I so despise?* The few memories Kari had of her father—more impressions than concrete memories—tumbled about in her mind, in conflict with her aversion to all things "Christian."

*Daddy!* Kari's whole sense of love, completeness, and security was tied to the memories of his embraces, to the peace she experienced when she remembered being held in his arms.

*Daddy was a Christian?*

Clover didn't seem to notice her disconcerted manner. He looked down at his notes and frowned. "I regret to tell you this, Miss Kari, but Mr. Peter was something of an avowed atheist. While he took pains to conduct himself in the utmost respectable fashion, he held what might be described as a deep bitterness toward Christianity."

Kari's mouth twisted. *So I have something in common with Peter Granger, my great-uncle? How ironic.*

Clover was still talking. "When Mr. Michael professed his faith in Christ, Mr. Peter was . . . shall we say, displeased. Mr. Michael, however, held to his convictions. He began attending church regularly and became quite ardent in his beliefs."

Clover took a moment to wipe his brow. "This part of my narration may sound terribly incongruous, Miss Kari but, as it turns out, *I* was that new young friend who invited him to church. It was my father who took him under his wing and mentored him in his faith."

"You. And your father." The words that fell from Kari's mouth were flat. Cold.

Clover cleared his throat. "The fact that our family introduced Michael to Christ and encouraged him in his faith caused a sizeable rift between our father, Leonard Brunell, and Mr. Peter. Mr. Peter continued to act as our family's financial advisor, but the two of them did not speak outside of his office for years.

"In public, Mr. Peter was quite cold toward us. Unfortunately, Mr. Peter's relationship with Mr. Michael also declined.

"When Mr. Michael graduated with honors from college preparatory school at age eighteen, he was accepted into Washington and Lee University to study business. He attended there for three years. During that time, he grew in his faith and became active in many outreaches.

"Just before his senior year, he felt that the Lord was calling him into ministry. After graduation, he wanted to go to Bible college. This, even though Mr. Peter had made no secret that he planned for Mr. Michael to work with him and succeed him in his business.

"I remember well when Mr. Michael announced his plans to Mr. Peter. It was a dark day. Mr. Peter declared that he would not pay Mr. Michael's senior year tuition if he persisted in his plans and if he continued his association with our family. He felt we were to blame for his ongoing estrangement from Michael, you see."

Clover met Kari's gaze with sad eyes. "As a young man I was one of your father's closest friends, Miss Kari. Mr. Peter's declaration meant the end of our friendship. Mr. Peter was so incensed and intractable on this point that the relationship between Mr. Peter and Mr. Michael grew more and more tenuous."

"You knew my father that well?"

"Oh, yes, my dear. Another reason I, personally, am so confident in proceeding with the probate of this estate is because, Miss Kari, you have the look of your father.

"Mr. Michael had blue eyes—extraordinary eyes, I might add. You have those same extraordinary eyes, Miss Kari. You have his eyes, his curling golden-brown hair, and many of his facial expressions. You are tall and slender like him, too. The resemblance is quite uncanny."

*Daddy's blue eyes! Yes, I remember!* Kari looked Clover in the face and unconsciously slid her hand across the table toward him. "Clover, would you be able to tell me more about him . . . later?"

"It would be my honor, Miss Kari." Clover patted her hand and squeezed it gently.

"But . . . but then what happened?" Kari had been drawn into the drama to the exclusion of the others in the room.

Clover again looked down. "What happened? Well, after much soul searching, Mr. Michael decided to strike out on his own, Miss Kari. He did not return to university. Instead, he set out to make his own way, and . . . he never returned. He was, I believe, about twenty-two years old when he left."

The large clock in the corner of the conference room ticked away steadily as Kari digested this information.

*All because of his 'faith'?* Kari felt resentment rising. *He cut ties with his only family for his 'faith'? I grew up entirely without family because of* **that***?*

Washington took up the narration. "Miss Kari, you already know where you were born—Las Cruces, New Mexico. What you perhaps do not know is how your parents were occupied in Las Cruces at the time you were born."

"You know?" Kari perked up. "Can you tell me? Can you tell me what my father did for a living? Where we lived?"

Washington looked to Clover before going on. "We know a little, Miss Kari. The little we learned was enough to help us form a timeline from when he left New Orleans until about 1951. Two years ago we located the Bible school from which he graduated in 1936. By digging in some very old school records, we were able to trace him to a small church where he interned after graduation and became the church's youth leader.

"Later he pastored a little church in South Carolina where, apparently, he met and married your mother, Bethany. We even have a copy of their marriage license, but the only information we have about her was that . . . she was an orphan."

Kari squeezed her eyes closed. It was too much—and not enough!

*Daddy! You were a minister? It's not bad enough you were a Christian that you had to also throw your life away as a minister? And not a scrap of information about Mommy?*

Washington, unaware of Kari's distress, kept speaking. "Michael Granger pastored three churches in the following years. When we traced him to Las Cruces—where you were born—we found that he had been the associate pastor of a small Spanish-speaking church. The aging widow of one of the church's deacons remembered your parents and told us that he and your mother came to their church to learn Spanish and prepare to be missionaries in a Spanish-speaking country."

"Missionaries!" Kari was astounded—and appalled.

"Yes, ma'am." Washington nodded and removed a letter from his folder. "I have a letter from that church's denominational headquarters. It tells us that in 1953 Michael and Bethany Granger were commissioned to teach and assist pastors in the nations of Nicaragua and Honduras. They and their little daughter, KariAnn, age one, left for the mission field in early fall."

"Nicaragua and Honduras . . ." *Then it's no fluke, no special aptitude, that I learned Spanish so easily . . .*

"They remained in Central America for five years, but in 1958 they were required to return to America for a sabbatical . . ."

"That's when they died." Kari was surprised that she had spoken the words aloud. "October. The fall of 1958."

"Yes. We believe they had not been back in the country for more than a week when they perished."

The many possibilities that *could have been* rained down in Kari's imagination. The life that *might* have been and *should* have been had her father not insisted on his own way, *insisted on being a Christian—*

Quite suddenly the air in the conference room was too thin, and Kari felt she could not catch her breath. "Excuse me," She pushed the chair back and got to her feet. "I need . . . some air, please."

She bolted toward the door, holding the wall as she escaped, the edges of her vision dimming. She drew deep, choking breaths as she raced through the hallway, flying past Miss Dawes' office, stumbling through the foyer and open work area with all its watching eyes, and out the front door.

The air outside was heavy with moisture and the scent of flowering trees and shrubs. Her chest heaved as she tried to pull deep breaths into her lungs. Kari dropped onto the steps and sat with her head down. All she could think of was what Clover had just told her.

*Daddy was a Christian.*
*A stupid, stupid Christian!*

*How could you, Daddy?*

# CHAPTER 5

"Miss Kari?"

Kari had half expected Miss Dawes to come find her and drag her back, sniffing and *tsking* over her appearance. But it was Owen Washington who squatted at the bottom of the steps below Kari and peered up at her with concern.

"I'll be all right," Kari muttered. "Just give me a minute." She was still lightheaded, but she knew it would pass soon.

Washington nodded and said nothing. He stood and went to the other side of the wide steps leading up to the entrance and leaned against the railing, soundlessly whistling.

When Kari got to her feet, Washington took a few steps in her direction. "Still dizzy?" he asked, ready to steady her.

"A little. Thank you." Kari sighed. "How much longer will this take, do you think?"

"Depends on how you feel," he answered. "The partners cleared their entire morning but we still have a lot to cover."

"And I'm wasting their time, is that it?"

"I'd hardly call it a waste of time. *The Seniors*, as we call the three senior partners, only work part-time these days, mostly guiding the direction of the firm. They don't keep office hours and rarely do any of the work. However, the chance to close the Granger estate lit a fire under all three of them. They've been in the office all week, barking orders and getting ready for today's meeting."

He chuckled. "Besides, Mr. Clive requires frequent restroom breaks these days. Your timing was perfect. I think he's good for another hour now."

"He is, is he?" Kari grumbled. Under her breath she muttered, *"Old geezer."*

Washington's laugh was loud and spontaneous. "He's a cool old guy, but 'old geezer' about sums him up. How about you? Are you good for another hour?"

She sighed. "I think so. I'm just . . . this wears me out when it happens. But I'll be fine."

"If you say so. But, if I may suggest something? Please remember that *you* are the client, and we are here to serve *you*—not the other way around, yes?"

Kari nodded, looking dubious.

"When we go back in that room, I recommend that you enter it boldly with no more than a, 'Thank you for your indulgence.' Sit right down, look Clover in the eye, and say, 'Please continue.' Nothing else. Think you can do that?"

Kari laughed and shook her head. "Like I own the place, huh?"

"Exactly. Can you do that? You're here to receive an inheritance, remember?"

"An inheritance. Ha! Well, I'll give it a try. What do I have to lose other than my dignity? Oh, wait. I've already lost that."

Washington grinned. He opened the front entrance doors and Kari marched inside, her chin up, looking straight ahead. By the time he opened the door to the conference room, Kari was able to do just as Washington had suggested.

She stared at the wall while Washington held her seat and slid it up to the table. She murmured a "Thank you for your indulgence" and "Please continue, Mr. Brunell" using the same words Washington had suggested.

*Why, butter wouldn't melt in my mouth*, she sneered. *Scarlett O'Hara could not have done it better.*

Clover responded with a courtly nod and Kari thought she glimpsed something like approval in his eyes. "Certainly, Miss Kari. Gentlemen, are we ready to proceed?"

Clover addressed her again. "Miss Kari, I would be delighted to tell you much more about your father in private at a later time. Now, if it suits you, we will read your great-uncle's will and give an accounting of his estate."

"Yes, that would be fine." Kari was grateful for Clover's offer.

She tipped her chin up until it was level with the table and again fixed her eyes on the back wall. She focused all of her energy on keeping her body composed and her chin up.

"Very good," Clover responded. He gestured across the table. "Mr. Jeffers, would you please read the will?"

"Why, I certainly will, Clover. It would be my pleasure. And Miss Kari, if at any time a point is unclear, please just wave your little hand and ask your question." Jeffers' personality was sweet and homey, his voice crackling with age.

Kari, whose work had often involved complex documents, nodded and said nothing. *I know how to read,* she bristled, keeping her face impassive.

Jeffers lifted some papers, held them about ten inches from his face, and began to read. Kari, with her eyes on the ivory watered-silk wallpaper across the room, zoned out as he read the date of the will—June of 1957—and the usual "being of sound mind and body" and other introductory legalese.

She began paying attention when he intoned, "I am an unmarried man, having never married, and I have no children, living or dead. My only living relative is Michael Daniel Granger, born February 2, 1911, the only child of my late brother, Willis Granger, deceased prior to Michael's birth.

"I hereby bequeath the entirety of my estate to Michael D. Granger. Should his death precede mine or, should his death occur before my executors locate him, I bequeath the entirety of my estate to his offspring."

Kari swallowed but kept her gaze fixed on the back wall. She clamped her teeth together to keep her expression neutral.

"I have had no communication with my nephew for many years now, a situation for which I assume all responsibility. If, at the time of this reading, Michael is present, I wish him to know how deeply I regret our estrangement. It is my hope that he will find it in his heart to forgive me and my unwillingness to allow him to choose his own path."

Tears pricked the backs of Kari's eyes and her clamped jaw was no longer working to keep her emotions under control.

*Great-uncle Peter forgave her father? Forgave him for becoming a Christian?*

The pricking in her eyes threatened to overflow and spill out; Kari's jaw, clenched as tightly as she could manage, was trembling.

*Daddy could have gone home? Oh, Daddy!*

Jeffers droned on, and Kari heard, "If at the time of this reading, however, Michael is not present, it is only because the many investigators I have hired over the years have been unable to find him. I say this because I have been searching diligently for him these past twenty-four years.

"I have lived through many troubling times, including two terrible wars. The world we live in has, in many ways, been turned upside down, making it even more difficult to find Michael, and I am now eighty-five years old. I don't know how much longer I will be around, for, to my everlasting surprise and displeasure, I confess that I am growing feeble.

"I am therefore making it the responsibility of the firm charged with executing this will to continue the search for my nephew and heir. I have made adequate financial provision for this responsibility, and I charge my executors with the following instructions and requirements:

"One: They are to maintain my home and properties in the manner and style I have maintained them, keeping them ready for Michael's return.

"Two: They are to manage the finances and holdings of my estate in the manner in which I direct in the attached codicil.

"Three: My estate shall not, under any circumstances, be subject to sale or probate until it has been bequeathed upon Michael or his direct descendants, except as directed below.

"Four: If, after fifty years of following these directives, Michael or his descendants have not been located, the entirety of my estate will fall to my executors.

"I am depending upon Brunell & Brunell to execute my requirements faithfully. Leonard Brunell, his sons, his brother, and his nephew profess to serve a God who is faithful. By that same God I charge him, his family, and his firm to be equally faithful to the responsibilities and duties which they have willingly undertaken and for which they will be generously compensated."

Jeffers looked up then. "That concludes the reading of the will."

Tears were streaming down Kari's face although she stared steadfastly through them toward the back wall. *Why? Why am I so emotional; why is this affecting me so?*

"Perhaps another brief recess?" It was Clover's voice. Murmurs of assent followed him. The room emptied.

A gentle hand rested on her shoulder for the briefest moment. "We know you're hurting, Miss Kari. You have had considerable turmoil in your life lately. It's all right to cry. You go right ahead now, hear?"

She heard Clover shuffle through the door. When it clicked shut she leaned her forehead on the hard surface of the venerable conference room table and wept. She wept harder than she had in a very long time.

Kari knew that her sobs had to have been heard by those outside the door—heard for quite a while. Clover had placed a box of tissues near her elbow before he left her alone to cry.

She had finished a few minutes ago and was now sopping up her tears with handfuls of the tissues.

"Miss Kari?" Owen Washington peeked into the conference room. "May I come in?"

"Yes." Kari wiped her nose a last time.

"Would you care to use the ladies' powder room to wash and cool your face?"

"Yes, that would be good." Out in the hallway he directed her to a ladies' room close by. She bathed her face in cold water and felt better immediately. When she returned to the conference room, they were waiting for her again.

This time Kari took her seat without a word and nodded to Clover.

"This last portion of our meeting today should be easier, Miss Kari. Clive has prepared a detailed rendering of the estate, which he will read aloud. You may follow along with your own copy."

Clive passed around bound copies of the document and Clover placed one in front of her. Kari's eyes were red and tired; she did not open it, deciding to just listen.

"The details in the document are quite specific and complete—exhaustive, I should say," Clive opened. "I will read the simplified listing on pages twenty-three through twenty-six. Please do stop me if you have a question."

Clive donned a pair of half-spectacles, peering over them at her and then through them at the list. He reminded Kari of Santa Claus perusing his Christmas toy list.

"Well, then, shall we begin?" He cleared his throat one last time. "Item one, the house and its furnishings on Marlow Avenue. Item two—"

"I beg your pardon," Kari hadn't realized she was going to speak.

"Yes, miss?"

"A house? Is it empty, then? I mean, unoccupied? Is that what he meant in the will by 'maintain my home'?"

"Yes, miss. No one has lived in it since Mr. Peter's passing. Brunell & Brunell keeps the house, its furnishings, and the grounds in well-serviced order—the roof, the furnace, the plumbing. In short, everything. The furnishings are protected, of course, but the covers are shaken and the house dusted and swept weekly."

"It would take a few days to ready it for you to occupy," Jeffers inserted, "but not long."

Kari paused and frowned. "But are the, er, taxes paid up?"

"Of course, Miss Kari." Clive looked at her expectantly, as though waiting for a real question, something of any depth or difficulty.

"And the mortgage?"

"I believe . . ." Mr. Clive consulted his notes, "Yes. Mr. Granger paid cash for the house when he bought it. The house has never been mortgaged and is completely unencumbered."

Kari was stunned. *I own a house? A paid-off house of my own?*

Clive continued. "Item two, commercial properties—" Clive read off a long list of legal descriptions and physical addresses. "Item three . . .

Kari tried to follow what he said but with each "item" he listed, the words flew from his mouth and stuck to her brain, kicking and screaming for attention—like a fly stuck to flypaper struggles to free itself.

Rental properties scattered throughout New Orleans.

A hotel named "The Grand Marquis."

*Wait—that's the hotel where I'm staying . . .* Kari heard but could not process the list as Clive droned on.

Holdings in stocks, bonds, and municipal funds.

Precious metals.

Utilities and commodities.

Oil and natural gas wells.

And bank accounts.

All eyes at the table were staring at her. "I'm sorry. Did I miss something?"

"Yes, my dear. I requested that you open your packet to page thirty-three."

Kari stared at the copy in front of her before slowly turning through until she arrived at page thirty-three.

"As you can see from the note at the top, the value of the estate's various assets are enumerated and calculated from close of business one week ago. The estimated total value of the estate is the figure" (he pronounced it, 'figger') "at the bottom."

The page swam before her eyes but when she could make out the numbers set in bold font at the page bottom her heart lurched.

"This can't be right," she stammered. "This *can't* be right. It's— it's too much." She used her fingernail to count the number of numerals and commas: *Two* commas. *Nine* numbers.

*Millions.*

*No. Hundreds of millions.*

She looked to Clover for help, imploring his assurance that it was a mistake. He stared back, his eyes steady. Understanding. Sympathetic.

"I believe I mentioned that Mr. Peter was quite good with his money," Clover murmured. "We've followed his practices and much of the detailed advice he left for managing his holdings. And my son Oskar has done well since he was placed in charge of the assets ten years ago."

"But—" Kari didn't finish. She stared at the sheet in front of her, her finger running down the page, through each item and its relative value. An uncontrollable giddiness was taking hold of her. She kept shaking her head. When she looked up, Washington was watching her, a grin tugging at his mouth, his happiness for her apparent and unfeigned.

Very, very slowly she smiled back.

The room began to relax then. "Congratulations, Miss Kari." Jeffers stood and offered his hand to her. "I know it will be an adjustment, but we are all quite happy for you. Quite happy!"

Clive was a bit more formal. "We must get through probate, and that is sometimes an ordeal. But the estate is in good shape and all the paperwork is ready. Taxes will take a sizable slice, of course, but we have planned and prepared for them as well." He gathered his papers and shuffled them into his portfolio; then he, too, offered his hand to Kari.

Kari turned, in a daze, toward Clover.

"So," he murmured. He was smiling, the twinkle creasing the folds about his eyes more than usual. "Not just a spoon collection, hey?"

# CHAPTER 6

The conference room emptied except for Kari and Clover. He was still smiling, but his mouth held that hint of sympathy Kari had seen earlier.

"Miss Kari, if you agree, I propose that we take the car this afternoon and I show you the house you will inherit. Does my suggestion meet with your approval?"

Kari fumbled around in her spinning thoughts for a moment. "I—yes; I certainly have nothing better to do. But . . . it seems I am taking up a great deal of your time, Clover."

Clover chuckled. "My dear, this estate has been our firm's largest client for decades, and we draw fees from the estate for its executorship. My time is quite devoted to its administration, as is my son Oskar's time. We *certainly* have time for you—even a great deal of time."

Clover fixed Kari with an intensity from which she was unable to look away. "Miss Kari, the probate will take a number of months, yes, but we have no doubt of its outcome. As of this moment, Brunell & Brunell, rather than serving solely as the executor of this estate, now serves *you* as the estate's sole heir. I think you have not quite yet grasped . . . the change in your circumstances."

Kari tore her eyes away from Clover, her head shaking a slow "no" to the implications of what he said. "I . . . ." She had no words left.

Clover again laid a light hand on her shoulder. "It is too much to take in all at once, I warrant, Miss Kari. Shall we do this? Shall we put the enormity of your new circumstances aside for the rest of the day? Tomorrow I have set aside time for us to meet again—you, myself, and Oskar—to discuss particulars.

"Shall we see the house this afternoon and let your cares go by the way until the morrow? Nothing of any import need be decided until probate is over, months from now, as we mentioned. You have ample time to think on and plan how you will go forward."

Kari nodded, relieved. "Yes. See the house. That would be . . . lovely."

Clover helped her from the town car and signaled the driver to wait for them. "We took the liberty of having the house more thoroughly cleaned and set in order a few days past so that you would see it as it should be seen," he murmured.

VIKKI KESTELL

Kari stood on the sidewalk and stared toward the house. It was a wide, two-story structure not, she admitted to herself, as fine as Clover and Lorene's Colonial, but breathtaking to Kari in any regard.

*I own this? I own this house?* Kari kept shaking her head.

According to Clover, they were a distance from the truly wealthy historic homes in the city, but Kari was in awe and a bit giddy over *this* house. *Giddy?*

*When have you ever been "giddy" or even used such a word?* she questioned herself. *That doesn't sound like you.* With an internal caution against allowing her newfound circumstances to go to her head, she followed Clover.

The house was constructed of beautiful chiseled stone that had weathered to a pale golden patina. The house was roofed in pink or rose colored slate. Clover led her to the front entrance centered under a great portico supported by eight pale gold posts.

The portico was enclosed waist high (except for where the steps led up to the entry) in the ornamental wrought iron so common to the Garden Area. As she tried to take it all in, Kari realized that every window on the ground floor was also covered in beautiful but protective wrought iron.

Kari was used to doors and windows protected by wrought iron, Albuquerque's break-in rate being what it was, but nothing as ornate as what protected this house.

They stepped into a large foyer where, with the press of a few buttons, Clover deactivated an alarm system. "This house has sat unoccupied for twenty-seven years. We have done our duty to ensure that it remained undisturbed by thieves and vandals."

Kari looked up and turned in a circle to take in the beauty above her. The ceiling of the foyer was high—at least fifteen feet. Its edges and corners were coved and corniced, and the ceiling plaster itself was intricately carved. A glimmering chandelier hung from the center of the ceiling, still at least ten feet above the parquet floors.

Her eyes swept up to the rail of a mezzanine where the stairway reached the second floor. The wide staircase, on her right, wound to the mezzanine, its rounded, polished banisters beckoning upwards.

Kari tore her eyes away. A door straight ahead was open, so Kari glanced through. She saw a room that had obviously been used as an office. The desk and chair and bookshelves were inviting, as though their owner had merely stepped away for a few moments.

Clover beckoned her. Two wide doors on the left opened into a small sitting room or old-fashioned parlor. Beyond the parlor lay a sizable living room and a large dining room.

Kari sniffed the air in the house. It was pleasant—neither musty nor stale—with a lemony tang.

"A very fine family, the Bodeens, are caretakers here," Clover continued. "Three generations of Bodeens have cleaned and maintained the house and its grounds, first for Mr. Peter, and then for us. Oskar oversees all aspects of the house now. The groundskeeper lives in a small house at the back of the yard and also keeps watch on the house.

"We have cared for the house and its furnishings all these years, as specified by Mr. Peter," Clover was murmuring. "Every object in the house has been photographed and itemized in detail. The furniture is kept draped in protective cloths but is uncovered and dusted, polished, or vacuumed as appropriate on a weekly basis. Three times a year we do repairs and preventive maintenance."

Kari stared around at the beautiful furniture and the dining table and chairs gleaming with fresh oil. Her gaze wandered over lamps, paintings, carpets, and other décor.

*All this is mine?* Kari couldn't grasp it. Her eyes passed over a tall stack of white dust covers folded and left on the seat of a side chair.

"We store the items that are more susceptible to decay, such as carpets and paintings, in a special room we built in the attic," Clover's hand pointed up, "those things to which Louisiana humidity could do damage. We installed a de-humidifier in that room to keep moisture from becoming a problem. Because we knew you were coming, we had the Bodeens bring them out of storage and place them where they belong so you could see them as they ought to be seen."

Clover led her slowly through the rooms on the ground floor until they entered the kitchen through a wide, swinging door. There, Kari gaped. Someone—a long while ago, she realized—had taken the time to make the room a delight—the soul of the home.

The kitchen's cupboards, all heart of pine, glowed with warm light and rose from above the counters all the way to the high ceiling.

*Why, even as tall as I am, I would need a ladder to reach those uppermost cupboard doors,* Kari noted.

Copper-bottomed pots and pans of every size and shape hung from iron hooks over an authentic butcher block island. Bright crockery lined several rows of shelves. The floor was of hard wood and shone spotlessly.

A bay window overlooked the back yard. Around the inside of the window were built-in heart of pine benches and a half-round table forming a charming, cozy nook.

*Did Daddy eat his breakfasts at this table?* Kari wondered. *Did his mother serve him cookies and milk here after school?*

Clover opened cupboards and drawers to display their contents. "Every dish, every piece of cutlery, every glass. All maintained and accounted for. Of course, they were boxed up until a few days ago."

He pointed to the stove—a black, commercial-sized gas range. "About ten years ago we upgraded the wiring, plumbing, and gas lines in the house. We had the chandeliers and this gem," he placed his hand on the stove's cold surface, "upgraded as well. The pilot lights and the gas to the stove are turned off, naturally."

Kari opened a door and found brooms, mops, cleaning supplies, and the odd gadget. Then Clover turned the deadbolt in the back door and pulled it open, stopping to show Kari something. "We took the original exterior doors down and had them and the doorframes "re-engineered" so to speak," he chuckled.

"The doors are solid wood—but now they are banded in steel with reinforcing plates. We also replaced the doorframes with metal ones, and then placed the original wood trim over and around them. These modifications should keep the doors and jams from splintering should someone attempt to break in."

He pointed to the lock. "And these are twin deadbolts, custom made for these doors and frames." His long fingers motioned to the bay window. "The doors and all the windows are wired into the alarm system. We upgrade the system every two years to keep up with advances. I can scarcely conceive of all the new things they dream up these days."

On the covered and screened rear porch, Clover gestured again. "That's the garage just there behind those shrubs. Over yonder, almost hidden in the trees, is the groundskeeper's cabin. Toller Bodeen is our current groundskeeper. You will see him around during the day, most likely."

Kari looked where Clover pointed and nodded when he commented, but it was all too much to retain.

*I would like to spend some time here just wandering about,* she decided. *I want to see this house through Daddy's eyes and imagine him here. Maybe I will keep a few things as keepsakes for when I return to Albuquerque.*

In Kari's mind she was already negotiating with the new owners to buy back her house—the house she had worked so hard to make her home. If all that Clive had listed in the estate was *true*, surely she would have enough money to buy back her house? Because Kari fully intended to return to Albuquerque.

Clover ushered her back inside and opened a door behind the wide swinging entrance to the kitchen that Kari hadn't noticed. He switched on a light and she peered up a narrow staircase.

"These are the back stairs," Clover murmured, "but I would much rather take you up the front way. It's quite lovely, especially during the day."

Kari followed Clover back through the house until they reached the foyer. He led the way up the wide staircase. Kari ran her hand along the banister, its perfect, graceful curves and supple wood delighting her fingertips.

At the first landing, she looked up and saw more of the foyer's architecture repeated above her head. A stained glass window graced the outside wall there—at just eye level. Kari reveled in the blues, purples, and greens of a peacock looking over his shoulder and down upon his fully fanned plumes.

"Breathtaking," she whispered and grinned.

Clover was smiling at her approval. "I particularly enjoy these stairs myself."

The staircase wound higher. The steps turned and Kari stepped onto a second landing. An intricately paned window, this one set in plain glass, provided natural light.

Kari turned left, took three more steps up, and followed Clover onto the wide mezzanine overlooking the foyer. She paused a moment, looking down on the foyer.

*Did Daddy lean over this banister on Christmas mornings, excited for the festivities below?* she wondered as she reluctantly trailed after Clover.

The second floor enclosed four substantial bedrooms and two bathrooms. Clover led her into what had to have been the master bedroom. "Mr. Peter had a bathroom installed *ensuite* in his last years," Clover murmured. "It is, I confess, in need of modernizing. That is something I wager you will enjoy doing yourself."

Kari started to comment—but stopped as what he said sank in. Things that had been impossibilities were becoming possibilities and they were rushing into her head all at once. It was as though the earth was shifting under her feet, and she was losing her balance. So she said nothing.

*But I'm not staying here,* she reassured herself, trying desperately to reestablish her equilibrium, *because this*—all this!—*is not me.*

*So I'm not staying here.*

*Am I?*

# CHAPTER 7

Kari was exhausted when the long day was over, but she was also "wired." Nothing she tried seemed to calm her down or slow her racing thoughts. The looming inheritance and its responsibilities settled like an immense weight in the pit of her stomach.

At the same time, oh, the *possibilities*—the many things she could do or see—stretched endlessly before her, and her mind jumped from one idea or thought to another, like water skittering and spitting its way across a red-hot stove top.

She ate a late dinner alone in the hotel dining room, went for a long walk, and then wandered around the lobby for a while trying to relax. When she returned to her room, still unsettled, she knew she could not put off calling Ruth any longer.

Kari didn't know how to tell Ruth that not only was the whole "inheritance thing" real but it was more than either of them had imagined. And Ruth's words, prophetic in hindsight, rankled under Kari's skin:

*I have been praying for you over this whole inheritance thing, and I truly believe that something good is going to come of all this. Something wonderful and good from God himself.*

*God*, Kari snorted, deriding the word. As she scoffed, she felt a prick in her conscience, a tiny but firm warning. She looked inside, wondering what it was. She brushed it aside and dialed Ruth's number.

"Well, it's about time!" Ruth grumbled when she picked up. "I've been waiting on pins and needles all day! In fact, I'd already given up and gone to bed." Kari heard springs creak through the receiver as Ruth scooted to the edge of her bed.

"I'm sorry; I couldn't call earlier," Kari lied. "It's been a bit . . . overwhelming." *Well, that part is true.*

Ruth was quiet, and Kari knew that she was sensing Kari's disquiet. Ruth's ability to see her more deeply than Kari believed she let on was one of Ruth's endearing—and exasperating—qualities. Ruth called it "spiritual discernment." Kari didn't know what to call it—except *extraordinary*. And sometimes downright annoying.

"Do you want to talk about it?" Ruth asked softly.

Kari hemmed a moment before plunging in. "Well, I met with the lawyers this morning. Actually, with the three senior partners."

There. That would be Ruth's first clue.

"The three senior partners." Now Ruth sounded wary. Good.

"Uh-huh. And their lead investigator, Owen Washington. He's the one who found me."

"All right." The line was quiet as Ruth waited for Kari to continue.

"So . . . it's pretty big, Ruth." Kari's words were bare whispers across the miles.

"The estate is big?"

"Uh-huh."

With those two syllables, Ruth felt things between her and Kari shift. Things would be . . . different now. Ruth waited again.

Finally, she cleared her throat. "Do you mind telling me, ballpark, how big? You don't have to, of course. It is your business. Private. Personal and all."

"No, I . . . it's . . . scary big, Ruth. Scary. I-I'm terrified."

Kari could hear Ruth's concern. "Why? What have they done?"

"Done? Nothing. It's . . . I mean, the estate's probate will take a while, couple of months or more. But then . . ."

"What is it you are afraid of, Kari?" Ruth was always, if anything, to the point.

"The responsibility, I guess. Clover—that's Mr. Brunell—took me to see the house today and it is . . . huge. Gorgeous. Beautiful."

"The house?"

"I, uh, one of the things I inherited is a house. And, no. There are no back taxes owing."

"Well, that's good, isn't it? And no 'other shoe' poised to drop, like you are afraid of, right? You will own your own house outright. See! That's a good thing—a God thing! It's what you've wanted—a home. A real home of your own."

*A home isn't just a house, Ruth; it is where your family is,* Kari objected without speaking the words. *All I find in that house are the remains of what should have been my family . . . but isn't. Too late for that now.*

Ruth babbled on. "Of course the house isn't here in Albuquerque. Are you thinking of selling it? I mean, that way you could buy a home here in New Mexico near your friends—if selling that house clears enough money, that is."

*Oh, I'm pretty sure it would clear enough money to buy anything I wanted in Albuquerque.*

Kari exhaled. "Well, one thing I'm considering is changing my name. Back to Granger. You'd asked me, when the divorce was final, if I would keep David's name. I wouldn't mind having Daddy's name again. It would mean something."

"I like the sound of that, Kari," Ruth murmured. "I'm sure it would comfort you."

"Um . . . and there's more. More to the inheritance. Lots of . . . assets and stuff."

"Lots of assets." Ruth spoke the three words solemnly, and the line went dead quiet. Many beats of Kari's heart passed before Ruth ventured another question. "Kari, did they tell you how much you are going to be worth when everything is said and done?"

"Yeah. I, um, don't recall the exact number. I have a report with it somewhere here in my room. I just counted commas and . . . numbers."

"Commas and numbers."

Kari exhaled once more. "Two commas and nine digits."

Sitting up straight on her bed in Albuquerque, Ruth blinked and her mouth opened, but nothing came out. She reached for her Bible, pulled a recent church bulletin from it, and in its margin scribbled a dollar sign and the number "1" followed by eight zeros. She slowly penciled in two commas.

Two commas, nine digits.

$100,000,000.

The lowest amount it could be.

"No way," she breathed.

As low as Ruth's words were whispered, Kari caught them. "That's why I'm scared, Ruth. It's too much. It's . . . blowing my mind."

In Albuquerque Ruth was still staring at the scribbled number.

Kari was scheduled to meet with Clover and Oskar in the morning. She slept fitfully and woke before dawn. She showered, dressed, and went down for an early breakfast. When Oskar called for her at 9 a.m. she was waiting.

"Good morning, Miss Kari. Sleep well?" Oskar Brunell was perhaps in his late forties. He had the same lean and lanky build as Clover and silver was already streaking his hair, but he also possessed Lorene's amazing gift of making comforting small talk.

As their driver wound his way through morning traffic toward Brunell & Brunell, Kari relaxed.

*If I can trust anyone, I can trust Clover and Oskar,* her heart assured her.

*Oh? Don't forget,* a strident voice inside cautioned, *Clover and Oskar are just two more Christians, bent on converting you—just like they got to Daddy.*

The thought disturbed her. *Will I have to weigh every suggestion and every thoughtful gesture against a hidden agenda?*

She shook her head and frowned. *That just doesn't add up,* she admitted, checking her interactions with them against the suspicious suggestion.

Kari realized that Oskar had witnessed her little internal *tête-à-tête* as it played out across her face. He was watching her, concerned.

"Sorry," she mumbled. "I guess I have a lot on my mind."

"You wouldn't be human if you didn't," he replied in his quiet way.

Miss Dawes was not waiting for them this morning. Oskar led her straight back, through the gauntlet of inquiring, appraising looks, stopping at his father's office. "We'll be in the conference room when you are ready, Father," he murmured.

Oskar held out the same seat Kari had sat in yesterday and poured her a glass of water. Clover joined them immediately.

"Miss Kari. Good morning. How are you today?"

"I didn't sleep as well as I would have liked," Kari admitted.

"I'm sorry. I hope you will become more comfortable in the next few days. Shall we begin?"

Clover outlined the services Oskar had been performing on behalf of Peter Granger's estate. Kari nodded at all the right times, feeling the weight of each task as he listed it. Then Clover surprised her.

"Miss Kari, if I may be so bold, Brunell & Brunell has been handling your properties and accounts for many years. We can continue to perform these same services until such a time as you wish to make a change.

"Admittedly, we draw fees for overseeing your home and other properties and for managing your financial holdings. As you become more familiar with your inheritance you may wish to take personal oversight of aspects of them—such as, initially, oversight of the Granger home—*your home*. We can advise you in any matter or—" Clover leaned closer, "you are perfectly free to take your business elsewhere.

"What I am hoping to assure you of is that *you need not fret or be anxious*. Brunell & Brunell will not be legally released from our obligations as executors until probate closes. Afterwards, when we have been released, you may continue to use our firm as long as you wish. Is this clarification at all helpful?"

Kari released a long sigh. *So much you cannot know*, she thought. "Yes. Thank you. I appreciate your candor."

"Very good, then," Clover smiled. "Brunell & Brunell is legally still employed by the estate until probate ends, at which time we can sit down again and make any changes you wish. We hope you will remain with us in New Orleans until then."

Kari frowned. "What? I mean, I don't know how I can do that, Clover. Back in Albuquerque I had just moved out of my house and I don't have an apartment yet. I'm staying with some friends but I can't impose upon them for long. I don't yet have a job, I won't receive my share in the equity of my ex-husband's and my house for a few more weeks, and I have bills coming due."

Oskar and Clover stared at Kari and then exchanged mildly confused looks.

"What I mean is that I'm proverbially 'cash-strapped' right now," she was quick to add. Kari's cheeks and neck grew red. "I can't afford to continue staying at the hotel—or anywhere else in New Orleans for that matter."

Clover, after another unspoken exchange with Oskar, cleared his throat. "Miss Kari, Brunell & Brunell as the estate executor has discretion with regards to disbursements from the estate. We would be pleased to help you set up a personal bank account here in New Orleans and deposit an amount in it that should suffice for the next few months. We can arrange for the bank to issue you a credit card at the same time."

He searched for the right words. "My dear lady, you really do not need to be concerned about finances anymore. You have, er, *plenty of money*—more than enough—to remain in New Orleans, at *The Grand Marquis*—it will soon be your hotel, after all—or, if you care to, you may move into the Granger house as soon as it can be readied for you."

Frowning, Kari answered. "I am only one person and I don't need much. I'm not a spendthrift, and I don't want to be one. Ever."

She looked up and Clover smiled with something like respect. "I am certain you are in no danger of becoming a spendthrift, Miss Kari," he murmured.

He turned to Oskar. "Will you arrange your time today to take Miss Kari to the bank?"

"Certainly." Oskar inclined his head toward Kari. "Are you available following this meeting?"

Kari leaned her forehead on her hand and stared at the table. *My whole life is changing,* she realized. *My whole life. Will I even need an apartment in Albuquerque . . . afterwards?*

"Miss Kari?" Oskar was waiting for her answer.

"Yes. I'm quite available," she murmured. "And would it be possible for me to spend some time in the house again today? No one need accompany me—if you feel that's all right. I just want to . . . get better acquainted with it. Where Daddy lived."

"I think that is a splendid idea," Clover responded with enthusiasm. He turned to Oskar again. "Will you also provide her with keys to the house?

"Of course."

Clover transitioned to another topic. "So. That is settled. Now . . ." as Clover opened a file in front of him his demeanor shifted subtly. He reached for the telephone on the conference room table and pressed a button. "Miss Dawes? Please send him in."

A moment later the door opened and Washington entered, tipping his head toward Kari. "Miss Kari."

"Good morning, Mr. Washington." Kari smiled a genuine welcome and he took a seat next to Oskar, placing a thick folder on the table.

"You know, Miss Kari, that Mr. Washington is the investigator we charged with finding Mr. Peter's heirs?" Clover asked.

"Yes. You said so."

"Quite right. And I did promise to tell you everything of your father that I could?"

Kari grew excited. "Oh, yes! I so wish to know more of him."

"Perhaps I may take you to lunch soon and share some of my memories of our youth together," Clover suggested. "But we should first hear from Mr. Washington and what his investigation uncovered. I should warn you that in the course of Mr. Washington's investigation, a few . . . curious facts came to light. In the spirit of complete transparency, we wish to apprise you of these curious, er, inconsistencies, although we do not yet know what they mean. Mr. Washington?"

"Thank you, Mr. Brunell. Miss Kari, after Mr. Peter's passing, Brunell & Brunell took possession of all the personal papers found in his house." Washington opened the folder before him. "Among those possessions were found Mr. Peter's birth certificate and those of his sister-in-law and your father, Michael Granger." He was fingering the documents.

"Oh, may I see them, please?" Kari reached her hand for them. *I just want to hold them!* she rejoiced.

"Certainly, Miss Kari." Washington handed them to Kari who received them with itching fingers. Kari spent a few moments perusing them, noting that her father had been born in Atlanta, Georgia. *Atlanta!*

She didn't notice the uncomfortable quiet in the room for several moments. "What is it?" She looked from Washington to Clover and back.

"I was not hired by Brunell & Brunell until late 1987—three years ago—to locate Mr. Michael or his heir and . . . the prior investigator apparently did not verify the birth certificates."

"What do you mean by 'verify'?" Kari asked, confused. "Why would that be necessary?"

"I'm certain the prior investigator thought the same thing, but I prefer a more, shall we say, *exhaustive* approach. I telephoned each of the offices of the county clerks that issued the certificates where the originals should have resided."

"*Should* have resided?"

"Um, yes. In each instance, the clerk could not locate the original record. After consulting the senior partners, I personally visited each of the county offices and made a more thorough search for the originals," he explained. "To our surprise and chagrin, no original documents could be found."

"No original documents?"

"Miss Kari, no records of these births exist except on the papers you hold. I also looked for the parents listed on the certificates. I could find no trace of them either—no birth or death certificates, no marriage licenses, no records at all of the parents listed.

"We also had the death certificate of Michael's father, your grandfather, and traced it back to the city that issued it. Like the three counties of origin for the birth certificates, the city of your grandfather's death had no record of his decease."

Kari's jaw hung slack. "But . . . what does that *mean*?"

"We're not sure it means anything at this date," Clover inserted in a calming voice. "It may mean nothing at all. The chain of inheritance from Peter Granger to you is unbroken and we certainly will not challenge it, nor will we . . . muddy the water by publicly making the uncertain nature of these certificates known as they *do not bear* on your right to inherit, but . . . well, we felt *you* had a right to know."

"But know what? What can this mean? Are you saying these papers are not real?" She held the certificates in her hands as she turned to Washington. "What do you think?"

He nodded. "It is my considered opinion that these are forgeries—very clever, very professional, but forgeries nonetheless."

Kari slumped back in her chair. "But if they are forgeries, then . . . then who is Peter Granger? Who is Michael Granger? And for that matter, who am I?"

"That is a question that, in the almost four years I have been on this case, I still cannot answer," Washington managed. "As far as the world knows, Peter, Alicia, and Michael Granger are just who those certificates say they are—and *you* are undeniably Michael's daughter. We know that your birth certificate is legitimate. I have verified it so."

Clover stepped in, his calm voice soothing Kari's nerves. "Miss, Kari, do you recall how we told you that when Mr. Peter passed away we took all personal papers from the house?"

"Yes, I do."

"Oskar, do you have that box we spoke of?"

Oskar replied in the affirmative and produced a small cardboard box that had been out of sight on the chair beside him. He stood and placed it in front of Kari.

"What is this?"

"It contains all the photographs we found in the house. Pictures of your father as an infant, growing up, and as a young man. Your grandmother and uncle."

Kari found herself clutching the box as if it would vanish. "Pictures . . . of Daddy?"

"Yes, ma'am. You take them back to the hotel with you, hear? They are yours now."

Kari could not fall asleep that night. She had gorged on the photographs, had feasted on each one until she was almost ill.

The pictures of her father as a young man meant the most to her—she *knew* this man even if in the images he appeared younger than she'd remembered him. She could almost hear his voice and feel his arms wrapped about her.

She studied his likeness and compared herself to him—same light brown hair shot with gold. Same eyes. Same nose. Kari was even tall like he was—shorter than him, of course, but tall for a woman.

But when she looked at the few photos of Alicia, Kari no longer saw a resemblance—not between her and her son; not between her and Kari.

*He must resemble his father, Willis Granger,* Kari decided. *Willis Granger—my grandfather.* She spoke the name aloud: "Willis Granger—my grandfather." She had so much more family today than she'd had just days ago before arriving in New Orleans!

Then Kari studied the single family portrait in the box: A sepia-toned image set in a folding cardstock frame. According to the stamp on the back, it had been taken in 1925.

Kari did the math. *Daddy was fourteen.*

She examined the three members of her family together: Alicia seated in the middle, Peter Granger to one side and Michael to the other. Michael's hand was placed on his mother's shoulder, a gesture of affection. Peter Granger's hands were clasped behind him. He seemed a little disconnected from Alicia and Michael. It was the only image of Peter Granger in the box. *Curious.*

When she could look at them no more, the images danced in her head. Kari frowned a little and studied the family portrait again. *Daddy doesn't really favor his uncle, either,* she realized. *And what about the birth certificates? What is that about?*

In some ways, coming to New Orleans had created more questions than answers. And instead of feeling filled and satisfied, all her staring at the photographs had left her empty.

*I still feel alone,* she confessed. *Even with all this "stuff," I still have no one and I don't know who I am.*

She pondered her feelings objectively for a change. *All my life I have been by myself. No family. No one. I thought I might be coming home, but that sense of connection I had hoped for isn't here. Instead, I feel even farther from the truth.*

Sure, she was going to inherit Peter Granger's fortune—*but who was this man?* The secrets Clover had confided to her—the birth certificates that attested to Peter Granger, Alicia Granger, and Michael Granger's identities but, when traced back to the hospitals and county records of origin, *did not exist?*—troubled her more deeply than she had allowed Clover or Oskar to know.

Kari lay awake until near dawn, her thoughts swirling around in her head until the knots they had twisted into brought on a pounding headache. She arose around four, took two aspirin, and crawled back under the covers. The air conditioning kept her room at a pleasant temperature, neither too hot nor too cold, and yet she shivered and rubbed the back of her neck where the knotty pain was worst.

# CHAPTER 8

The aspirin must have worked, because Kari at last fell into an exhausted sleep. When she awoke the clock on the stand next to the bed read half past ten.

*At least that blasted headache is gone,* Kari sighed. She showered, dressed in jeans and her favorite boots, and made her way, bleary-eyed, to the little café down the street from the hotel.

"Coffee, please. *Café au lait,*" she begged when the waitress passed by. Clover had given her ample cash with which to buy her meals in the hotel's classy restaurant, but Kari felt more comfortable in this mom and pop café.

"Long night?" the waitress asked. "Ya look wrung out, hon."

"Long night but short sleep," Kari replied, scrubbing at her eyes. *I need to start jogging or hiking again. I'm getting stiff and lazy.*

"I'll get y'all's coffee right away, hon. And y'all need our fresh beignets, too. I'll jest bring a plate."

Kari brightened at the prospect of one of the piping hot confections. While Kari was sipping her first cup and licking powdered sugar from her fingers, she scanned through the list of furnishings from the house she'd compiled, the pieces she thought she might like to keep. Other items there called to her, but she doubted they would "fit" in any home she might rent—or even *buy*—in Albuquerque.

*I won't have the class of home these furnishings deserve,* she fussed inwardly, *but I hate to think of selling any of these precious things. I don't know if I should sell the house, for that matter! After all, it's paid for; I could just . . . move in, I suppose. For a while.*

The idea of truly living in such a house tantalized. On the other hand rattling around in the large house by herself in a strange neighborhood—in a strange city!—also gave her a mild case of the creeps. And, after all, did she even want to live in New Orleans?

*Like, who do I know in New Orleans?* she asked herself. *Not one person other than Clover and his family! And what about Albuquerque? Would I up and leave my friends there?*

Then she had to ask herself the real question, the one she had been avoiding. *Just who do I have to go back to in Albuquerque?*

Only Ruth, the Esquibels, and a few old co-workers. The truth was distressing and, before she could catch her thoughts, the same old tune started up: *I'm alone. I have no one—*

"Stop it!" Kari spoke the words aloud, snapping herself out of her reverie and out of her spiraling thoughts. She was sitting in the coffee shop and her outburst had drawn curious looks.

She took a sip of coffee and made herself "try on" the idea of staying in the house—*just until I figure out what I want, what I should do.* As she turned the idea over in her mind, it surprised her to discover that it seemed right.

*If I stay in the house, I will feel more 'at home' than I do at the hotel,* she reasoned. *I can take my time and think things through. No need to rush. No pressure.*

The more she thought on it, the better the decision fit. Even the expense of opening the house faded. She had to keep reminding herself that she had money now. *Plenty of money,* Clover had insisted. Plenty of money to open the house and make it livable again.

*But I can't—I won't!—allow the money to change me,* she promised herself. *I will not be rash or impulsive with it. That would feel . . . wrong. Selfish.*

Not for the first time, Kari wished the inheritance had been minor, enough to help her through until she could get back on her feet, but nothing more. She felt the weight of all the holdings Clive had listed during the reading of Peter Granger's will growing heavier by the day and felt nearly crushed by the impending responsibility Clover had hinted at.

*I can stay in the house for now,* she decided, *but I swear I will not become the stereotype* nouveau riche, *crazed with spending and ostentation.*

With that decision made, Kari decided to return to the house when she finished her late breakfast. After the meeting yesterday, Oskar had taken her to the bank to open a new checking account and apply for a credit card.

Oskar's whispered message to one of the account managers brought the bank manager running. He introduced himself and personally assisted Kari. She shivered as she recalled the transfer form Oskar filled out and the balance the bank manager penciled on the top line of her check register. He also handed her several hundred dollars in twenties. Kari had tucked them into her wallet, trying to shake the sense of unreality.

Afterwards, Oskar had taken her to a car rental office where he'd signed for a car for her. Of all things, it was another *white* vehicle, as unexciting and blasé as the Reliant parked at the Esquibels' in Albuquerque.

*Someday I'm going to have a nice car, one that I personally select,* Kari promised herself, warming to the idea. *Nothing outlandish. Just nice—and not white! A car, after all, is something I need, not something I just want.*

As Oskar had bid her goodbye yesterday, he had pressed a ring of keys into Kari's hand. "Every key you need for your house should be on this ring," he assured her. "I understand the Bodeens have replaced the dust covers on the furniture, but you may move them if you wish."

*For your house.* She shook her head just thinking those words again.

As she had passed through the parlor, living room, and dining room yesterday, she'd seen that Oskar had been correct: The Bodeens had re-covered the furniture but they had not taken the carpets and paintings back to their attic storeroom. Then Kari had spent the rest of that day wandering "her" house, making notes and noodling ideas.

She had been over the entire house, including the attic, but she had not yet explored the garden in the back or seen the inside of the old garage. This she would do today.

Kari paid for her coffee and beignets and walked back to the hotel. The valet brought her rental around and she set off for the house, fairly confident she could find her way back to it.

After only one wrong turn, Kari arrived. She parked in the driveway but near the front of the house. Before she used the key Oskar had identified as belonging to the door, she rehearsed to herself how to disarm the alarm. Then she was inside.

The house was growing familiar to her and she went straight back toward the kitchen. There Kari rummaged in the broom closet for a flashlight Oskar had told her she would find. With it in hand, she unlocked the back door and stepped onto the screened and covered porch.

Toller Bodeen (*who names their child Toller, for heaven's sake!*) kept the grounds beautifully pristine. Kari was entranced by the aged trees, their gnarled old trunks dripping Spanish moss. She spied the roof of Toller Bodeen's cabin peeking through the branches.

On the side of the house nearest the kitchen, at the end of the long cobbled driveway, sat the garage. It was detached, as was customary around the time the house was built, and sat far back on the lot.

The garage, like the house, had been built of chiseled stone mortared together. As she circled around its outside, it became apparent to Kari that someone had taken pains to see that the building was secure: The garage's automobile door was newer, quite strong, and locked from inside. The lone window at the back of the building had a sturdy grate bolted over it. The garage's side entrance was protected by a barred, steel security door set in a steel frame. A heavy deadbolt kept the security door locked. Kari had rattled every entrance.

"Good morning, ma'am."

The voice took Kari by surprise, and she stood up, feeling guilty, to see who spoke to her.

"Sorry, ma'am. Din't mean t' startle you. I'm Toller. You must be Miz Hillyer?"

The man was medium sized, thin, with black hair and a permanently sunburned face. Kari could scarcely see his eyes, creased as they were, but his mouth was pleasant and welcoming.

"Yes. I am." She wiped her hand on her jeans and held it out.

"I'd shake with ya, but my hands are filthy, ma'am." He apologized and held his hands out for her to see. "Been workin' over that flower bed just there." Toller nodded and Kari looked where he pointed.

"Well, please don't let me interrupt you," Kari replied. "I'm just looking around, getting familiar with the place."

The man nodded and offered, "Anytime ya'd like me t' show you th' grounds, ya just holler, hear?"

"Yes; thank you." As Toller strode across the lawn, Kari tripped up the back porch and into the kitchen where she dug in her handbag for the set of keys Clover had given her. She grasped them and returned to the side door to the garage.

Kari tried several keys until she found the one that fit the deadbolt. Once the barred door opened, she found that the same key fit the deadbolt on the wood interior door.

She switched on the flashlight she'd found in the kitchen and pointed the beam inside. The interior was dim and dust motes floated in the flashlight beam, but the garage wasn't as dirty as she had expected it to be. It, too, bore the look of regular cleanings.

Kari's mouth formed an "o" as the beam fell upon an automobile parked inside. Clover had said nothing about a car! The car was set on blocks and completely enclosed in a custom-fit canvas cover that molded to the car like a glove.

Kari's eyes roamed hungrily over the shape of the car, sucking in her breath when she spied two large fins at the rear—two very distinctive fins.

"Classic . . ." Kari murmured, growing excited. She dropped the key ring on a tool bench and worked her way around the car until she found a way to loosen the cover in front. She slid the canvas up and back until the grill was exposed. The Cadillac chevron and emblem shone dully but the glossy red paint glimmered in the glow of the flashlight.

"Cadillac! Candy-apple red." Kari was beside herself. She had to see more. When she found the "Coupe de Ville" letters and emblem on the side, she was ecstatic.

Kari knew next to nothing about cars, but she shivered with excitement at the thought of owning such a fine vintage auto. *I must call Clover this afternoon and find out if the car can actually be driven,* Kari promised herself.

She recalled the nondescript white Chevy sitting in the driveway and her equally humdrum Reliant in Albuquerque, sniffed with disdain, and then chuckled. *Why, I'm a car snob!* she laughed. Taking care not to scratch the finish, she tugged the car's cover back into place.

Nothing else of interest caught her eye in the garage. She opened a tall closet at the end of the building and looked over the usual collection of yard and garden tools. They had not been used in quite some time and were finely furred with rust.

*Mr. Bodeen must store the tools he uses elsewhere.* Kari closed the closet and moved the beam around the interior once more.

Then she pointed the flashlight up. Instead of rafters, she saw a crudely finished ceiling and the dangling, knotted end of a rope. Training the light on the rope, she realized it was attached to a long trapdoor.

*I wonder if anything is up there,* Kari mused. She had been more than a twinge disappointed in the house's attic. The special room Clover alluded to was built to keep the room at an ideal temperature and humidity for storing carpets, paintings, books, and other perishable items. The storage room took up half of the attic's available space.

The rest of the attic contained none of the mysterious clutter of trunks and antiquities Kari's imagination had conjured, only neatly stacked boxes and a few extra dining chairs. Altogether disappointing.

Kari pulled on the rope. The long trap door was hinged. With a creak—and a cloud of dust—it swung down to the garage floor. Built onto the inside of the door was a ladder, set at an angle like a mini staircase.

Kari stared up the ladder. Dim light shone down through the trap door's opening. She itched to see what was up there but the dirt . . .

She returned to the kitchen and gathered a whisk broom, some work gloves, and a clean dusting cloth before sprinting back to the garage. "Here goes nothing." She folded the dust cloth into a triangle and covered her hair with it, pulled on the gloves, grabbed the small broom and the flashlight, and climbed the ladder to the garage's attic—which, by the looks of it, hadn't been swept in a while. She knocked down a couple of cobwebs before she dared stick her head into the attic space.

Using the flashlight, she scanned around the low room. The pitched roof wasn't insulated or finished; its bare boards over the pitched rafters formed the ceiling, but the roof seemed in good shape. Kari noticed where a workman had patched a leak at one time.

At the end of the attic was a single window set in the stone wall. It was round with panes like pie slices. As dusty as the window was, quite a lot of afternoon light shone into the small attic, and Kari could see that the room was empty with the exception of some old luggage and antique chests or trunks.

The trunks were as alluring as a treasure map. *Maybe I'll find some fun old clothes,* she grinned.

She climbed into the attic room and made for the trunks. Kari, wary of spiders or other creepy crawlers, was glad she was wearing gloves, jeans, and boots.

The suitcases were empty; the two trunks were both locked. Kari remembered the set of keys Clover had given her. They were on the workbench, below. She clambered down the ladder, snagged the key ring, and climbed back up, and carefully looked over the collection of keys.

"Yes! Some of these keys *have* to fit these trunks!" she laughed aloud. Before long she had unlocked the two chests.

The first trunk was empty and smelled of mothballs, but she hit pay dirt in the second trunk, the one with a domed lid. As she opened it, the scent of lavender mixed with expensive perfume wafted upwards. She inhaled deeply, reveling in the intertwined fragrances.

The trunk had a deep tray insert that rested on narrow rails attached to the inside walls of the trunk. She studied the removable tray for a moment. Then, with utmost care, she unfolded the top layer of tissue paper between her and whatever was packed inside.

As she folded the tissue back, the sheets broke and crumbled, but underneath them she spied several beautiful old gowns, each folded inside its own layers of tissue paper. Kari's heart quickened and she exhaled, anticipating the fun ahead.

*I can't take these out with nowhere clean to lay them,* Kari realized. *But wasn't there a stack of—* She scooted down the ladder, this time leaving the garage and taking the steps to the kitchen two at a time. In the dining room she grabbed a dust cover from the stack left folded on one of the dining chairs. She took the cloth outside, shook it for good measure, and raced back to the garage.

Kari spread the long dust cover on the attic floor and turned back to the tissue-wrapped dresses in the trunk. Just like the top layer, the paper crumbled when she lifted out the dresses, but the gowns were in wonderful shape. She laid each dress carefully on the dust cloth, reveling in their full-length display.

*Alicia wasn't very tall,* she observed, noting the length of the dresses. *I must have gotten my height from Daddy's daddy, Willis. Willis Granger.*

When the tray was empty, she lifted it out and placed it on the dust cloth also. In the depths of the trunk she found neatly arranged boxes. She lifted every box out and examined its contents, finding three exquisite hats, two pair of evening shoes, and an assortment of beaded handbags, each one a work of art. Kari was thrilled.

As she opened the handbags, she was rewarded with elegant, elbow-length gloves with pearl buttons at the wrists, tiny cut-glass perfume bottles, and a gold-plated compact with the name "Alicia" engraved on its cover.

*Alicia Granger,* Kari marveled. *My grandmother. These are her dresses and handbags—placed here after her death?* Suddenly, the treasure Kari was unearthing took on dearer meaning.

Lastly, at the bottom of the trunk and in a corner, was tucked a fabric-covered item. Kari lifted the item out—it was a long scarf, tied about some sort of box.

The scarf was a diaphanous woven silk, purple and red, shot with gold and silver threads. "Priceless," Kari murmured, holding an end of the fabric to the light, marveling as it shimmered.

Taking pains not to snag or tear the scarf, Kari undid the two knots. Within the scarf's folds she discovered a carved cedar box—a miniature hope chest—perhaps only eight by ten inches and five inches deep.

Kari picked it up. *What will be inside?* she queried herself. *More finery? Precious jewelry? A bundle of old love letters written between Alicia and Willis Granger?*

But the box was locked. The box's brass hasp was folded over its corresponding staple and was secured by a tiny brass padlock.

A simple paper seal was glued all the way around the box—encompassing it. The year *1957* was scrawled large in faded ink across the seal. Kari puzzled over the box for a moment.

*Odd. This box was sealed in 1957?* She stared at the dresses and handbags. It was a moment before she realized why she was puzzled.

Because Alicia Granger had died in 1927 and, presumably—because of the fragile condition of the tissue paper—these wonderful dresses had been packed away not long after her death.

*Did someone put this box at the bottom of this trunk long after these dresses and bags were packed away?* She frowned, still puzzling over it. It would have been simple to lift the tray out of the trunk, place the box at the bottom of the trunk under the boxed hats and handbags, and replace the tray without disturbing the dresses packed in the tray.

Then the import of the carved cedar box dawned on her: *Why, someone deliberately hid this box here. Someone locked it, sealed it, and put a date on it. Then they hid it at the bottom of this trunk. But whatever for?*

The seal read 1957. Kari thought she had heard the year 1957 spoken recently, but she couldn't put her finger on where or when. *When did I hear the year 1957 lately?*

The mystery only made Kari want to open the box more.

Fumbling with the key ring, Kari looked for a key to match the tiny lock—there was none, of course. Such a small key would not have fit on the much larger ring.

She sat back on her heels to think. She glanced at the trunk, now empty. Not knowing why, she leaned over the trunk and felt along its inside walls. Nothing.

She examined the inside of trunk's domed lid. Nothing.

Then she ran her hand along the inside of the lip of the trunk's lid—the lip she could not see because the lid was open and the front of the lip was facing down.

That's when she felt something, something stuck. It felt like a little envelope, perhaps only one inch by two inches, attached to the inside wall of the lip.

She tugged at a corner of the envelope, but it was fixed—glued—quite securely. Kari grabbed the key ring and slid one of the keys under the envelope. It popped free.

It was as though she knew what she would find. When she lifted the folded flap of the little manila envelope and turned it over, a miniscule key plopped into her hand. She fit it into the lock and turned it.

With a click, the lock separated. She pulled it off and was able to easily lift the box's hasp from the staple. All that remained was to break the seal around the box. Kari hesitated, unsure of doing just that.

She swallowed and looked about the attic again. *This is mine. All of this is mine,* she reminded herself. *It is all right for me to open this, because it is mine.*

She used a longer, sturdier key to slice through the paper seal and eased open the box lid. The inside of the box was dry and dust-free, smelling of aged cedar oil. Lying in the box was only a cloth bag with a drawstring closure. She lifted the bag out.

She couldn't stop thinking that someone had taken care to hide the box and its contents. With trembling fingers she loosened the drawstring tie, opened its mouth, and drew out its contents onto a corner of the dust cloth.

First her fingers encountered and pulled out a thick envelope, the lettering on it so faint that Kari could not make it out. She turned it over—it was sealed, with more faded writing across the seal—and set it aside. She reached into the cloth bag again and drew out a small book. The book's faded leather cover was chipped and cracked and its pages rustled as Kari placed it on the cloth and stared at it.

*No jewels or finery. No love letters tied in a ribbon.*

Kari picked up the book, hoping not to break the spine as she eased it open, but the spine retained some of its suppleness. She turned to the first page. The ink was still bright, and she easily read the words penned in a fine hand,

*Rose Thoresen*
*My Journal*

❧ ✻ ❧

# CHAPTER 9

In the fading afternoon light Kari turned that first page and read, *Journal Entry, April 25, 1909*. The date stunned her. *1909! Eighty-two years ago!* Kari turned her eyes back to the yellow-edged page. In a small, flowing script, Kari read,

*Journal Entry, April 25, 1909*

*Dear Lord, as I arose this morning I felt led to chronicle this new endeavor upon which we have embarked. I confess though, that as this new day begins, I also need to pour out my heart to you.*

*We have been so pressed in the past 48 hours. It was not until this morning I realized what I had lost in the fire: The only likenesses of Jan I possessed and the few photographs I owned of Joy as a baby and as she grew up. All of them burned in the lodge with everything else. Oh, Lord! Grief, heavy as a great rock, struck my heart at this realization.*

*So I pick up pen and ink and pour my sorrow onto this page. Father, please help me to bear the loss. I recall with gratitude that Søren and Meg still have a few photographs of Jan and one in particular of Søren and Joy together when she was a toddler. Thank you, Lord, for reminding me. I will ask them to have reproductions made for me, no matter how costly.*

*I must also acknowledge a great truth, if only to you. I acknowledge that had I been given a choice between keeping my precious mementoes or gaining the freedom of these even more valuable treasures—I speak of these young women, Lord!—I **must** have chosen these women.*

*For on those whom you have poured your Son's lifeblood, you have also placed the most value. Can any earthly treasures be worth more? No, Lord, they cannot.*

*So I commit today, Lord, to honor these young women with the care I would have given my precious photographs. Strengthen me to care with all my heart, I pray, Lord God!*

At the first lines, Kari's brows drew together. *Just what I need. Another religious weirdo preaching at me.*

But as she continued reading, the tale on the page drew her in, especially the part about the fire and the lost photographs, the only ones she owned of . . . Jan and Joy?

*Who were Jan and Joy to this woman?* Kari wondered. *Her children?* As she read and reread the entry she couldn't help but compare what she read with her own experience. *I have no pictures of Mommy and I had none of Daddy until just recently—only my memories of him.*

Her heart went out to the woman whose words she read. "Rose," Kari whispered. "Rose Thoresen. I feel your pain."

The tiny glimpse into this woman's life—this *Rose Thoresen*—stirred something in Kari. She read the page again, moved and intrigued.

Kari stared at the page, no longer seeing it. *The freedom of these even more valuable treasures? I speak of these young women?*

What could it possibly mean?

*For on those whom you have poured your Son's lifeblood, you have also placed the most value. Can any earthly treasures be worth more?*

Those two lines struck Kari deeply. "Your Son's lifeblood," she murmured.

And then it seemed that the light in the attic went out, leaving her in the dark. Kari gasped, but her reason soon prevailed: The late afternoon sun had at last dropped below the bottom of the attic window.

Kari fumbled around and found the flashlight she had brought up the ladder. She shone it on the contents of the trunk she had unpacked.

"I cannot leave these priceless things lying out," she muttered. Neither could she repack the dresses the way she had found them without risking damage to them—the tissue paper so carefully folded around the dresses had fallen to bits.

Kari placed the journal and the unopened envelope in the cloth bag, returned the bag to the cedar box, and took them first into the house. She brought back another dust cloth, folded the dresses inside the two sheets, and carefully carried them down the ladder. The boxed hats, shoes, and handbags she left in the trunk. They would be fine until later.

It was nearly seven-thirty in the evening and twilight was upon them. *I need to contact someone familiar with the proper care of such aged clothing,* Kari reflected, *but I won't find anyone this late in the day.*

She went into the dining room and looked at the long, cloth-covered dining table. *That will work.* She gently deposited the gowns on a chair and then, on the table atop the clean cloth, she tenderly laid out each gown and covered them with other cloths.

It was while she was laying out the gowns that she finalized her decision. *In the morning I will tell Clover that I am going to live in this house—for the time being. I will ask him to make the arrangements to have the house readied for occupancy.*

*And tomorrow I can ask Oskar or Clover for a recommendation regarding these gowns,* she thought. Then she remembered the Cadillac. *And ask them about the car!*

She locked up the garage and house, set the alarm, and stood on the front porch thinking. In her hand was the carved cedar box. She was not about to leave that in the house! In fact, she could not wait to get it back to her hotel so that she could read more from the book she had found.

As she opened her car another thought came to her, this one somewhat troubling: *Who was Rose Thoresen and why was her journal hidden at the bottom of Alicia Granger's trunk?*

Kari spent hours that night reading Rose Thoresen's journal, completely caught up in the family and events Rose had described on the journal's pages.

*I had no idea that girls back then were often kidnapped and forced into prostitution!* Kari was appalled but experienced a vicarious thrill as Rose described rescuing many such women.

She wrinkled her nose as she thought of Albuquerque's "war zone," the area on and around Central Avenue near the fair grounds, so notorious for streetwalkers, drugs, and gang violence.

*Surely raping, beating, and enslaving girls in prostitution doesn't happen today . . . does it?* Kari's forehead puckered as a few doubts and questions crossed her mind.

She returned to the journal, and much to Kari's surprise, even the way Rose interwove her prayers with the goings-on and often troubling events of "Palmer House" fascinated her.

*She puts little distinction between her concerns and her prayers,* Kari mulled, *as though she were having conversations with God, as though she knew God . . . on an intimate footing . . . as though her faith were a tangible thing and God were nearby, actually listening. That is not how I've thought of Christianity.*

By the time she finished reading Rose's journal, the clock read two-thirty in the morning. Kari only stopped because the journal had come to an abrupt end. The last entry was April 12, 1911, and yet many blank pages remained in the little book.

Kari stared at the last entry, chagrined and frustrated. Her mind was filled with unanswered questions: *What became of Rose Thoresen? What became of her daughter Joy? What about Joy's husband, Grant, and their little baby boy, little Edmund, named after their dear friend?* Rose had described Grant's illness, and the prognosis had not been good.

Kari was vexed. *What could doctors possibly do for heart disease back then? And what about Mei-Xing and her little daughter? Were they kept safe from Shan-Rose's awful grandmother, Fang-Hua? What became of them—and Breona and Tabitha and Sara and . . .*

Kari sighed, keenly disappointed. In the space of hours she had become intimately involved in so many lives—only to have their stories cut off with no explanation! None!

Reluctantly, Kari laid the book aside and climbed into bed. She lay with her eyes open in the dark pondering the mysterious Rose, the two unusual and amazing years she had chronicled . . . and her faith.

*If I were to ever believe in God,* Kari confessed, *I would want it to be real like that, real all the time, like how it was real to Rose.* She sighed. *But I know better—I will never be talked or tricked into believing in a god who is so heartless in the face of so much suffering. So it does not matter.*

*Only . . . I wish I knew what happened to Rose.*

Without realizing it was happening, Kari had grown possessive feelings for this woman. *Perhaps there is a way to learn more about her,* she thought as she drifted off.

Kari woke the next morning filled with plans. Before she had breakfast, she changed into shorts, a t-shirt, and running shoes and left the hotel by a side door.

Twenty minutes of running showed her how difficult jogging in New Orleans summer heat would be, even in the early morning. She was soaked when she returned to the hotel and slunk through the lobby, avoiding the disparaging eyes of the front desk manager.

She showered, ordered breakfast, and called Clover at home as soon as she knew he would be up and around. "Clover? Yes, good morning! Thank you; I've had a lovely time the last two days wandering all over the house, exploring all its 'wonders.'"

She listened, smiling, as he enthused with her over the house. "I also went into the garage yesterday," she inserted when he took a breath.

"Ah-*ha*! And did you find the car?"

"Oh, I did! And, Clover, it is gorgeous! Can it ever be driven, do you think?"

"My dear, the engine has only a few thousand miles on it. Not even properly broken in, I suspect. Mr. Peter bought it brand-spanking new in 1959 but, because his strength was declining, never did drive it much. When he passed away in 1964, we found that the tires had gone bad—ruined from disuse.

"We hired some boys who specialized in long-term auto dry storage to prepare it properly. They drained the engine and crankcase, removed the battery, and put the car on blocks. Covered it, of course, and mouse-proofed the garage.

"We'll need to locate a vintage car specialist as those good ol' boys have been out of business for fifteen years. We'll have the specialists tow the little beauty to their garage and put it to rights for you."

"Oh, thank you! I can't wait to see it then." *And drive it!* she enthused.

"Clover, I've been thinking. I've decided to stay here during the probate. Would you please make the arrangements so that I can move into the house?"

"My dear, I am delighted to hear this! It was Mr. Peter's express wish that Michael come back to live in his childhood home. Since it cannot be him, I am glad it is you. I shall have Oskar call the Bodeens right away. He will also arrange for the plumbing to be flushed out and tested and the gas turned on. You shall have things to do, also, you know."

"What will I need to do?"

"I will have Oskar call on you to help you make a list. You must choose one of the bedrooms for your use and purchase a new mattress for the bed, buy all new linens for it and the bathrooms. A myriad of little things before you move in. Perhaps you would like to repaint and paper. Just put it all on your credit card and we will take care of the bills."

"I-I . . . just go and buy whatever I like?"

"My dear, again, *plenty of money*. You buy for yourself and the house whatever you like. In fact, buy yourself a new wardrobe while you are at it. Use the card."

"Um, I have no idea where to go . . ."

"Ah. Quite so." Kari heard him tapping a pen on his desk. "Would you care for Lorene's company? She knows just where to go for what. I don't wonder but she would love to help you shop—bearing in mind that my girl is no spring chicken anymore."

"Do you think she would? Oh, I will be careful with her, Clover, I promise. We can do a little at a time, if that works best for her."

"Then give her a call. She will be elated. Now about that lunch we talked about. Are you available Friday?"

"Yes! I so want to hear more about Daddy."

"Then let me pick you up, say around 11:30 Friday morning? We'll go somewhere special."

"Thank you, Clover."

Kari went on to tell him about the trunk in the garage's attic filled with Alicia Granger's exquisite dresses and handbags. "Can you suggest someone who could help me to properly preserve these beautiful things?"

"Yes, yes, I believe so. Let me look them up. I will give them your name and number."

Kari inhaled and then blew out her breath. Yesterday she had nothing left to do in New Orleans; today she was inundated with tasks and activities that would last days if not weeks.

Then she remembered: "Oh, I almost forgot! Clover, I found something else in that trunk, a woman's journal. Did you ever hear the name 'Rose Thoresen' before?"

"Is that whose journal it was?"

"Yes. I-I've read it already. I hope that's all right."

"What are the dates in the journal?"

"It starts in 1909. More than eighty years ago. At the end, she had just become a grandmother."

"Well, then, Miss Kari, we can't expect Rose Thoresen to still be living and, as the journal is among your uncle's things, I see no harm in your reading it. But to answer your question, no; I've never heard that name. Perhaps a relation to Alicia Granger?"

"Maybe . . ." but Kari was deep in thought again. *If Rose Thoresen was related to Alicia, wouldn't Rose have mentioned her? Anyway, why hide the book in a box, lock and seal it up, and hide it at the bottom of Alicia's trunk, beneath her gowns?*

It was a tantalizing mystery!

Kari said her goodbyes to Clover automatically. As she hung up the receiver, she was already reaching for the cedar box and the sealed envelope.

She peered at the faded writing on the envelope, turning it this way and that to get more light on it. "Still can't make it out," she muttered. "Part of it looks smeared."

She stared at the envelope until the name Owen Washington came to her. "Owen! He's an investigator—surely he would know how to make the writing on this envelope readable?"

"Owen Washington." He spoke with that warm, honeyed NOLA drawl Kari had learned to love.

"Mr. Washington? This is Kari Hillyer calling."

"Miss Kari! It is good to hear you. How are you doing?"

Kari appreciated the concern she heard on the other end of the line. "Actually, I think I'm adjusting, but only because I'm taking things a day at a time."

"The best way to live, in my opinion."

"Thank you."

Kari told him of her decision to stay in New Orleans for the time being. "I shall be stumbling about town for a few weeks buying mattresses and towels, I suppose, but I have decided to move into the house as soon as it can be readied."

"I am glad you are staying, Kari. I hope you'll make your home here, but that is a premature hope, I think. After you've fallen in love with NOLA, you may think you could not live elsewhere. Now, what can I do to help you today?"

Kari explained to him about the trunk, the journal, and the sealed envelope with faded ink. "Whatever is written on the envelope must be important, because there is writing across the seal, too. I can't read what it says because the ink is so faint and scratchy."

"Why don't you just open the envelope?" he asked. "Perhaps the contents will explain themselves."

Kari thought about his suggestion. "I guess I wouldn't feel right about it. I'd like to read the outside first. That's why I called. Would you know how to make old ink readable again?"

"That's not usually too difficult, and I have a friend, another investigator, who has a little home laboratory. Would you like me to call him?"

"Yes, please! I would really like to know what it says."

"I'll call you back then."

Kari hung up and started making a list. "I need to go back to the house and choose a bedroom," she realized.

That afternoon she met Oskar at the house and they toured the four bedrooms on the second floor. The logical choice was the master bedroom with the bathroom "ensuite" as Clover had called it, but Kari didn't think she'd be comfortable sleeping in Peter Granger's bedroom or his bed—even with a new mattress!

Even if nearly three decades had passed, something about the man gave her the shivers.

"When Mr. Peter added the bathroom to his bedroom, he incorporated what had originally been Mr. Michael's nursery," Oskar mentioned. "That was in the 1930s. Although the bath was remodeled in the 1950s, it is sorely in need of an upgrade."

*The nursery! Where Daddy's mother rocked him to sleep and where he played with his toys as a little boy. Maybe later I will have it all remodeled, especially the bathroom,* she considered.

She was finding it easier to think about spending money from her father's inheritance from his uncle—now *her* inheritance from her father.

Kari studied the room Alicia had lived in until she died. Then she looked over the guest room. All the bedrooms were of ample size. Of course, the bathroom was at the end of the hall.

*I can deal with that,* Kari decided.

Oskar stood outside the last bedroom door and gestured. "I understand from the Bodeens that Mr. Michael moved to this room when he was a very young man. It is much larger than the nursery was."

The idea of sleeping in her father's room *did* appeal to Kari. *It's where he grew up,* she thought, *where he slept. Where he grew to be a man. The walls he was so familiar with. Even his furniture.*

Michael Granger's furniture was all golden maple, bright and cheery—a bedstead with four short posts and a headboard, a nightstand, a large dresser with deep drawers, and a wardrobe.

"Yes, I'll use this room, for now," Kari announced, looking around and envisioning a new comforter and matching curtains, perhaps new wallpaper and paint.

As she said the words aloud, she exhaled, and felt a burden lift. It was as though she'd made a correct decision, like things were right and something good was just ahead, like—

*Like what Ruth said,* Kari admitted. *Like what she said she prayed for me, that God would bring something good out of this.*

*But is God even interested in doing good things, wonderful things, for people?* she whispered to herself, thinking of the prayers of her childhood. *More importantly . . . is he interested in anything good when it comes to me?*

# CHAPTER 10

Clover's long, black town car pulled up in front of the hotel at 11:30 Friday morning. Kari was ready. He took her to Antoine's in the French quarter (Clover referred to it as just "The Quarter") where they were seated in a large dining room with high ceilings, tall windows curtained in French sheers, wonderful wood trim throughout, and tables set with white cloths and stylish place settings.

Kari loved the elegance and history of the old restaurant. She studied those who dined near them, realizing again how underdressed she was—even in the best clothes she owned—to move in Clover's circle.

*Not that he is stuck up or a snob,* Kari admitted. *It is just such a different culture here.*

"May I recommend the three-course lunch special?" he inquired.

"Please. I wouldn't know what to order here."

When the waiter went for their first course, Kari didn't have to wait long for Clover to address what she was most hungry for.

"Would you like me to share my memories of your father now, Miss Kari?" he asked.

"Yes, please."

He smiled and stroked his silver goatee for a moment. "Well, let's see. I met Michael when he was about fifteen years old and I was nearly sixteen. I remember, because not long after we met, his mother became ill.

"What was he like then? Michael was a strong, independent young man, somewhat given to getting himself into trouble."

"What sort of trouble?"

"Oh, he skipped classes, took up smoking for a time, and generally rebelled against his uncle. That sort of thing. They had a love-hate relationship at the time. Michael loved him; his uncle loved him back, but Mr. Peter, if you recall my saying so, was not an easy person to get close to."

"How did you meet my father?" Kari asked. She was breathless with anticipation.

"My father, Leonard Brunell, took me with him to call on Mr. Peter at his office. Michael happened to be there and, while the adults were talking, we struck up a conversation.

"We attended the same college prep school, so we recognized each other, but we ran in different crowds at the time. I liked Michael right away."

"Why? What about him did you like?"

"Well, he was a natural-born leader, for one thing, with an engaging personality. Mr. Peter didn't like that Michael was outgoing and friendly in a trusting way. As I came to know later, Peter trusted no one, and he didn't want Michael trusting anyone either.

"When Michael's mother Alicia became ill, Mr. Peter's response was very different from Michael's. Mr. Peter heard the prognosis and accepted it with little emotion, while Michael struggled to accept that nothing could be done for his mother.

"Mr. Peter made sure Alicia had the best care including around-the-clock nurses but, as his way was, he treated the situation as a problem in logistics rather than responding with compassion for Michael's impending loss. Michael felt alone in his grief.

"Michael and I were close friends by then. We took classes together and collaborated on our schoolwork and projects. He would often be at our house doing homework—that is, until Alicia became ill. As long as she was ailing, I went to their house to do homework. Michael wouldn't leave the house except when necessary.

"After she passed, it was the opposite. Michael couldn't stand being in the house knowing she was gone. He started staying the night with us—until Mr. Peter made it known that Michael didn't have his approval to do so.

"Mr. Peter began directing Michael's schooling more closely after Alicia passed—all to shape Michael to someday work with him and eventually take over his business. Michael, on the other hand, hated financial work. He was wonderful with people, though.

"High school graduation was a relief for Michael. He went off to college and, I suppose, to find himself. He became involved in campus ministries and soon emerged as a young leader.

"And you know the rest of the story," Clover finished, "At least as much as I know. I'm sorry I can't fill in the blanks."

"Clover, I've been thinking about something." Kari looked down at her plate, avoiding his eyes—eyes that always seemed to know what she was feeling. *Kinda like Ruth,* Kari realized. "I, um, you know I'm divorced?"

"Yes. I know."

Kari fixed her eyes on the fancy window poufs. "I don't want to keep my married name of Hillyer . . . but I also don't want to go back to my adopted name, Friedman."

"I can understand that."

Kari looked at him now. "After two failed marriages and an adopted 'family' that was more dysfunctional than the foster care system, I don't even *know* what my name really is, Clover. In a way, I've spent my whole life trading one name for another."

He didn't say anything, but his pale blue eyes were compassionate. Kind.

*Simple kindness is going to kill me,* Kari thought, trying not to choke on her emotions.

"I . . . would it be legally possible for me to get the Granger name back?"

"Of course, Miss Kari. I think it would be most fitting, don't you? Would you like us to take care of it for you?"

"Yes. Thank you," Kari mumbled.

"It will take a few months, I believe, but the process is straightforward."

"Good. The sooner the better."

Oskar, true to his word, ordered the work that needed to be done on the house so Kari could move in. By the middle of the second week, sooner than Kari had expected, he called to say that the house was ready.

"Miss Kari? Oskar Brunell here. Good news! The plumbing has been checked out, the gas turned on, and the Bodeens have done a thorough cleaning.

"I've also taken the liberty of having a telephone line installed under your name. Presently the house has only one phone, but the phone company has upgraded the system and added these new modular phone jacks to every room in the house. You can purchase additional phones and plug them in wherever you would like them."

"Oskar, that is wonderful—thank you so much!"

"My pleasure, Miss Kari."

Kari still could not move in until she had readied a bedroom to sleep in, so over the next two weeks Kari shopped. *And shopped.*

*For someone who has never shopped—except when absolutely necessary—I am getting pretty good at this!* Kari laughed to herself. For an instant the parsimonious budget David kept her on flashed before her.

*All so he could wine and dine his mistresses!* Kari pressed her lips into a tight line and pushed the hurtful memories aside.

Under Lorene's guidance and knowledge of New Orleans' stores, Kari bought a good mattress, box spring, and pillows. Then she chose a bed set that she adored—comforter, dust ruffle, and pillow shams—of deep, dusty mauve, beige, and cream.

Then they bought complementary linens—three sets!—and filled the bathroom with towels, a thick bath rug, and shower curtain and liner; soaps, bath salts, and aromatic oils; and a wealth of vitamins, cold medications, toothpastes, mouthwash, shampoos, and other toiletries.

"We could stock a third-world drugstore with all this," Kari grumbled. She stopped complaining when she saw how personal and inviting her bathroom looked.

Then Lorene called a friend who was an interior decorator. Aided by (and sometimes in spite of) the two of them, Kari chose paint and wallpaper for her bedroom. Within days, her father's old room was transformed. No longer a young man's room, it was transformed into a woman's boudoir, comfortable and tasteful without being frilly or fussy.

"I love it," Kari admitted, sinking down on the bed.

And then Lorene took her shopping for clothes.

"I'm really more of a jeans and boots girl," Kari protested as Lorene pulled her into some rather "snobbish" shops.

"My dear, you're not a girl; you're *a woman*. While jeans and boots are comfortable and carefree—you may be surprised to hear that I own a few pair of comfortable jeans myself—*a woman* requires both definition and taste to exemplify who she is in the world. And you are somebody, you know."

"Because I suddenly have money?" The words, almost spoken in anger, came out with a cough as Kari managed to choke on her tone.

*Clover and Lorene have money, but I would never dream of calling them snobs, social climbers, or aristocratic. They simply aren't.*

"Not at all, Kari. You were somebody when you had nothing. You *are* somebody because God *made* you somebody.

"People who are insecure in who they are don't understand that God made us in his image and likeness. That makes us somebody, somebody special. We're not to be haughty or proud or act higher than others who are also made in his image and likeness, but we *can* be secure in his love for us."

Lorene smiled at Kari. "After all, God set his seal of love upon us by pouring out his Son's blood for us. That makes us valuable. *Somebody*. And we should act like it."

Kari, laden with shopping bags, almost stumbled. *For on those whom you have poured your Son's lifeblood, you have also placed the most value. Can any earthly treasures be worth more?*

It was déjà vu, the most unlikely of coincidences.

*Right?*

Kari didn't know anymore. She was experiencing far more "coincidences" lately than she cared to scrutinize too closely.

At the end of their shopping day Kari owned three beautiful ensembles with coordinated shoes, stockings, handbags, and jewelry. And Lorene had pounced upon colorful blouses, sweaters, and slacks, declaring, "This is perfect for you, Kari! The color suits you to a 'T.'" or "With your long legs, you can wear these charming cropped-style pants."

Kari also had lovely new underthings and nighties and a score of accessories—scarves, gloves, and belts—"extras" she'd never dreamed of spending such money on before.

Tomorrow she had an appointment with someone whom Lorene assured her was the *best* stylist in New Orleans. "He will add grace and chic to your hair, Kari, although it is naturally thick and such a gorgeous color already!"

*I have worn my hair long and trimmed it myself for so long,* Kari thought, *that I can't remember the last time I went to a salon.*

Lorene mentioned other outings she intended to schedule—one for makeup, another for a manicure—but Kari, keeping a close eye on the gracious older woman's energy, replied, "I hope you will give me a few days to catch up, Lorene. All of this gallivanting around has worn me to a frazzle."

Lorene murmured her assent, and Kari thought she noted a touch of relief around Lorene's mouth.

Kari said goodbye to her hotel suite to spend her first night in the house. She climbed between her new sheets and read from Rose's journal until she could no longer keep her eyes open.

She yawned, placed the journal in the drawer of her nightstand where it would be safe—and then slept like the proverbial baby.

When she woke in the morning she stared around her bedroom, appreciating how it looked in the early light. She reveled in the thought that it was hers.

*Mine,* she thought. *This room is mine. This house is . . . mine?* She wasn't quite ready to say "mine" about the house. It still felt like Peter Granger's house, not hers.

She sniffed. *Is that coffee?*

Slipping into jeans and a t-shirt, she padded down the back stairs to the kitchen. The scent of fresh-brewed coffee . . . and something else, something very delicious . . . wafted up the staircase.

*If this is a cooking and coffee-making burglar, I wonder if we can come to a mutually satisfying arrangement: He pilfers a priceless antique and leaves me with food and liquid treasure.*

Kari sniffed again and opened the stairway door leading into the kitchen. A tiny woman engulfed in a large apron stood before the open oven door. She was pulling out a tin of something . . . *popovers?* Kari's mouth began to water.

"Good morning," Kari said.

The woman shrieked and dropped the tin into the sink. "There! Ya skeered th' wits outta me!" She turned, holding her hand over her heart.

"I was thinking something similar when I woke up and realized someone was in the house with me," Kari answered evenly.

"What? Mr. Oskar din't tell ya he hired me t' do fer ya?"

"No; Mr. Oskar didn't tell me he hired anyone to 'do for me.'" Kari's eyes flew over the small woman. She was small, thin, and her hair, under a worn kerchief, was black with silver strands throughout. Something in her mouth, the shape or set of it, reminded Kari of someone but she couldn't quite place who.

The woman lifted the tin of popovers from the sink. "There. Not many ruint. Plenty for yer breakfast."

She set the tray on a hot pad, pulled off the oven mitt, and offered her hand to Kari. "Azalea Bodeen. I'm Toller's mom. Been lookin' forward t' meetin' ya."

Kari shook hands, muttering, "Kari Hillyer. I would have been looking forward to it myself if only I'd been told."

Silently she started planning just how she'd bawl out Oskar for scaring her out of several years of life.

"Said I sh'd start today, Oskar did. Din't know he'd not told ya. Would ya like coffee first?"

"Indeed I would," Kari relented. Azalea poured and handed her a thick mug and Kari hung her nose over the cup, inhaling the nutty aroma. Then she tasted it.

"Ohhh."

"Good, yeah? M'husband always liked m' coffee real well. I'll have breakfast on th' table in five minutes, Ms. Hillyer."

"Kari. Please call me Kari." Kari was already on her way to the table, sipping Azalea's magical brew, her stomach calling for popovers.

Kari called and regaled Ruth that night with her tale of meeting Azalea. They laughed so hard, Kari had tears running down her cheeks.

"I'm not kidding—I smelled that coffee and thought, 'If that's a burglar, I'm going to make him an offer he can't refuse.'" Kari wiped her eyes. "She's about as plain and as plainspoken a person as you will ever meet, Ruth. But her popovers? To die for."

"Well, I'm jealous. I'd love someone to 'do' for me."

"I don't know. I'm so used to doing everything myself. I don't think I'm 'aristo' enough to have someone wait on me. At least Azalea's attitude isn't subservient. I couldn't handle that."

"No; that wouldn't be your style, Kari. So what else have you been doing?"

"Would you believe shopping? Lorene Brunell has taken the bull by the horns with me and has about worn me out! We've been going here, going there, trying on this and that and the other. I have a completely new wardrobe with more clothes than I've ever owned in my life."

"No! The shame of it!" Then Ruth growled, "Now you listen here, Kari Hillyer: If you are grumbling and whining about shopping—even an iota—you just call your dear friend Ruth. I'll come and relieve you of your heavy burden pronto."

Kari could hear Ruth muttering to herself, "*I* could sure use a new wardrobe. *I* could sure use a makeover! The nerve of her—complaining!"

Ruth's good-natured ribbing was comforting to Kari. *I am so blessed to have such a good friend,* she realized.

Then she frowned. *Blessed? The Bible belt must be rubbing off on me.* And she shuddered a little.

Over the following days—with Kari insisting on a reasonable pace—Lorene pushed ahead with her shopping and makeover goals. Kari looked in the bathroom mirror and, in spite of her reluctance, thrilled over what the stylist had done with her hair. The man had kept the length but had layered her hair and trimmed its sides in front so that they curled gently, framing her oval face.

"You have wonderful hair, Miss Kari," he'd murmured, "and such striking eyes!" The style looked classy but it was perfect and easy to maintain.

Kari glanced down. Her nails were now a soft, muted pink and she looked comfortable but fashionable in black cropped slacks, black slip-ons, and a loose sweater.

The doorbell rang; Kari smiled at herself in the mirror and ran down the stairs to answer it.

"Miss Kari?" It was Oskar's unmistakable voice outside the front door.

"Oskar! It's so good to see you. What brings you here?"

He backed away from the doorway and gestured grandly toward the driveway. "Your chariot awaits, madam."

Kari glanced at the driveway and did a double take: There sat the Coupe de Ville, its top down, cherry-red paint and chrome trim glowing in the sun.

"Oh, Oskar!"

She raced down the steps, almost tripping over her own feet. She had been out of the house when Oskar had the car towed away three weeks ago, and she hadn't seen the Caddy's interior before. Now she ran her hands over the white leather, supple and creamy, amazed at how good it looked and felt.

She walked around the car, taking in every detail. "Brand-new white sidewalls," she breathed. "Wow." The wheel rims sported the glowing red Cadillac emblem, the chrome-topped fins sparkled, and "Coupe de Ville" was spelled out in chrome above the trim on the rear panels.

"The Peters Brothers almost paid *me* to do this job," Oskar joked. "Really, though, they put a rush on it and loved every minute of getting your car road-ready. They even made me quite an offer for it."

"What! It's not for sale, is it?" Kari almost panicked.

Oskar laughed. "No, ma'am, it surely is not. It is all yours." He dangled the keys and Kari grabbed them the way a child grabs candy.

"Can I drive it, then?"

"Waalll," Oskar drew the word out as long as he could and lapsed into an overdone Southern drawl. "I'm thinkin' them Peters boys din't put all that-there effort into it so's you could park it in th' drive jest t' gawk at it all th' day."

He reverted to his usual voice. "Want to take her for a spin?"

"And how!"

Kari soon realized that the car was bigger—larger and just *more*—than anything she'd driven. She took hold of the steering wheel—half white and half shiny red. It felt stiff and hard in her hands but turned easily.

*Power steering!* Kari gloated. *And power windows!* The Cadillac even had two-way seat adjustment!

She examined the interior minutely, noting the classy pin-and-button tucked upholstery and the heavy use of chrome—more chrome than she'd ever seen in a car. Every part of the dash was surrounded by sparkling chrome: the speedometer that proudly boasted 0 to 120 miles-per-hour, the clock, the radio, and the trim that bled onto the door interiors.

Kari stared at the speedometer in awe. "Will it really go 120 miles an hour?"

Oskar climbed into the passenger seat. "This vehicle has an 8-cylinder, 390-cubic-inch engine with a 4-barrel carburetor, Kari," he grinned. "It'll go, all right, mind my words. Jack Peters told me to tell you, too, that the engine is still in factory-new condition. Never was broken in properly. He suggested a nice, leisurely road trip at about seventy miles an hour to do the trick.

"And you'd better brush up on your parallel parking. This boat will take some getting used to," Oskar teased.

Kari and Oskar drove for half an hour, and Kari raised her eyes to the open sky above her, breathing deeply of the moist air.

*A nice, leisurely road trip?* Kari had seen advertisements for a new movie about two women taking a road trip in a 1966 Thunderbird convertible. In the posters she'd seen, the women were wearing sophisticated-looking sunglasses, scarves, and *attitude*.

*What was the film's name? Thelma and someone.*

Kari felt the sudden urge to shop. *I need designer sunglasses*, she laughed. *And a couple of delicious-looking scarves.* She placed her elbow out the open window and leaned back, one-handing the steering wheel. *I already have the attitude.*

After their drive, Kari and Oskar returned Kari's rental car and Kari dropped Oskar at his office. When she returned home, she parked the Coupe de Ville in the garage. She pulled down the garage door and locked it, sighing in satisfaction.

"Mighty fine automobile, Ms. Hillyer," Toller Bodeen called to her from where he was deadheading a flower bed. When he said "automobile" he placed emphasis on each syllable.

"Thank you, Mr. Bodeen!"

*No doubt about it,* Kari blushed with delight. *I'm in love with a Cadillac!*

That night, across the miles Ruth guffawed. "You have a *Cadillac*?"

"Oh! I hadn't told you? It was in the garage and had been sitting there since Great-Uncle Peter bought it in 1959. It only has a few thousand miles on it."

"A Caddy."

"Not just *a* Caddy, a *vintage* Caddy—a Coupe de Ville— *convertible*, Ruth! I can't tell you how I love this car. It's like the best part of all of this."

When the words came out of Kari's mouth she realized it was true. The car felt like freedom while the "estate" felt like a tub of cement hardening around her ankles. But when she was in the car, driving, she felt alive and free—without cares. Just wonderfully, wonderfully free.

# CHAPTER 11

Owen Washington called Kari later that evening. "Are you ready to read that envelope?" he asked.

"Oh, yes, indeed! What do I need to do?"

"Meet me at this address at nine in the morning." He rattled off directions and they hung up.

Washington was waiting in front of a modest home when Kari arrived the next morning.

"Good morning, Mr. Washington," Kari called. She couldn't stop grinning because instead of looking at her, he was ogling her car.

"*My word.* Where did you come by this gorgeous ride?" He walked all the way around the car, admiring it and shaking his head as he did.

"Would you believe it was in Peter Granger's garage? Clover says Daddy's uncle bought it new and hardly drove it. It's been sitting on blocks in dry storage since Great-Uncle Peter died. Isn't it sweet?" She ran her fingers over one of the rear fins.

"It's a beaut," he admitted, tearing his eyes away. "Well, then. Did you bring that envelope?"

"I have it right here, Mr. Washington." Kari pointed to a small box she carried under her arm.

"Miss Kari, would you mind calling me Owen? I would take it as a kindness."

"It would be my pleasure, Owen. And thank you."

His knock on the door of the house was answered by a tall, long-boned woman. "Good morning, Priss. Wayland at home?"

"Shore is, Owen. Come on in now." She held the door open and Kari followed Owen into the house. "Wayland! Wayland, honey, Owen is here."

Owen's friend, Wayland, was a large man—both tall and wide—but he moved with the grace of a dancer. He grabbed Owen in a bear hug. Kari, not used to seeing men hug each other, stared—a little in awe, a little uncomfortable.

"And who's this pretty lady, Owen?"

"Priss and Wayland, this here's Ms. Kari Hillyer."

Kari shook both of their hands and smiled; she found right away that she rather liked both Priss and Wayland.

"I understand you have some faded writing you wants t' read?" Wayland asked.

"Yes, sir. I do."

"Right this way, then,"

Wayland had his laboratory in the back of his garage. What for most men would have been a workbench for mechanical tools or yard work, Wayland had turned into a finely organized worktable for his chemicals and lab tools.

Kari scanned the counter with its two microscopes, Bunsen burner, and various pipettes, slides, spoons, and tongs, all tidy and in their places. Above the bench she saw a shelf stocked with rows of neatly labeled glass jars and bottles.

At Wayland's gesture, Kari placed the cedar box on the table and removed the cloth bag. She gently pulled out the envelope and handed it to Wayland, who had slipped on disposable gloves.

"Let's see what we got here, now." Wayland studied the front and then the back, his long fingers as graceful and agile as the rest of him. "Should be easy enough . . . but first we'll get us a camera ready." He reached inside a drawer and removed a sophisticated-looking camera. He inserted a roll of film, wound it, and set the camera on the bench.

"What will you do with the camera?" Kari was curious.

"We'll take some pictures of th' writing when it comes clear, just in case it fades again after th' solution dries."

"Oh! How very ingenious."

"That's Wayland for you," Owen agreed.

Kari watched, intrigued, as Wayland mixed a few droppers of two different chemicals in a small jar. Then he dipped a fine brush in the solution and touched it only to the end of the line of writing on the front of the envelope.

"A little test area, see?" he murmured.

The blue of the ink instantly materialized.

"It works! I think it's an 's'!" Kari breathed.

Owen peered over her shoulder. "Yes ma'am. It sure is."

Wayland stroked the solution across the entire line of writing. As the ink appeared, he took several shots with the camera.

"Looks t' me that this is ol'-fashioned fountain-pen writing, Miss Kari," he grunted, leaning in close for another shot. "And like th' nib on that pen was broke, too. See all them scratches on th' paper where th' ink don't flow smooth? Where th' writing goes thin?"

Kari hardly heard him. She was staring at the name that had—almost miraculously—appeared on the envelope:

Joy Thoresen Michaels.

*Joy Michaels. Rose's daughter!*

"Joy Thoresen Michaels," Owen read aloud. "You know who that is?"

Kari didn't seem to hear him. She was still staring at the envelope, wondering who had left it.

The puzzle was growing more curious.

"Shall we do th' other side now?" Wayland asked Kari.

"Yes, please," she whispered.

Wayland dipped the brush in the solution and gently brushed it across the writing that crossed the seal. The scratches he'd alluded to were worse on the back and the ink had bled from the broken nib. Whole letters and parts of letters had ink "blobbed" over them. The three of them watched the ink clarify, leaving these letters and illegible smears:

"Jo  i  ael . Pers  al  nd C  fid n  al."

After a moment, Kari translated the words aloud. "Joy Michaels. Personal and Confidential."

"I think you're right," Wayland muttered. While he was snapping photographs, Kari stepped away from his bench shaking her head, deep in thought.

*Joy Michaels. Personal and Confidential. Who wrote those words? Who hid the journal and this envelope—together—in the trunk? And why?*

The obvious candidate, of course, was Peter Granger—but what possible connection could there be between Great-Uncle Peter and Joy Michaels?

"Miss Kari?"

She turned to look at Owen. "Yes?"

"Do you know who this 'Joy' person is?"

Kari glanced down, her possessiveness of Rose's journal making her cautious: She wanted to keep the journal and its precious story to herself. Kari felt Rose's journal too . . . intimate an experience to share with someone else.

"I might have heard of her."

Now it was his turn to be puzzled. "Might have heard of her? *Might* have?"

Kari sighed, unable to make up her mind what to tell him.

Wayland had finished taking the pictures and was winding the film out of the camera. "Miss Kari, here's th' film for you to develop. Do you want to open th' envelope now? Pretty sure I can do it 'thout tearing it."

"No!" Kari startled both of the men.

"I-I'm sorry. That came out wrong. What I mean to say—and not *shout*—is, I don't feel comfortable opening this envelope. It is, as it says, personal and confidential."

Wayland shrugged. "It's your call, Miss Kari," but Owen was still studying her, a speculative look on his face, as Wayland looked from him to Kari and back.

"Where should I send th' bill?" Wayland asked, to break the awkward silence.

"Write it up now, if you like. I'll see that it gets paid," Owen answered.

"Thank you." Kari nodded her thanks to Wayland and then whispered to Owen, "Could we go somewhere to talk? Privately?"

Owen bent his head once. They waited without saying anything as Wayland wrote and handed Owen the bill and saw them out of the garage and down the drive to the curb.

"Well? Where would you like to talk?" Owen murmured.

"Over coffee?" Kari wanted a few minutes to decide how much of her private mystery she would share. How much *of Rose* she would share with someone else.

"All right."

Fifteen minutes later they were seated in a quaint café sipping *café au lait* and waiting for fresh beignets. Kari knew Owen was watching her, waiting for her to open the conversation.

"I want to tell you something, Owen," Kari began, "but it is something that is important to me. Please don't laugh and please tell me that you will respect my confidence."

"Certainly, Miss Kari. If it's important to you, I would never make fun of it."

"You might change your mind when you hear it," Kari sighed.

"No; you have my word." He held up his hand as though swearing an oath.

"Well, all right then." She lifted her cup, savoring the first sip of the creamy beverage. "A few weeks ago when I found the Caddy in the garage, I also found a little attic room above."

"Find some treasure up there, did you?"

Kari frowned. "You're laughing."

Owen sobered immediately. "I'm sorry. You must have found something up there that means a lot to you."

"Yes, I did. I . . . I found an old journal."

"An old journal? Like a diary?"

"Yes, like that. The woman it belonged to was named Rose Thoresen."

"As in Joy Thoresen Michaels? That Thoresen?"

"Yes. Joy was Rose's daughter. I found the envelope where I found the journal."

"And?"

"And . . . I've read the journal. It was written over a two-year period—1909 to 1911. The thing is . . . the thing is, something about Rose has become quite dear to me. I can't explain it, Owen, except to say that she—Rose—seems so real to me . . . and what she writes about is, well, incredible."

Through two cups of coffee and a piping-hot beignet, Kari rehearsed to Owen all she'd learned about Rose Thoresen. "At first I thought Jan and Joy were her children, but later, in other entries, I realized that Jan was her husband and that he'd recently passed away. She missed him very much, Owen. I ached for her loss!"

Then Kari told Owen about the women Rose and Joy had rescued from two "high-class" brothels in a little mountain town outside Denver named Corinth. She told Owen about Joy's husband Grant, lost at sea, but returned to her long after he was thought dead.

"Owen, when Rose wrote that Grant was alive and had found his way back to Joy, chills ran through my body. I . . . broke down and cried. It was too wonderful."

Kari went on to describe the empty house Martha Palmer had given them in Denver, how they and those with them had worked to make it livable again and make it a home and a refuge for fallen women.

She blinked against sudden moisture. "Rose wrote about this young girl, Martha Palmer's only child, how she became mentally deranged as she grew up. How she was left in the care of trusted servants and nurses . . . and one of them violated her.

"The little mad woman was pregnant and no one knew it. Then she began to miscarry and . . . she didn't know what was happening—because she was innocent! Completely naïve. She went to the attic of the house where she often played and lay down there . . . and died."

Owen's eyes were large. "All this is in that journal you found?"

"All this and oh! So much more, Owen! More than I could tell you right now. But then the journal just stops! After April of 1911 there are no more entries."

Kari stared at her coffee. "Owen, I know you are an investigator and you were assigned to find me. You must . . . know a lot about me."

He didn't say anything, but he nodded his head.

"Then you know I was in foster care . . . you know Will and Nell Friedman adopted me."

Again he nodded.

"I . . . they didn't have a good marriage. They didn't really want a child; I think they thought adopting me would help their relationship, but it didn't. I don't know, but I've always thought it would have been better if I'd been left in foster care. I ended up back there anyway."

Kari vowed she was not going to get teary in front of Owen and swallowed down the choked feeling in her throat.

"Did you know I've been married? Twice?" She was ashamed to look at Owen. "Twice!"

"Yes, Miss Kari. I know." His voice was soft, not judgmental. "It was your recent divorce decree posted in the Albuquerque Journal that led to me finding you at last."

"It was?"

"Yes'm."

Kari sipped on her coffee, wondering how to say what she was trying so hard to express. "I've never had a home or a family, Owen. Never. I always have this *feeling*, this feeling in my-my *gut*, in the deepest part of me, that I am alone—by myself in the world. Always alone."

The words were coming in a rush now. "Even coming here, to the city and the very house where my father grew up, learning so much about him, seeing pictures of him, being around the things he touched, even the bed he slept in . . . it just isn't enough. It hasn't changed that feeling. It hasn't fixed the fact that I am always *alone*.

"When I read Rose's journal, she talks about her family—and even the people who live at Palmer House—with such love and caring, and I long to be cared for like that! I crave what she wrote about. Sometimes when I'm reading her words I even feel a little bit like I am right there with her—even if it is just in my imagination."

Kari had to stop. She was trembling and her voice shook. She chanced a fleeting glance at Owen and was dumbfounded to see tears filling his eyes.

"I'm so sorry, Owen," Kari began. "I shouldn't—"

"No, Miss Kari. It is all right. I just feel your pain. Here," he tapped his chest. "I'm sorry you are alone in the world. It's not right. Even the Bible says, *It's not good for man to be alone.*"

Kari laughed but tears squeezed out of her eyes at the same time. "I really don't get the whole 'the Bible says' thing, Owen. I really don't. If it's 'not good for man to be alone,' then why does God let it happen? And I guess that . . . is just another confusing, confounding question for another day.

"I . . . I only wanted to explain why the journal and this envelope are so important to me. I think I got a little sidetracked. A *lot* sidetracked."

"Not a problem, Miss Kari." Owen signaled the waitress. "More coffee? Thanks."

While the waitress was pouring the coffee and hot milk, Kari took a deep breath and got her thoughts straight.

"Owen, two things about Rose Thoresen's journal hold me in their grip. They hold me so tight I can't seem to stop thinking about them. The first is, what became of Rose? And Joy? And all the rest of them? I want to know, and I wonder about them . . . rather obsessively, I'm beginning to think."

She was quiet for so long that Owen had to ask, "And the second thing?"

Kari sighed. "Oh, well. I'm not sure I can explain and it's rather like going down that slippery slope again, but . . . you see, Rose has this way of talking . . . to God in her journal. She would write out the day's events and—in the very same sentence—*the same breath*—she would talk to God as if he were right there next to her, listening and answering.

"See, I know that's not *possible*, but something—something about how she *thought* she knew God was there and listening—has sunk hooks into my soul. I don't know how else to express it."

"Kari."

"Yes?"

"Kari, what makes you think knowing God like that isn't possible?" Owen was looking at her intently, and Kari, once caught in his gaze, could not look away.

"But-but it's not true, is it? It couldn't be, right? I mean, if it were *true*—if God was real *like that*—wouldn't everyone know by now? If you could know God like *that*, wouldn't it change *everyone's* life?"

Kari's voice, without her meaning to, had risen to a higher pitch. "I mean, wouldn't this be the very *meaning* of life?"

Owen just looked at her.

And Kari stared back, noting the creases in his honest black face, the sprinkling of gray in his glossy hair. The conviction in his eyes.

"Owen?" Kari swallowed. "Is this the type of Christianity Daddy found? What Rose wrote about?"

"I cannot speak for him or for Mrs. Thoresen, Miss Kari. I can only speak for myself."

"You? You, too?"

"And my sweet wife Mercy. And Priss and Wayland. And Clover and Lorene. And Oskar.

"But . . . it can't be, can it? . . . Wait. Is that what made Daddy so stubborn against his uncle's wishes?"

"I can only assume so, Miss Kari. I never met him, but Clover knew him well—and Clover and his father did lead your daddy to Christ, after all—and it is what Clover has told us."

"I . . . but if it's *true*—if it *can* be the way Rose wrote about it—then wouldn't more people be like her? Why wouldn't everyone know God the way she did?"

Owen's smile was tired. "It is up to each individual to respond to God the way Rose did, Miss Kari. But in my experience, it is both sad and astonishing how hard people fight against Jesus when he calls to them."

He sighed and scratched the stubble just starting to show on his cheek. "I may be taking liberty in saying this, Miss Kari, but . . . haven't *you* been fighting Jesus as he calls to you?"

She gasped as the implications of what he said hit her.

*All the judgments I've made about Christians. All the snide remarks I made to Ruth every time she tried to tell me . . . and I know I hurt her! The way I reacted when Clover told me about Daddy's conversion to Christ . . . and the way I sneered at* **him***, at God himself?*

Kari heard Ruth's words again and swallowed.

*I have been praying for you over this whole inheritance thing, and I truly believe that something good is going to come of all this. Something wonderful and good from God himself.*

The tiny warning Kari had heard or felt when she'd scoffed at God came back even stronger, and a chill jittered down her back. She swallowed again.

It was as though all the laws of nature she'd taken for granted her whole life were proving to be lies. Everything firm upon which she had based her life was disintegrating and dropping out from under her. Kari was grasping for something solid on which to stand, but the floor was gone. And she was falling.

*Have I been wrong all along?*

"I-I need to go," Kari muttered weakly.

Owen, looking apologetic, tried to say something, but Kari waved it away.

"I . . . we're fine, Owen. I just need to think. I need to think and I need to figure this out." She threw some money on the table. "Thank you. I-I so appreciate you."

Without looking at him she stumbled toward the door.

# CHAPTER 12

How Kari got home was beyond her. She sat in the living room of Peter Granger's house staring at nothing, but hearing Owen Washington's voice ask, "Miss Kari . . . haven't *you* been fighting Jesus as he calls to you?"

She must have turned that simple sentence over in her mind a dozen times, looking at it from every angle, until she opened the little cedar box and laid Rose's journal on her lap. She sighed and stroked the cracked cover, trying to imagine what Rose might have looked like. Kari randomly opened the book.

*Journal Entry, September 12, 1909*

*We attended Calvary Temple again this morning. Thank you, Lord! I have been so nourished and strengthened by the worship and the pastor's messages. This morning he spoke on eternal life using John 6:67-69:*

> *Then said Jesus unto the twelve,*
> *Will ye also go away?*
> *Then Simon Peter answered him,*
> *Lord, to whom shall we go?*
> *Thou hast the words of eternal life.*
> *And we believe and are sure*
> *that thou art that Christ,*
> *the Son of the living God.*

"'The words of eternal life,'" Kari huffed. "What does that even mean?" She scanned down the now-familiar page and read, *He called those who wished to surrender to Jesus to the altar to pray. Thank you, Lord!*

Kari shook her head in confusion. "He called them to the altar to pray? To surrender to Jesus? How would you do that?"

She thumbed gently through the pages and read from an entry dated February 7, 1910.

*Tonight I confess I longed for Jan's strong arms to hold and comfort me! So many trials are upon us, and I just wanted to run from them, run into Jan's embrace and hear him say "Nei, Rose; I have you."*

*Lord, we are pressed out of measure, above strength. We cannot trust in ourselves and so we trust in you, Lord, the God which raiseth the dead.*

"'We trust in you . . . the God which raiseth—*raises?*—the dead . . .'" Kari's puzzlement increased.

She read on, stopping at March 30, 1910. "Flinty died," she murmured, saddened for a gentle old man she'd never even seen. She studied the long Scripture passage Rose had taken the time to write out in longhand. "You have such beautiful penmanship, Rose," Kari whispered, but her eyes were scanning the verse, looking for something, some clue.

> *But I would not have you*
> *to be ignorant, brethren,*
> *concerning them which are asleep,*
> *that ye sorrow not,*
> *even as others which have no hope.*
> *For if we believe that Jesus died and rose again,*
> *even so them also which sleep in Jesus*
> *will God bring with him.*
> *For this we say unto you*
> *by the word of the Lord,*
> *that we which are alive and remain*
> *unto the coming of the Lord*
> *shall not prevent them which are asleep.*
> *For the Lord himself*
> *shall descend from heaven with a shout,*
> *with the voice of the archangel,*
> *and with the trump of God:*
> *and the dead in Christ shall rise first:*
> *Then we which are alive and remain*
> *shall be caught up together*
> *with them in the clouds,*
> *to meet the Lord in the air:*
> *and so shall we ever be with the Lord.*

Kari's reflections turned toward her parents. "Them that sleep in Jesus. Surely that is a euphemism for death?" She read on. "Yes. That's what Rose explains in the next paragraphs."

*Dear Maria did not quite understand that "them which are asleep" refers to those who have died and left this life, but Grant explained it so beautifully. He said, "When we die, our bodies fall asleep, to rest and wait for the return of Jesus. When he awakens us, our bodies will be restored, not to their fragile former state, but to one that is incorruptible and eternal."*

"Does this passage mean that Jesus will awaken Daddy and Mommy? Their bodies will be restored like Grant said?"

The idea fired Kari's imagination. For long minutes she visualized seeing them, just as she had remembered them that last night. She saw herself running—running to them—and them catching sight of her and running to embrace her!

As they drew near, Kari could see their happy faces and their arms reaching for her, just as they had that last night—

Something about the thought of *that last night*, the last time she had seen them, tugged at her mind. Kari grasped at the thread, so close, so near, only to encounter a familiar rush of anxiety. Of dread.

*I haven't had a panic attack since that first day at Brunell & Brunell!* Kari realized, her throat closing on her, choking her. She fought it, turning her eyes back to Rose's journal and the words she had been reading.

She read further, *How you fed and strengthened us with the Bread of Life in that moment, Lord! We have so much hope for eternity.*

"Hope for eternity . . ."

*Is eternity a real thing?* Kari pondered. *Can we hope for something beyond death?* She realized that her heart yearned to believe that eternity was real and that she would see her parents again.

"You have the words of eternal life," Kari repeated from the early passage.

*He called those who wished to surrender to Jesus to the altar to pray.*

"Surrender to Jesus?" Kari closed Rose's journal and sat thinking, wondering if Jesus was real, if surrender to him were possible.

At almost the same time a realization intruded, one that snapped her attention elsewhere.

*Wait. I saw them the night they died?* Kari's eyes widened. *I saw my parents the night they died?*

She grew still, stunned, knowing she had remembered a piece of her past that had been eluding her for more than thirty years. "I *remember* seeing my parents the night they died," she breathed.

The scene was dark with occasional streaks of light, and Kari intuitively knew it was nighttime. The glimmer of light racing toward her was—

Kari gasped. "I was there. The accident on the highway—I was there! I was standing on the side of the road in the dark!"

As she struggled to see more of that night, dread began to course through her body. Kari was angry with herself for forgetting all these years, and she pushed at the anxiety and fought against *The Black*, the fearful curtain that always fell between her and the forgotten truth.

"No! No, I don't want to forget! I want to remember!" she screamed.

"*Jesus*, please help me!"

Abruptly, the dark, the panic, and the breathlessness—

Ceased.

Kari, gasping but in complete control of herself, jerked her eyes open, staring around the room, peering into corners and shadows. "What just happened?" she whispered.

*I asked Jesus to help me . . .* she thought. *Is it possible . . . that he did?*

She paced the living room thinking, going over what she'd seen. *I remember being at the scene of the accident that killed my parents. I suddenly remember being there. Why? Why today? Why do I remember that now?*

The other realization that came to her in a rush was so obvious that she spoke it aloud.

"What else have I forgotten?"

She sat on the arm of the sofa and reached for the telephone sitting on the end table. She dialed Ruth's number from memory and listened to the phone ring. On the fifth ring Kari was about to hang up—until a breathless Ruth picked up.

"Hello?"

"Ruth. It's Kari."

"Hi, stranger. Sorry it took so long to pick up. I was just seeing a client to the door."

"Oh. I'm sorry—I didn't even look at the time."

"No problem! What are you up to?"

"Funny you should ask . . ." Kari muttered. "Do you have a minute? May I ask you a question?"

"Shoot."

Kari took a breath. "Ruth, is it possible that my panic attacks happen because I'm about to remember something I've forgotten? . . . Something perhaps traumatic?"

"Did you have a panic attack? Is that why you're asking?"

"No; that is, I almost did, but . . . something sort of amazing happened."

"Tell me?"

"I was . . . reading and thinking and suddenly I remembered my parents reaching for me and it was night—*that night*—the night they died. I remembered that it was dark and I was on the side of the road. I could see the lights of oncoming traffic on the other side of the road."

"What? You were there when your parents, er, the accident happened? But I thought it was a car crash? How could you have been on the side of the road? You weren't in the accident, were you?"

"Ruth, I don't know. I can see them coming toward me and then nothing. I tried to remember more and then the panic started coming on and that black curtain came down. It's like something bad is about to happen and my brain just short circuits it so I don't remember."

"Are you all right? Did you pass out?"

"No; the crazy thing is that the panic just *stopped*. That's one of the . . . reasons I called to talk to you."

"It did?" Kari could hear Ruth's dubious but hopeful tone.

"Yes, I, er . . . Ruth, when the panic started in, I-I asked Jesus to help me. I . . . is that even possible? That he would help me, I mean?"

The silence on the other end of the line was deafening, and Kari got on her feet and started to pace again.

"Glory be to God," Ruth finally managed. "You asked Jesus to help you and the panic stopped?"

"Yes . . . and there's a little more. I was actually reading something." She picked up the journal and found the entry she was looking for. "I was reading some words from the Bible and thinking about them, thinking about what they said. It was, 'you have the words of eternal life' and a different place where it talks about 'the dead in Christ shall rise first.'"

Kari sighed. "I was wondering if it could be true. I was thinking about my parents and if Jesus would raise them from the dead and if I would see them again and then—without trying—I remembered."

"Kari, slow down. No; wait, I need to sit down."

Kari heard Ruth's ample backside slump into her office chair.

"All right. Let me get this straight. You're reading the Bible?"

Ruth made the idea sound so incredible that Kari laughed. "Not exactly. I mean, yes, the words are *from* the Bible but they are quoted in another book."

"All right . . ." Kari heard Ruth blow out a big breath and then shuffle through her appointment book. "Listen, what is happening is wonderful, and I want to talk to you about it further, but I have another client coming any moment. Can you call me this evening? Don't say 'no,' because I know you can."

Kari laughed again, for some reason feeling lighter in her heart than she had in a while. "Yes; I'll call you. I . . . I want to tell you about something I found."

"About seven then? I'll make a pot of tea, throw on my nightgown, and curl up in my chair with my cat. We can talk as long as we want."

That evening Kari, a little ashamed of herself for holding back on Ruth, told her about finding Rose Thoresen's journal and the letter addressed to Joy Thoresen Michaels. She then related the conversation she'd had with Oskar—and the passages in Rose's journal that had led to her memory breakthrough.

"Rose's writings are changing the way I look at God," Kari admitted, "the way Christianity could be."

"You mean the way God is so real to her?"

"Yes; that's it exactly. Not religious—but *real*."

"It wasn't possible for us to truly know God before Jesus came to earth, Kari. He came to open the way for an *intimate* relationship with his Father."

Ruth paused to sip her tea. "It's just that most Christians don't understand that Christianity is not rules and regulations but love and obedience in *response* to that love. Either that or they aren't sincere in their surrender to the Lordship of Christ. Some people only want a nodding acquaintance with him.

"As a result, well, some 'Christians' are probably God's worst P.R., you know? They profess to 'know' him, but they only know *of* him. Big difference."

Kari thought about what Ruth was saying. "You said 'surrender to the Lordship of Christ.' I read something like that in Rose's journal— and I couldn't figure out what it meant. How do you surrender to a God you can't see?"

"Ah. I hear you. I think of it as 'Close Encounters of the Spiritual Kind.' God is real, but he is a spirit. We are spirits, too, but our spirits live—at least temporarily—in a physical body and in a physical world.

"Jesus put it this way, 'You must be born again of the Spirit.' I think this means first, that your spirit, the part of you that yearns for God but has been damaged by sin, needs to be reborn—made clean and made new."

Ruth answered Kari's next question before she could ask it. "So *how* does that happen? That's the second point. When you surrender to the Lordship of Jesus—when you make him the ruler of your life—the Holy Spirit comes and makes your spirit alive and clean. Then he stays and lives in your spirit so that you have that continual communion with God."

"Wait. God the Father and Jesus. Now the Holy Spirit?"

Ruth chuckled. "We have a lot to talk about, Kari, but we've been on the phone for an hour and a half. Your long distance bill will be right through the roof."

"Apparently I can afford it," Kari drawled and snickered. And then sighed. "I miss you, Ruth. I wish you could come for a visit."

Ruth grew quiet. "Does this mean you aren't coming back to Albuquerque, Kari? Will you stay and rule your little empire from New Orleans?"

"My little empire? Wow. Some days I wish it *were* just little. I still can't grasp it all. And I don't know yet, Ruth. I just don't know. Right now, while I'm waiting for probate to close, I . . . I'm thinking about doing something . . . daring."

"Oh? What might that be? A cruise around the world? Do tell. And take me with you!"

Kari giggled. "No; nothing exotic like that. The thing is, I don't need to find a job anymore and I won't have any legal obligations until that pesky probate closes—which could still be months, according to Clive and Clover.

"So I'm thinking about taking a little road trip. Oskar tells me my Caddy's engine needs to be properly broken in, and a road trip is just the thing to do it."

"Road trip? Would you come here for a visit? That is a long drive for a woman to take alone."

Kari, thinking of how she longed for an open road ahead of her and the freedom and time to think it would afford her, ignored Ruth's last comment.

"Yes, I definitely want to see you and Anthony and Gloria. And I need to go through the storage unit and decide what to keep and what to sell or give away. But Albuquerque would just be the first stop on the trip."

"Wait. Hold the phone. Where are you thinking of going?"

Kari dithered. "I'm thinking . . . of Denver."

"Denver? Who do you know in Denver?"

Kari tried to find the words to explain. "No one, not really. But . . . I'm wondering if I could, you know, find out what happened."

"Happened where? Happened to whom?"

Kari sighed. "I want to find out what happened to Rose Thoresen, Ruth. I want to see if Palmer House is still standing and, if it is, if they are still using it to help young women escape prostitution.

"If it's still there, I might be able to, I don't know, help them financially? I should use some of the money I will inherit for good, shouldn't I? And if Palmer House is still there, maybe someone can tell me more about Rose and Joy and the others."

"Just trying to be the objective friend here, Kari, but you sound a little obsessed."

"I know. And I might be! But so what? I'd really like to find out, you know? And that's the thing Clover keeps drilling into me."

Kari lowered her voice in her best Clover imitation drawl: "*Miss Kari,* he says, *you have money. Plenty of money. You need to learn to use it. Do some things you've always wanted to do. Enjoy yourself a little.* Of course he also says, *Now don't go overboard; be moderate and responsible, hear? But do have some fun.*"

"Well, yes, I suppose he's right, but couldn't you just hire Anthony or Owen Washington to do the searching? I mean, Owen is the investigator who works for Brunell & Brunell, isn't he? Didn't he find you?"

"Yes, he is, but no. No, I want to go there myself. Rose said that Martha Palmer and her husband built that house, so there has to be a property record to match it. If there is, you *know* I will find it. I wasn't a librarian all those years for nothing! And, I think, from Rose's description of the house, that I will recognize it when I see it. If it's still standing, of course."

"Hmm." Ruth thought for a moment. "When are you thinking of doing this?"

"Well, it's almost July now, and let me tell you: Summer in NOLA is *hot* and *humid.* Ech! I'm used to summer in Albuquerque. You know—'it's a dry heat' and all that. This humidity is killer."

"So soon?"

"Yes. Maybe I could spend the Fourth with you? Or right after? Then I could head on up I-25 to the Mile-High City."

"Albuquerque is higher than Denver," Ruth muttered.

"Yeah, by a bit, but *Mile-High City* was already taken."

"Whatever."

They both laughed, and Kari sipped on the last of her tea, finally diving in. "Ruth, do you remember the question I asked you earlier today? We never did talk about it."

"Ah. About whether your brain was keeping a traumatic memory from you?"

"Yes. Exactly."

"I'll be honest, Kari. I've wondered that since we met. Sometimes, when children experience something horrific, they protect themselves by blocking it out. Unfortunately, whatever was blocked usually finds a way to seep through in one way or another. Often, the blocked trauma is sexual in nature. It's why I asked you, for example, if any of your stepmother's boyfriends had molested you."

"That can't be it, though, can it? I mean Nell didn't allow the men she brought home near me."

"Right; we've established that. So it could be something else. And here's where Ruth cautiously floats another spiritual truth out there, Kari—in case you want to ready yourself to tell me to go fly a kite."

Kari cringed as she remembered the disrespect she'd shown Ruth in the past and recalled the nudge she'd received—from God? from her conscience?—for her scoffing remarks.

"No. No, I won't be doing that, Ruth. Please tell me."

On the other end of the phone Ruth's brows went up. "Really?"

"Yes. I'll try to listen with an open mind. Heart. Whatever."

Again, on the other end, Ruth was surprised. "Thank you, Kari. Well . . . what I was going to say is that when people are born-again and made new—like Jesus talked about—many times the Lord will begin to heal their emotional wounds. Whether that healing happens immediately or as they grow in their relationship with Christ, they can ask for and believe that God will heal them of every wound, even a broken heart."

Kari covered her mouth with her hand. *What was it Rose had written? 'Lord Jesus, I am so glad that you came to heal the brokenhearted'?*

Kari swallowed back unexpected tears. *There has to be something to this,* she admitted. *Too many coincidences. Too many "random" occurrences that could not possibly be random. Could they?*

❧ ✳ ❧

# CHAPTER 13

Kari parked the Caddy in front of Brunell & Brunell and tripped up the wide steps to the front entrance. She turned and grinned at the sight of her convertible sparkling in the afternoon sun. Then she swung open the heavy door and walked inside.

The air conditioning was heavenly. Kari stopped, smiled, and let it swirl around her. When she opened her eyes the receptionist was staring at her.

"M-Ms. Hillyer! G-Good afternoon. We weren't expecting you."

Kari removed her Sophia Loren sunglasses and let her new scarf, a sharp sky-blue-and-black print, slide off her head and pool around her neck. "No, I don't have an appointment, but I understand Mr. Brunell—Clover—is in the office today. Would he be available for a short moment?"

"I-I will certainly check, ma'am." The woman punched a few buttons and whispered into the phone.

Only moments later Kari heard the click of heels coming toward them. *Miss Dawes, no doubt,* Kari thought with a wry twist to the corner of her mouth.

"Ah, Ms. Hillyer! How nice to see you." The woman's dark eyes swept over Kari from head to toe and then back—startled and a little unsure. Once again she scrutinized Kari and, to Kari's surprise, smiled approvingly. "You are looking quite smart, if I may say so, Ms. Hillyer."

Kari was wearing one of the ensembles Lorene had helped her select and coordinate—a white, sleeveless linen sheath set off by a wide black belt cinching in her waist, the gorgeous blue and black scarf draped about her neck. Black pumps completed the look and showed off her long legs to perfection. Her hair was trimmed and styled, her nails perfect.

For a moment Kari didn't know how to react to Miss Dawes. And she became conscious of the fact that the receptionist was regarding her with something akin to awe.

*Well, I guess I've "improved" a bit,* she admitted. So she squared her shoulders. "Thank you, Miss Dawes. You're very kind. Can you tell me if Clover could spare a moment? If he is available, I would like a word with him."

"For you? Certainly, Ms. Hillyer. Right this way."

Kari couldn't help but compare the first time she had followed Miss Dawes across the expanse of the office area and down the long hall past the partners' offices. She had glanced at the sea of faces and seen curiosity. Today she saw something different—admiration? Respect?

Clover stood to greet her when Miss Dawes showed Kari into his office. "Miss Kari! What a pleasure to see you again." He looked her over. "Why, you are perfect, my dear. Quite perfect."

Kari blushed. "Thank you."

He took her by the elbow and showed her to a comfortable chair. "Well, what can I do for you this morning?" He sat down opposite her.

"I've come to ask if it would be a problem for me to be away for a short while."

"A problem? You mean with the probate?"

"Yes; I guess that is my question."

"No, it should present no problem. How long do you anticipate being gone?"

"I'm thinking . . . two weeks? I'm going to drive to Albuquerque to see friends and take care of some business." Kari didn't mention the primary reason for her road trip: Denver and the search for Rose Thoresen.

"You would drive there by yourself? I confess I am old-fashioned, but the thought of you alone on the highway all that distance . . ."

"I had thought to take only interstate roads and make a hotel reservation about halfway."

"The problem, my dear Miss Kari, will be navigating the many parts of the interstate that are incomplete as yet. Just getting out of New Orleans can be difficult if one is not familiar with the city."

Kari knew how protective Clover was of her and appreciated his concern. But she was not going to be talked out of the trip. She said nothing and waited.

He nodded at her silence and thought for a minute. "Perhaps you would allow us to plan your outbound itinerary?"

"I would be happy for your assistance," Kari admitted, surprised at how relieved she was.

"Well, then, I shall make the arrangements. When would you like to leave?"

"I was thinking the Monday following the holiday?"

Clover went to his desk and thumbed through a desk calendar. "Ah, yes. July 8. We will draw up a route for you and I will have Miss Dawes make hotel reservations. If I were driving and wished to stay on the interstate network, I would take I-55 north to Jackson where it joins I-20 westbound to Shreveport and then Dallas.

"It will add some time to your trip, but will keep you on good, four-lane road. From Dallas I would take I-35 north to I-40 and I-40 west into Albuquerque. Three days of relatively easy driving—about six or seven hours a day with hotels in, say, Shreveport and Oklahoma City. How does that sound?"

"It sounds perfect, Clover. Thank you."

"Very good, Miss Kari. And now I'd like to ask you a question."

"Sure, Clover. What?"

"Miss Kari, would you care to accompany Lorene and me to church on Sunday with brunch afterwards? Oskar and his wife will be joining us."

Kari felt trapped. *Am I ready for the church thing? Is this where it's all headed?*

Clover must have seen her reluctance. "Please don't worry about hurting our feelings, Miss Kari. You come if you'd like or, if you'd prefer not to, we will understand."

Kari fidgeted a moment longer then just blurted, "Yes."

If he was surprised, he couldn't have been any more surprised than she was.

*Yes? I said 'yes'?*

*What?*

Where had that come from?

But Clover's eyes had lit up and he was smiling and Kari could not—*would not*—say anything to dash his pleasure. He wrote the directions to their church on a card with the time of service and Kari found herself in the company of Miss Dawes being escorted to the front door.

*Nicely done, Clover,* she grumbled to herself. Then Kari realized she'd never been to church. Ever. Well, except for a few weddings. But church as in "church service"?

She'd rather have been tied to a chair and staked over a hill of red ants.

And yet, when Sunday arrived, Kari got up, showered, dressed, fixed herself a light breakfast, and pointed the Caddy toward the Brunell's church.

As she drove, a question occurred to her: *Is this the same church Daddy went to?*

The building was constructed of brick with white painted trim and a tall steeple. It was not, as Kari had expected, an ornate or wealthy-looking edifice. In fact, as she entered the church lobby, she found the inside to be as commonplace as the outside and the people as commonplace as she might find on the streets of NOLA or Albuquerque.

Lorene spotted her and nudged Clover who greeted her. "Miss Kari! We're so glad you came." He directed her to a pew and she nodded to Oskar and his wife.

Kari watched the people and the service with interest, no longer nervous as she had been for the past few days or even this morning. She stood when the congregation stood and sat when they sat, nothing making much of an impression on her until about the fourth song.

The haunting melody was taken up *a capella*, softly at first, and then rising, slow and majestic, climbing in fervor.

*Our God . . . is an Awesome God . . . He reigns . . . in heaven above*

Kari shivered and chills ran down her back as the power of praise built. *Is God truly an awesome God?* she wondered. *What is it like to know a God who reigns in heaven above?*

When the minister took his place behind the pulpit to bring the message, Kari was waiting expectantly. The minister began to read,

*When Jesus came*
*to the region of Caesarea Philippi,*
*he asked his disciples,*
*"Who do people say the Son of Man is?"*
*They replied, "Some say John the Baptist;*
*others say Elijah; and still others,*
*Jeremiah or one of the prophets."*

*"But what about you?" he asked.*
*"Who do you say I am?"*
*Simon Peter answered,*
*"You are the Messiah,*
*the Son of the living God."*

The minister, a young man of possibly thirty or thirty-five, repeated the question: "Who do *you* say Jesus is?" he asked.

"In this passage, Jesus was making an important point. He was showing his disciples that it doesn't matter what *people* say. For example, when people say 'Jesus was only a good man' or 'Jesus was only a prophet' or even 'Jesus was a fraud and a liar,' it is not *their* opinion that matters."

His voice shook with conviction. "It does not matter because on the day each of us stand before God Almighty, he will not ask us who *people* say Jesus is. He will not ask who your parents say Jesus is. He will not ask who your spouse says Jesus is. He will not ask who your friends say Jesus is.

"No, on that day when you stand before God to give an account of your life, God Almighty will only ask *you* who you say Jesus is. When Jesus asked the disciples, *But what about you? Who do you say I am?* Peter answered, *You are the Messiah, the Son of the living God.*

"And Jesus replied to Peter, *Blessed are you, Simon son of Jonah, for this was not revealed to you by flesh and blood, but by my Father in heaven.*"

The minister looked out over the congregation. "Today Jesus is asking each of us, *Who do you say I am?* And I am repeating Jesus' question to you: Who do *you* say Jesus is?

"This is the question each of us must consider and give an answer to. If you are ready to confess that Jesus is the Messiah, the Son of the living God, if you are ready to make him the Lord of your life, I invite you to come forward, pray with me, and surrender your life to him."

Kari stood with the congregation, struck by the pastor's words and how similar they were to Ruth's. *Who is Jesus?* she pondered. *And surrender? What is this surrender to him? What does it mean?*

As the service closed, a number of individuals went forward to pray with the pastor. Kari twisted in her seat to see what was happening up at the front of the sanctuary. She was curious as to what they were saying to the pastor and what he was saying to them.

*Who do you say I am?* That question stayed in her thoughts.

As a piano and organ began to play in the background, Kari honestly considered Jesus and his claims for the first time. *Is he truly the Son of God? Is there actually a God who is a Father? Is Ruth right and anyone really* can *know Jesus and know his Father?*

She felt as though something were tugging at her, nudging her to dig deeper. But then the congregation began to sing and their voices swelled sweetly in a haunting refrain. The only words of the song Kari could remember later were

*Our God . . . is an Awesome God . . . He reigns . . . in heaven above*
The endless chorus tumbled through her veins for days after.

*Our God is an awesome God . . .*

# CHAPTER 14

## JULY 1991

"Don't worry 'bout a thing," Azalea assured Kari as she set a plate on the little table in the breakfast nook. "We been takin' care o' this place 'long time now. You don't need t' worry 'bout a thing."

"I know. I won't fret, truly. Thank you—and thank you for getting up early to bake muffins!" Kari's stomach growled in appreciative anticipation as she picked up a hearty honey-bran muffin and sliced it in half.

"Were nothin'. You need a good, hot meal afore you get on the road." Azalea recharged Kari's coffee cup and went back to the stove.

Thirty minutes later Toller put Kari's luggage—a beautiful new Louis Vuitton suitcase and overnight bag—in the trunk of her Caddy, closed the lid, and made sure it was locked.

"Y'all got directions t' get out of NOLA?" he asked. "This town is a mess o' roads."

"I have these directions Clover gave me," Kari waved a sheet of paper, "and this map once I clear the city."

He plucked the paper from her hand and scanned it. "This is good. Keep th' top on th' Caddy up now, 'till you're on the highway, hear?"

Toller had painted a bleak picture of some of the neighborhoods she would pass—and had reinforced Clover's stern admonition, "Under no circumstance do you diverge from the directions I've given you. A woman alone and in a car like this one makes you a tempting target in some places." He had lectured her on safe and unsafe driving practices before he was done.

*Like I was a kid!* Kari laughed. Then she smiled fondly. *Like I was his kid.*

Her smile grew. *I actually rather like that idea.*

At last Kari pulled away from the house, waving to Toller and Azalea and, with her first five turns burned into memory, started on her way. An hour later, when I-51 became I-55, Kari breathed easier. She exited at a large truck stop, used the facilities, and put the Coupe de Ville's roof down.

"I am really on my way," she smiled. The warm, moist air first from Lake Pontchartrain and then Lake Maurepas flowed over her as she pointed her Caddy north toward Jacksonville, Mississippi.

Her stylish new handbag—more like a tote bag, given its size—rested on the floor in front of the passenger seat. Inside her handbag was the small cedar box and, nestled within it, was the cloth bag containing Rose's journal and the unopened envelope addressed to Joy Michaels Thoresen.

Kari turned on the Caddy's radio and twirled the dial looking for some music that "fit" her mood, something that was right for the drive. She hit a few rock stations. Maybe it was the time of day, but nothing seemed to suit her.

She'd moved the dial up and down the length of the station frequencies twice and was almost ready to quit looking when she heard that haunting melody:

*Our God . . . is an Awesome God . . . He reigns . . . in heaven above . . .*

Kari's hand came off the knob. *Was it just another coincidence?*

When the song ended, Kari switched the radio off. "Great," she grumbled. "Now I'll have that song stuck in my head all day."


By the time Kari rolled into Albuquerque on the third day of her drive, she was ready to be off the road, ready to rest her eyes and body somewhere familiar. She checked in at the downtown Marriott, delivering her luggage to a bellboy and her Caddy to the valet.

Safely in her room, Kari picked up the phone. "Ruth? I'm here at last."

Ruth's happy voice on the other end of the line was infectious. Knowing she was only a few minutes away from Ruth caused Kari's smile to grow into a grin.

"May I take you to dinner this evening? Yes; my treat. How about the Ranchers Club?"

The Ranchers Club of New Mexico was one of Albuquerque's finer restaurants, known for its ambiance and service as well as food. Ruth's voice on the other end signaled her enthusiastic approval and they made arrangements to meet at six.

Kari showered and changed into one of her new simple but elegant outfits—beige slacks and a beige, cream, and gold top. The outfit hung just right, emphasizing her tall, slim figure, and it *breathed*, so that Kari felt cool even in the heat of the early evening. She added a wide gold chain and gold earrings.

As Kari brushed out her long hair, she silently thanked Lorene again for insisting on taking Kari to have her hair styled. The cut framed her face perfectly, and her earrings gleamed and dangled just a little, subtly complementing the golden shimmers in her hair.

When it was time, Kari went down to the lobby and waited for the valet to bring her car. Now in familiar territory, she drove away from the hotel, caught I-25 down to the interchange of I-25 and I-40 (known locally as the Big I), and exited just beyond, to make her way back toward the Ranchers Club.

She was just about to hand her keys to the waiting valet when someone called her name.

"Kari?" The voice of the man who spoke her name was incredulous.

Kari froze. She didn't need to see him to know who it was. *David.*

She turned toward him. He and Beth Housden were standing arm-in-arm just outside the restaurant. Both of them were gawking.

*What are the odds?* Kari asked herself cynically. *Well, fine. We'll just get this bit of unpleasantness over with and I won't need to fear it in the future.*

Kari smiled a tight, uncomfortable smile. "Hello, David. Hello, Beth."

Beth Housden's eyes narrowed and she screwed up her mouth as she looked Kari up one side and down the other. "You're looking . . . different, Kari." The cattiness of her comment was unmistakable.

"Yes. You look fabulous, Kari!" David had forgotten the woman at his side. He blinked as if to clear his vision.

Kari remembered then how much her clothes and hairstyle had altered her appearance. Suddenly she felt confident. And she didn't miss the moment David's eyes slipped past her to rest on her Caddy.

"Is that *your* car?"

Kari forgot who she was speaking to for a moment. She turned her eyes on her car and grinned. "Oh, it is! Isn't it sweet? A 1959 Cadillac Coupe de Ville convertible. I've just driven it up from New Orleans."

David's eyes popped. "Wow. Is it ever! But how did—"

If possible, Beth Housden's mouth shriveled further as she interrupted David. "It was *so* nice seeing you, Kari." She pulled on David's arm. "But, we need to be going. *Now*, darling."

David nodded, hesitating. He looked at Kari once more before he gave in to Beth's tugging. "It was nice seeing you, Kari. Really."

Was that regret she saw? Kari wasn't sure. She handed her keys to the waiting valet and watched, dispassionately, as David and Beth walked across the parking lot to David's car.

*Funny. Watching David walk away with another woman doesn't even faze me.*

David had left her more than a year ago now. The last time she had seen her former husband was at the divorce proceedings in January. It was now mid-July. Six months had passed.

*He looks the same; he hasn't changed,* Kari mused. And then she knew: *But I have.*

She strolled up to the restaurant's hostess, inhaling deeply, glad of the trial she had just passed, and more glad of the revelation she had received.

*Yes! Somehow I've changed,* she rejoiced, *and I'm changing still!*

In the softer light of the restaurant Kari spied Ruth's happy, dimpled face and her heart leapt. *Oh, thank you for this dear, dear friend,* she rejoiced.

Again, it dawned on her. *Just who am I thanking?*

Over the next week Kari visited often with Ruth and once with Anthony and Gloria Esquibel. She made a point of giving Anthony a check that would clear her account with Esquibel Investigative Services in full. She added $1,000 as a bonus.

"You don't need to do this," Anthony expostulated.

Kari hugged him. "I want to, Anthony. No, I need to. I would not have survived this last year if it hadn't been for you and Gloria taking me in, taking me under your wings . . . introducing me to Ruth. This check is little in comparison to what you and Gloria have done for me."

That gesture opened Kari's eyes to some of the benefits of her new circumstances. *I can help others,* she realized. *I could help a lot of 'others'!*

Ruth suggested one way she could help. "What will you do with your other car, Kari?"

"The Reliant? Sell it, I guess."

"Well, if you don't dearly need the money, may I offer an alternative?"

Without naming names, Ruth described a client of hers. "She's just come out of an abusive marriage and has two small children to support. Her husband left her with the rent unpaid and without a vehicle."

Kari didn't even need to think about it. *How long ago was I without hope for my future?* She remembered her depression and fears all too well.

"Can I give the Reliant to her, Ruth? Will that help?"

"More than you know, Kari."

On her second day in Albuquerque she also went to her storage unit and opened it up, thinking she would sort through its contents. Instead she considered the remnants of her old life and recognized that she no longer needed any of it.

Nor would she be returning to Albuquerque to live.

She'd gone to look at their old house, hers and David's, and found that the new owners had already made drastic changes to the landscaping she had struggled so hard to do on her own.

*It's nice,* Kari admitted. *Nicer than what I'd done.* And she let go of the house again, this time for good and without regrets.

Now she knew that she needed nothing of what she'd left in Albuquerque except her papers. She found the short file cabinet right where Anthony had said it would be.

*I need a box,* she thought. *No, a couple of boxes. Not large ones; just two good, sturdy boxes.*

She re-locked the storage unit and drove to a U-Haul rental store. There she bought two boxes to hold the contents of the file cabinet.

When she returned to the storage unit she unloaded the file cabinet into the boxes—her birth certificate, adoption papers, employment and job search records, letters of recommendation, tax returns, divorce papers, and a mostly empty scrapbook containing the paltry news clippings reporting her parents' accident and copies of her parents' death certificates. She folded the boxes closed and placed them into the trunk of her car where they would be safe.

After staring at the inside of the storage unit a little longer, she made up her mind. She again locked the unit. This time she drove to the nearest Goodwill collection center.

"I recently moved and put all of my furniture and household items into a storage unit," she told a manager at the drop-off area. "Now I'm back to close out the unit and I've decided I don't need any of it. I would like to donate it all. Would you be able to send a truck to empty the unit?"

They agreed upon a day later in the week and a time Kari would meet them at the unit.

That evening, as Kari and Ruth sipped sweet iced teas on Ruth's covered patio and watched a monsoon storm form to the north of the city, Kari told Ruth her decision. "I'm not coming back to Albuquerque to live, Ruth," she whispered.

"I already knew, Cookie," Ruth smiled back. "God has something different in store for you."

"Well, I don't know what it is yet," Kari confessed, not appreciating that she'd agreed with Ruth's statement, not snapping to the fact that she'd acknowledged God's role in the direction of her life.

"Not to worry," Ruth answered. "He knows what it is and whatever it is, it will be good."

Kari halfway believed her.

"So. From here you will go on to Denver?"

"Yes. I think, from the information Rose gives in the journal, I can search property records and find an address for their house in the city."

"And if you find the house?"

Kari didn't answer immediately; she was wondering herself.

"I think I would like to see it, Ruth, even if I can't go inside. Rose described it so perfectly . . . and I would like to see if it matches her description. Of course, it might not even be there anymore, but I'd like to know."

"And then?"

Kari sighed. "I'd like to know what became of all of them. I know they have all . . . passed, and I know it's not likely I'll find much about them, but again, I'd like to try."

"Say," Ruth sat up. "I would love to see it—Rose's journal. Any chance you have it on you?"

"Actually, I don't go anywhere without it," Kari was a little embarrassed. "I'm nearly terrified to leave it in my hotel room, so I carry it in my handbag everywhere I go."

She opened the large bag and removed the cedar box. She took the cloth bag from the box and tugged at the drawstring. Giving the cracked leather of the book a gentle caress, she handed it to Ruth.

Kari said nothing, only sipped her tea and watched for long minutes as Ruth read the first several pages and then skimmed ahead to stop and read whole entries.

"Wow." Ruth's eyes were filled with tears. "This woman's ministry is amazing."

"*She* is amazing," Kari added. "I am so . . . inspired by her and . . . touched by how she writes."

"She has a deep walk with the Lord," Ruth agreed. "I can understand why her journal means so much to you. And the way she loves and shares Jesus with these girls! Oh, my. It's powerful."

Kari swirled the little tea and ice remaining in her glass. Her voice slipped into a whisper. "I find myself a bit jealous of those girls, Ruth."

Ruth looked at Kari, curious. And then empathetic. "This Rose is like a mother to them."

"Oh, yes. When I read how she writes about the girls and about her own daughter, Joy, even about Mei-Xing . . . well, I long for that kind of love and care, too."

"I understand, Kari." It was all Ruth needed to say.

Kari knew Ruth did understand.

*Thank you for Ruth,* she breathed again.


The week ended, and Kari grew restless, ready to be on her way. She picked up Ruth for a goodbye lunch. "I'm ready to pay my debt." Kari cracked a cheeky grin as they nibbled on chips and salsa after they'd ordered.

"Oh?"

"I think, all things considered, that I should admit that some pretty wonderful things have happened to me since May. You promised me that if I came back from New Orleans and something wonderful hadn't happened, you would treat me to lunch. Right here at Little Anita's on Juan Tabo, I believe."

"I forgot!" Ruth laughed. "Wow. Hey, wait! Wasn't there something in that promise about flying a kite, too?"

"Don't push your luck."

When they finished their lunch, Kari drove north on Juan Tabo and turned left on Comanche.

"Where are we going?" Ruth mumbled. She had her head leaned back on the seat and was reveling in the cool breeze washing over the Caddy.

"Just a short detour," Kari murmured.

Several blocks later they arrived at Loma del Rey Park. Ruth sat up and looked around. "What are we doing here, Kari?"

"Just this." Kari unlocked and opened the trunk. From it she took the neatest—*the coolest*—kite she had been able to find in Albuquerque.

Ruth was chuckling. She was giggling. No; she was downright howling with laughter.

"I figured I owed you this, Ruth!" Kari shouted as she ran with the kite toward the middle of the grassy field. She held the kite high over her head and started letting out the string.

The air caught the kite, lifted it, and Kari walked quickly, letting more string roll from the kite spool. Ruth chased behind her and then they were screaming like children, running as the kite gained altitude and shot into the sky.

The kite was striped in bright colors and trailed a long purple tail. It soared, higher and higher, brilliant against the flawless New Mexico sky.

Kari handed the spool to Ruth and, arm-in-arm, they watched the kite mount on the wind.

# CHAPTER 15

The next day was Sunday and Ruth had asked her to church, but Kari had declined. "I want to start looking for Palmer House in the property records first thing Monday morning, so I need to leave early tomorrow."

The drive to Denver took longer than she expected. Even though she had left Albuquerque by 7 a.m., she was on the road close to eight hours, counting lunch and restroom breaks.

The city's late Sunday afternoon traffic was light; still, Kari was relieved when she exited the six-lane freeway and found her way to the Brown Palace Hotel. She checked in and, gratefully, sent her car to the safety of valet parking.

If she'd learned one thing on her drive from New Orleans to Albuquerque, it was that her car was a magnet for attention. People ogled her ride. Some shouted questions or kudos at her as they drove past her or when she was stopped at a light. If she was parked anywhere, they all wanted to *touch* the Caddy.

*Keep your hands off my car!* she wanted to shout and, on occasion, did. Hotel valet parking would be the best place for her beloved Cadillac while in Denver, she decided.

The Brown Palace hotel fronted Tremont Place and occupied the triangle-shaped block bounded by Tremont, 17th, and Broadway. After consulting a map of the city and talking to the concierge, Kari decided that tomorrow's objective was within walking distance.

*I won't drive my Caddy to look at property records in the morning and leave it on a curb or in a public parking lot where someone could ding a door or worse.*

It hadn't yet occurred to Kari that she was becoming a bit obsessive regarding the Coupe de Ville.

In the morning Kari left the hotel lobby, timing her walk to coincide with the opening of Denver's public buildings. She turned left on 17th and headed for Broadway where she turned south at the pie-shaped corner. She found that the day was warming quickly, aided by the heat of so many vehicles in Denver's thick weekday traffic.

A few but long blocks later Kari, now hot and sticky, was wondering about the wisdom of walking. Then she arrived at West Colfax—where it took her many impatient minutes to cross.

*I will take a cab home. Walking around downtown in this heat is just crazy,* she admitted with a rueful laugh. After navigating West Colfax, she found her way west through Civic Center Park to Bannock. She could see Denver's City and County Building on the far side of the street.

She climbed what seemed like a hundred steps to the building's entrance and stood within its foyer glad of the air conditioning. She consulted the directory and looked about for the stairs leading down to a lower level.

Kari spent the rest of the morning in the building's basement poring over property records. The county's old records had been transferred to microfilm and were sorted by location and legal description rather than by owners' name. All Kari had to go on in her search for Palmer House was the information Rose Thoresen's journal provided her—a house built by Chester and Martha Palmer, presumably in the late 1800s, on the west side of old Denver.

*At least I know where not to look,* Kari mused, ruling out everything east of the river and everything developed after 1900. *And, with my work experience, I am certainly adept with microfilm!*

Kari was confident that once she found the right property record, it would also have the property address. And once she had an address, she would be able to find it and verify that it was the right property using the characteristics Rose Thoresen, in her journal, had assigned the house: A three-story Victorian set deep within a corner lot, with a covered porch that spanned the front of the house leading to a gazebo off the house's corner.

*Gables, turrets, and dormer windows,* Kari recited to herself. *Gables, turrets, and dormer windows.*

She used the phrases to drown out the nay-saying questions running in the background: *What if the house was torn down? What if it burned? What if I find it is a rundown apartment building now—or a warehouse! What if it is only a vacant lot?*

Soundlessly, Kari chanted, *Gables, turrets, and dormer windows,* and pressed on in her search.

Still, she was dazed when, in less than two hours, she scrolled past yet another record, stopped, backed up, and stared at the name, *Chester H. Palmer,* upon a property deed. Kari fumbled in her handbag for her notebook. She laughed at how her hands trembled and wondered again why finding the house Rose had called "Palmer House" seemed so vital, why this search goaded her with such . . . significance.

"I don't *need* a reason that makes sense," Kari muttered under her breath. "For once in my life I can do as I please, simply *because* I please." Even as she transferred the address of the property to her notebook, she heard Clover Brunell's parting words to her.

"Miss Kari, you know that you are now a wealthy woman. Take a little time to get used to the idea. Stay in nice hotels and eat in nice restaurants. Do a few things you have been putting off or spend a little time on something you care deeply about."

Kari was certain that Clover's last three words to her were part of what drove her: *Something I care deeply about? I have not one thing in the world that I care about! Not one person, not one thing.*

Well, that was not quite true anymore. In fact, she had to admit that in the last year she had found a number of people she cared deeply for and who cared for her: Ruth, Anthony and Gloria, Clover and Lorene, Owen and Mercy Washington, Oskar and Deborah Brunell. Even the Tollers.

*But no family*, she insisted, stubbornly holding to self-pity. *I need something more than just friends.*

The thing Kari had convinced herself she cared most about, foolish as it might be, was the mystery of the woman whose journal Kari had now read many times. *I don't care what anyone thinks,* she groused. *I want to know! I want to find her.*

What had become of Rose Thoresen, her daughter, and her daughter's husband and child? What had become of their work with former prostitutes? What was it that inspired this woman, Rose Thoresen, and gave her such hope? More than that, what was it about her that intrigued Kari so?

If she found Rose's house—*Palmer House*—would she find any answers?

Kari studied the address she had copied into her notebook and double-checked the microfilm record to ensure that she had written the address correctly. She took a deep breath, closed her notebook, and tucked it into her handbag, her hand grazing the cloth bag in which she carried the faded journal. She rewound the spool and turned off the microfilm reader.

"All done, then?" The clerk hovered near Kari. "Find what you were looking for?"

"I think so."

*I hope so. I hope I find . . . something . . . to care about.*

"Thank you for your help," Kari smiled.

The clerk nodded and gathered the spools. "I'll take care of these."

Kari trod up the stairs to the courthouse's main floor, across the rotunda, and out into the heat and sunshine. She had the house's address memorized now, but she stood on the sidewalk, irresolute. The voices she'd ignored pushed through her defenses, assaulting her.

*Why go further on this wild-goose chase? This woman, Rose Thoresen, has been dead—must assuredly have been dead—for decades now! What do you expect to find?*

"Perhaps I will find the rightful owner of this journal," Kari said aloud. Even as she uttered the words she cringed. The last thing in the world she wanted was to give up Rose Thoresen's diary! It was her talisman; it had become her quest.

*Well, I won't mention anything about Rose's journal,* she decided. *That way no one will ask for it and I won't feel obligated to return it!*

Kari gripped her handbag and began walking with no direction in mind. When she reached the corner of Bannock and West Colfax she stopped. Traffic along the street that fronted the courthouse was thick and slow; West Colfax cross-street traffic was worse.

As Kari waited with the traffic for the light to change, she spotted a cab on Colfax, one lane away, stopped at the light. The driver was alone in his vehicle.

She didn't think; she just acted. She ran through the lane of stopped cars, pulled open the cab's door, and slid inside.

"Hey! You don't cross lanes to get in! I got to pull over to the curb to pick up a fare," the driver hollered.

"Can you take me to this address?" Kari rattled off the street and numbers, ignoring his protest.

"Yeah, yeah, lady. I get a ticket, though, I'm blamin' you."

The light changed and the cab surged forward with the flow of traffic.

It wasn't a long drive. Ten minutes later the driver wound through a neighborhood that had certainly seen better days. The area was half residential and half industrial; the block they were driving through had warehouses surrounded by chain link fences on one side of the street and rundown houses on the other. It was a depressing sight.

The driver ducked his head out the cab's window, looking for street signs. They turned right at a corner, drove two blocks, and then turned left onto a new street. Kari saw the street sign and knew they were getting close. Her heart thudded in her breast as she watched the house numbers roll by.

They passed a beautiful old park, somewhat neglected. A path wound from the sidewalk into the park and rambled in and out of aged pine trees.

Past the park, the neighborhood seemed to improve a little. Everywhere Kari's eyes darted, the homes were large and of the age she expected. Some of the houses had been converted to apartments; others showed their age. A few had been restored with care.

Kari realized the corner she was looking for was only two blocks farther. She held her breath as the cab drew near the intersection.

There. Kari knew it immediately. Set far back in the oversized lot and surrounded by a gated iron fence, the house had once been the queen of the neighborhood . . . Now it was an elderly dowager, long in the tooth.

"That's it," Kari called to the driver. She hardly noticed when he slid up alongside the curb—her eyes were fixed on the old house.

She stared through the tall gate and up a long walkway. The house's age did not diminish its stately lines nor did its aged appearance distress her. In her heart it looked exactly as Rose described it in her journal the evening Rose, Joy, and Joy's husband Grant had first seen it. That evening when Martha Palmer had given the house to them.

"Well?"

Kari jumped. "Oh!"

"You getting out here?" The cabby glanced at the house and back. "You know the folks what live here?"

"No, not exactly. That is . . ."

The driver let his impatience show a bit. "If you're getting out, that'll be $7.75."

Kari dug in her handbag for her little purse and counted out eight dollars. "Keep the change."

"Well, gee, thanks." He got out and opened the door for her.

When he drove away, Kari was standing on the sidewalk, still gazing through the gate and up the walkway. Too late, she realized she didn't have a return ride to her hotel and she whirled back—but the taxi was long gone. She shook herself and turned to gaze at the house again.

*It is just as you described it, Rose,* Kari thought. *What a beautiful house this must have been! It still is!*

She reached through the gate and unlatched it. It swung open on oiled hinges.

*Well, someone must still live here,* Kari decided. She swallowed, trying to frame just the right words she would use to introduce herself. After dithering for too long, she started down the walk. As she got closer, she realized that, while the house's paint was faded, it had been touched up—repeatedly, Kari noted—and the yard maintained, even if indifferently so.

She climbed the steps and stood before the house's entrance. The door was immense, constructed of solid wood. A heavy brass knocker faced Kari at eye level.

"Cool," she breathed. She noticed a doorbell but could not resist using the antique knocker. Kari raised and dropped it, thrilled by its deep and melodic thud. She dropped it a second time, reveling in its powerful note.

For the first time since leaving the courthouse, Kari smiled. She looked up and down the long porch. Ivy had twined itself around the railings and up the posts, but obviously someone trimmed it and swept the porch regularly. The door was clean and the knocker shone—*someone* still cared enough to polish it!

At the corner of the house the porch opened onto the old gazebo; it, too, was covered in vines, but the ivy had been cut back from the gazebo's archway.

*Oh, Rose!* Kari sighed. *Someone still sits there, perhaps on a hot July evening like this one will be.*

Kari's examination swept back to the door. An old metal sign hung off to the side, the lettering worn but legible. She pondered the three words: *Lost Are Found.* The shabby sign seemed in contrast to the shining door and knocker.

"Huh," Kari murmured, thinking the words "Lost Are Found" were vaguely familiar.

Straightening her shoulders, Kari waited. Echoing from far back in the house, Kari heard a woman's voice holler, "Coming!"

The door opened and Kari was face-to-face with a slender young Asian woman—a girl, really. The lids of her dark eyes were outlined in heavy black, emphasizing the eyes' deep luminosity.

The girl's hair—cut short—was teased and sprayed into a few spiky points. She was dressed in tight jeans and a black t-shirt, and she chewed and cracked a piece of gum, waiting for Kari to speak.

"Hello. I, um. My name is Kari Hillyer."

Kari stared at the girl. The girl stared back.

"All right, then . . . *Kari Hillyer*. What are you selling? 'Cause we're not buying."

"Selling? No, no, I'm not selling anything." Kari shook her head for emphasis.

The girl looked Kari up and down and then cocked her head to one side, still waiting.

Kari roused herself to speak again. "I'm terribly sorry to intrude . . . I, um, actually, I'm doing some research on someone who lived here—in this house—years ago now, a Rose Thoresen. I was wondering if anyone living here can tell me anything about her?"

The girl blinked at Kari and her gum-chewing jaws slowed.

Kari, growing a little lightheaded, inhaled deeply and added, "If not Rose Thoresen, then perhaps her daughter, Joy Thoresen Michaels?"

The girl continued to blink and stare, but the gum chewing had stopped and her lips had parted slightly.

"Mixxie, who is it, dear?"

The voice that called from behind the girl was cultured and aged. For several beats, the girl did not respond.

"Mixxie?"

The voice drew closer, and Kari sensed, more than heard, a whiffling or shuffling in the wide foyer beyond the doorway. The girl, keeping an eye on Kari, turned a bit and whispered something Kari didn't understand.

*Chinese?* Kari wondered.

The shuffling stopped. "*Shén?*" The single word hinted at doubt.

The girl repeated herself and waited. The shuffling resumed and, as the girl called Mixxie stood back, Kari saw a tiny woman move into the light of the doorway. She walked with the aid of a cane, accompanied by the soft sound of her embroidered slippers sliding over parquet.

The old woman—Kari saw at a glance that she was elderly—peered into Kari's face, studying her with almond-shaped eyes. Kari, her heart pounding, took another deep breath and studied her in return.

The old woman's expression was serene, and her ivory skin, stretched over delicate bones, was still lovely. Kari could tell she had once been a woman of outstanding beauty.

Without thinking, Kari blurted, "Are you, by any chance . . . Mei-Xing Li?"

Kari's attention was jerked in Mixxie's direction as the girl loosed an expostulated curse word.

"Mixxie." It was said gently, but the girl sighed and nodded.

"I'm sorry, Auntie."

"I accept your apology, Mixxie. Now, please; ask our guest to join us in the great room." With that, the woman turned and began her slow shuffle into the shadowed depths of the house.

As Mixxie did another top-to-bottom examination of Kari, her jaw resumed its work on the piece of gum in her mouth. "You better not be trying to scam my aunt," she hissed.

"She's your aunt?" Kari was gnawing on her lower lip, both thrilled and anxious that she had been invited inside the house.

*Palmer House!* The anticipation caroming around inside Kari made her stomach lurch.

"My great-aunt," Mixxie admitted. "Follow me. And don't you touch anything. *Not anything.*" She poked her finger at Kari to make her point. "*I'll be watching you.* You better not have sticky fingers."

"I assure you—" Kari started to say, but Mixxie had already disappeared into the badly lit interior. Kari closed the front door behind her and hurried to follow.

As her eyes adjusted to the dim light, Kari's mouth opened in astonishment. The parquet floors of the foyer glowed with a waxen sheen. The walls of the hall were papered in a subtle brocade.

She barely registered a tall vase tucked into a niche as the foyer widened and she caught a glimpse of the house's main staircase far down the hall. The wood of the banisters and steps shimmered, curving up and away from the first floor.

Mixxie had turned right through a set of double doors. Kari tore her attention from the staircase and followed her into a very large room where she stopped still, astounded further.

For as much as the owners allowed the exterior of Palmer House to show its age, the interior of the house was vibrantly alive, immaculate, and richly decorated. The great room Kari entered had two seating areas arranged around the two fireplaces, one at each end of the room.

The room's furnishings were of a quality Kari had never dreamed of—at least before that fateful letter from Clover—and she was certain that the pieces of art and bric-a-brac gracing the walls and shelves were priceless.

"Come in. Please take this seat near me."

Kari found the old woman sitting on an exquisite settee near the fireplace closest to the room's doors, her knitting piled on the settee next to her. The woman gestured Kari toward an arm chair set at an angle from the settee.

A large glass bowl of fresh cut flowers—mostly lilies, gladiolus, and chrysanthemums—sat on a table between the settee and chair. Their perfume scented the air.

Kari sank into the indicated chair and sniffed in appreciation. Mixxie, who seemed uneasy with Kari's presence, fidgeted over the back of a chair off to Kari's side.

"Do you enjoy flowers?"

Kari turned her attention to the old woman. "Yes, ma'am, I do. I'm from Albuquerque. Gardening can be a little problematic there, but I always did my best."

"Albuquerque? And what did you tell my great-niece your name was?"

"Kari Hillyer, ma'am. Er, it will be Kari *Granger*, soon. I recently divorced."

The old woman set her head on one side, the very gesture Kari had seen Mixxie make. She studied Kari for a time. Kari waited without speaking.

"A few moments ago you asked me if I were Mei-Xing Li."

Kari nodded.

"I haven't heard her called by her maiden name in many years. It was quite a shock to hear it from . . . a stranger."

"Then you are not Mei-Xing?" Kari's regret was palpable.

*Well, what in the world did I expect?* she scolded herself. *Mei-Xing would have to be in her late nineties or nearly one hundred years old, wouldn't she?*

Kari realized that the old woman was watching her closely as she chided herself. A look of concern crossed the woman's brow and then disappeared.

"You . . . seem as though you are quite disappointed, my dear," the old woman breathed, "as if you were personally acquainted with her?" Another look of concern flickered across her face.

"No. No, of course I don't. Know her, I mean. I apologize." Kari watched her hostess with the same intensity as the old woman studied her. "It's just that I-I . . . read her description somewhere and you seem to . . . that is, her description could easily fit you."

As the old woman's expression changed from concern to puzzlement, Kari felt her emotions begin to sink.

*I am such a fool! This is so stupid!*

Kari didn't notice that the old woman was struggling to reach for a glass tumbler of water on the table, but Mixxie did. She jumped to place the glass in the woman's hands.

Kari saw then that her hostess was trembling. Mixxie muttered several sentences in what Kari assumed was Chinese to her great-aunt, ending in English, "Please let me send this woman away, Auntie. She has disturbed you." Mixxie shot Kari a glare that had Kari on her feet.

"I am *so* sorry! I-I didn't mean to cause her any distress—I will leave immediately."

Kari had taken only a step when the old woman, with more strength than Kari thought her to have, ordered, "No! You will stay."

Mixxie's mouth tightened and she stared hard at Kari, but the old woman pressed her niece's hand. "I wish her to stay, Mixxie. Please."

Kari glanced between Mixxie and the old woman. When Mixxie huffed and dropped her eyes, Kari reseated herself.

The woman sipped the water and patted Mixxie's arm. "I am all right. Sit down, dear." She looked at Kari again and said, "You asked me if I were Mei-Xing Li."

A spark bloomed in Kari's breast. "Yes. Did you know her?"

"Of course, my dear. She was my mother. My name is Shan-Rose Liáng."

Kari's jaw dropped and tears sprang to her eyes. "Shan-Rose! Of course! That's why you look just like Mei-Xing!"

Shan-Rose and Mixxie exchanged confused looks.

"You are starting to creep me out, lady," Mixxie hissed.

"Stop it, Mixxie." Shan-Rose Liáng's tone did not brook an argument, but Mixxie continued to glare at Kari with open hostility.

Shan-Rose, on the other hand, leaned toward Kari with interest. "My dear, you said you read a description of my mother. May I ask where you read this description?"

Kari sucked in her breath, annoyed with herself. "I, um . . ." She did not answer the question and Shan-Rose waited, too polite to repeat herself. She picked up her knitting and set to work, but she glanced up at Kari, letting her know that she was waiting for Kari's reply.

Kari drew her handbag into her lap, still hesitating. She glanced up and found Mixxie's eyes fixed on her, glittering with antagonism. Kari's grip on her handbag tightened.

*What if I show them the journal and they try to take it from me?* Kari debated with herself.

*Just don't let them take it, Kari,* she answered back. *No matter what.*

Armed with that decision, Kari opened her handbag and drew out the cloth bag. She worked at the drawstring until it opened and then drew out the journal.

"It's all in here," she whispered.

Mixxie snaked out a hand to take the book but Shan-Rose rapped her knuckles with a knitting needle before her fingers touched it.

"Manners," Shan-Rose growled low in her throat. She placed her knitting next to her on the settee again. "May I hold it?"

Kari shot her eyes at Mixxie and issued a silent warning: *You even think about grabbing this book and I'll deck you, little girl. Just try me.*

Mixxie got the message and sat back with a sniff.

Shan-Rose, in the meantime, had placed the book on her lap and carefully opened it. She turned to the first page, the page Kari knew by heart.

*Rose Thoresen*
*My Journal*

Shan-Rose's mouth dropped open and she uttered an exclamation in Chinese. Then her eyes snapped up to meet Kari's.

"Where did you get this?"

"I-I, um, found it."

"*Where* did you find it?" Shan-Rose demanded. For an old lady, she sounded a lot tougher than she looked.

"What is it, Auntie?" Mixxie scooted close to Shan-Rose and tried to peer over her shoulder. Shan-Rose, without letting the book out of her hands, pointed to the inscription.

Mixxie read it and stuttered, "*W-what the—*"

"Mixxie!"

While the girl stared at Kari as though she'd seen a ghost, Kari reached over and tugged the book out of Shan-Rose's hands. She clasped it to her chest with both hands. "I found it. That's all you need to know."

Shan-Rose replied in a no-nonsense voice, "No; that is not all I need to know, young woman. That book belonged to my grandmother."

"She wasn't your grandmother," Kari shot back. "Even *I* know that."

"No; not my natural grandmother, that is true." As Shan-Rose stared at the book Kari held protectively, she looked as if she regretted her outburst. "But she was certainly the grandmother of my heart."

A moment later, she whispered, "I apologize, Ms. Hillyer."

Kari, too, was sorry. *This isn't going at all like I'd hoped,* she thought. "Please. I-I'm sorry. Call me Kari. Perhaps we can start over."

"Yes, I would like that." Shan-Rose, breathing heavily, turned to Mixxie. "Please go fix us some tea, Mixxie."

Mixxie eyes were large and unsure, but she nodded and slipped from the room.

"Mixxie is overprotective, Kari. I apologize for her rudeness. And my own. But, while she is gone, I hope you will speak freely. You may trust me," Shan-Rose coaxed Kari. "Can you not tell me where you got this journal? It has been missing a long time."

"Missing?"

Shan-Rose nodded but did not explain. She only studied Kari again, looking for something, and making Kari uncomfortable in the process.

Kari licked her lips, debating whether or not to trust the old woman . . . who had been only months old when Rose had written about her last.

*Rose loved her. Rose loved her mother, Mei-Xing. I can't believe I'm here, in this house . . . where it all happened . . . but Rose loved her.*

*And I love Rose,* her heart echoed. *I should trust Shan-Rose. For Rose's sake.*

"I'm not lying. I did find it," Kari said softly. "In an old trunk in a garage."

"I see. A garage." Shan-Rose thought briefly. "May I ask in what city or place this garage was?"

Kari nodded. "New Orleans. Louisiana."

"New Orleans." Shan-Rose slumped against the back of the settee and closed her eyes. It seemed to Kari that, whereas just minutes ago the woman had been stronger than Kari had suspected, she now appeared fatigued. Frail.

"Auntie?" Mixxie had returned with an old-fashioned tea tray that she placed on the low table near the flowers. "Auntie?" She spoke in Chinese, sounding a little worried, and Shan-Rose opened her eyes a moment and then closed them.

"I am just tired," she whispered.

"I think you should leave now," Mixxie said to Kari. She wasn't angry when she said it, just concerned for her aunt. "She needs to rest." She still looked at Kari strangely.

Kari nodded and placed the journal back in the cloth bag and the bag in her purse. Shan-Rose, though, her eyes still closed, whispered something to Mixxie.

Mixxie protested, but Shan-Rose was insistent.

"She . . . wants you to come back," Mixxie repeated with obvious reluctance. "Tomorrow. Can you come back tomorrow?"

"Yes, I suppose I can," Kari answered. *It's why I came here, after all,* she reminded herself. *I came to find out more about Rose.*

"If I come back, will you tell me about Rose?" she asked Shan-Rose. "And about Palmer House?"

"Yes. I will," Shan-Rose murmured, opening her eyes then letting their lids drop again. "I will."

Kari glanced at Mixxie and raised her eyebrow in a question.

"She is best in the mornings," Mixxie answered. "Say, around nine?"

Kari left the house and stood on the sidewalk staring up at the house. Her emotions were torn. *I'm not disappointed,* she told herself. *I won't allow myself to be disappointed. Tomorrow will go better. Tomorrow I will learn more about Rose.*

She walked in the general direction of her hotel. *Tonight I'll make a list of questions to ask Shan-Rose. First I need to find a pay phone and get a taxi.*

Back in the house, Mixxie helped her Aunt to bed. They had turned what had once been the house's parlor into Shan-Rose's bedroom, so the walk was not far.

"You'll feel better after a nap, Auntie," Mixxie whispered, tucking the old woman into her bed.

"Yes. Thank you, my dear girl," Shan-Rose managed.

Later that evening, when Mixxie had gone to the kitchen to fix their dinner, Shan-Rose reached for the telephone and dialed.

"Quan?" She spoke in Chinese. "Something important has happened, and I must see you. Can you come this evening?"

She listened. "I will be fine. I had a good rest this afternoon. Please come. And bring An-Shing. No, no. It must be tonight. *Very* important."

She listened. "Yes? Around seven o'clock, then. I am certain you will be glad you came."

# CHAPTER 16

When Kari arose in the morning, her spirits were high. *Today Shan-Rose will tell me more about her namesake, Rose,* she rejoiced.

*Shan-Rose! I can't believe I've met her. I want to know everything about Rose; about Joy and Grant and Baby Edmund; about Mei-Xing; about Breona, Mr. O'Dell, Marit, Billy, and Will; about Tabitha and Sara—oh, and everyone!*

Kari was so excited and nervous that she had trouble eating her breakfast. She also dithered over bringing the journal with her or leaving it in her hotel room—but then she worried someone might take it from her room!

*You are getting a tad bit paranoid about this book,* Kari reprimanded herself. Yet the thought of losing Rose's precious words hurt her more than she cared to admit.

Kari decided to wear her hair down but pulled back in a large clip. Clips that would hold all of her thick hair were hard to come by; the faux tortoise shell one she wore today was a favorite.

She stepped from the hotel lobby into the bright Denver sunshine and gave the valet her claim check for the Caddy. A few minutes later the valet, a young man with an infectious grin, stepped out the car and held the door for her.

"Awesome ride," he enthused.

"Thanks; I think so, too," Kari answered. She drew on her Sophia Loren's, flipped her long mane back, and tossed him a cheeky grin. He laughed and waved as she pulled away.

Kari drove straight to Palmer House, now confident of how to get there. She pulled up to the curb behind two other cars. Three more were parked along the curb across the street.

*Who's having a party?* She looked around at neighboring houses but saw no activity. As she opened the gate and walked toward the porch, it dawned on her that the cars might mean others were in Shan-Rose's house, and she was immediately a little anxious.

She stared at the front door. *No one had better try to bully me into giving them Rose's journal,* she fretted, *because I won't give it up, and that's final.*

She was about to ring the doorbell when she heard footsteps behind her. Whirling, she faced a Chinese man, quite spry but likely near or in his seventies.

It was hard for Kari to tell his age; his face was smooth like Shan-Rose's, and he smiled pleasantly. When he smiled, his eyes all but disappeared.

He bowed. "Ah, you must be Ms. Hillyer. I'm late, as you can see. Why don't we just go in?" He opened the door and gestured for her to go in before him. As she passed, he reached for something and Kari caught the movement out of the corner of her eye.

The man touched the rusted sign hanging next to the door with the tips of his finger and, bowing his head reverently, murmured something.

*What is that about?* she wondered. From down the hall, Kari could hear the murmur of many voices. *Maybe I should be freaking out about now,* she added, but then Mixxie appeared, frowning.

Kari was beginning to think her face was stuck that way.

"Who let you in? Did you think you could just open the door and waltz—Oh! Grandfather. I didn't see you."

Mixxie bowed—*actually bowed*—to the old man, although Kari was finding it hard to think of him as *old*, for he seemed bursting with energy.

"Mixxie, Ms. Hillyer is our guest."

Mixxie reddened under the implied rebuke. "Yes, Grandfather. I apologize, Ms. Hillyer." She bowed to Kari but ruined the effect by sticking her tongue out at Kari on the way up. The old man—Mixxie's grandfather?—had stepped across the foyer and into the great room and missed the display.

"Charming," Kari muttered. Not waiting for Mixxie, she followed the man through the double doors. And stopped dead in her tracks.

*Is it Chinese New Year and I didn't get the notice?* Kari stared around the room. It was filled with men and women—fifteen or so—all Chinese.

*No, that's not true,* Kari realized. A couple across the room were Anglos like Kari. And with the exception of Mixxie, no one else in the room appeared to be under the age of forty. The doors to the dining room were open and people were eating or serving themselves from a breakfast buffet.

The room stilled as they noticed her.

Kari stood in the doorway, unmoving. *They decided to host a brunch and forgot to invite me. Either that or I'm the main course.*

A middle-aged couple broke away and came toward her. The man held out both of his hands. "Ms. Hillyer? Welcome. Please come in. I am An-Shing Liáng. This is my wife Fen-Bai." He nodded curtly in Mixxie's direction. "I see you have already met our daughter, Mixxie."

*I feel for you . . .* Kari cut her eyes toward the girl. *Yup. Still frowning.*

An-Shing took Kari's hands in his and studied her a long moment. "I hope you don't mind. When Aunt Shan-Rose mentioned you would be returning this morning, some of us wanted to meet you. So she invited a few family members."

*A few? To meet me? Stranger and stranger.*

Fen-Bai shook her hand and whispered a greeting. Others lined up behind her, each one shaking Kari's hand and giving his or her name. Each one scrutinizing Kari.

*What are they looking at?* Kari didn't know what was happening, and she didn't like it. With every nerve on edge, she did her best imitation of Lorene Brunell, enduring the introductions with stilted graciousness but promptly forgetting every name. Almost.

*Quan Liáng—his son, An-Shing? and An-Shing's wife, Fen-Bai Liáng? Relatives of Minister Liáng?*

It was all a blur until the other Anglos in the room reached her. "Hello, Ms. Hillyer. My name is Sean Carmichael. This is my daughter, Alannah Carmichael."

*Carmichael?* Kari stared at both of them. "Are you related to Pastor Isaac Carmichael?"

Sean also looked to be in his seventies. He smiled. "I am his son. Did you read about him in the journal you found?"

Kari's face froze. *Ask to see that journal and I'm out of here,* she dared.

His expression changed to one of concern. "I'm sorry. Have I offended you?"

Kari flushed. "It's just that I didn't expect to see anyone today except Shan-Rose and Mixxie . . ."

"Of course. We have . . . overwhelmed you. Please. Sit here and make yourself comfortable." He gestured to a chair and Kari eased her way toward it, wondering if she should just bolt for the door instead.

Kari sat down and clutched her handbag on her lap. Sean Carmichael's daughter, Alannah, whom Kari judged to be only a few years older than herself, took a seat near Kari.

"Aunt Shan-Rose told us that you are very protective of Rose's journal."

If possible, Kari's grip on her handbag tightened, and Alannah noticed.

"We are not going to take the journal from you, Ms. Hillyer. It isn't ours to take, you see. I want to assure you that we would not try anything . . . underhanded."

"If you say so." It was the only thing Kari could think of to say. From across the room, Shan-Rose caught Kari's eye and gestured to her. "I think Shan-Rose is asking for me." Kari was glad to get away, even though she was feeling a little more comfortable with Alannah.

"Of course. You should go to her," Alannah agreed.

Kari walked past several staring people on her way to the chair in which Shan-Rose indicated Kari should sit. Some of them whispered together in Chinese while studying her.

*I'm starting to feel like a bug under a glass.* Kari reached Shan-Rose and sat down.

"My dear, I am so sorry," the old woman whispered, placing her hand on Kari's. "I called my brother last evening and told him about your visit. The next thing I knew, caterers were here this morning setting up breakfast for twenty! What a hullabaloo."

Kari almost burst out laughing. *Who says 'hullabaloo' anymore?* she chuckled to herself.

Shan-Rose didn't notice Kari's mirth. "Have you eaten, Ms. Hillyer?"

"Oh, yes. I have, thank you." *Like I could swallow anything while under this microscope!*

About that time Quan began calling softly for everyone's attention and the room quieted. "Everyone is refreshed, I hope? Good. Perhaps we can begin now?"

*Begin what?* Kari thought, darting her eyes around the room.

"Ms. Hillyer, I'm sure you are wondering why we have gathered to meet you. My sister has told us a little about you and that you have found Rose Thoresen's missing journal. This is great news to all of us who remember her, and even those of us who only know her as part of our family's history."

Kari looked from Shan-Rose to Quan. "He's your brother?" she whispered.

"Oh, yes," Shan-Rose replied. "I assumed you knew."

"You have a question, Ms. Hillyer?" Quan asked.

"No, but—I mean, I didn't know you were Shan-Rose's brother." She looked between them. "Rose's journal only covers two years and ends in 1911. I didn't know Mei-Xing married anyone." She frowned. "Wait. Your last name is Liáng, not Li?" She asked Shan-Rose and Quan at the same time.

"Yes," they both answered. A little laughter rumbled from the others.

"Ms. Hillyer," Shan-Rose explained, "Our mother, Mei-Xing Li, married Minister Yaochuan Min Liáng in the spring of 1912 . . . after everything happened, and he adopted me."

"Oh! She did? She married Minister Liáng?" Kari was thrilled. "And were they happy? Rose loved Mei-Xing so much . . . and I have been wondering what became of Mei-Xing."

Tears sprang to Shan-Rose's eyes. "You know of my mother only through Rose's eyes and words? This touches my heart, Ms. Hillyer. Your visit is bringing back many happy memories."

Shan-Rose touched a tissue to her eyes and answered Kari's question. "Yes; I would say that Mother and Father's marriage was very happy." She nodded at Quan. "Quan is my youngest brother. He assumed Father's pulpit when Father grew too feeble to pastor. We also had two sisters and a brother. We are the only two siblings left now. Our sisters and our brother have gone to heaven before us, but we have many nieces and nephews—some of whom are here—and they have many children and even grandchildren."

Kari saw a few heads nod and then she realized . . . "So the others here are Mei-Xing's grandchildren?"

"That's right," Shan-Rose smiled.

"And you?" Kari asked the old woman. "Your name is still Liáng. You didn't marry?"

"No, my dear," Shan-Rose chuckled. "I was far too busy trying to change the world to marry."

"Well, this is just fascinating," Alannah spoke aloud. A murmur of agreement went around the room.

Kari fastened her eyes on Alannah. "If you are Isaac Carmichael's granddaughter, who did he marry?" she asked.

"Breona," several voices replied at once.

"What? Breona!" Kari shook her head slowly. "Wow. That is *so* cool."

More soft laughter reassured Kari and she began to relax.

"Our families—the Liángs and Carmichaels—have been friends now for how long?" Sean Carmichael looked to Quan and An-Shing.

"At least eighty years," An-Shing answered.

"Perhaps a little longer than that," Quan added. "And it is quite amazing to hear you talk of these departed friends and relatives with such intimate knowledge, such passion."

"As Shan-Rose said, I only know them through Rose's eyes," Kari explained, "but I came to love Rose through her journal and to love those *she* loved. I am so anxious to hear more, to fill in the gaps and learn what happened afterwards. I drove all the way from New Orleans just to see if Palmer House was still standing . . . and if, by some chance it was, to see if anyone knew of or remembered Rose Thoresen and could tell me anything more about her, about Joy and Grant, about Mei-Xing—oh, about everyone I read of in her journal—"

"Thoresen," someone interrupted. It was Mixxie. "Her name was 'Tor-eh-sen.' *Not* 'Thor-eh-sen.'" Her words dripped sarcasm.

"Mixxie!" Quan's rebuke cracked in the quiet room. "That was quite unnecessary and you will apologize to our guest. Now."

Mixxie's face suffused with color and she would not meet Kari's eyes. "I apologize." The words grated like glass in her throat.

*That had to smart,* Kari gloated, thoroughly irritated with Mixxie's hostility. At the same time she tried out the correct pronunciation. "Tor-eh-sen. I had no idea I was saying it wrong all this time."

"I'm sure it is not a problem, Ms. Hillyer. But speaking of time," An-Shing, with a reproachful glare at his daughter Mixxie, turned the conversation, "we are all quite interested in how you discovered Rose's journal. Could you tell us when you found it?"

Kari sensed the subtle shift in the conversation. Her defenses armed themselves and she held them at the ready. "Let's see. It hasn't been that long . . . this is mid-July, so perhaps three months ago?"

"Ah. I see," An-Shing smiled and bowed that "half-sort-of bow" Kari had seen now several times. "Auntie told us a little of how you found Rose's journal, but we would all be most pleased to hear it again. Could you tell us how you came to find it?"

Kari wanted to resist their intrusive questions. She stared warily from person to person in the room, wondering what was going on, until she reached Alannah.

"Kari," Alannah assured her again. "No one wishes to take Rose's journal from you, but . . . it has been missing a very long time. We are only curious as to how you found it. I would love to hear you tell us. Please?"

Kari still sensed something odd emanating from the eager expressions aimed at her, but she relented. It was easier to look at Alannah and talk to her, so she did.

"I lived in Albuquerque until recently," she began. "A law office in New Orleans contacted me in April and said I had inherited my great-uncle's estate."

Kari was leaving a lot out. *They don't need to know my personal business,* she decided.

"Part of his estate was his home. It was built around the turn of the century and has a separate garage in the back. I . . . found a trunk in the garage filled with my grandmother's clothes. Her evening gowns. Beautiful handbags and gloves. That sort of thing."

Alannah was listening intently. Kari chanced a glance around the room and saw the same intensity in the others. Her narrative stumbled to a stop. *What is going on?*

"Very nice, Kari," Alannah encouraged her. "Please continue."

Kari gathered her thoughts. "Um. At the bottom of the trunk I found a small wooden box. Inside was a cloth bag. A book was inside. I opened it and found the inscription: *Rose Thoresen. My Journal.* You know the rest."

"The inheritance came through your great-uncle?" Quan asked the question softly.

"Yes. It was his house."

"Do you happen to know how he knew Rose Thoresen? How the journal came to be in his possession?"

Kari sighed. "You know, I have asked myself that same question. My grandmother, Alicia, died in 1927 so I assumed her clothes were packed away soon after she died. But the box at the bottom of the trunk had been put there long after that."

"Oh? How do you know that?"

"I know it was put in later," Kari said, "because the box had a seal on it—a strip of thick paper glued around it with the year '1957' written on it. I have no idea why."

"And your great-uncle did not know her?"

"I really can't say. I never met him. I didn't even know *he* existed until recently."

Her listeners stirred and turned questioning looks toward Quan. "I pray you will forgive our inquiring minds, Ms. Hillyer, but can you tell us how it is that you did not know of your great-uncle before the attorneys contacted you?"

Kari sat back and stared at him. "I'm not sure that I am comfortable with how personal your questions are becoming, Mr. Liáng."

He sighed. "I am so sorry, Ms. Hillyer. I apologize for our intrusion . . . it's just that . . . well, we're trying to figure out how Rose's journal turned up so far away. Can you understand and forgive us?"

Kari thought about it. It irked her that she was baring her family's business in front of a room of perfect strangers. Well, perhaps not *complete* strangers . . .

*What harm will it do?* she decided.

"If I tell you what you are asking, will you let me ask you about Rose? Will you tell me about her?"

"It would be our pleasure, Ms. Hillyer," Quan agreed. "Anything you wish to know."

Kari looked around. The twenty or so in the room were waiting for her to continue. "My parents died when I was six."

Her words hung there because suddenly Kari's tongue dried up in her mouth. "I am so sorry, Kari," Shan-Rose touched her hand gently. A little angry, a little embarrassed, Kari jerked her hand away.

"Whatever. It was a long time ago."

If she didn't sound heartless, if she didn't make herself *be* heartless, she would break down. *And that,* Kari vowed, *I will not do in front of these people.*

She gritted her teeth and ground out, "A few months ago, out of the blue, some attorneys from New Orleans sent me a letter. It was the first time I'd heard of a 'Great-Uncle Peter.'"

Quan cleared his throat. "You've not had an easy life, Ms. Hillyer. I'm so sorry we have opened old wounds."

She shrugged and clutched her handbag in her lap. The thought of Rose's journal, safe inside, helped her to calm. *Her words always comfort me,* Kari realized.

"Ms. Hillyer? May I ask a question?" It was Sean Carmichael.

Kari shrugged again.

"Your father . . . God rest him. How old . . . do you know in what year he was born?"

*What sort of a question is that?* Kari frowned and looked up at Sean. His expression was sincere.

*Whatever.*

"Daddy was born in 1911. His mom was a widow. They lived with her husband's brother. Uncle Peter."

"Your father was born in 1911?"

Every eye was on her.

"Yes. February 2, 1911."

Shan-Rose murmured something to herself. An-Shing and Quan began whispering together and a few of the group stood up and joined them. Kari heard a few words, but they were in Chinese.

*They might as well speak out loud, for all I can understand,* Kari groused.

Sean and Alannah Carmichael said nothing; they kept looking at her, and Kari noticed that Alannah was grasping her father's hand.

Then there was Mixxie. Even though she said nothing, anger and antipathy radiated from her toward Kari.

*What have I done,* Kari wondered, *to warrant such strong emotion from this annoying girl?*

The whispering stopped and people resumed their seats. Kari noticed that they were all looking at her again.

"What? What is it?" she demanded.

"Ms. Hillyer, would you do us a great favor?" Quan spoke quietly, seriously.

Kari was about out of patience. "Well, what?" she snapped.

"We would like to discuss, uh, some family business for a few minutes. Would you care to join Mixxie in the kitchen? She would be delighted," Quan skewered Mixxie with a stern look, "to keep you company and serve you some iced tea."

Then he looked expectantly at Kari.

"Wait. You want me to go sit in the kitchen?" Astonished, Kari turned to Shan-Rose. "You asked me to come here this morning. You said you would tell me about Rose! This is . . . not right!"

"Oh, we will, my dear, we will. I promise," Shan-Rose soothed Kari. "But—and just for a few minutes—we would like to discuss something important. Without you."

Incredulous, Kari stared at her and then around the room. Alannah was nodding, trying to encourage Kari to just go along with the request.

"Whatever." Kari jumped up and, in a huff, marched toward the door. She jerked her head at Mixxie. "This had better be an outstanding glass of iced tea. And not instant, either!"

She stalked out of the great room with Mixxie on her heels. "Which way?"

Mixxie turned toward the back of the house and Kari followed, disgruntled and not a little confused.

Sean and Alannah listened to the babble of Chinese as the Liáng family members all sought to voice their opinions at the same time.

"Right now I'm rather sorry I didn't make an effort to learn Mandarin." Sean raised his brows and slanted his eyes toward his daughter.

"In other words, you'd like me to translate the mayhem?" Alannah chuckled, "Just because I *did* make the effort?"

"You made the effort to be a good police officer. In this city, knowing Chinese is an edge, just as knowing Spanish is. So. What are they saying?"

Alannah listened for a minute. "Well, some of them are wondering why Kari's father's birthday doesn't exactly match Edmund's. An-Shing suggested that Dean Morgan wouldn't have been stupid enough to use Edmund's exact birth date."

"I would have to agree with that," Sean nodded.

"Pretty much all of them think Kari has no clue."

"I agree with that, too. Who's the holdout?"

"Peng. He thinks she might be an opportunist, a gold digger, playing us."

"Hmm. I don't know. She doesn't look like she's hurting any financially. And she says she just inherited her 'great-uncle's' estate? Are you going to check that out?"

"I certainly am. I need a few more details to go on. I'm going to offer my services to give Kari a tour of the house. I'll ferret out what I need while we talk. Then I will make some inquiries."

"Do you have sources in Louisiana?"

"I know someone who does."

The discussion among the Liángs seemed to wrap up. Quan and An-Shing walked over to Sean and Alannah. "This is a *most* momentous turn of events, don't you agree? How long our families have been praying! So many years! And now God, in his own timing . . ." Quan's voice cracked a little. "It is most humbling to see his hand at work."

The three of them nodded.

"Did you hear our discussion?" Quan asked Alannah.

"Yes. I agreed with most of it."

"Do you have a means of investigating Ms. Hillyer's 'great-uncle' whose estate she says she has inherited?"

Alannah nodded. "I will gather a few more details and then it should be fairly easy to check out her story. Do you think this 'great-uncle' of hers is—"

"After all this time, I'd rather not form an opinion; I'd rather have facts," Quan answered. "The very mention of Dean Morgan's name has become synonymous with conjuring the family boogey man." Quan looked as if he'd tasted something sour.

"What will you tell the others?" Sean asked Quan.

"I will call tonight and tell them everything we know so far." He looked to Alannah. "The more you can verify, the better."

"And what will you tell Kari?" she asked. This was the sticking point in the discussion she'd listened to.

Quan studied the floor, thinking. "I favor letting this play out a bit longer. The question is, does she really know *only* what is in that journal? I suppose Peng could be right—she could somehow have uncovered our families' shared history and be playing us along—but what profit in that could there be, after all?"

He stroked his chin. "For what it's worth, that's not what I believe. I trust the Holy Spirit to give me good discernment. Peng, as you know, is not as devoted a follower of Christ as we could wish. He is quite . . . *distrusting*.

"Besides," Quan added, brightening. "Just look at her! Those eyes? Have you seen pictures of Joy when she was younger? Of course, they weren't in color, but I knew her and I remember . . ." His voice trailed off.

"So we shouldn't say anything to her about . . . ?"

"I think we tell her only what she asks for. If possible, we skirt around the . . . issue. Let the others see her first and decide."

Kari and Mixxie sat at the kitchen table in silence. Kari looked at Mixxie and finally spoke, if just to break the wall of ice. "Your family is a bit old-fashioned."

The girl snorted and cracked her gum. "You . . . have no idea." She eyed Kari and then looked away, drumming her fingers on the table.

"So . . . Mixxie is a cute name. Different. I've never heard it before," Kari tried again. "Is it a nickname?"

Mixxie cut a glance at Kari, suspicion oozing from her narrowed eyes. "The family saints cast long shadows," she muttered cryptically.

*Huh?*

"Uh, sorry—I don't understand."

"You came in here yesterday asking my great-aunt if she were *Mei-Xing Li*, as if—*as if!*—Mei-Xing Li would still be alive in 1991? Even *our* family saints don't live to a hundred!"

She added in a snarl. "That woman's shadow has hung around my neck like a millstone all my life.

*Mixxie.*

*Mei-Xing?*

"You're named for her?" Kari breathed. "Your name is Mei-Xing?"

"*Don't* call me that. *Ever.*"

The kitchen went silent, the atmosphere icy again. Kari studied the worn wooden table, wondering how old it was, wondering if Rose had sat at it, had sat in her chair.

*It's the same room, even if it's not the same furniture,* she consoled herself.

"Still, it must be great to *have* a family." Kari ventured further, hoping to raise the temperature a notch.

No response other than the fingers tapping in time to some unheard beat.

"I don't know what having lots of relatives is like," Kari added. "See, I don't have any family at all."

*Lame,* she ridiculed silently. *Pathetic.*

She cast around the kitchen, trying to imagine Rose and Breona having coffee together in the early mornings before the rest of the house awoke. She was really getting into it, envisioning Marit rolling out her famous ginger cookies, when she realized the tattoo on the table had stopped—and had been replaced by Mixxie's "evil eye" drilling into her.

"Don't even start with your phony sob story," she hissed. "The whole 'I don't have a dime' and 'you must be my long-lost family' is *wasted* on me. Got it?"

Kari drew back at the girl's vehemence. "I-I'm sure I don't know what you mean—"

"I said, *got it?* Don't waste your breath on me. In fact, just *shut it* altogether."

Kari exploded. "I've had just about enough of your vile attitude and lack of manners, *little girl.* Where I come from, *children* don't speak unless spoken to and when they *are* spoken to they answer 'yes, sir' or 'yes, ma'am' or they *keep their yaps shut.* I suggest you do the same before I *shut yours for you.*"

Mixxie's mouth went slack in shock. Kari could see Mixxie's wad of gum, pale green, on the back of her tongue.

*Disgusting.*

While she still had control of her hands and hadn't committed battery, Kari stormed out of the kitchen and down the long foyer. She stood in front of the double doors leading into the great room. She was shaking with rage and frustration and almost flung open the doors. Almost.

*This is by far the weirdest—and rudest—experience of my life,* she fumed.

Instead of barging in, she turned around and paced to the foot of the beautiful staircase and stared up to the landing, one hand on her hip. The wood was polished until it burned with an inner fire. The carpet runner was classic Victorian, all brilliant budding and blooming flowers.

*I'd so love to go up and look around,* she yearned. *I know just which room Rose used. Perhaps Shan-Rose will allow me to. Or maybe she will ask one of the relatives to take me on a tour?*

The doors to the great room opened and Kari, reluctantly, turned toward them.

"Ah, Ms. Hillyer." It was Fen-Bai, Mixxie's mother. She looked around. "Mixxie isn't with you?"

"Your daughter has quite the mouth on her." Kari was blunt and didn't care that she was. "I decided not to keep her company in the kitchen any longer. Speaking of 'longer,' how much longer will this family confab take? Shan-Rose invited me here today to talk about Rose and about Palmer House, but so far all I've gotten is *grilled* by all of you."

Kari waved her hand in the direction of the great room, and did not mask her irritation.

"Just so. I am so sorry. Yes; Mixxie is quite a handful, and I apologize both for her behavior and for our leaving you to her, er, *devices*. Please accept my humble apologies for all of us."

Kari looked aside and decided to shelve her annoyance. "All right. I accept your apology."

She sighed. "It's just that I have come a long way to learn more about this amazing woman. I mean, I didn't even know I was pronouncing her name wrong. *Tor-eh-sen,* is it? Shan-Rose promised to tell me about her. I imagine there aren't many still alive who can."

Kari's voice had grown plaintive at the end and Fen-Bai gave her a strange look.

"And what is *with* the way all of you keep looking at me?"

Her question was cut off, though, as the doors to the great room opened. Quan nodded to her. "Ms. Hillyer? Will you join us again?"

Kari shot a glance at Fen-Bai and then followed Quan into the great room. They were all watching her again, one or two speculatively, but most with simple curiosity. And acceptance?

Shan-Rose patted the arm of Kari's chair so Kari walked over and sat down.

"Ms. Hillyer, you came to Denver to discover what you could of Rose Thoresen and the others who lived at Palmer House. We're so glad you did. In fact, we believe the Lord himself directed your steps, and we have truly enjoyed making your acquaintance.

"We will be taking our leave in a few minutes. However, Alannah has agreed to stay and give you a tour of the house. I hope you will enjoy doing this?"

He looked for Kari's agreement and she nodded vigorously. "Yes, I certainly would."

"While she is doing that, I believe my sister will take a short rest. Then, after lunch, she would be pleased to share many memories with you, but we feel there are others who can—and who would be honored—to tell you even more."

Quan smiled a little. "We would like to send you on to RiverBend, Nebraska, Kari."

Kari caught her breath. "Isn't that where Rose and Jan lived?"

"Yes, it is. And you—I mean, *they*, that is, Jan and Rose and Joy— still have much family there. We will call ahead and let them know you are coming."

Kari blinked. "That is so very . . . nice. But won't they, I mean, they don't even know who I am—won't that be quite an imposition?"

Quan smiled wider and Kari decided she really liked this old man. "My dear, leave it to me to let them know," his smiled deepened further, "*who you are*."

He placed a reassuring hand on her arm. "Please trust me: They will be quite happy to see you."

# CHAPTER 17

Quan looked around the room. "Shall we conclude this family gathering with prayer?" Heads nodded and a few replied, "Yes."

"Very good." Quan bowed his head and prayed softly, "Father God, you truly are the God of all grace! And we are so grateful for this day and for answered prayer. You are faithful, Lord! Your ways are past finding out."

*The God of grace!* Kari's ears perked up. *Where have I heard that expression before? Oh! In Rose's journal! She wrote of Minister Liáng always praying to the God of grace. I wonder what 'grace' means.*

Quan added, "I thank you, Lord, for giving us direction in this matter. I thank you for the confidence we have to follow where you lead. Amen."

As the prayer ended, people began making their goodbyes. Quan drew near and asked Kari for her hotel name and room number. "I will call you this evening, Ms. Hillyer, after I've made arrangements for you in RiverBend."

"Are you sure I won't be imposing?" Kari felt uncomfortable pushing herself on strangers. "I can get a hotel—I don't want to be a burden."

"I don't believe RiverBend has any hotels, Ms. Hillyer. The railroad rerouted its tracks some years back, so no trains go through the town anymore. It was always a small town, and it is even smaller now. However, I can guarantee that the Thoresens living in RiverBend would be pleased to meet you and tell you more of Rose's history."

"But . . . where would I stay?"

"Will you allow me to make arrangements for you? I will make inquiries and I am sure things will sort themselves out by this evening."

Kari thought a minute. "Well, all right. If you say so."

"Very good. Can you stay in Denver tonight and tomorrow night? I will personally bring you driving directions tomorrow."

The house emptied out leaving only Shan-Rose, Mixxie, Kari, and Alannah in the great room. Kari still clutched her handbag close, unwilling to even chance the loss of Rose's journal.

"Ms. Hillyer," Shan-Rose murmured, "I trust you and Alannah will enjoy yourselves while I rest? I give you the run of the house. Then Mixxie will prepare a nice lunch for the four of us and we can talk further."

"Yes, ma'am," Kari answered. She itched to explore the house. *I will pretend that Rose is still here, perhaps just around a corner*, she fantasized.

Mixxie went off with Shan-Rose to help her to bed so Kari turned to Alannah. "I don't mind saying that was the strangest 'meeting' I've ever experienced, Alannah."

"Goodness—I have no doubt! I love the Liáng family, though it may take a Westerner a minute to adjust to their conversational 'style.' I grew up with them, you see, so I forget how abrupt they can sometimes seem."

"So Mei-Xing married Minister Liáng." Kari shook her head. "That sounds just like the perfect ending, doesn't it?"

"Minister Liáng and my grandfather, Isaac Carmichael, joined forces, so to speak, and had one of the largest ministries in Denver." Alannah's mouth curved as she remembered her happy childhood. "They grew a single church into thousands of believers in Christ—all colors and races. Mei-Xing and Breona were on the front lines with them, too, leading many women to Christ and standing against the vice that still grips this city today. Shan-Rose followed in their footsteps."

"Are you involved as they were?" Kari asked.

Alannah chuckled. "I am, but from a different perspective, Kari. I'm a police detective. Vice Squad."

Alannah watched Kari's reaction closely; Kari seemed genuinely surprised, but Alannah sensed no guilt.

"You? Wow. I would never have guessed. I imagine it is difficult for you—as a woman?"

"It is, but I come from tough stock, people who cared very deeply for this city." Alannah smiled and returned the conversation to her family. "I still recall the Liáng-Carmichael ministry partnership and how effective those two couples were, what love and fellowship they had for each other. Our families, the Liángs and Carmichaels, are entwined—like brothers, sisters, and cousins all wrapped into one."

"That is amazing." Kari was remembering Rose's description of Calvary Temple when those from Palmer House began attending.

"Rose couldn't have written a better ending than for Mei-Xing to find happiness after all she'd been through." Kari shook her head and grinned. "Just like a fairy tale."

"I was very interested in *your* tale, Kari," Alannah mentioned casually. "It seems like you've just had one of those storybook events. What? Inheriting a long-lost relative's estate? How improbable is that?"

"Believe me, I know. When I got the letter from the attorneys asking if I was Michael Granger's daughter, I thought it was a scam and nearly threw it away."

Alannah made a mental note: *Michael Granger. I will need to do some digging.*

"I know a few lawyers in New Orleans. Just on an off chance we know the same ones, what was the name of the law office that contacted you?"

"Brunell & Brunell. One of the senior partners, Clover Brunell, actually grew up with Daddy. He and his wife Lorene and their son, Oskar, have become dear friends."

"No; I don't know them. But he knew your father?" Alannah had to calm herself. *This is too good to be true.*

"Yes, he did. It has been so wonderful hearing him tell me about Daddy."

And then Alannah glimpsed the loneliness that Kari lived with. *If that's not real pain, I'll eat my badge.*

"Shall we walk through the house now?" she suggested. "Feel free to ask questions as we go along."

"Yes, let's! I'm particularly interested in seeing Rose's room."

Alannah frowned a little. "You know she hasn't lived in this house for many years, right, Kari? Decades."

Kari sighed. "Yes. I figured as much, but I didn't know for sure . . . how things ended up. So, what about the ministry of Palmer House— the outreach they had to rescue prostitutes? How did the house change from Palmer House to just being Shan-Rose's house?"

"Ah. That I can tell you. Do you know how Palmer House started?"

"Yes; Martha Palmer heard Rose and Joy speak and gave them this house for their work. It was in Rose's journal."

"Right. So, they used Palmer House for their outreach to women for many years, even after Joy branched out."

"Branched out? I don't know about that."

Alannah trod carefully. "Okay; taking a little side track but still answering your question, did Rose's journal say anything about Joy's husband, Grant?"

Kari sighed again. "She wrote how sick Grant was. His heart. They didn't have the miracles of modern medicine we have today. I-I almost hate to ask what happened to him."

"Yes; I understand it was very sad. He died in 1911. Not long after the journal you found ended."

Kari mulled over Alannah's words. "Poor Joy! How she must have grieved!"

Alannah looked back and remembered her grandmother repeating the story; remembered too, how every time she told it, tears would fill her eyes. "I've heard Joy grieved deeply. I've also heard how amazing her faith was. How she put her pain to work for the Lord."

Kari found that she didn't mind so much that Alannah was talking about God—just like Clover and Ruth and Owen seemed to do all the time. "Tell me?" she begged.

"A few years later, she and her husband—"

"Wait! Her *husband*? She remarried? Who?"

Alannah grinned. "Joy *did* remarry. She married Edmund O'Dell several years after Grant died. What a story that is! I can't even go into all the details, but O'Dell—that's what everyone in the family called him—was head of the Pinkerton office here in Denver for many years before he was promoted and they moved to Chicago."

"They moved to Chicago? But what about Palmer House?" Things were going much too fast for Kari.

"That's what I'm trying to get to. First Mei-Xing married and moved out; then Breona. When Joy and O'Dell married and Joy moved out of the house, Rose was left to carry most of the burden of it alone. Billy and Marit stayed on, of course, and Sara became something of Rose's right-hand. From what I've heard, the Lord seemed to bring the right people at the right time to help.

"Through Breona and Mei-Xing and their ministry on the streets of Denver, many fallen women came to Jesus. A large number of them lived at Palmer House where love, God's word, and time healed their hearts and prepared them for independent lives.

"By the time the O'Dells moved to Chicago, the house had grown to be too much for Rose—she was, after all, getting on. I think she was in her seventies by then.

"So, the Lord raised up Sara and two other women to continue in Rose's place, and Rose moved with Joy and her family to Chicago. It was during their time in Chicago that Joy expanded her ministry."

"And Rose? I mean . . ." Kari didn't want to ask; she didn't want to hear of Rose's death.

Alannah heard Kari's sorrow as she alluded to Rose's final days. "Later . . . much later, she wanted to go home . . . to RiverBend."

*I need to be careful of what I say,* Alannah realized, *for more than one reason. Kari seems to honestly have feelings about Rose.* "Rose died in her sleep one night, at a good old age. Like the Bible says, she was gathered to her ancestors."

Kari nodded very slowly, taking in the details of what she already knew to be certain.

Alannah watched Kari closely to see if what she spoke of was already known to her. "Did you know that prior to running the Denver Pinkerton office, O'Dell had specialized in finding kidnapped children?"

Kari nodded again, thoughtful. "Yes, but not just children, right? That is why he was so effective when Mei-Xing disappeared."

"God had his hand all over that, Kari. Edmund O'Dell would have been the first one to tell you that if God hadn't intervened, they would never have found Mei-Xing. It almost broke Grandma's heart when her dearest friend disappeared."

Kari was drowning in information, and just then she realized who Alannah's grandmother was. She stared at Alannah with fresh eyes. Noting Alannah's raven hair and eyes, she blurted, "Breona was your grandmother! You get your black hair and eyes from Breona?"

"Ah! Yes, but not just from Grandma. Our family—my siblings and I—were handed a double dose of the 'Black Irish.'"

"What do you mean?"

Alannah laughed. "Ready to get even more confused? Joy and Edmund O'Dell had four children: Matthew, Jacob, Luke, and Roseanne. What I mean by 'double dose' is that while my father was a Carmichael, my *mother* was an *O'Dell*—Joy and Edmund O'Dell's daughter, Roseanne. Their youngest.

"Mom didn't inherit Joy's brilliant blue eyes, though." She slanted a look at Kari. "Only one of Joy's children did. Mom got her dark hair and eyes from Edmund O'Dell. And I? I got the double dose."

"Oh, wow." Kari clapped her hand over her mouth. "I know I've said 'wow' about ten times, but *wow*!"

Kari and Alannah laughed together, comfortable in each other's company. They were finally walking up the staircase to the upstairs, and Kari had reached her saturation point. "Wait. I'm sorry—this is all so confusing. Rose said in her journal that Joy and Grant's son, Edmund, had Jan and Joy's blue eyes. So Edmund O'Dell . . . he adopted Baby Edmund?"

Alannah cast a sharp look Kari's way but saw nothing to indicate guile. In fact, as they emerged on the second floor, Kari was engrossed, taking in every room and every detail.

Alannah stalled and then said, "Um . . . O'Dell promised Grant that he would raise Edmund as his own." *That's not a lie, Lord,* she added silently.

"So you were going to tell me what ministry Joy started." Kari, unwittingly, brought the conversation back around, but not necessarily onto a safer track.

"Her ministry is, uh, actually more of a movement. It's called *Lost Are Found.* Dedicated to finding missing children. It dovetailed very nicely with the work of helping women and girls escape human trafficking."

"*Lost Are Found.* Like pictures on the back of milk cartons back in the 1980s?"

"Like that."

"I saw the *Lost Are Found* sign out front and I *knew* those words sounded familiar. But human trafficking? I haven't heard it called that before."

"As it turns out, many children who go missing end up in the hands of human traffickers—those who sell children into the sex trade. That made *Lost Are Found* a very real sister ministry to Palmer House."

Kari felt her stomach lurch. "Children? No. That's sickening!"

"Yes," Alannah murmured, "I know. It is what I deal with on a regular basis."

She turned the conversation back to Joy and O'Dell. "Joy and Edmund O'Dell were instrumental in reuniting many parents with their lost children. They led a number of these families to Christ. I am proud that they were my grandparents."

Alannah kept glancing at Kari, evaluating her responses. *I've been a detective for a decade,* Alannah thought, *and I know how to read faces. Nothing. Kari knows nothing about . . .*

She shook her head. *The more I listen to her, the more I think that her story has to be on the up-and-up.*

They didn't talk much as Kari wandered through the second floor. Alannah got the impression that Kari just wanted to be left alone to look and think . . . which was exactly right.

Kari opened the door into the bedroom that had once been Breona's and Mei-Xing's. She saw the evidence of it not being occupied for some time. The two twin beds in the room were stripped, their mattresses removed. The décor was pure 1970s: Boldly flowered wall paper, curtains, and shag carpeting in oranges and yellows, brightly painted dressers, and a single desk. The room contained no personal items and smelled stale and musty.

Kari walked to the windows. They overlooked the front yard of the house, the iron gated fence, the sidewalk, and the street. She tried to imagine Breona standing at this very window and seeing O'Dell below—bringing home Mei-Xing, rescued and restored to those who loved her by the miraculous hand of God.

*Are you there, God?* Kari wondered. *I have come to believe that you were here, at Palmer House, at one time. Do you still reveal yourself to people like you revealed yourself to Rose?*

She and Alannah walked the halls of the second floor in silence, looking into every room except the one Kari knew had been Rose's.

*I will save it until last,* she decided.

Alannah let Kari wander freely and did not interrupt her introspection. After a bit they climbed the stairs to the third floor together, to the rooms built into the towers and turrets. The rooms were largely the same as those on the second floor—a mish-mash of dated furniture and décor.

While the main floor of the house was cared for and warm with human presence, the neglect and abandonment that pervaded the second and third floors wore on Kari, distressing her. The rooms and halls smelled of age and disuse; their emptiness echoed the aching loneliness in Kari's breast.

When they returned to the second floor and Kari reached the bedroom she knew had been Rose's, she stopped at the closed door. She didn't open it; she merely placed her hand on it and shut her eyes.

Sensing the tender import of the moment, Alannah backed away and said nothing. She watched the play of emotions washing Kari's face.

*Oh, Rose,* Kari mourned. *Oh, how I wish you were still here— that I could know you personally. That I could talk to you. I think that is what I long for and why I came all this way. I have so much I want to ask!*

Kari gulped as her throat tightened and tears formed. *I guess what I really wish is that I could ask you about your Jesus. How did you learn to know him so well? Is knowing him what made your heart so loving, so compassionate toward the plight of others?*

She squeezed her eyes even tighter. *Will I ever know your God as you knew him, Rose? Yes—I admit it! I was wrong! If he was here for you, he **must** exist! And if he was here for you, then I must—somehow—find him! But this house is so empty now!*

Kari's fingers traced the design on the door, finding that the intersecting rails formed *a cross* on the door's face. She opened her eyes and stared at the wood grain in front of her. The symbolism gripped her, and a solitary tear streaked its way down her cheek.

*I won't open this door,* she vowed. *I won't open it and be disillusioned by how the room looks and smells inside, all these years later. I want to just remember standing here, as though she were on the other side, waiting for me. Waiting to tell me everything I long to know. Waiting to hold me as though I were one of her lost girls!*

*Rose! I wanted you to hold me like that!*

She covered her eyes with her hands and sobbed her heart into the wood of the door. Her tears flowed, unchecked, soaking her face, leaking through her fingers.

Until something startled her out of her grieving.

Kari blinked. A sacred Presence seemed to reach out for her, touching her gently, sweetly.

From behind the door—but also from around her—a Voice whispered. *You were wishing for Rose to be here and speak of Me, but I am already here, Kari. I have always been . . . here . . . where you are . . . waiting for you.*

*I Am.*

Kari froze, terrified. Astounded. But the Presence flowed like peaceful water, all around her. She closed her eyes and let it wash over her.

*In a manner of speaking, I am on the other side of this door—and more, Kari. I am on the other side of the vast gulf that separates us. And I am knocking.*

Kari's lips parted. *Are you Jesus? Am I just imagining you—or are you really him?*

The Voice swelled. *I am the One who is called Faithful and True, the One who reigns and rules as The Lion of the Tribe of Judah. I sit forever upon the throne of David. And I am here: Behold, I stand at the door and knock. Only you can open the door. Open and find me.*

The strength in Kari's legs gave out and, before an amazed Alannah, she crumpled, more or less onto her knees. Something constrained Alannah from going to Kari's aid. God's very attendance restrained her and urged her to pray. She dropped to her own knees.

"O Jesus," Kari wept. "Oh, please! Yes! I want you to come in! I want you to come in!"

*O Lord!* Alannah breathed. *What marvelous thing are you doing here? Please bring Kari into your Kingdom this day, I pray!*

Kari wept, her face pressed against the door, her hot tears staining its wood. She wept and she heard the words of Rose's journal beating a rhythm in her soul:

*Surrender. Surrender to the Lordship of Jesus. Surrender. Surrender to Jesus.*

The wall of doubt and willfulness within Kari crumbled and gave way. With all the broken pieces of her heart, she surrendered.

# CHAPTER 18

Kari didn't know how long she knelt, pressed against the door to Rose's old room. Her tears had dried. No voice spoke to her again. But within her soul a light flickered and burned, warming her, soothing her.

"O Jesus," she whispered. "O Jesus. Thank you."

*Holy!* Kari's heart thumped. *Holy! You are holy, Lord!*

The sacred presence of God in that hallway lingered. Kari became aware that Alannah, too, was on her knees, several feet away, her hands clasped, her eyes closed, her mouth moving in silent words.

*She feels him, too,* Kari realized. *Jesus.*

*Holy!* Kari's heart called again.

Kari drew a deep breath and slowly stood to her feet. Alannah opened her eyes and stood with her.

"What happened, Kari?" Alannah breathed. "God did something, something wonderful. I know. I felt him!"

"You're a . . . Christian, right?" Kari answered.

"Yes. I am."

In those two words, Kari heard that Voice again . . . *I Am.*

"I . . . he . . . Jesus." The tears Kari thought were finished flowed again. "He spoke to me! From the other side of the door, he said, *Behold, I stand at the door and knock.* He said, *Only you can open the door.*"

"What did you do?" Alannah's eyes had also filled and were overflowing.

Kari looked down for a moment. "I said *yes.*" She smiled with trembling lips. "I said *yes* to Jesus. I kept hearing those words from Rose's journal: *Surrender to Jesus.* I said *yes.*"

Alannah touched Kari's arm. "You will never be the same, Kari. From this day forward. Now I know and have no doubts that God himself led you to find Rose's journal and led you . . . here."

The two women walked down the long staircase together. "If you don't mind," Kari murmured, "I think I'd like to go sit in the gazebo? Would that be a problem?"

"Not at all." Alannah walked outside with Kari and they found seats in the vine-shaded gazebo. "Aunt Shan-Rose's room is just here," she whispered, pointing to the windows.

Kari nodded. She wanted to be quiet anyway. They sat for a long while, both of them re-living what had happened in the dank hallway upstairs.

"Alannah," Kari asked at last, keeping her voice low, "How did Palmer House end? How did it come to be Shan-Rose's?"

"Will you walk around the yard with me, Kari?"

Alannah took Kari's hand and folded it into the crook of her arm so that they were walking arm-in-arm. Surprisingly, Kari felt comforted by her gesture of companionship. They wandered through the old pine trees in the front yard and meandered along a path that led down the side of the house to the back.

"Martha Palmer died in 1917," Alannah said, quite out of the blue. "I hear that when she passed, everyone was shocked to learn the contents of her will.

"She left an ample amount to her great-nephew—her only living relative—and a tidy little stipend to a Mr. Wheatley, an dear and trusted old friend of Joy and Grant's."

"Mr. Wheatley! Oh, yes. I read quite a bit about him from Rose's journal." Kari nodded, satisfied to hear the elderly gent had been taken care of in his last years.

"Martha left her house—not Palmer House, but the one she lived in for many years—to Mei-Xing and Minister Liáng's children. The rest of it, the bulk of Martha Palmer's fortune—considerable in those days I hear—was not left to Mei-Xing, as some had expected."

"Oh?" Kari glanced at Alannah, a little surprised to find her watching her. They stopped their stroll and Alannah faced Kari.

"She left only her house and a small amount of money to Mei-Xing. The remainder of her fortune was placed into a trust. The trust was to pay a set amount for Palmer House's expenses each year as long the ministry was in operation. The remainder was to be paid out to two individuals, beginning in the twenty-first year of each of them."

"Who were those two people?" Kari asked.

Alannah observed her closely as she replied, "Shan-Rose Liáng and Edmund Thoresen Michaels."

Kari didn't know why she felt Alannah was waiting, watching for her response. She shrugged her shoulders. "That was quite marvelous of Mrs. Palmer—especially paying the expenses of Palmer House. Rose mentioned several times in her journal how difficult the finances were."

*Rose prayed her heart out, is more like it,* Kari added to herself.

Then she thought of something. "So what happened to the house's ministry, anyway?"

Alannah smiled and took Kari's hand again. "The house became too difficult to maintain. It cost a fortune to heat and cool and lacked some of the modern amenities the ministry needed. Moreover, there just weren't as many girls coming into it as had before.

"The board of directors—yes, they had a board by then—decided that a smaller, more modern facility would work better. They rented a newer five-bedroom house and moved the ministry there. Sadly, it did not work well. Somewhere along the way, the original vision for this ministry got lost. The leadership's approach became more humanistic rather than God-breathed."

"God-breathed?" Kari was unfamiliar with the term.

"Did Rose describe some of the wonderful things God did in the early years of the ministry? Did she write about women's lives being miraculously transformed?"

"Oh, yes! To be truthful, that was what first engaged me in her journal. In her first entry she wrote—I have it memorized, you see—:

*For on those whom you have poured your Son's lifeblood, you have also placed the most value. Can any earthly treasures be worth more? No, Lord, they cannot.*

Kari shook her head in wonder. "It was the first time I had heard how much value God places on *people*. I didn't understand what it meant the first time I read it, but today I feel like she wrote that about *me*!" The tears threatened to fall again and Kari choked up.

Alannah gave Kari's arm an understanding squeeze. "I know. I know just what you mean. Those words she wrote? She wrote them under the influence of the Holy Spirit—as though God himself had breathed on them. That was how Palmer House was birthed and why it was successful for so long."

Alannah huffed. "Then the board of directors, over many objections, placed leadership of the new house in those who had no idea what the power of God could do. They relied on programs and methods instead of God's word and his power.

"However, Martha Palmer's trust was set up under strict guidelines. The new leadership couldn't meet the requirements to continue the funding and lost it. Our family felt the Lord was leading us in another direction, so we let go of it, knowing that God's heart was guiding us.

"You see, according to what I've heard and later observed, from the time she was a teen Shan-Rose had a powerful call of God on her life. Her entire life, she has been on the front lines, working with women in prison, in drug addiction, in prostitution—you name it, she was there, leading the way. She never married and she never veered from her calling. I admire her more than any woman I know."

Alannah sighed in remembrance. "Anyway, when the board of directors of Palmer House moved the ministry from here, Shan-Rose asked her siblings to buy her out of her part of the house they had inherited from Martha Palmer. Shan-Rose took her share and the money she had left from Martha's trust fund and bought *this* house.

"She used it in a limited manner as it had been intended for several years. But about fifteen years ago, when she was nearing seventy, she more or less retired—after her siblings begged her to slow down.

"She lived here alone until last year, still ministering a little outside the house but not having women live here with her. Then the family insisted she either move in with one of them or have someone live here full time to care for her. Shan-Rose picked Mixxie, which was quite a shock to us all, given Mixxie's attitude and behaviors.

"Everyone was equally surprised when Mixxie accepted. Well, she needed a job and wanted to get out of her parents' house, but I think Shan-Rose has ulterior motives." Alannah grinned. "It's my opinion that Shan-Rose will work on Mixxie until she gets what she's after."

Kari made a face. "That *girl*! I almost slapped her, Alannah; I won't deny it. She said some pretty rude things—even some strange things about me."

"Oh?" Alannah feigned mild curiosity. "What sort of strange things?"

Kari shrugged. "She was raving about how I came in here with a sob story saying I didn't have any money and something about my saying you guys were my long-lost family. First of all, I certainly never asked for money or even hinted at such a thing! I have my own money and I sure don't need anyone else's! Second of all, I'd like to know how I could be related to the Liángs! Um, *hello*! If you've got eyes, you can plainly tell that I'm not even remotely Asian, right?"

Alannah cut her eyes at Kari. *Nothing, Lord. She really hasn't a clue!*

Alannah picked up the pace of their meander around the house and asked in a playful manner, "So you have your own moolah, huh, lady? Don't need ours?"

Alannah laughed but at the same time she was digging for information. "Despite how this place looks, Shan-Rose has little left and the rest of us are all just working slobs."

"No, I don't need anything," Kari muttered. "To quote my attorney, I just inherited 'plenty' from my great-uncle. He left me a home in New Orleans, too."

"Really? How nice." They walked in relative silence again, but Alannah's brain was whirring in high gear. "New Orleans is a wonderful place. What part of town is your house?"

"I'm not familiar enough with the city to say what area it's in. It's on Marlow Avenue, 2787 Marlow Avenue, if you know where that is."

Alannah made careful note of the address. *I need to make the trip to NOLA for myself,* she decided. *I want my own boots on the ground to ferret out exactly what is and isn't true. And who was this "Great-Uncle Peter" anyway? I have my suspicions, but we need proof.*

Kari and Alannah joined Shan-Rose and Mixxie in the dining room for a late lunch. "We usually eat in the kitchen," Shan-Rose confessed, "but having you here is a special occasion."

*Me? A special occasion?* Kari glanced at Mixxie and ran up against her perpetual scowl.

"Tell me what you thought of the house, my dear," Shan-Rose invited. "And help yourself to some of that salad."

Kari thought for a minute. "I confess that the upstairs is rather sad-looking after all the years of use and now . . . nothing." She dithered, shy about saying anything more.

"Will you tell her what happened upstairs?" Alannah asked. She was staring at Kari, telling her it was all right.

"Something happened?" Shan-Rose fretted. "Oh, dear. I told Quan that the roof could be leaking up on the third floor!"

"No; it's nothing like that, Shan-Rose." Kari didn't want the old woman worrying. "It's a . . . *good* thing that happened."

"Oh?" Shan-Rose seemed to sense the momentous tone of Kari's response. "Will you tell me?"

Kari did want to tell, but maybe not in front of Mixxie who seemed to heap scorn on everything she did not like or understand. She glanced once at Mixxie and then turned back to Shan-Rose.

"I—that is, *we*—had finished looking at the house, everything except Rose's old bedroom. I knew which one it was, you see, from the descriptions she put in her journal. Anyway . . ."

Kari's words trailed off a moment as she placed herself back in that hallway, outside Rose's door. "I was standing at her door, but the other rooms were so . . . different from what they used to be . . . that I decided I wouldn't open the door to Rose's room and be disillusioned. Disappointed."

Shan-Rose nodded, saddened. "I understand. It's not the same for me anymore, either." She placed her tiny, frail hand on Kari's and patted it gently.

"Well, I was just standing there . . . sort of, I guess, talking to Rose. Oh, not talking *to* her; I know she's not there and not a ghost or anything—that would be silly. But I just stood in front of her door and wished that I could talk to her."

*I wished she would hold me,* Kari admitted to herself, *like she used to hold her girls, the girls of Palmer House. How I wanted to be one of her girls!*

"I told her I wished she were there to tell me about Jesus. But then I heard." Kari stopped, the words thick in her throat. "I heard *Jesus* calling to me! To *me*! He said he had always been there and that he was standing at the door and knocking and I should let him in."

Kari looked from Shan-Rose to Alannah and back. "That sounds crazy, doesn't it? That Jesus should be on the other side of the door? But I know he was there! And he asked me to surrender. And I did! And I felt him inside of me! You felt it, too, Alannah, didn't you?"

Mixxie made a show of rolling her eyes. Kari ignored her and saw that Alannah and Shan-Rose did, too.

"Oh, yes! I did feel it, Kari. I felt the presence of God in that hallway," Alannah agreed. "I was on my knees praying because I could feel he was doing something powerful, something wonderful, even though I didn't know *what*. But what you heard him say to you? What he asked you to do? That isn't crazy at all, Kari."

"Right," Mixxie grumbled, "'cause we don't do crazy *here*."

No one paid her any attention.

Alannah went into the great room and returned with Shan-Rose's Bible. She had it opened toward the back. "You see this passage? Read what it says."

Kari took the worn book and looked where Alannah's finger was pointing. She read aloud,

> *Behold, I stand at the door, and knock:*
> *if any man hear my voice, and open the door,*
> *I will come in to him, and will sup with him,*
> *and he with me.*

"But that is almost exactly what Jesus said!" Kari was so excited she was stammering. "How can it be the same thing?"

"Because whatever God does will always agree with what he has already said," Shan-Rose answered. "After he has promised something, he doesn't change his mind and go back on his word, like people do."

"Why are the words printed in red?" Kari asked.

"Everywhere Jesus himself is speaking is printed in red," Mixxie sneered. "Can't believe you don't know *that*."

"Mei-Xing Liáng!" Shan-Rose's rebuke was loud and sharp. "You do not sneer at what God himself is doing or has done! What he has done in Kari is *sacred* and is *not* to be ridiculed."

"What a crock! It's *all a crock*! And I can't stand it anymore—*you* least of all," Mixxie spat the last words at Kari and ran from the room.

Kari blinked, unsure of what had just happened but realizing that Mixxie's anger was more than about her coming to Palmer House.

Shan-Rose sighed. "Please don't be offended by Mixxie, Kari," she advised, stirring her tea and sighing again. While Shan-Rose seemed perturbed, Kari thought she also seemed resolute. "Mixxie is running as fast as she can from the Lord. Anger is her defense, but you cannot outrun the God who created you."

Kari nodded. "Someone said to me not long ago, 'It is both sad and astonishing how hard people fight against Jesus when he calls to them.' I relate, because honestly . . . I have been fighting against him a long time. My whole life, in fact."

Shan-Rose placed her hand on Kari's again. "And he never gave up on you, did he? No matter how fiercely you fought him, he still heard you when you called to him. That's the way our God is."

She picked up her fork but stopped to reflect. "A family that is committed to the Lord has tremendous power to pray for family members who have lost their way. Or have been lost *to* them. It is our motto, you know, the Thoresens, O'Dells, Liángs, and Carmichaels: *Lost Are Found.*

"Our families are tied together by the blood Jesus shed for us, by our shared service in the Lord, and by our shared troubles. We do not give up, Kari. We have *never* given up on those who walk away—or on those who were taken from us. We—Joy and O'Dell, Isaac and Breona, Grandma Rose, and my mother and father, and our families—have lived by this motto for as long as I can remember."

Kari thought she saw Shan-Rose and Alannah exchange the most fleeting of glances but she wasn't sure. She turned her eyes to her plate.

*Lost Are Found? I thought that was the name of Joy's missing children's ministry.* It seemed to Kari that another facet of that simple phrase was hidden from her in a manner that Shan-Rose and Alannah understood but she did not.

Kari was saying goodbye, getting ready to take her leave. She was exhausted physically but oddly at peace otherwise. "Shan-Rose, was Quan serious when he said I should go to RiverBend and visit Rose's family?"

"Oh, yes, Kari. Quite serious."

Kari thought for a moment. "Alannah, do you know where Grant Michaels is buried? For that matter, where Joy and O'Dell are buried?"

Alannah, who was also readying to leave, looked to Shan-Rose. "Grant's grave is here in Denver, isn't it, Auntie?"

"Yes; Riverside Cemetery, I believe. I have a faint memory of going there with Mother and Father when I was a little girl. We met Joy, O'Dell, Grandma Rose, and several others to place flowers on his grave. I think it was right before Joy and O'Dell married."

"Would you like to go there?" Alannah asked Kari.

"I very much would. Quan asked me to stay another day and night before leaving for RiverBend. I could go to the cemetery tomorrow."

"I work tomorrow, but I believe Fen-Bai would be delighted to take you."

"Do you think so?"

"Let me call her. I'll let you know this evening."

"Thank you." Kari turned to Shan-Rose. "And I want to especially thank you, Shan-Rose, for opening your home and your . . . heart to me. Visiting here today meant so much to me."

"Kari, you have no idea what a blessing *you* are to all of us. When you knocked on that door yesterday, it was an answer to prayer."

"It was?" Kari didn't understand, but Shan-Rose just nodded.

"Revisiting the history of our families has been good for all of us," was all she added.

Alannah escorted Shan-Rose to her chair in the great room and kissed her on the cheek. "Will you be all right here, Auntie?"

"Oh, my, yes. Mixxie will be along as soon as you two leave. She might spit and snarl, but she has been very good to me."

"All right then."

Alannah gestured for Kari to walk out with her. Kari thanked Shan-Rose again and followed Alannah out. She paused on the front porch and looked at the worn sign hanging by the door.

"Alannah, I saw Quan touch this sign on his way in this morning. It looked as though he were praying when he touched it."

"Hmm." Alannah didn't answer for a moment "Well, it is, as we've said, something of the motto of our four families and of other friends who were also involved in . . . that period. Perhaps he *was* praying. Giving thanks."

"Giving thanks for what?" Kari asked. She touched the faded letters with her own fingers, feeling the grit of the letters' roughened outlines.

"For God's amazing, unfailing faithfulness, would be my guess," Alannah answered softly.

Alannah went directly to her station and straight to her desk where she made some phone calls and filled out pages of HR paperwork. Then she headed for her boss's office.

"Hey, Captain? You have a sec?" Receiving a nod, Alannah closed the office door behind her.

"What do you need, Carmichael?" The Captain didn't look up; he kept his eyes on the stack of papers in front of him, his pen moving over them methodically.

"I need to take some leave. At least three days. Possibly four."

Now he did look up. "Oh? When?"

"Tomorrow through Friday. Family business. I should be back in the office Monday. Well, Tuesday at the latest. Depends on how it goes."

He blew a frustrated huff. "You just took most of today off, didn't you?"

"Like I said, family business. I have the time on the books."

"Fine. But only if you can work out coverage."

"Already did, Cap."

"All right; fill out the paperwork for my sig—" He stopped when Alannah handed him two sheets.

"Ready for your signature, sir."

"Always a step ahead, eh, Carmichael?"

"That's how I like to play it, sir."

Alannah went to her desk and called her travel agent. "Yeah; I'd like to confirm that round-trip ticket to New Orleans. Yes, first flight out tomorrow, returning on Friday, the twenty-fifth."

"Your seat is still available. I can have your tickets ready in an hour."

"You close at six? I'll pick them up just before," Alannah promised.

Kari ate dinner in one of the hotel's restaurants. She sat alone but did not feel alone. She replayed, over and over, her encounter with . . . Jesus on the second floor of Palmer House.

*Jesus! O, Jesus.* Each time she thought or said his name, her insides seemed to warm and she felt a strange absence of anxiety— often her normal state. And she felt oddly . . . *all right*. Stable. Content. At peace.

*I don't feel that continual aching inside . . .* Kari ate her meal lost in thought. She was actually afraid to "poke" at the peace she was enjoying, afraid—just a little—that it would prove too fragile to stand up under scrutiny.

Later, back in her room, Kari waited for Quan's phone call. While she waited, she did something she'd never dreamed she would do. She began opening drawers in her room—dresser, nightstand, and desk.

The desk was where she found what she was looking for: A Bible, placed there by "The Gideons."

*I don't know who or what The Gideons are,* Kari shrugged, *but I'm grateful they left this here.*

She opened it and thumbed through the index, having no clue where to begin or what she wanted to find. *Perhaps I'll just look for Jesus,* she decided. Starting at the beginning, she paged through, growing discouraged as, page after page, she found no mention of him.

The phone rang. "Hello?"

"Ms. Hillyer? It is Quan Liáng calling."

"Oh! I'm so glad you called, Mr. Liáng. As a minister, I know you can answer this! Could you please tell me where in the Bible to find Jesus?"

After being momentarily thrown, Quan was elated. "If you are reading the Bible for the first time, Ms. Hillyer, I recommend that you begin with the four gospels."

"The four gospels? Are they near the front?"

"No. Ah, does your Bible have a table of contents, by any chance?"

"Oh. Let me look." Kari went to the beginning again and paged until she found it. "There's an Old Testament and a New Testament and a list of books in each."

"The four gospels are the first four books of the New Testament," Quan told her. "Matthew, Mark, Luke, and John. Start with those. You'll read all about Jesus in those four books."

He explained, "The gospels are four different accounts of Jesus' life and ministry. Two accounts are from his disciples—they were firsthand witnesses to Jesus' ministry. Those books are Matthew and John. Mark is believed to be Peter's account as recorded by the young man the Book of Acts called John Mark. Luke was a companion to the Apostle Paul on his missionary journeys. Church history teaches that he interviewed multiple eyewitnesses to write his account."

"Wow. Thank you." Kari already had her finger in the start of Matthew.

*I have a lot to learn,* she thought.

"So, Ms. Hillyer, I made several phone calls last night and today, letting our friends know that you had, er, found Rose Thoresen's missing journal. Everyone I spoke to is very eager to, um, make your acquaintance. They would like you to come to RiverBend the day after tomorrow."

"Really?" Kari was dumbfounded.

"Really. Søren and Ilsa Thoresen, great-grandchildren of Jan Thoresen, own one of the original Thoresen homesteads, and they would love for you to come and stay with them for a few days."

"These are great-grandchildren of Jan and his first wife then?"

"Yes; brother and sister, two of the nine grandchildren of Søren Thoresen, for whom our present Søren is named."

"Well." Kari looked around the room, indecisive. "If you think it's really all right."

"These people are the salt of the earth," Quan reassured her. "Wonderful folk, wonderful followers of Christ. What do you think?"

"Well," Kari said again. "I guess so. How long will it take to drive there?"

"It's going to be eight hours or more unless you put your foot down on that Cadillac I saw you park at Palmer House."

"Hmm. I *might* have done that a few times on the way here from Albuquerque," she grinned.

Quan chuckled. "Well, plan on a good eight hours. Are you doing anything for dinner tomorrow evening? Perhaps you would join some of the Liángs and Carmichaels out for dinner?"

Kari was enthusiastic in her response. "I would love that!"

A half an hour after Kari hung up with Quan, Alannah called.

"Good news, Kari! Fen-Bai said she would love to take you to see Grant Michaels' grave. She will pick you up at your hotel tomorrow after lunch—one o'clock."

Quan dialed a number from his library at home. It rang only twice before a voice answered, "Hello?"

"Matthew? It's Quan."

"Yes, old friend. I've been waiting on pins and needles to hear back from you."

"Did you get in touch with everyone? Are they all coming?"

"More than you would think. The entire clan is electrified. Are you sure? Are you sure she's . . ."

"Alannah left for New Orleans early this morning. Kari gave her the name of her attorney—the firm that is handling her 'great-uncle's' will. She also mentioned the name of her father: Michael Granger. You know Alannah. She will leave no stone unturned. We hope to learn the truth—the incontrovertible truth—before next weekend."

"Will Ms. Hillyer stay that long in RiverBend, do you think?"

"I think so. Søren and Ilsa will do their best to make her feel welcome and to keep her interest."

"Quan, I have to tell you that I have been trembling most of the day. The import of this! How I wish Mother and Father were here to see it! I know they are rejoicing in heaven, but how I wish they were here with us."

"I am grateful that the three of *you* are still here, my friend, you three, her father's half brothers! I'm sorry Roseanne is not."

"Yes. We would wish her here, too. I am comforted to know that she is watching from heaven with Mother and Father. So, tell me again, Quan. What is she like, this Kari Hillyer?"

"Well, she looks incredibly like Joy, only her long hair is not blonde but light brown. And she is strong like Joy, too. I can see her determination. However, she has also been beaten up by the world. Two divorces, I gathered, the latest one just this year. Kari believes that she has not a relative in the world, and that has left a bit of hopelessness lingering in her eyes."

"Not a relative in the world! God willing, that will all change next Friday. I hope it will not overwhelm her too much."

❧ ✳ ❧

# $\mathcal{C}$HAPTER 19

Alannah rolled her bag from the claim area to one of the car rental desks. "I'd like a small sedan if you have one," she asked, "and I would like to purchase a detailed map of the city if you have one of those, too."

Armed with a car and a map, Alannah considered her first move. It was after eleven in the morning, Louisiana time, and the July heat was already oppressive.

*I will get to my hotel, turn on the air conditioning, call Brunell & Brunell, and make arrangements to meet with her attorney—either this afternoon or first thing tomorrow,* she planned.

Alannah let herself into her hotel room and threw her bags on the bed. She switched on the air conditioning, reveling in its rush of cold relief, then went straight to the phone, checking her watch first. *Nearly one o'clock,* she noted. *Perhaps they will see me today.*

If what Kari had related to her about her recent inheritance were true, Alannah did not doubt that one of the senior partners would scramble to make time to see her. *Especially after I drop my opening bomb on them.*

Alannah had thought carefully of how to ensure that she saw a decision maker at the Brunell law offices—someone high enough up the ladder to tell her what she needed. In this situation, she was not averse to throwing her weight around a little to get the result she desired.

Her dialing was rewarded with a prompt answer: "Brunell & Brunell. How may I direct your call?"

"This is Detective Alannah Carmichael, Denver Police Department," she opened in a brisk, authoritative voice. "I am calling in regards to Ms. Kari Hillyer, who is, I believe, a client of this firm?"

If Kari were the A-list client that Alannah was now convinced she was, she hoped the combination of "detective," "police," and "Ms. Kari Hillyer" would inject a little alarmed energy into the receptionist.

It did. So electric and breathless was the receptionist's response that Alannah felt she could almost see her on the other end jump from her chair and stand to attention.

"Yes, ma'am. I will connect you with Miss Dawes, executive assistant to the senior partners. Please hold."

She put Alannah on hold and Alannah, gratified at the immediate response, waited.

"Good afternoon. This is Miss Dawes. How may I help you?"

"Miss Dawes, this is Detective Alannah Carmichael of the Denver, Colorado, Police Department speaking. I recently made the acquaintance of a Ms. Kari Hillyer as she visited Denver. I believe she is a client of this firm?"

"She is. However, that is the extent of the information I am at liberty to disclose, Detective Carmichael. Client-attorney privilege, you understand."

What Alannah understood was that Miss Dawes' words were carefully scripted to protect the privacy of the firm's clients.

"Yes, of course, Miss Dawes. However, I am calling today because I have reason to believe that Ms. Hillyer is intimately connected to a *felony* committed in our city. I would like to speak directly to her attorney, if I may. In fact, I am here in New Orleans for that purpose."

"Felony? What felony?" Miss Dawes' professional veneer cracked ever-so-slightly.

"I'm afraid that is the extent of the information I am at liberty to disclose," Alannah answered smoothly. "Except to her attorney. In person. Client-attorney privilege, you understand."

"I see." Miss Dawes paused only momentarily. "Mr. C. Beauregard Brunell is not scheduled to be in the office today. However, may I take your number and ring you back?"

"Certainly."

Alannah hung up and waited. She was patient, however, knowing that she'd lit a fire under Brunell & Brunell and would hear from them soon.

When Miss Dawes called back, she was once again professional and aloof. "Mr. Brunell has agreed to see you this afternoon at 3:30, if that is convenient for you?"

"It is. Please thank him for seeing me so promptly and tell him I will be there at that time."

*And so we begin,* Alannah reflected.


Kari had passed the morning in her room reading the four gospels as Quan had called them. She was surprised at the voracious appetite she seemed to have developed for hearing about Jesus.

Each time she encountered his own words, printed in red, she pored over them, wondering at some of the unorthodox things he said but feeling oddly strengthened by them.

Kari ordered a light lunch to be delivered around noon. Afterwards, Fen-Bai came by the hotel to pick her up. The old Riverside cemetery lay alongside the South Platte River and was larger than Kari had expected. Fen-Bai drove them through the entrance and then began to wind around inside the park until she reached an unspoken location and parked.

"This is a splendid historic cemetery, Kari. Many of Denver's founders are buried here," Fen-Bai told her. "When I called yesterday, they provided me with the location of Grant's grave. We are closest to it here. It's just a short walk in that direction."

Kari followed Fen-Bai, noting as they walked the many old headstones they were passing. Some of the headstones had sunk into the soil and were tilting a bit to the side. The writing on other stones was worn, so that the inscriptions were hard to read.

"This part of the cemetery is filled, of course," Fen-Bai said quietly, "but many people come to pay their respects and to look at the history of Denver through the lens of those who sleep here."

Fen-Bai stopped and pointed. Kari, her feet suddenly heavy, walked forward. The simple headstone read,

*Grant Aubrey Michaels*
*Beloved Husband and Father*
*1878-1911*

Kari stared at the stone and tears smarted in her eyes. *They were real, all of the people Rose wrote about!* she truly grasped.

*Rose was real. Grant was real. Joy was real—and she ached and shed real tears when her beloved Grant died. Oh, Joy! I'm so sorry for your loss. I can only hope that you found happiness again with Mr. O'Dell.*

Tears were streaming down Kari's face now. Fen-Bai drew near and gently touched Kari's shoulder. "Nothing makes us more aware of how brief and fragile life is than visiting the grave of someone who is no longer with us," she murmured.

Kari took a deep breath and swiped at the moisture wetting her face. She looked around at the many other graves nearby, searching.

*Why, where is Joy's grave?* she wondered in dismay. Pondering the question and the likely answer, she frowned. *She must be buried with O'Dell somewhere else . . . but how sad that is! Grant is here alone?*

She thought deeply about it for several moments. *But if Grant was a Christian, then all the verses Rose wrote in her journal about Jesus coming back and raising those who loved him from the dead apply to him, too.*

*So . . . I suppose where we are buried doesn't truly matter? Jesus will find us wherever we are? And is Grant really here, in this grave, anyway? Or is just his body here and his spirit already with Christ? Lord, I have so many questions and so much to learn and understand.*

Kari rested one hand on Grant's headstone. *I wish I had known you, Grant Michaels,* she said silently. *To those who knew and loved you, you lived a life that . . . honored God. Would that someday those I know might say the same of my life.*

After a moment she turned and hugged Fen-Bai. "Thank you, Fen-Bai, for bringing me here. I'm ready to go now."


Alannah had less than two hours to kill before meeting with Kari's attorney. *I will see if I can locate this house she inherited from Peter Granger.*

She pulled out the map she'd bought at the airport and scanned the long list of street names in the legend, looking across and down to the correct grid, finding Marlow in tiny print.

"2787 Marlow Avenue should be here," Alannah mumbled to herself, "and I should be able to drive there, take a look and a couple of photos, and make it to my appointment."

She threw her camera into her bag and ran a pick through her mane of curling black hair. Her hair, however, had frizzed and poofed into ridiculous proportions.

"Blasted humidity," she complained. She gave up on her hair and, grabbing her bag and a sizeable briefcase, raced to her car, setting the map on the passenger seat next to her and the briefcase on the floor.

Forty minutes later she cruised slowly down Marlow Avenue, looking for the house Kari Hillyer had said she inherited from her great-uncle.

*There it is.* Alannah eased up to the curb and gawked.

"That is some house," she muttered. The house was old, beautiful, and immaculately preserved. The grounds were impressive.

"No wonder she said she didn't need our money," Alannah admitted, "not that we have any!" To herself she added, *Well, Kari, so far so good. This part of your story checks out. We'll know more soon, though, I'll bet.*

She turned the car toward the law offices of Brunell & Brunell.

At 3:30 precisely, Alannah walked up the steps to the imposing front entrance of Brunell & Brunell. She carried her handbag and the briefcase and introduced herself to the receptionist. "Detective Alannah Carmichael to see Mr. Brunell."

"Yes, ma'am. I will ring Miss Dawes."

The click of high heels upon marble announced the approach of Miss Dawes. The attractive, well-groomed woman looked Alannah up and down before issuing a crisp, "This way, please, Detective."

They traversed a large, open room where lawyers and their assistants were hard at work. On the other side Miss Dawes turned down a long hall. After passing several offices, Miss Dawes opened the door into a conference room. Four men waited for Alannah.

"Detective Carmichael? I am C. Beauregard Brunell. May I introduce Jeffers Brunell and Clive Brunell? We three are the senior partners of Brunell & Brunell. And may I introduce Mr. Owen Washington, our lead investigator?"

The three men nodded to her and she nodded back. *Three senior partners? And a lead investigator? All showing up on short notice? Kari, I am impressed,* Alannah thought.

C. Beauregard Brunell gestured to a seat at the commanding conference table. Alannah placed her briefcase on the table and seated herself.

"How may we help you today, Detective?" C. Beauregard Brunell, while civil and pleasant, was on his guard. His drooping blue eyes gave nothing away.

Alannah, taking the measure of the men in the room, for the most part approved of what she saw. *Breaking through their need to protect Kari and her privacy will be my biggest task,* she acknowledged to herself.

"Gentlemen, just yesterday morning I met Ms. Kari Hillyer in Denver, Colorado. She gave me to understand that this firm represents her?"

"That is correct, Detective," C. Beauregard Brunell stated. He said nothing more.

"Thank you," Alannah responded evenly. "Kari is a lovely woman and I already consider her something of a friend."

She went straight to the point. "I understand your firm's legal obligation to protect Kari and her privacy, so what I propose is that I tell you a story. A true story. You will find this account . . . interesting, to say the least. Even, perhaps, incredible. Afterwards, you may wish to contribute to the, er, storyline."

The four men glanced at each other, curious but also cautious.

"Very well, Detective. We are listening." Apparently, C. Beauregard Brunell would be the spokesman for the group.

Alannah popped open her briefcase and removed a file folder and a bound scrapbook. She closed the briefcase and placed it on the floor next to her chair. She laid the file folder open in front of her, smoothing it so it lay flat.

She made eye contact with each of the men before saying, "On April 12, 1911, a heinous crime was committed in the city of Denver."

"April 12—*1911?*" The firm's dark-skinned investigator was surprised into speaking.

"Yes, that's right. 1911. May I proceed?"

They nodded, but C. Beauregard and the investigator, Owen Washington, exchanged concerned glances.

"On April 12, 1911, the infant son of a Mr. and Mrs. Grant Michaels was abducted just outside a Denver park. Two men, personal security guards, were shot and killed during the commission of this crime. One woman was shot but survived."

Alannah opened the scrapbook and held it towards the men, moving it from right to left so the four of them could take turns reading various headlines from the Denver Post.

"I can tell you that the baby's kidnapper was subsequently *identified*, but not apprehended. Sadly, the child was never recovered.

"The kidnapped child was born on January 19, 1911, and was, at the time of the kidnapping, nearly three months old. The Pinkerton Agency, in cooperation with local police, assigned its most experienced agent to the investigation, a man whose specialty was missing persons.

"The investigation uncovered and verified several facts. The first fact: As I mentioned, the kidnapper was identified. He was a man known to the child's family, one *Dean Morgan*, born *Regis St. John* in Seattle, Washington, also known as *Shelby Franklin* and other aliases. This man was an embezzler and con artist of no small degree, wanted in several states.

"The reasons behind the kidnapping, however, were personal and vindictive. The story is quite involved. I will not go into those details at present for the sake of time."

The room was quiet as the partners and Washington absorbed Alannah's words.

"The second fact: Evidence indicated that Dean Morgan hired a woman to be wet nurse to this infant. It is believed that they traveled together, just the three of them, by automobile when fleeing the State of Colorado.

"The third fact: This information will bear directly on why I am here. During the kidnapping, it was believed that a small book was accidentally taken with the child. It was in the child's buggy and may have been folded into the baby's blanket and picked up with him when he was taken."

Alannah hesitated for effect. "That book was the journal of Rose Thoresen."

Jeffers and Clive did not respond to Alannah's last sentence, but Clover and Owen gasped at the same instant.

"Mr. Brunell, I see you are familiar with this book," Alannah said quietly, looking at the attorney on her right. "Kari Hillyer showed the journal to me, knowing nothing of my involvement in this case."

Clover was staring at the table, his mouth working, his thoughts in chaos. Jeffers and Clive glanced nervously between Clover and Owen, perceiving that the two knew something they did not.

"Clover?" Jeffers asked timidly. "Do you know anything about what Miss Carmichael is saying?"

Clover held up his hand to his brother, shaking his head just once, fighting to gather his thoughts and wits. "Detective Carmichael, if you please, just what is *your* involvement in this, er, case?"

"That is a good question, Mr. Brunell, and I am happy to address it. You see, Mrs. Michaels, the mother of the child, was Joy Thoresen Michaels, daughter of Rose Thoresen. *Rose Thoresen was the child's grandmother*."

She waited as Owen and Clover processed the information. Jeffers and Clive still watched, out of the loop but observing the drama with keen interest.

Alannah continued. "Sadly, only a few months after the abduction, the child's father, Mr. Grant Michaels, passed away. Four years later, in 1915, Mrs. Michaels remarried. She married Edmund O'Dell, the same Pinkerton agent charged with finding the baby.

"I would like to mention here that Mr. O'Dell and Mr. Michaels were such close friends prior to Mr. Michaels' death that Mr. and Mrs. Michaels named their baby after Mr. O'Dell. The child's name was Edmund Thoresen Michaels."

"Detective Carmichael?" The interruption came from Owen Washington. "I believe Mr. Brunell requires a moment. Clover? Are you all right?"

Clover was looking more ill than Owen had ever seen him. Clover turned unseeing eyes toward Owen. "I must—we must hear the rest, Owen. We must."

Owen agreed with reluctance, but hurried to pour him a glass of water and bring it to him. "If you say so, Clover, but drink something first." He took the seat next to Clover and watched him with anxious eyes.

When Clover had sipped on the water, he looked at Alannah. "Please continue, Detective."

Alannah glanced into her notebook. "This is the most concise account of the crime I can render; a more substantial recounting would take hours. But there is a bit more I believe you should hear."

She cleared her throat. "You asked to know my involvement? I will tell you. Edmund and Joy O'Dell went on to have three sons, Matthew, Jacob, and Luke. They are in their seventies now. Edmund and Joy O'Dell's fourth child and only daughter, Roseanne O'Dell, has since passed away. However, when she was a young woman she married Sean Carmichael, my father. Roseanne O'Dell is my mother."

Alannah stated, matter-of-factly, "I believe Kari Hillyer to be the daughter of Edmund Thoresen Michaels, known to you as Michael Granger. That makes her *my cousin*, my half-cousin.

"Our four families—the Thoresens, the O'Dells, the Carmichaels, and our friends, the Liángs—have been searching for Edmund Michaels now *for eighty years*. My grandfather, Edmund O'Dell, went to his grave not having fulfilled his promise to Grant Michaels to find his namesake, baby Edmund Michaels. He died, however, proclaiming that God would prevail and that Edmund *would* one day be found. It is one of the reasons I became a police officer."

She flipped opened the scrapbook again. "This book is filled with newspaper clippings documenting the abduction and the investigation, including the evidence implicating Dean Morgan as the kidnapper."

Alannah looked all around the table. Jeffers and Clive were trying to keep up, but she could tell that the investigator, Owen Washington, and the other Mr. Brunell, the one Washington called "Clover," were tracking with her perfectly.

She turned in the scrapbook to the page she wanted. "In 1909 Dean Morgan was arrested for quite a number of criminal offenses, in particular the crime we now call human trafficking. His crimes were found out and he was arrested—largely due to the efforts of Joy Thoresen Michaels to expose him.

"Morgan awaited trial for his crimes in the Denver county jail, where these mug shots were taken, until he managed to escape in November of 1909."

She turned to Clover. "Mr. Brunell, I understand that you knew Michael Granger personally in your youth. I also understand that you reached out to locate Kari because Michael Granger's purported uncle, Peter Granger, was this firm's client and Kari stood to inherit in her father's place?"

"Yes," Clover whispered.

Alannah spun the scrapbook so he could see it. She tapped Dean Morgan's fading mug shots. "Is this the man you knew as Peter Granger?"

Clover turned his eyes to the page where Alannah's finger rested and stared at the grainy photographs. He did not need to study them long.

"Yes. This is the man I knew as Peter Granger."

"Clover?" It was Clive's voice that broke the tension in the room. "Clover, I don't understand what you are saying about Mr. Peter. Do you know what is going on?"

"Yes." Clover rubbed his long fingers over his face. "Yes, I believe I do know what is going on. I—that is, *Miss Kari*—was exploring in Mr. Peter's garage and found a journal in the attic. It was written by a Rose Thoresen"

"It's pronounced *Tor-eh-sen*," Alannah corrected, not unkindly. "Kari also pronounced it with a 'th' instead of a hard 't' when she told us about finding the journal."

"I see." Clover took a deep breath. "The journal does explain your coming here to see us."

"She found a journal. How does that get us here?" Clive insisted, now a bit peeved.

Clover answered mechanically. "Clive, you know that Miss Kari went on a road trip? She planned this trip because she was somewhat taken by the woman whose journal she read. She wanted to go to Denver where Rose Thoresen—pardon me, *Tor-eh-sen*—lived and do some research. She hoped to find out more about her life, if she could."

"Yes. She found the property records and address of the house Rose Thoresen had lived in—and that is how she found us. All of us, the whole of our four families, know that Rose's journal was taken at the same time Edmund was abducted. It is part of our family lore, you see.

"However, we never knew what became of it. It could easily have been tossed out—and that was the most likely scenario. But some family members held onto the hope that Rose's journal went with Edmund and might, someday, lead him back to us."

She smiled a little. "When Kari showed up out of the blue two days ago with Rose's journal in hand, well, you cannot imagine the consternation and speculation it raised!

"And, I must say, once we *saw* her? Two elder members of the Liáng family who knew Joy in their youth say that Kari has *very much* the look of her grandmother, especially her unusual blue eyes. Also, those who knew baby Edmund in the three months before he was taken attested to and passed down to their children and grandchildren the knowledge that he, too, carried the unusual color of his mother's eyes. Thoresen eyes."

"Yes," Clover whispered. "Michael Granger had those blue eyes. He was my best mate in our teens and early twenties. I knew Kari was his daughter the second I saw her."

"I understand you lost touch with 'Michael' many years ago?"

Clover tipped his chin. "Yes. He and his uncle had a falling-out over Michael's faith in Christ."

"His faith in Christ?" Alannah trembled. *O Lord! Are you not too wonderful?*

"Oh, yes. Michael became a follower of Christ not long after his mother—I mean after *Alicia*, the woman he *thought* to be his mother—passed away."

Clover sipped his water. "But Peter Granger? He despised Christianity. He forbade Michael from following Jesus. Michael, to his credit, would not be turned from his faith. The issue of Michael's faith drove a wedge between them, and Michael eventually left home to pursue the call of God on his life."

Alannah was overcome and had to momentarily cover her face with her hands. *O Father! Just as Joy and O'Dell prayed and believed right up to their deaths, you kept your hand on Edmund! You drew him to yourself! You called him to you! O Lord. Your ways are past finding out!*

She rubbed her eyes and tried to bring her attention back to what was being said.

Clover finished, his voice soft and rough, "We never heard from Michael again. It took Mr. Washington here, and his efforts, to locate him just last year—or rather locate the notice of his death in an Albuquerque paper. From there, he was, at last, able to trace Miss Kari."

Clover frowned. "One thing I don't really understand, Detective. You say that Peter Granger—or Morgan or whatever his real name is—was a criminal? A con man and embezzler?"

"Yes."

"And yet the man we knew was something of an intellectual and a financial genius. I cannot fathom *why* he would resort to criminal activities when he was so obviously talented at making his fortune honestly."

Alannah thought about it for a moment. "If I recall correctly, Dean Morgan grew up quite poor and, at an early age, fell in with criminal elements, in particular, a Seattle family—the Chens—known for its activities in gambling, prostitution, and drugs. I suppose, once set in a wrong direction, Morgan just continued in that way."

Clover sighed. "Mr. Peter's past does, I suppose, explain his guarded manner all those years."

Washington inclined his head toward Alannah but asked Clover, "Shall I tell her?"

"Yes. Of course. This changes everything."

Clover turned to his brother and cousin. "Jeffers and Clive . . . I kept you in the dark regarding what Owen is about to disclose, I'm sorry to say."

Alannah again rubbed her eyes and looked expectantly at Washington.

He smiled at her. "You see the hand of God in all this, don't you, Detective Carmichael?"

Alannah shook her head slowly and started to grin back. "I am . . . *overcome* by the God of grace, Mr. Washington."

Owen nodded. "We love Miss Kari, Detective. She is a very special woman in many ways, but . . . she grew up entirely without family and has felt alone from the time her parents died when she was six until even now. Being without family is her deepest sorrow. Does all that you are telling us mean that she will now *have* family? *Real* family?"

Alannah's laugh was a little tongue-in-cheek. "Family is both a blessing and a curse at times, don't you agree, Mr. Washington? Like the old saying goes, 'you can choose your friends but not your family.' What I can tell you—what I can *promise* you—is that Kari will soon have more family than she can likely handle."

A knowing chuckle went around the room, and then Alannah sighed and brought them back to task. "But you were going to tell me something, Mr. Washington?"

"Ah. Right. Just this: When I came on staff at Brunell & Brunell, I took over the search for Michael Granger or his offspring. In the process of acquainting myself with the case, I reexamined all of Peter Granger's personal papers stored in Brunell & Brunell's files.

"Among them I found birth certificates for Peter, Alicia, and Michael Granger and a death certificate for Peter's brother, Alicia's supposed husband and Michael's father. I called the county clerk for each certificate, hoping to discover additional family information in adjacent records.

"However, in all instances, there were *no* records of their births or any record of Alicia's husband's death in those county files. It turns out that the birth certificates and death certificate were all forgeries, and quite good ones."

"I see." And Alannah did see. "We never found a trace of Dean Morgan once he left Denver, but I understood from what my grandfather told me that Morgan was exceptionally adept at changing identities."

She pondered what she'd been told for several minutes. "How I wish Grandpa O'Dell could have lived to see this day."

"Detective?" Clover had recovered and he was flipping through the scrapbook, reading newspaper accounts and clipping after clipping.

"Yes?"

"Does Kari know? Have you told her?"

"No. We are gathering the four families outside RiverBend where Rose and her husband lived and Joy was born. We will tell her just before then—now that you have confirmed Kari's identity for us."

"When?" Clover asked the question. "When will you tell her?"

"Next Friday before the family converges on RiverBend the following morning. And I will be returning to Denver tomorrow—that is, if there is nothing left uncovered at this point?"

"I don't believe anything is left uncovered," Clover said, thoughtful. "This information does not change Kari's ability to inherit since she *is* Michael Granger's daughter, whether that is his real name or not. It will complicate the probate process while identities are sorted out and delay its closure a little, but it can be overcome."

Clover stood to his feet. "Detective. We owe you a debt of gratitude for Kari's sake, and I wonder if you would allow me a great favor?"

"What is that, Mr. Brunell?"

"Would you allow me to be present when Kari is told? I think she trusts me. At this time she knows me better than she yet knows her own family. I may be of help assuring her of the truth when it is revealed."

Alannah returned to her hotel exhausted and elated at the same time. She thought how helpful it would be to have Clover Brunell present when they revealed the truth to Kari on the following Friday.

*Who names their kid Clover, for heaven's sake!* Alannah chuckled.

Clover had assured Alannah that he and possibly his wife would attend. Owen Washington had also asked if he could come.

Putting all these people up in RiverBend presented a logistical problem—as they knew from past family reunions. A few of the Thoresens had extra bedrooms, but Matthew was asking as many attendees as could manage it to bring their campers, fifth wheels, or trailers. When the clans were gathered, Søren and Ilsa's pasture would resemble an RV park.

It was going on six o'clock in Louisiana, but was not yet five o'clock in Denver. Alannah dialed Quan's number from memory.

Alannah's voice was shaking. "Uncle Quan? I met with Kari's attorneys and it is true—all of it. Kari's 'Great-Uncle Peter' was Dean Morgan, and her father, Michael Granger, was baby Edmund."

She heard Quan's long sigh of relief over the long-distance line. "You are certain?" Emotion roughened his words.

"Yes. I'm positive. Kari's attorney knew Peter Granger personally and identified him from the old mug shots I have."

"It is all so . . . incredible! After all these years . . ." His voice trailed off as he tried to absorb her news.

"And guess what?" Alannah added. "This attorney even knew Edmund! They were friends as boys and young men. You won't believe what he told me . . ."

When they finished talking and hung up, Quan immediately called Matthew. "Alannah has confirmed it—Kari is Edmund's daughter! And there is more . . ."

Kari was in the lobby at six that evening when Quan said he would pick her up. An-Shing and Fen-Bai were in the car also.

"Hello, Fen-Bai!" Kari was happy to see the woman again. "Hello, An-Shing."

"Good evening, Ms. Hillyer," he answered.

"I hope everyone will just call me Kari," she replied. "I am done with the Hillyer name anyway. Kari is just fine."

They met Sean Carmichael at the restaurant. "Oh! Isn't Alannah joining us?" Kari's disappointment was visible.

"She had to leave town for a few days," was all Sean said on that score. "She did, before she left, tell me what a blessed time she had with you at Palmer House."

"She did?" Kari wondered if the "blessed time" Alannah had related to Sean included a rendering of what Kari was now calling her "God Encounter." That experience was so precious to her that she didn't know if she wanted it spoken of lightly or shared with everyone.

"She merely said that you toured the house, had some good conversation, and that you were deeply touched."

Alannah had *not* spoken to anyone about what she'd witnessed on the second floor of Palmer House. She, too, felt it such a sacred experience that she was still reflecting on what she had seen and what Kari had experienced.

As dinner progressed, Quan often found himself studying Kari. Armed with Alannah's news, he could scarcely keep himself from blurting it to Kari.

*Lord, help us to reveal this secret to Kari with compassion,* he prayed. *What we tell her this weekend will turn her life upside down—for good, I believe. Nevertheless, it will be a shock to her. Please help us to be tenderhearted as we reveal this truth to her.*

When Quan returned Kari to her hotel he gave her scrawled driving directions to RiverBend and to Søren and Ilsa Thoresen's farm. "Their farm is a few miles from town but the roads aren't too bad."

Kari frowned. "Gravel roads?"

Quan smiled. He clearly saw the wheels turning in Kari's mind as she considered the information and its impact on her car. "Keep your speed way down. The roads will be dusty, but if you drive reasonably there will be less of a likelihood of chipping the paint on your car."

"All right. So these Thoresens? They are really expecting me tomorrow?"

"Yes; they said they have a room ready for you and they hoped you would stay for a few days on the farm, just relaxing and getting the feel of the place."

What Søren *had* said was, "This is a working farm, Uncle Quan! What am I supposed to do with a city woman for a week and two days? Yes, I'm so glad we've solved the mystery of Edmund's kidnapping and I'll be happy to meet another cousin and all, but you know how we're struggling to stay afloat here."

"I know, Søren, I know. She may surprise you, though. I think she will chip in and end up being a help. Just do whatever you need to do to *keep her there* until we arrive next Friday ahead of the family gathering. Whatever happens—don't let her leave before then!"

# CHAPTER 20

The bellboy finished putting Kari's bags in the trunk of her Caddy and Kari thanked him, handing him a five-dollar bill, something she'd seen others do.

*This tipping generously is a little hard to get used to,* Kari reflected, glad she had thought to have a little cash in her wallet. *David was too stingy to tip except when he was trying to impress someone, and I never had the money—or much opportunity. Being wealthy is going to be an adjustment in more ways than one.*

Kari tipped the valet, too—the same valet who had complimented her on her car yesterday. He grinned and saluted; Kari laughed out loud, slipped on her sunglasses, and pulled away from the hotel. She had tucked her large handbag, with Rose's journal safe within, under the passenger seat.

Kari drove north toward a ramp that would put her on I-76. It would lead, eventually, to I-80 eastbound. According to Quan's directions, she would leave the interstate somewhere in the middle of Nebraska and find her way to her destination on smaller roads.

*I'm on my way now, going to RiverBend where Rose and Jan married, where Joy was born, where they lived on a homestead, for heaven's sake!* She was excited for the trip and the opportunity to see Rose's old homestead, but she was less than enthusiastic about meeting more total strangers just so she could talk to them about Rose.

*Particularly after my odd experience with the Liáng family!* she thought with a laugh.

She would do it, though, because Quan had already made the arrangements and, as he had said, the Thoresens would be disappointed if she did not come.

*It will be all right,* she assured herself. But it was that glow down in her belly, the warmth that seemed to overspread her, even calming her normal anxieties, that was truly reassuring. It seemed as though her new relationship with God was already impacting so many things in her life.

She thought about what she'd read in her hotel room's Bible last evening. Some of it was astonishing; some of it was wonderful. Some of it just confused her, but Quan said not to worry too much about the confusing parts, to just keep reading and that clarity would come over time.

This bit, though, had thrilled Kari to the marrow of her bones:

*Marvel not at this:*
*for the hour is coming,*
*in the which*
*all that are in the graves*
*shall hear his voice,*
*And shall come forth;*
*they that have done good,*
*unto the resurrection of life;*
*and they that have done evil,*
*unto the resurrection*
*of damnation.*

*This is like what Rose wrote about,* Kari breathed, amazed. *The resurrection of life!* And for the first time she realized that her surrender to Jesus had saved her from hell and had made her a candidate for the resurrection. For seeing her parents again.

When her mind had grasped this sea change for her future, she could not help it: She burst into joyful, grateful tears, crying again and again, "O, thank you, Jesus! Thank you, Jesus!"

Then, after breakfast this morning, at the last instant of her packing, she realized that she would have to leave the hotel's Bible behind—and she had almost panicked. She called down to the front desk in a dither.

"Hello? Yes. Kari Hillyer in 207. Can you tell me if there is somewhere nearby to buy a Bible?"

A muddled silence greeted her.

"Hello?"

The woman at the desk had likely *not* been asked that before and floundered a moment. "Uh, Ms. Hillyer, let me just ask the assistant manager. He's right across the hall."

As it turned out, the assistant manager knew of a bookstore that was down the street and around the corner; however, it would not open until 10 a.m. Kari needed to be on the road much sooner than that.

"I'll just buy one the next time I see a bookstore," she told herself, but she worried a little about it because she didn't want to go a night without dipping her heart into the words that were stirring her so.

Kari drove out of the mountains of Colorado, marveling at the vast land spread before her in the morning light. The foothills gave way to the plains, bathed in purples and gold and a vast land stretching into the distance.

The sun grew too warm on her head by eleven in the morning, so she pulled off the road and put the roof of the Caddy up. She kept driving; an hour later she stopped in a small town and got a bite to eat for lunch.

Still hours later Kari left the highway by means of a lonely exit ramp and overpass that put her on the other side of the interstate. She began to drive along a dusty but paved road that fronted the highway on one side and low, undulating hills on the other. Following Quan's directions, she drove over railroad tracks and turned north into a land spread with wheat and corn fields with the occasional glimpse of farmhouse and barn.

Kari crossed over some old, disused tracks and, caught by surprise, found herself in the town of RiverBend. The "town" was not much more than a main street with a line of buildings on both sides, a few of which were closed up.

She noted a small grocery, hardware store, post office, library, and café open for business. She drove through a blinking yellow light and stopped at the café to get a soft drink to go and to use their facilities.

The café's inside door was propped open and Kari caught the flow of cool air blowing through the screen door. As Kari reached for the screen door's handle she stopped short, astounded and in awe. Just to the left of the door was an aging metal sign.

Kari's fingers traced the words: *Lost Are Found.* She was amazed to see the sign here in RiverBend, but beyond her surprise, the sight of the three words etched new meaning in Kari's heart. *I was lost . . . and you found me, Lord!* she marveled. *You truly* ***are*** *an awesome God!*

A young woman, maybe just a girl, spoke from within the cool shadows of the café. "It's a hot one. Can I get you something cool to drink?"

The girl opened the screen door for Kari and saw that she still touched the sign nailed to the building's outside wall. She seemed to study Kari before saying, "Do you know what that sign means?"

Kari's smile was half amusement, half chagrin. "I'm learning it means more than just one thing."

"Oh?"

Kari's hand dropped from the sign and she stepped into the welcome coolness of the little restaurant. "Yes. And I was surprised to see one here. I saw my first one on Monday. In Denver."

"Palmer House, right?" The girl, her blonde hair cut short in a manner that reminded Kari of Mixxie, was still appraising Kari as she stepped behind the old-fashioned wooden lunch counter.

The café was empty except for the two of them. Kari took a seat on one of the bar stools at the counter. "That's right. How do you know about Palmer House?"

The girl smiled. She picked up a blender jar and started adding ice, frothy juice, syrups, and ice cream to it. "I'm Sunny. My great-grandmother Esther owned this place. It was a clothing store back in the day. It's been passed down, four generations now."

She stirred the ingredients before screwing on the blender's bottom. "In fact, I practically teethed on this counter when I was a kid. From what my grandmother told me, Esther and a good friend of hers moved here from Denver and had quite a number of tales to tell about Palmer House and . . . how they owed their lives to Rose and Joy Thoresen."

"Esther? No kidding!" Kari leaned her elbows on the counter. "I've read about Esther. So she's your great-grandmother, huh?"

Sunny grinned. "Yup. The skeleton in the family closet. Except she never shied away from talking about her past."

"And Rose Thoresen! I'm in RiverBend sort of researching her life." Kari looked around. "I mean, what are the odds I'd just run into someone else whose ancestor knew her? I can't believe how much she impacted the lives of others."

Sunny ran the blender without saying anything and poured the contents into a tall glass. She added a straw and a maraschino cherry, set the glass on a napkin, and slid it in front of Kari. "Here you go. On the house."

"What? I mean, you didn't have to—"

"It's my pleasure, Kari. It's my own little concoction; I call it my 'Summer Sizzle Solution.'"

Kari stared at her and did not reach for the drink. "How did you know my name?"

Sunny wiped the counter where a little condensation dripped from the glass. "Mixxie called me. Said I'd see you rolling into town shortly." Sunny jerked her head toward the door. "Said I'd know you by your ride. Hard to miss a classic red Cadillac."

"Mixxie." The name fell from Kari's mouth dripping with derision.

"Yeah, that's our Mixxie. Some folks don't have a suspicious bone in their body. Mixxie and I have been friends a long time, but I'd say Mixxie hasn't a bone in her body that *isn't* suspicious. What do you think?" Sunny's eyes twinkled with suppressed mirth.

"I'd be hard-pressed not to agree with you, Sunny. Mixxie and I didn't exactly . . . hit it off."

Sunny laughed aloud and Kari joined her. "Yup. Now I *know* you've met our Mixxie," Sunny grinned.

Still laughing, Kari took a sip of the drink Sunny had made for her. "Wow. This is fabulous."

"Thanks."

Kari sipped on the frosty drink and thought about what Sunny had told her. "So, I'm still a little hazy about the whole 'Lost Are Found' movement. Alannah and Shan-Rose said Joy started it. Isn't it about finding lost children? Is that why you have a sign out front?"

Sunny nodded. "Yes, but as you said, the term has more than one meaning." Her eyes glinted as she bent another examining look on Kari. "To the women Rose and Joy rescued from prostitution, it meant redemption."

*But, that's like me!* Kari realized. "So is that why you have a 'Lost Are Found' sign next to your door? Because your great-grandmother was one of the women Rose and Joy rescued?"

Sunny looked away. "Yes, she was, even though she came here to RiverBend instead of living at Palmer House. But 'Lost Are Found' meant more than that. To Joy and her husband the words had a deeply personal meaning."

Sunny slanted a peek at Kari. "The phrase became a talisman of sorts among the Thoresens and their many friends, so Billy and Mr. Wheatley made the 'Lost Are Found' signs. A lot of the families put them next to their doors. Parents to children, down through the years, the signs remained as symbols. To remind them . . . and, later, us."

"Remind them of what?"

Sunny shrugged. "That God would be faithful to his promises . . . and return something that had gotten . . . lost."

Kari looked up from her straw. "Huh. So what got lost?"

Sunny shrugged again. "You're going on to Søren and Ilsa's, aren't you?"

Kari faltered a moment before answering. *I'm sure getting tired of everyone knowing my every move,* she grumbled within herself. "Yes. I'll be staying with them a few days."

"Well, the Thoresens can fill you in on all the details. It's a family thing, after all." Sunny clamped her lips together, turned her back on Kari, and started cleaning the blender. "You know, some of us younger ones stopped believing in the whole 'Lost Are Found' myth."

With her back still to Kari, Sunny muttered, but loud enough for Kari to hear, "We may have to reconsider that decision."

Kari finished her drink in silence. She thanked Sunny again and walked outside. Up and down the street she saw only a few cars parked at the curbs and two individuals walking.

As she put the car roof down and climbed into it, she was pondering the uncomfortable and intrusive fact that Mixxie had called ahead to alert Sunny of Kari's arrival. When Kari turned the key, she was thinking on all Sunny had told her about the 'Lost Are Found' signs and chewing on Sunny's last, cryptic words.

When she drove north out of town she was still puzzled. *This is— by far—the strangest bunch of people I have ever met,* she decided. *Nice, yes. But strange.*

Kari drove out of the little town and onto an endless prairie sea. *This land goes on forever!* she marveled in fearful awe. *How in the world did the settlers who came here ever find their way? Even with roads, if I didn't have directions I would be terrified of getting lost!*

The pavement had ended at the edge of town and turned to dirt and gravel. As Quan had suggested, she drove slowly. For what seemed like miles and miles.

At each marked and unmarked "intersection" she checked the directions Quan had given her and made the appropriate turns. The road started to rise and, abruptly, the Caddy crested a hill. Kari found herself driving along the edge of a bluff and spotted a lazy stream rolling along below her. From the bluff she could see the prairie for far around and she was spellbound. Feeling 'on top of the world,' she even picked up her speed.

She came to a gentle curve in the road that looked like it might start down the other side of the bluff. So engrossed was she in the far-away sights that she did not realized a truck heavily loaded with baled hay and riding the center of the road was rounding the curve from the other direction until they were nearly nose to nose.

Kari jerked her steering wheel hard to the right; at the same time the truck slammed on its brakes. As Kari's car started to pass the truck, a bale of hay, rocked by the truck's sudden stop, tumbled off the top of the load—onto Kari's car.

Dust and hay flew everywhere.

"You *idiot!*" The words flew from Kari's mouth as she stared—appalled—at the damage. The Caddy's hood was scratched and dented; the windshield was cracked and crazed. The bale of hay had seemed to explode on impact and was scattered everywhere, including inside of her car.

A lot of the scattered hay was attached to Kari—in her hair, on her clothes, even in her mouth. She spit hay and dirt and coughed.

The farmer standing just behind the driver's door (Kari hadn't even looked at him yet, so engrossed was she in the damage to her *car*) said nothing, but Kari had the impression that he was shaking his head and rubbing the back of his neck.

She turned in her seat and cut loose. "You *idiot*," she repeated. "You think you *own* this road? Look what you've done to my *car!*"

He was studying her and, still without saying anything, reached over her seat and plucked a strand of hay from her hair. Kari looked down and saw that she was covered in hay.

It was, quite *literally*, the final straw.

She pushed open her door, shoving him backwards, all the while directing a string of obscenities at him. Kari didn't even know where she'd picked up half the words she used, but use them she did.

And how.

The man found his tongue then. "Whoa. I hadn't expected such nasty words from such a good-looking woman."

Kari glared at him and felt her face flushing as another burst of anger flooded her—this time directed at herself. Along with the anger flowed guilty regret.

*Here I thought Jesus had come into me and he'd changed me,* she fumed. *Some change! I—* Her anger gave way and crushing despair took its place. *Oh, no! What have I done? What if he won't stay with me now?* she questioned. Anxiety rose in her throat.

*What if I've driven him away? O Jesus! Where are you? Please don't leave me! I'm so sorry! Please don't leave me! Please! Don't—*

She couldn't breathe. The panic clamped down as the old voices and her old fears swept over her chanting, "We don't want *her!* We don't want *her!*"

*O Jesus!* The blood pounded in her throat. Her heart thundered and she began to gasp. As her sight dimmed, Kari clutched at the arm of the man next to her.

And then, of course, she passed out.

❧ ✳ ❧

# CHAPTER 21

She was sprawled in the dirt road when she woke up, gravel poking the back of her head and a shadow looming over her.

"Kari! Kari, wake up!"

Cold water trickled onto her face. Unfortunately, some ran down her nose and she started choking. Coughing to clear the water running down the back of her throat, Kari sat up and realized that the shadow was a man in a straw hat.

"Back off, buster! You're too close!" Kari complained. She coughed a few more times. "What were you thinking? Were you trying to drown me?"

The man stalked a few steps away, jerked his hat off his head, whacked it across his thigh, and ran his hand across the back of his neck and then up his neck and over his head. He was facing away from her, but Kari could still hear him growling angry words.

Kari looked around. She sat between the two vehicles, covered in dust and hay and, if she wasn't mistaken, would soon be sporting a bruise on her backside from her abrupt impact with the graveled surface.

She crawled to her knees and grabbed the handle of her car door, using it to haul herself up. As she usually was after a full-blown panic attack, she was jittery and weak.

"How about you sit down in the car for a few minutes?" The man was back and Kari nodded, grateful that he opened the door and steered her onto the seat.

When the wave of weakness passed, she sighed. "I'm sorry. Sorry I hogged the road, sorry I yelled, sorry I cussed."

"Are you sorry you just scared the ever-living *crap* out of me?" he demanded.

Kari shook her head. "It was a panic attack. Takes me a few minutes to get over it. No big deal."

His voice rose. "Yeah, well how was I to know that? I thought you'd had a heart attack or something! In case you hadn't noticed, we're not exactly near a state-of-the-art medical center!"

"For heaven's sake! Quit barking at me!" Kari yelled.

Then she looked at him, really looked at him. Piercing blue eyes stared out of a face weathered by the wind and sun. His hair was cut short and bleached white with golden red streaks.

He looked to be in his early to mid-forties. Beneath his glare of indignation Kari perceived worry. A heavy weight of worry.

She softened her tone. "I-I'm all right. Truly. It's just . . . " Her eyes swept over the damage to her car again and, without notice, she burst into tears. "It's just my *car*! My beautiful C-C-Caddy!" she sobbed.

"Yeah. That is a real drag." He laid a comforting hand on her shoulder. "Don't worry, Kari. I've got a good friend who specializes in classic cars. I'm pretty sure he can get it fixed up, good as new."

Kari sniffed. "Really? Is he far from here?"

"No; lives a couple of farms that way." The man pointed west. "Just beyond the McKennies'."

"Are you sure that he . . ."

"That he knows what he's doing? Being farmers doesn't make us all backward hicks," he growled. "For your information, Jeff is a certified mechanic and holds some pretty prestigious awards for his vintage restorations."

"All right. Sheesh. I just needed to know. You don't need to get all defensive." Then Kari frowned, suspicion creeping into her mind. "Hey! You just called me 'Kari.' How did you know my name?"

The man smiled, but it was a tired smile. "Uncle Quan said you'd be driving a classic Cadillac. Bright red. Not too many of those on these dusty back roads." He held out his hand. "Søren Thoresen. You'll be staying with my sister and me. And it looks like for longer than just a few days."

*Oh, fine! Way to go, Kari!*

She blushed as she took his hand. "I'm Kari Hillyer." She reddened further. "Well, of course I am," she muttered. "Listen, I'm really sorry about the swearing . . . I thought I was past that . . . and all."

He looked bemused. "Past that?"

"I mean, I'm a Christian now. *Was* a Christian anyway. Just a few days ago. I thought . . . I didn't think I would be cussing any more. Guess I ruined it. Everything."

Søren watched sadness flit across her face. He gave a knowing grunt and looked away.

Kari followed his gaze out into the deep prairie and gawked again. *It's magnificent,* she realized. *No wonder Rose loved it!*

"So what you're saying is that you are a new Christian? Is that right?" Søren asked, still staring out across the vista afforded by their vantage atop the bluff.

"Um, yes. Just since Tuesday."

"And this is Thursday. Wow. So a whopping two days now?"

"Yes." Kari gritted her teeth. *This guy pushes my buttons but good.*

He looked over to her and saw that her irritation masked a sense of loss. "And you think that by cussing a blue streak just now you have driven Jesus away?"

Kari turned to face him. "Well . . . yes. How did you know?"

One corner of his mouth tipped up, but the smile didn't reach his eyes. "*Well*, your face told me, Kari Hillyer. But have no fear. Jesus is pretty hard to get rid of, especially once you've let him in."

Palpable relief washed over her. "Really? Are you sure?"

"Oh, *I'm sure.*" His words were tinged with irony. "But just for your future reference, when you became a Christian, it was your eternal spirit that was immediately saved and made clean before God. The rest of you? Your bad attitudes and bad habits? It takes a lifetime for God to work out his salvation in each of us. And no; he doesn't leave us or let us go while he's working on us."

He muttered as an aside, "Nor does he let up."

Søren looked out across the prairie again. "It's a process the Bible calls 'sanctification.' Our job is to read the Bible, pray, and learn to hear and heed the voice of the Holy Spirit. Little by little, the work God does *inside* of us changes our hearts and our desires. Those changes *inside* eventually show up on the *outside*—in our behaviors. Change happens from the inside out. It's a miraculous transformation. Does that make sense?"

Kari stood next to him, staring into the distance, peace filling her heart. "So . . . so he won't leave me?" *Like everyone else does?*

"Jesus? No. He won't leave you. He promised, *I will never leave you nor forsake you.* When you know you've done something that displeases or saddens him, be quick to tell him you're sorry *and* to ask him to help you. Then move on."

Kari sighed, relieved. At the same time they turned and faced each other. "Thank you, Søren," Kari whispered. She stared into his face, wondering how he'd come to such wisdom.

He gave a half laugh. "You're welcome. Now . . ." he gestured to her car. "Let's get this mess cleared away, shall we?"

He hauled what remained of the hay bale off the side of the road and dumped it there. Kari busied herself pulling handfuls and clumps of hay out of the car's interior. She grimaced at the damage to the hood and front window but she also prayed.

*Lord, I'm so sorry I had such a fit over this car. I guess . . . I guess my love for it got to be too important, huh? Maybe this is you helping me to put things in the right order? You first. Everything else after? I'm sorry. Will you please help me, like Søren said?*

She glanced at herself in the rear view mirror. "Ugh!" She spent a few minutes pulling hay from her hair and wiping dust from her face.

"You ready to go?" Søren, arms folded, leaned against his truck door.

"Yes; where to?"

He heaved a sigh. "You follow me out to Jeff's place. We'll leave your car with him; he can call us later and give us the damage. You can ride with me back to our farm. I'll drop you, turn around, and finish delivering this load."

"Where are you taking it?" Kari was curious.

"Out to the interstate and then about thirty miles west."

It dawned on Kari how long it would take him, what with first dropping her car and then backtracking to drop her. "I've really messed up your day, haven't I?"

"Yup. But it can't be helped, so let's get going."

He climbed into his truck and Kari into her car. When she'd turned around, she followed behind, eating his dust the whole way.

*I'll be washing dirt from my hair for a week,* she thought glumly.

About twenty minutes later they pulled into a long drive and up to a barn-turned-garage. A red-haired man of about fifty came out to greet them.

"Hey, Jeff. This is my . . . friend, Kari Hillyer. She's had a little mis—"

Jeff cut him off and never gave Kari a second look. He only had eyes for the Caddy. "Whoo-ee! Look at this baby! Are you crazy? What in the world did you do to her?"

"Uh, *she* had a little run-in with a bale of hay."

"Whatareyou, *nuts?*" As Kari got out, Jeff pored over the car, inside and out. "This car is in mint condition," he muttered.

"You mean it *was* in mint condition," Kari huffed, digging her handbag out from under the passenger seat.

Then she shot Søren a repentant look. "Sorry," she muttered. He just shrugged.

"Well, it will take a few weeks to do the work, but you won't know the difference when I'm done," Jeff answered, still checking out the car, even the trunk.

"We'll take those." Søren grabbed Kari's bags from the trunk. "Can you give her an estimate, Jeff?"

"Take me a day." He looked at Kari. "Where can I reach you?"

"His place, I guess. Only, I won't be there for 'a couple of weeks.' Probably only a couple of days. I'll need your number so I'll know how to reach you after I leave."

"It'll be pricey," he warned. "Can't skimp on anything or it'll ruin her."

"Oh, I'm good for it," Kari answered, "as long as the work is done properly."

"Oh, I'm good for it—as long as the work is done properly," Søren mimicked her.

Kari folded her arms and stared at him. "Are you always so rude?"

"Are you always so prissy? Makes a man think you're a whiney, useless city woman. Come on. I've got a long drive ahead and chores to do afterwards."

She had to climb to get up into the high cab of Søren's old truck. The seats were as dusty as she was. "Good thing I wore my jeans today," she muttered, slapping more dirt from her thighs.

They turned around and, after another twenty minutes, they were driving the edge of the bluff and Kari recognized the curve where their "meeting" had resulted in the damage to her car. Then they were rolling down the other side.

She gasped. Below them ran the same little stream she'd seen from atop the bluff. On the left, the bluff curved gently away from the stream creating a wide hollow between it and the creek. A cluster of trees gathered alongside the creek and others dotted the hollow. She thought she'd never seen so picturesque a setting.

As the road descended, Kari studied an old house sitting in the hollow of the bluff. The house listed dangerously to one side. Its paint had been scoured clean by the wind and its rock chimney was crumbling, but a wraparound porch still stood strong. Kari thought it looked like the porch was keeping the rest of the house from falling down.

*Did someone actually live there at one time?* she wondered.

A couple hundred feet or so from the old house she spied the charred stumps of some outbuildings and a discolored cement pad nearby. It took a minute for Kari to realize that a house had once stood on that pad.

"What happened there?" She pointed to the scene below.

Søren scowled. "Fire. Started in the barn. Took the house and the other outbuildings. Nothing left but the original homestead house."

Then they were at the bottom, headed toward a sturdy bridge built high over the creek. Kari's mouth opened as she saw the realtor sign where the road led toward the listing house: *For Sale*.

"Who owns this place?"

If possible, Søren's scowl deepened. "We do. That is, a branch of the family does. Us and others."

They didn't say another word as they drove over the bridge and alongside a long, fenced pasture that fronted the other side of the creek. Cows and a few horses and goats browsed in the pasture.

At the end of the pasture Søren turned up a lane that led to a white farmhouse. Kari studied what she could see of Søren's farm with interest: A huge red barn at the top of the pasture; lots of smaller sheds and pens; a large vegetable garden not far from the back of the house, and a long green lawn that sloped toward the road and east, up a low rise covered in neat rows of fruit trees.

As Søren stopped, Kari saw that the lane they were on continued north, past the house, leading to another farm not far away. And beyond both farms, to the east, lay well tended fields of alfalfa, wheat, and corn.

Barking dogs greeted them and a woman in worn jeans and a work shirt emerged from a door at the back of the house.

"Here you go." He climbed out and pulled her bags off the load of hay.

"Aren't you even going to introduce me to your sister?" Kari glared at him.

"I don't have time. Besides, you were going to just drive up and introduce yourself anyway, right? Have at it. I need to deliver this hay and be back here for chores." He jumped back into the cab, his long legs making it look effortless.

Kari was left standing alone with her bags as three dogs alternately sniffed her and bayed, running circles around her.

"Stop your noise, you ornery dogs, you!" The woman, her long red hair flowing in a single braid down her back, came down the porch steps and walked out to meet Kari. She shook Kari's hand and grabbed one of the bags. "You must be Kari? I'm Ilsa. What happened to your car? Uncle Quan said you had a Caddy. Hey! You dogs—*shut it!*"

They climbed the porch steps. Ilsa was already in the kitchen and hadn't given Kari even a breath of a pause to answer her. She stopped and turned when she realized Kari had stopped on the back porch.

Kari was stopped outside the screen door. Her hand was tracing the familiar words on the sign fastened beside the door: *Lost Are Found.*

*So beautiful!* Kari completely related the words to her new life in Christ. *I wonder if anyone has an extra sign I can take home with me. If not, I'm going to have one made!*

She stepped inside just as a young boy with golden-red hair raced into the kitchen from somewhere else in the house. He skidded to a stop when he saw Kari.

"Wow. Who're you?"

"Max, this is Kari Hillyer. Remember we told you she was coming for a visit?"

He stared at Kari. "You're pretty," he blurted. "I like your eyes, too. They're really blue like mine."

"Max, mind your manners," Ilsa replied, giving him a light tap on the head.

"Yes'm. Sorry."

"It's all right. Thank you for the compliment," Kari answered. She realized that Max did have brilliant blue eyes like . . . Søren?

"Is Max your son, Ilsa?"

"No; I'm not married. Never have been. Max is my nephew, Søren's son."

"Really?" Kari didn't know why she'd said "really" as though it weren't possible.

"Yup," Max answered, staring raptly. "My mom up and left when I was four. I'm eight now."

He grinned up at Kari, but his revelation earned Max another light rap on the head. "Don't be telling family business to new friends," Ilsa scolded.

"Yes'm. Sorry," he muttered again. Then he brightened. "How long're you going to stay? Wanna see my pig? I got a goat and a horse, too."

"You do? I, um, I'd love to see all of them," Kari answered politely.

"Why don't we get Kari settled, first," Ilsa injected. "Kari, you will have the bedroom off the living room, just through here."

Ilsa led the way toward a swinging door, and Kari glanced around the large kitchen before following. Along two walls that met in the near corner of the room she saw a wealth of cupboards and counters and a huge stove. To the side of the back door was a large kitchen table and well-worn benches under a picture window that looked out on the lawn.

*This room is so homey and lived-in,* she decided. *It feels like the heart of this house.*

Someone had built a screened-in porch off the end of the house. It, too, overlooked the lawn and the orchard. The door into the porch was on the wall on the other side of the table and benches.

As Kari followed Ilsa, her eyes fastened on the carved shelves that ran across the wall's entire length: The shelves were covered in ornate painting—colorful flowers, vines, and patterns—and crowned with beautiful crockery.

She stopped to admire the painted shelves. "Extraordinary," she said aloud.

"Rosemaaling," Ilsa called over her shoulder. "This house was originally built by Jan Thoresen and his brother Karl 'bout a hundred and twenty-five years ago. Most of the house has been added onto or completely redone. At one point, our folks had the whole thing jacked up so they could pour a proper foundation and redo the plumbing."

Her voice echoed from beyond the doorway and its swinging door. "But those shelves? Jan carved those himself. And the rosemaaling? The painting was done by Elli Thoresen, Jan's first wife. That there is real history. No one touches that."

*Elli! Jan's first wife!*

Kari, whose mouth was hanging open, was grateful for the bits of Thoresen family history Alannah, Quan, and Shan-Rose had recited to her. And now this! She followed Ilsa's voice through the swinging door into a long living room. She spied an open door near the middle of the living room and peeked inside.

"This will be your room," Ilsa said. She plopped Kari's suitcase on a chair. "It has a bathroom just through there. Part of this room was once Jan and Elli's, but it's been expanded, rebuilt, and remodeled a couple times. Hard to know anymore what's original and what's not."

She stood in the doorway and waved at the living room. "And this room is about three times the size as it was when first built, but it's still nice to think of how our ancestors lived here when the prairie was completely wild and untamed."

Ilsa suddenly smiled at Kari and her eyes crinkled with pleasure. "We're so happy you've come to spend a little time with us, Kari. And we're excited to see the journal you found. We know it is in good hands with you. Now, feel free to unpack into this dresser here and the closet. I imagine you'd like a shower, too. When you're done, why don't you join me in the kitchen? We can talk while I fix dinner."

"Thank you," Kari breathed. Ilsa's sudden warm welcome was a relief, even more so her words, "We know it is in good hands with you."

*Maybe I'll be all right here for a few days . . . since I'm stuck anyway until I get my car back.* She frowned, momentarily smarting again over the vision of the Caddy's cracked windshield and the scratched and dented hood.

*Nope,* she warned herself. *You first, Lord. Everything else comes after you.*

An hour and a half later, showered, her long hair washed and dried, Kari pulled on a clean pair of jeans and a soft, well-loved t-shirt. She tugged on her ropers last.

*At least I'm going to be dressed comfortably here,* she smiled.

She started to pass through the living room on her way to the kitchen but stopped, struck dumb by what she saw. One entire wall was devoted to family photographs. From left to right, across the wall, she observed what could only be a pictorial history of the Thoresen family.

She started at the beginning with a family portrait: A huge blonde man, a tall woman with sweet eyes and a crown of braids, a young tow-headed boy, and his younger sister.

The next family group was comprised of a second mountain of a man (who could have been the fraternal twin of the blonde man in the first portrait!) along with his wife, a daughter, and three small boys.

A few single photographs and tintypes were mounted near them. Kari inched slowly down the wall and came to a faded photograph of the same blonde man in the first family grouping—only many years later by the looks of it. His face had aged and was permanently creased by the sun and wind.

Next to him sat a slender woman with the steadiest eyes Kari thought she'd ever seen. Something calming and at the same time strengthening seemed to glow in the woman's expression. Beside her stood a young girl whose blonde hair hung free to below her waist. Her clear eyes held the same strength as the woman's.

"Jan and Rose and Joy," Kari breathed. "It *must* be!" She felt she had stumbled upon untold treasure. "Oh, Rose! Oh, I . . . I am so happy to see your dear face."

She touched the glass over the faded photograph and could not stop the tears that dropped from her eyes onto the hardwood floor.

"Rose," she murmured again, sniffing. "Now I'm so very glad I came here after all."

A polite cough brought her back to herself. She quickly wiped her eyes as Søren joined her.

"Jan and Rose Thoresen," he said softly. "And their daughter Joy."

"I had just figured that out," Kari sniffed. "I-I feel so blessed to see what they actually looked like."

Søren nodded, his expression solemn. "After reading her journal, you must feel that you know her."

"Yes." It was all Kari could manage.

Søren pointed to a small portrait down the wall. "Joy and her husband, Grant Michaels, on their wedding day." He cut his eyes toward her, watching her response.

Kari examined their likenesses closely. "They are both so . . . beautiful. Is there a portrait of them with their baby?"

Søren coughed. "Um, sadly, no." He dithered a moment. "Grant passed away before they were able to take a family portrait."

Before Kari could ask further questions, Søren stepped to the left and stopped before the second portrait on the wall. "This is Jan's brother Karl and his family, a few years after they homesteaded this land. Their last daughter, Uli, wasn't born yet when this was taken."

He took another step left. "And this is Jan and his first wife, Elli. This is their daughter Kristen and their son Søren."

He cleared his throat. "Søren was my great-grandfather. I am named for him. He lived here, in this house, until he died at a ripe old age—ninety-five, in fact. I was eight when he passed away, but I spent those eight years listening to him recount their first years on this land when he was just a boy."

He looked at Kari. "I don't know how they survived the work and pain and grief they endured. If it weren't for the Lord, I am convinced they could not have." He shook his head. "I have never known faith like my great-grandfather's. His life inspires me . . . even today."

"Tell me? I want to know everything."

Søren smiled, that one-side-tipped-up half smile that didn't touch his eyes. "Later? Perhaps after we eat? Ilsa sent me to fetch you. Dinner is ready."

Kari nodded. "All right."

"And beware and be warned, Kari Hillyer: Ilsa kept Max away from you these last two hours, but once we cross the line into that kitchen, all bets are off. You are on your own."

"Oh?" Kari looked confused.

This time Søren laughed and his eyes meant it. "Max has already said you're the prettiest woman he's ever seen and he's going to ask you if anyone is courting you yet."

"Oh, *that*."

Kari laughed and they entered the kitchen together.

# CHAPTER 22

Dinner that evening proved to be everything Kari had imagined about farm life—and a lot she had never imagined. Yes, Ilsa served pan-fried chicken from their own flock; home-grown potatoes, mashed and buttery; from-scratch biscuits and creamy pan gravy; and green beans from their garden—but she used a microwave to heat the green beans and served a frozen key lime pie for dessert.

"Hard to grow limes on a Nebraska farm," Ilsa observed with a straight face. Then she cracked up.

Kari had stuffed herself with dinner and replied through a mouthful of pie, "You won't hear any complaints from me!"

And Max, despite Søren's warnings, was quiet during dinner. Instead of chattering, he leaned on his elbow and stared dreamily in Kari's direction. Søren had to smother his laughter in a napkin.

Kari thought that with the day's work near an end, Søren seemed to relax a bit. The worry and weight she noticed him carrying earlier lifted, in particular, as he drew out an old Bible at the end of the meal.

"We read the Scriptures together after breakfast and dinner, Kari," he explained. "You are welcome to join us." Ilsa and Max had brought their personal copies to the table. "We take turns reading aloud and follow along in our own Bibles."

"I would love that, really," Kari was quick to respond, "but I don't have my own Bible yet. I was using the Bible I found in my hotel room and I haven't been anywhere I could buy one for myself."

"You don't have *a Bible*?" Max's eyes were as big as saucers. Those were the first words he had addressed to her since they sat down to eat.

"Well, I never thought I needed one until I became a Christian." Kari shrugged her shoulders, feeling a mite sheepish.

"When did you become a Christian?" he demanded.

"Max, don't badger Kari," Ilsa chided.

"But she's the one who said—"

"Max." It was one word, spoken softly by Søren, but it was enough.

"Yessir. Sorry."

"If it's all right, I'd like to tell him," Kari requested. "I'll keep it simple and short." She looked to Søren and he nodded.

"You see, Max, I wasn't raised in a Christian family. In fact, I don't have a family at all. I've maybe been inside a church three or four times in my life, like for weddings. So I really didn't know anything about Jesus until recently. And I just answered the door two days ago."

"You did what?" Max's face took on a confused expression and, as Kari looked around the table, she realized Ilsa and Søren wore the same bemused faces.

"Um, we'd love to hear about this 'answering the door,' too, Kari," Ilsa added carefully.

Kari glanced from Ilsa to Søren and back and saw they were sincere. "Well . . . I was upstairs in Palmer House, you see."

More confused expressions.

She sighed. "I was touring the house with Alannah Carmichael. You know Alannah, don't you?"

They nodded. "Of course," Ilsa murmured.

"Well, I figured out from Rose's journal which bedroom had been hers, but all the other bedrooms were so . . . *changed* from what she had described when she had lived there. You know. All *modernized*, but dated and ruined at the same time because of it. And, frankly, smelly with disuse."

She made a face and Max giggled. "Well, I didn't want to see how changed Rose's bedroom was. I didn't want what I had imagined ruined, soooo . . . because the door to her room was already shut, I decided I'd just leave it that way."

Their expressions hadn't changed much although Søren was beginning to look intrigued. Kari took a deep breath and pushed on.

"I was standing there, you see, in the hall outside Rose's bedroom. And I just, sort of leaned on the door and talked to her. To Rose."

She saw concerned looks cross between Ilsa and Søren and hastened to say, "Oh, I'm not being weird—I knew she wasn't there and couldn't answer me or anything. I just wanted to think of her, as though she were on the other side . . ." *Waiting for me. Waiting to hold me as though I were one of her lost girls!*

"I-I told her . . . that I wished I could have known her and that she could have told me about . . . Jesus."

Kari had to blink hard several times to keep the moisture forming in her eyes from pooling and spilling down her cheeks. She hadn't foreseen how retelling her encounter with Jesus would stir up those same emotions.

"I was just leaning against the door when . . . *Jesus* spoke to me."

"Really?" Max was in awe.

Kari nodded slowly. "He said, *You were wishing for Rose to be here and speak of me, but I am already here. I have always been . . . here . . . where you are . . . waiting for you.*"

"And then he said just *I Am.*" She looked at Søren, whose eyes had widened. "Does that mean anything? *I Am?*"

Søren nodded and whispered, "Oh, yes. Yes, it does."

Ilsa leaned toward Kari, as captured as Max. "Did he say anything else, Kari?"

Kari blinked again. "Yes. I remember everything and I think on bits and pieces of it all the time. One of the most beautiful things he said was, *In a manner of speaking, I am on the other side of this door—and more, Kari. I am on the other side of the vast gulf that separates us. And I am knocking.*"

Kari wet her lips. "And I wasn't sure . . . so I asked him: *Are you Jesus?* I wanted to be certain, you see."

She was nodding as she remembered. "I will never, *ever* forget his reply. He said, *I am the One who is called Faithful and True, the One who reigns and rules as The Lion of the Tribe of Judah. I sit forever upon the throne of David. And I am here: Behold, I stand at the door and knock. Only you can open the door. Open and find me.*"

Kari's voice dropped to a whisper. "He asked me to surrender my life to him. That was when I opened the door."

The kitchen was silent. Kari was locked away in the memory of her encounter with Jesus. A stunned Søren and Ilsa were absorbing what she had told them. Max was staring in wonder.

Until he broke the silence. "Wow. That is *so cool!*"

Kari stirred and let out a long breath. She caught Søren's eye and was surprised when he started to smile.

"I have to agree with Max."

"Me, too," Ilsa added. "Coolest thing I've heard in years."

"But there's still one thing wrong," Søren mused after a moment.

"Wh-what's that?" Kari looked concerned.

"You not having a Bible, that's what." He was already striding toward the stairs that led to the upstairs. He took them two at a time and Kari turned to Ilsa.

"Just wait." Ilsa flipped her copper-colored braid over her shoulder and grinned.

A few minutes later Søren pounded down the stairs. In his hand he held a black volume. "I hope you don't mind that it's a little used," he apologized. "But until you pick one out at a Bible bookstore, please feel that this is your very own."

Kari took the book from him and caressed it. "Thank you," she whispered.

"So," Søren said as he took his seat. "Shall we have our Bible time now?"

"Yup!" Max opened his Bible and Ilsa did the same.

Kari followed suit.


The next morning set the pattern for Kari's stay with Søren, Ilsa, and Max. The family rose early, and Kari forced herself to do the same. Half asleep, coffee in hand, she followed Max around the barnyard as he demonstrated how to feed the chickens, collect the eggs, milk their four goats, and "muck out the barn," as he put it.

Afterwards, she joined the three of them for breakfast—and had a hearty appetite to show for it. Just as with dinner, they took half an hour after breakfast to read from the Bible and pray. Kari brought her Bible to the table and tried not to flounder too much when Søren called out the passages they would read. Max helped her with that, too, showing her how to find the right book and chapter.

That morning, Søren led them to Philippians chapter 4. He read aloud,

*Not that I speak*
*in regard to need,*
*for I have learned*
*in whatever state I am,*
*to be content:*
*I know how to be abased,*
*and I know how to abound.*
*Everywhere and in all things*
*I have learned both to be*
*full and to be hungry,*
*both to abound*
*and to suffer need.*
*I can do all things*
*through Christ*
*who strengthens me.*

*Content! I'm learning to be content,* Kari decided. *I have had nothing and now I have quite a bit. Still, contentment has always eluded me. Now I'm learning that with Jesus, no matter what I have, I can do whatever I need to do—and be content while doing it.*

After breakfast when Max went out into the fields with Søren, Kari stayed with Ilsa and helped her clean, cook, work in the garden, and can the produce they picked together.

"It's July, so we have tomatoes coming out our ears. You know what that means, don't you?"

Kari racked her brain for the answer. "Um, no."

"What it means is all the BLTs we want! Breakfast, lunch, and dinner!"

Kari's stomach rumbled its appreciation and they both laughed.

"I must say it is so nice to have someone to keep me company and work with me," Ilsa commented. "You are a huge help! Why, we've gotten so much done, I think we should bake some pies this afternoon—what do you say to cherry and apple?"

At the end of that first day, Kari was exhausted but elated. She went to her bed early and discovered that getting up before dawn was a bit easier than it had been the day before.

That evening when Søren asked if he and Ilsa could see Rose's journal, Kari found that she was not fearful that they would take it. Instead, she felt she was sharing her treasure with those who would love it and value it as much as she.

"Will you read part of it to us, Kari?" Ilsa asked after they had both carefully handled it and read Rose's name on the flyleaf.

Kari nodded and selected a passage near the end.

*January 26, 1911*

*Grant and Joy have named their son Edmund, after our dear Mr. O'Dell. This honor speaks of the great friendship between Grant and Mr. O'Dell—and, truthfully, of Mr. O'Dell's friendship to us all.*

*I am happy for this precious man. I remember how hardened by the world he was when I first met him in Corinth—how skeptical, disillusioned, and cold the difficulties of his work had made him. Lord, you have done a great work in his heart!*

Kari paused, considering what she'd read. "Fen-Bai took me to see Grant's grave in Denver. Alannah told me that a few years after Grant passed away, Joy married Mr. O'Dell. She said that her mother was their daughter, Roseanne. Named for Rose, no doubt."

Søren and Ilsa both nodded, and Kari tipped her head a little in thought. "I understand Joy and O'Dell's other children are still alive. I would really like to meet them someday."

She ducked her head a little. "I have a confession to make."

"Tell us," Ilsa smiled.

*I really like Ilsa,* Kari thought at that moment. *Maybe it really is a God thing that my car is keeping me here with them for a few weeks.*

"Well, I have been afraid," she said softly.

Søren lifted his brows. "Really? Of what?"

"You see . . . I've been afraid that someone, some descendant of Rose's, would claim her journal and demand it back." She reddened. "You don't know how much I love this book. I don't ever want to give it up."

"Ah." Søren nodded. He had an odd expression, but Kari felt that he understood. "What will you do if, uh, someone does ask for it?"

"I don't know. I guess . . . I guess I would pray about it and do what is right, even if I don't like it."

"That sounds good," Søren answered, "but somehow I don't think anyone will do that."

Søren and Ilsa then regaled Kari in bits of family history they thought Kari would appreciate. "According to what's been handed down, Rose Brownlee arrived in RiverBend wearing the latest fashions for 1881."

"Brownlee? Was that her name before she married Jan?" Kari took notes as they talked.

"Yes; it was her first husband's name," Ilsa answered. "She had a bank manager drive her out to look at abandoned homesteads. In what we today would call 'a wild hair,' she up and bought one. She set the tongues of the whole community on fire by daring to live on a homestead by herself—a 'citified' woman completely unprepared for life on the prairie."

They talked on, adding details that fleshed out Kari's knowledge of Jan, Rose, and their daughter, Joy.

Later, when Kari had dragged herself into bed and was on the verge of sleep, she had a last thought. *No one has told me yet where Rose and Joy and O'Dell are buried. Or Joy and Grant's son, Edmund, for that matter. I will ask—*

She was asleep before the thought fully formed.

Kari hadn't realized that the next day was Sunday until Max thundered down the stairs after breakfast with his damp hair haphazardly combed.

"Kari? Aren't you going to church with us?"

*It's Sunday?* The day had started with chores, just like any other day! Kari raced to her room. Eying her choices, she decided that one of Lorene's picks would be most appropriate.

Dressing quickly, she entered the kitchen just as Ilsa did. Søren and Max were ready and waiting. Max sidled up to Kari and slipped his hand into hers. He smiled up at her and slowly winked. Kari had to turn her face aside and cough.

"Wow. You clean up good," Søren grinned.

Ilsa slugged him in the arm.

"What! She does, don't you think?"

That earned him another slug.

Søren opened the back door of a small sedan for Ilsa and Max and the front door for her. "Oh, I can ride in the back," she protested. "Ilsa should ride in the front."

"Just get in," Søren growled. "We're going to be late as it is."

The little church, just outside of the town, looked like it had leapt out of a classic movie: white clapboard, peaked roof, and steeple. The pews were filled and service had just started when they entered. The four of them slid into a row of extra chairs against the back wall.

Kari closed her eyes and sank into the old hymns being sung, all of them unknown to her but powerful in their words of praise and adoration. And then the congregation took up a new melody, their voices strengthening and swelling on the chorus:

*Our God . . . is an Awesome God . . . He reigns . . . in heaven above*

Kari was stunned—and then she was singing, raising her voice with the others, losing herself in the majesty of their corporate worship.

*O God! My awesome God!* her heart proclaimed. *I long to worship you in your heavenly dwelling place . . . someday.*

After the service ended and they were milling around on the church's lawn, Kari noticed how many tow-headed children raced about with Max. Eventually, several families sought Kari out and introduced themselves.

"Hey. I'm Dalia Thoresen; this is my husband Lars. You must be Kari." Dalia was plump, blond, and dimpled. Lars was, without a doubt, a Thoresen: tall and broad with sandy-colored hair and brows and piercing blue eyes.

"We're Søren and Ilsa's cousins, next farm over," Dalia added. "Those are our boys with Max."

"The next farm? You mean Karl Thoresen's homestead?" Kari expostulated. "Why haven't I met you before?"

"The very one," Dalia assured her. "We haven't been over because we're so busy with harvesting the corn and the garden . . . and because Søren didn't want us to bug you about Rose's journal."

"Does everyone know about the journal?" Kari wondered aloud.

"Everyone in the family, I imagine. It's pretty big news, what with—" She had started to add something but caught herself.

She laughed, a little embarrassed. "Well, just wanted to say 'hi.' We'll see you next weekend—"

Her husband pinched her arm.

She frowned and coughed. "I *mean*, we'll see you *around*. So nice meeting you, Kari."

Lars nodded and dragged her away.

Søren had sauntered up to Kari's side at the last moment. "Well done, Dalia," he muttered, glaring after her.

"What?"

"Nothing. Are you ready to go now?"

That afternoon over lunch, Kari remembered to ask Søren and Ilsa what she had been thinking as she fell asleep the night before. "Can you tell me where Rose is buried? And Joy and O'Dell? And Edmund Michaels?"

Kari saw Søren and Ilsa exchange a quick glance. She was certain Søren gave a curt shake to his head.

"I'm sorry. Was that wrong to ask?"

"Not at all, Kari," Ilsa smiled. "Søren will show you the family cemetery after dinner."

Kari helped Ilsa with the dishes while Max and Søren took care of some chores in the barn.

Then Søren and Max poked their heads in the back door. "You ready?" Søren asked.

Kari stepped out into the bright sunshine and followed Søren as his long legs ate up the distance from the house, down the lawn and up the slope to their orchard; Max stayed as close to Kari as her own shadow.

They climbed the low hill covered in fruit trees. At the top of the rise she saw what the trees had screened: a wrought iron fence surrounding a family cemetery. Søren waited for Kari and Max at the gate. Then he opened the gate and led them inside.

The plots were simple but well-tended. Kari was surprised how many graves there were—the area inside the fence was nearly filled.

"My father added to the fence and expanded the cemetery years ago, but still it is almost full. There's room for, perhaps, two or three more graves, but the family has decided that no one else should be buried here," Søren said quietly, "inside the fence. We will keep it as it is—the resting place of our pioneer ancestors."

He sighed. "We are talking about making a second cemetery just down the slope . . . if we stay here."

Kari frowned. "What do you mean 'if we stay here'?"

Søren shrugged. "Every year we are losing ground with our farms. Us, our cousins next door, other farmers in the community. Expenses are up and the prices we sell our crops and animals for are down. We need to modernize many of our operations, but we can't afford to—and yet we can't afford not to. It's a losing proposition."

He tugged off his hat and ran his hand over his neck and up the back of his head. Kari recognized the gesture now for what it was—an expression of stress. "But let's not talk about that right now," he muttered. "Come on. I'll show you what you were asking."

Max slipped his hand into Kari's and tugged her along. They followed Søren, who stopped at the first row of graves. "The first of our family to die in America was Karl Thoresen. Some horrible sickness came upon the two families, Jan and Karl's. Karl, Elli, and Kristen died within days of each other."

He pointed. "Karl's wife Amalie never remarried. She is buried next to him. Jan is there, between Ellie and Kristen. Hard to believe how long ago it was."

Kari nodded. All she could wonder was, *But where is Rose?*

Søren pointed out others, his namesake, Søren, and wife Meg, many of their children, some who died in their infancy, and other Thoresens whose names Kari did not know.

"Our side of the family got the red in our hair from Meg," Søren grinned. "Talk about a volatile mix. Meg, an Irish-American, and Søren, a Norwegian. That's hot tempered *and* stubborn."

"I would never have guessed," Kari muttered, dripping sarcasm.

"Careful," Søren growled.

In the back, in the last row, he stopped. "Here is where they laid Rose."

Kari knelt down and traced words on the simple stone.

*ROSE*
*Blake Brownlee Thoresen*
*1849–1935*
*Beloved Wife, Mother,*
*and Friend to Many*
*—I know that my Redeemer lives—*

"You have been a friend to me, too, Rose," Kari whispered. "Thank you. From the bottom of my heart, thank you."

Søren watched Kari, wondering at the emotions she was experiencing. When she stood, he walked a few steps farther. "Joy and Edmund O'Dell," he said softly, pointing. Joy's grave was between her husband's and her mother's.

"I remember Joy and O'Dell's sons saying that their mother wanted to be buried on Thoresen land. O'Dell, who lived a few years longer than she did, asked to be buried next to her."

"But Grant! He's . . . he's in Denver."

Søren nodded. "I know. That's a hard one to swallow. But in reality, he's in heaven. He understands. The fact is . . ." he shoved his hands in his pants pockets, and Kari smiled as Max followed suit, copying Søren exactly. "The fact is, life is not easy. It certainly isn't neat and tidy. Sometimes it's downright unfair. It's best to take the long view. The eternal view."

Kari pondered Søren's words and looked back at Joy and O'Dell's headstones. "They lived good, long lives," she murmured.

"Yes. And their long lives were lived *for* good," he answered. "Their examples are hard to live up to some days."

"Mixxie said something like that," Kari mused. "Something about the family saints casting long shadows."

Søren coughed on a surprised laugh. "That's a good way of putting it. The heritage they left us is both inspiring and daunting."

"Heritage." Kari turned the word over in her mouth. "It's not a term I have any experience with."

Søren shifted his eyes sideways toward her. "That could change. You never know."

They stood there until the July afternoon sun dimmed unexpectedly. Søren glanced up.

"Looks like we'll get a rainstorm in a couple hours. Maybe sooner." He gestured to Max. "Run on down to the barn now, Son, and get a head start on your chores."

"Okay, Papa."

Kari watched Max tear down the slope and then looked up and saw the clouds building. "Down in New Mexico we have summer thunderstorms that come up from the Gulf of Mexico or off the Baja. Monsoon weather we call it."

Søren chuckled. "Yeah. *Our* summer storms are often called 'tornadoes.' We keep an alert eye out for funnel clouds."

"Yikes," Kari muttered, glancing up again. "Søren, may I ask you a personal question?"

He shrugged. "Sure."

"When I came here last week, Max . . . said something about his mother."

"That she left?"

"Yes. That's what he said. I hope you aren't mad that I brought it up?"

He shrugged again, but Kari glimpsed that pain in his eyes she'd seen before. "Sharon knew what she was getting into when she married me."

"A farmer's wife; a farmer's life?"

"That. And the life of a Christian." He sighed. "She changed her mind. About all of it. One day she just announced that she was going 'in search of her dreams.' She put her things into the family car and drove away."

*Selfish, selfish woman!* Kari glowered inside. *How could you leave your son alone?*

"But . . . do you know where she is now?"

Søren didn't answer for a long time, and Kari was thinking they should get back to the house. She studied the darkening sky and smelled rain coming.

"She's in Los Angeles," he whispered. "In a cemetery in Los Angeles."

Kari's lips parted in horror. "She *died?*"

Søren nodded. "Drug overdose."

*Oh, Søren! Oh, I am so sorry!* Kari cried in her heart. Out loud she whispered, "And Max doesn't know."

"No. Not yet. I'll tell him in a few years. He doesn't really remember her . . . Ilsa gave up her life in Lincoln to come help me raise Max. He was only four when Sharon left."

He stared at his boots a few minutes. "I never did divorce her. Thoresens don't divorce. We marry for life."

He sighed again, and Kari heard the weight of his regret in that sigh. "I admit that it was my fault, Kari. I knew Sharon wasn't a committed believer. I even knew she was . . . unstable. Immature.

"I thought . . . I thought I could fix her, I guess. Could fix the character flaws that everyone else in the family knew could only change through a deep, growing relationship with Jesus—something she did not have."

Kari nodded. "I've been there."

When he looked a question at her, she took a deep breath. "You told me yours. I might as well tell you mine. I've been married . . . and divorced. Twice."

"*Twice?*" Søren's voice was rough. Surprised.

"Sad, huh? My first husband could never keep a job. I didn't understand why until I found out that he, too, had a drug problem. So I guess I understand a little about Sharon. Anyhow, I just kept working and paying the bills and thinking that one day he'd get a job that suited him and everything would be fine. Instead, he emptied our savings account and ran up the credit cards. It was three years before I got out from under the debt."

Søren was studying Kari intently. "And the other marriage?"

Kari wilted under his scrutiny. "We divorced this year. He-he made all the decisions, controlled all the money . . . everything, actually. And then I found out about . . . the other women."

Søren's eyes widened. "He cheated on you."

"Yes. With at least three women I know of. I hired a private investigator to document his infidelities. Even so, by the time it was all over, I was flat broke. I don't know what I would have done if Clover hadn't called me."

Søren's frown was skeptical. "Clover? Is that actually someone's name?"

Kari smiled, remembering her own disbelief. "C. Beauregard Brunell, managing partner of Brunell & Brunell, Attorneys at Law. The "C" stands for Clover. To quote his wife Lorene, *It's a Southern thang.*"

They were both chuckling as thunder broke overhead. They started down the slope together.

"So what was the phone call about?" Søren asked. "From Clover."

"Oh." Kari laughed aloud then. "The phone call, Søren, was the start of this amazing journey. Turns out my father's uncle left him his estate.

"Daddy and Mommy died when I was six. His uncle's attorneys hadn't been able to find Daddy until they uncovered the notice of his death earlier this year. After that, they found me and I inherited his uncle's estate."

Søren stopped on the grass and stared at her. "Wait. You inherited *an estate*?"

"It's no biggie," Kari said, evading the issue. "There's a house, and some other, er, *stuff*. And the Caddy! But that's not the best part. No. You see, I was exploring in the garage when I found Rose's journal at the bottom of an old trunk. It was when I read her journal that I began to learn about Jesus, to learn about being a Christian. When I started longing to know him myself."

Rain was pelting them as they reached the back steps.

"That," Kari added as they climbed up the porch, "*that* was the best part."

Each morning of the next week Kari rose in the dark with the others and helped Max do his first chores. Kari found that she was enjoying helping out. She was growing accustomed to the earthy smells, the quiet routine, the physical work, the early calm and stillness.

Tuesday morning breakfast wasn't quite ready when she and Max finished choring, so Kari grabbed a second cup of coffee and wandered outside. She found herself standing on the other side of the barn gazing across the pastures and across the stream. The rising sun warming her back lit up the abandoned homestead on the other side of the creek.

She heard steps behind her and turned her head. "Hey."

"Hey, yourself," Søren muttered. "What's up?"

"Oh, I don't know. I just . . . Something about that place over there draws me."

He snorted a laugh. "Guess I'm not surprised."

"Hmm?" Kari sipped on her coffee.

"You, Kari. It's like you are nothing if not 'all things Rose.' So, see that house over there that's falling down? That was the house Rose and Jan lived in. That land is the homestead Rose bought when she moved here in the 1880s."

Kari's head jerked up and she stared with new eyes down the pastures and across the meandering creek. *"That* is Rose's homestead?"

She whirled and faced Søren. "And you are *selling* it? But how can you?" Her shock and dismay—even indignation—were evident.

He dug his toe into the dirt where he stood. "I told you the other day. We are losing ground here. Even if we sell it and plow the money back into the farm, I don't know how long I can hang on here . . . I don't know if I will even be able to leave this place, *our heritage*, to my *son*."

His jaw tightened. "And Rose's land is not just ours—Ilsa's and mine—alone. Others also have claim to it. So when we sell it, we'll only receive a fifth of the proceeds."

"But-but it's *wrong* to sell it—" Kari turned in stunned disbelief toward the falling down house in the distance.

Søren held up his hand. "Please don't lecture me, Kari. You don't think I *know* that? You think I *want* to give up what our ancestors worked, bled, and died to build? It is killing me!"

Søren's voice broke and Kari glimpsed the pain he tried so hard to hide. Through his frustration and grief he shouted, "So don't lecture me, Kari Hillyer. *Just don't.*"

After he'd stomped away, Kari turned her eyes again to the land on the other side of the creek. It was still early and the light still soft. Even though the only building left standing was listing precariously, she could imagine it as it had been once: The little house tucked into the hollow of the bluff, flowers blooming in window boxes maybe, a green garden, certainly.

Before she knew it she was striding toward the lane, running down it to the road. It felt good to stretch her legs and gulp great lungfuls of air. Her long braid, a copy of how Ilsa wore her hair, bumped against her back as she ran. She moved into her jogging rhythm, despite wearing her ropers, setting a pace that would carry her across the bridge and onto Rose's land.

*These boots were made for walking,* she laughed, *not for running.* But she kept going.

Kari lengthened her stride. When her feet echoed on the wood of the bridge she slowed to a walk and took her time, trying to see the old place as perhaps Rose had seen it when she first arrived.

*Rose's land!* Kari wandered along the creek until she came near what remained of the burned out house and barn. She walked up the slope to them, seeing the pattern of what had been. She came nearer the house Rose had lived in.

Careful not to do anything unsafe, Kari peered through the windows. The house was empty, of course; *barren* was the word that came to her. The floor had rotted away and gaps showed between the wall boards.

*Yet wasn't it much like this when Rose first arrived here?* she wondered. *Didn't Ilsa say Rose and her neighbors, the McKennies, found a nest of snakes in the stove?*

She walked around the old house, staying clear of it, but examining it from all sides. Then she turned and stared across the creek toward Søren's land. Backlit by the sun, Søren's pastures and fields glowed and shimmered.

*So this is what Rose saw when she got up early like this,* Kari realized. She smiled, thinking about Søren's description of Rose and Jan's courtship.

*Oh, Rose!* she mourned. *I would give anything to keep your land in your family!*

# CHAPTER 23

Kari was lounging on a cushioned bench in the screened porch, sipping one last cup of coffee. She now loved the rhythm of a farming day, drinking her first coffee with Søren and Ilsa before the sun rose, helping with morning chores and breakfast preparations, soaking in the Scriptures that Søren and Ilsa read aloud as they lingered over the remains of the morning meal.

The Thoresens' house faced west and, from Kari's perch on the porch, her view included the barn, the outbuildings, the pastures running down to the creek, and—most significant to her—Rose Thoresen's old homestead on the other side of the creek, nestled in the hollow below the bluff.

Kari often slipped away from Max, her frequent shadow (and from everyone, to be honest), in order to stare across the creek at the old house listing so precariously. She would recall Søren's even, mellow voice recounting the twin tragedies of Jan and Rose's first marriages, then later how they had met, how they had fallen in love, the story of *their* marriage and family.

By the time Søren had finished telling her about Rose and Jan, Kari could see them clearly in her mind: Jan, tall and wide, blonde, blue-eyed, sunburned from years of farming this daunting land; Rose, slight but sturdy, grey-eyed, steady, new to her faith—*like me!*—and the two of them coming together to influence many future generations for Christ.

Kari had slipped into the living room many times to stare at the family portrait of Jan, Rose, and Joy that hung on the wall.

*What an amazing couple,* Kari mused. *What an amazing family. I am so honored to know of them.*

She gazed across the distance to Rose's old house, trying to imagine it as Rose had first seen it—even smaller and more primitive. She imagined Rose living there alone through the wild prairie blizzards with only her dog, a homely mutt Søren said Rose had named The Baron!

This morning, from where she sat in the screened-in porch, Kari frowned. She could just barely glimpse the realtor sign along the road, but even that glimpse rankled.

*This land should never pass out of Thoresen hands.* Of that she was certain, and she found that she faulted Søren—at least a little— even though he and Ilsa had again patiently explained the harsh facts of farming in the 1990s.

Kari's eyes shifted to the scorched foundation of what had been the newer farmhouse, now burned to ashes. *If there is a way for Søren and Ilsa to keep this land, they should do whatever it takes,* she grumbled.

Kari roused herself. *Well, I can't stay here lollygagging all day, not contributing. It's time for me to find something useful to do.*

She started to get up only to be jerked to a standstill. Stunned by the thought that had leapt into her head, she could only stand there . . . astounded by its audacity.

*But why not?*

Why not . . .

After lunch that afternoon, Ilsa started baking up a storm. Before many hours had passed, pies filled refrigerator shelves and jars of cookies lined the counters.

"What are all the goodies for?" Kari asked, curious.

Ilsa turned her back. "We might have company this weekend," she muttered, a little evasively.

"Oh." Kari wondered at Ilsa's sudden reticence and looked down at her hands.

*I'm overstaying my welcome,* she deduced. "Is it okay if I use your phone?"

"Certainly."

The only phone in the house was hanging on the kitchen wall. It had a long cord, so Kari dialed the number and walked through the swinging door into the living room, dragging the cord and receiver with her. "Hey, Jeff? Hi. It's Kari Hillyer."

She listened. "I'm fine, thanks. You? Oh, good. Say, I'm just wondering about my car . . ."

She listened for a while longer, making noncommittal sounds as Jeff talked. "So two more weeks? Really? Um. No, the money sounds fine. Do you take credit cards? No? Will you take a check?"

She listened again. "Well, if I give a check to you now, you can deposit it right away. That way it will have cleared and you'll have the money in hand before I take the car. Yes? All right; I'll bring it over. I'll get Søren to lend me his car."

She fiddled with the cord. "The thing is, Jeff, I feel like I'm imposing here. Is there anywhere nearby I can rent a car so I can go back to Denver until you have finished with the Caddy? Yeah. Well, I understand Søren and Ilsa have company coming this weekend—"

Then Kari realized that Søren was standing right behind her, listening. Arms folded. Frowning.

"Jeff? Hey, I need to go now. I'll get that check over to you right away."

Kari pressed the button to disconnect. "Hey."

"Hey yourself. Are you planning to leave?"

"Well, I, that is, Ilsa said you were expecting company this weekend."

"And?"

"Well, I really appreciate your letting me stay and all, but I shouldn't be in the way when your company comes—"

"You're not going anywhere."

"What?"

"First of all, you're not in the way and you won't be in the way this weekend. Second of all . . ." he scratched his head. "Well, I guess there's no 'second of all.' Just . . . you aren't in the way, we're enjoying your company, and you're helping—a lot. We want you to stay. Please. Just stay until your car is ready, all right?"

"But—"

"Just stay, Kari."

It was more of a demand than a request, but Kari decided that she didn't mind. She was loving the routine of the farm, loving their family life, after all.

"Well, if you think so."

"I do think so. Now. Did I hear you say you need to get a check over to Jeff?"

She nodded.

"Here are the keys to the sedan. Think you can find your way there and back without getting lost or clobbered by a bale of hay? —Ow!"

He rubbed his arm where Kari had punched it. "That hurt."

"It was supposed to."

That afternoon Kari drove to Jeff's farm. Before she handed him the check, she inspected the work he was doing: Jeff had removed the hood from the Caddy, sanded the paint from it, and hammered out the dents.

"Priming the hood is next. You won't know the difference when I'm done, Kari," he promised. "And I'm still waiting on the windshield, but it's coming. Be here mid-week, next week."

"I'm encouraged," Kari admitted. Jeff had also vacuumed the hay from the interior.

When Kari left Jeff's farm, she paused where his long driveway intersected the road. Then, instead of turning in the direction of the farm, she made a right turn and drove into RiverBend.


The following day started out just as the previous Friday had. The household rose early and worked hard, Kari working hard along with them. She noticed, though, that Søren and Ilsa seemed to have quickened their pace and were hustling to get the day's chores done early.

They both seemed a bit nervous or preoccupied and less talkative that morning, too—except for Søren barking orders at Max and at Kari.

At lunch she learned why.

As they sat down to eat, Søren cleared his throat. "So, Kari, Ilsa mentioned yesterday that we're going to have visitors this weekend. Some of them will arrive in just a couple of hours, in fact."

"Oh? Who might your company be? And is that the reason you are in such an all-fired rush today?" Kari glared at Søren, happy to let him know she didn't appreciate the rough side of his tongue.

He shrugged. "It is. And . . . I apologize for being so brusque. It's just that we can't take time off this afternoon to visit with them if we still have work to do."

"Oh. I didn't think about that. I understand." Kari nodded, forgiving him immediately.

*The life of a farmer is unrelenting,* she admitted. *No sleeping in, no weekends off, no holidays, no vacations.*

"Thank you," he whispered. His eyes met hers and something crossed between them and connected.

*How much of the weight of the world must you carry on your shoulders, Søren! I do understand, and I'm so sorry,* Kari thought, trying to tell him with her eyes.

Ilsa glanced between them and coughed politely. "Why don't you tell Kari more about our visitors, Søren? She shouldn't be caught by surprise." To herself she muttered, "There'll be surprises enough as it is this weekend."

Kari snapped out of the silent communication between her and Søren. "Surprise? Why? Who is coming?"

Søren pressed his lips together and searched for the right explanation. "Word of you finding Rose's journal has gotten around in the family."

Kari nodded, still waiting.

"The O'Dells would like to . . . make your acquaintance."

"The O'Dells? What, like, *all* of them?"

"No, that is, not today. Today just the O'Dell brothers. Joy and Edmund O'Dell's three sons." He glanced at her, nervous. "You did say you wanted to meet them, right?"

"Yes, but they are coming *here*? Today?" Kari jumped up. "Why, I'm a mess! I've been mucking out stalls! My hair is dirty! In fact, I *stink*!"

She directed a glare at Søren. "When do you expect them? And why in the world didn't you tell me sooner?"

"We expect them around three," Ilsa offered. "That's . . . a little over two hours from now."

Kari stared at both of them. "And why? Why are they coming here just to see *me*?"

To Kari's amazement, Søren started stuttering, but Ilsa replied smoothly, "It's all about the journal, Kari. All about the journal. I'm sure they will explain when they get here. Why don't you go ahead and shower? I'll take care of the dishes."

With a puzzled backwards glance, Kari scurried away.

Just before three that afternoon, a line of vehicles throwing up a haze of dust lumbered its way down the bluff on the other side of the creek. Kari, from her favorite perch in the screened-in back porch, watched as a sedan and three RVs—two motor homes and a fifth wheel—crossed the bridge and turned up the lane.

A few minutes later Kari lost sight of the vehicles as they pulled up to the front of the house. She could hear doors slamming and shouts of greeting. That was when Kari realized Søren was standing near her, his hands thrust into the pockets of his jeans.

"Kari?"

She turned and was alarmed at the pensive look he wore. "What is it, Søren?"

He fingered her sleeve. "Listen, whatever happens during this visit, will you trust God, Kari?"

Worried and a little touched, she studied him. "I can do that. But . . . is something wrong?"

He sighed. "Let's just say that something *was* wrong but it will be set right today. I just need you to know that we, Ilsa and I—and Max, too—are here for you. More than that, God has you. He has you *right where he wants you to be at this moment*, Kari. Trust him. Please just trust him, okay?"

Kari swallowed. She felt an all-too-familiar wave of anxiety tighten her throat but she refused to acknowledge it.

*Lord, I do trust you,* she prayed. *I don't know what is going on, but Søren is right. You have led me here and, as I've learned in this last week, I can . . . do all things through Christ.*

Ilsa walked toward them. Her smile was a bit tremulous. "They are ready for you, Kari."

Kari and Søren followed Ilsa toward the living room. As they walked Kari nervously reached for the comfort of Søren's hand and found that he had reached for hers at the same time.

Kari's first thought as she pushed through the kitchen's swinging door into the living room was not very charitable.

*Did I just step into a geriatric convention?*

A group of older-to-elderly men and women mingled among the furniture—and then Kari's mouth fell open in stunned surprise. "Clover? Lorene!"

She ran to embrace them both. "I don't understand! What are you doing—*Owen*?"

Owen Washington hugged her, too. "Hey, Kari. You are looking wonderful, girl."

"But . . . I don't understand . . ."

Søren bent toward her ear. "Just go with it, Kari, and trust God, okay? Like we talked about."

His whisper tickled her ear and as his words sank in, Kari nodded. "All right. I'll do my best."

"I'm here, too, Kari."

"Alannah! Oh, I'm so happy to see you!" Kari rushed to hug her.

"Kari, I'd like to make some introductions," Ilsa said quietly.

Kari pulled away from Alannah. In fact, she realized that the room had gone quiet as many sets of eyes studied her.

She swallowed. "Okay."

One of the elderly men stepped forward and held out his hand. "My name is Matthew O'Dell," he said by way of introduction. He had thick, steel-grey hair and dark eyes, eyes that studied her kindly.

"Kari Hillyer," Kari answered, her eyes large. "You are Joy and Edmund O'Dell's son?"

"I am. This is my wife, Linda. More of the family is on its way to RiverBend," he gestured, "our children and grandchildren, my brothers' families, and Roseanne's family, too."

"Wow. It will be like a family reunion," Kari stammered. "I didn't know I was visiting Søren and Ilsa during a family get-together. They never said or I would have left sooner. I don't want to be in the way."

"Actually, Kari, we're all here because of you." Matthew was still scrutinizing her, like Kari had been scrutinized many times in the last two weeks. "We understand that you found Grandma's journal and came all the way to Denver—and now here—just to find out more about her?"

"I—yes; I did find her journal. I'm very interested in learning more about her. She . . . her words have meant so much to me."

Kari's emotions sank. She was certain now they would take Rose's journal from her, and she was already bereft, blinking back tears of dismay.

*But after all,* she tried to remind herself, *who has more legal right to Rose's journal than her own grandchildren?*

"Perhaps," Matthew added, "perhaps you would be kind enough to allow us to see this journal you found? But more than that, we would like to get to know *you.*"

Kari brightened a hair. It almost sounded as though they didn't intend to demand the journal of her. "I would be happy to show it to you. Søren and Ilsa have been so good to me—they have recited so much of your family's history that I really feel that I know Rose, and Jan, and even your mother, Joy."

"I'm glad they have told you so much, Kari. We, my brothers and I, have come today because we also have some family history to share with you, some history we think you have not yet heard."

Matthew still stared at her—no, he was *fixated* on her—and Kari was as confused as ever as to *why* her visit should garner so much family attention. Nevertheless, she responded, "All right. I look forward to it."

Matthew, then taking possession of Kari's hand, introduced her to the others in the room. "Jacob and Ellen? This is Kari. Kari, this is my brother, Jacob and, his wife Ellen, and our other brother, Luke, and his wife, Thea."

Jacob and Ellen shook Kari's hand, studying her as intently as Matthew and Linda had. Luke, though, just smiled and squeezed her hand. "It's nice to finally meet you, Kari," he whispered.

*Finally?* Kari was lost.

She turned and found Søren right at her shoulder. "You're doing fine, Kari," he whispered. "Why don't you sit down?"

He led her to a chair and Kari saw that someone—Ilsa, she assumed—had rearranged the furniture in the over-large room into a much more intimate configuration. Kari sat down and looked for Clover and Lorene. They and Owen had taken seats a little behind her. Matthew, Jacob, and Luke were facing her. Their wives and Ilsa, Søren, and Alannah were seated behind them, just as Clover, Lorene, and Owen were behind her.

She was face-to-face with the three O'Dell brothers.

Matthew spoke first. "We asked Søren and Ilsa not to say anything ahead of time about our visit, Kari, because we didn't want you to feel too uncomfortable about our coming," he said gently. "Say, would you happen to have Grandma's journal nearby?"

"Yes. Just in my room, there." Kari pointed. She stood up, squared her shoulders, and added, "I'll get it for you."

During the short trip she prayed, *Lord, please don't let them take it! And I don't understand what is happening! Why are Clover, Lorene, and Owen here?*

Staring at Kari's back, Matthew's mouth parted just a little. "Amazing," he muttered.

Linda, at his elbow, nodded her agreement. "Yes, quite. How many times did we see Grandma Rose and your mama square up their shoulders and face whatever must be done *just like that?* So much like both of them!"

In her room Kari held Rose's journal in her hands and remembered what Søren had asked her: "Whatever happens, will you trust God, Kari?"

*Yes, Lord. I will trust you.*

She returned to the living room and, with shaking hands, gave the precious volume to Matthew. Then she realized that his hands were shaking, too.

Jacob and Luke peered over Matthew's shoulder as he opened it and read the inscription inside.

*Rose Thoresen*
*My Journal*

"It's true," Jacob breathed. "This is her missing journal!" He cut his eyes toward Kari again, this time with what looked like wonder in them.

Matthew turned to the back and paged forward until he reached the last entry. "Her last entry is dated April 12, 1911."

All three of them looked up and stared at Kari.

"What?" she whispered. "What does that mean?"

Matthew closed the journal and stood to return it to her. "Thank you, Kari."

Kari swallowed. "I can keep it?"

"As far as I'm concerned, yes," Matthew replied. "God saw fit to lead *you* to it and then lead you to *us*. I consider the journal to be yours."

He took a deep breath and looked around at his brothers, who both nodded. "Kari, I said earlier that we, too, had some family history to tell you."

He took his seat again so that the three brothers and Kari were quite close. The stillness of the others in the living room was palpable.

"Kari, you have read Rose's journal, haven't you? Did she write about Mei-Xing Li's disappearance?"

"Yes. Su-Chong Chen kidnapped her and held her prisoner for months. When Edmund O'Dell—your father—found her, Su-Chong was dead. O'Dell returned Mei-Xing to Palmer House but . . . but she was pregnant. With Shan-Rose."

"Very good. Then do you know, too, that Su-Chong was an only child? Do you know that Su-Chong's mother, Fang-Hua Chen, plotted to steal her son's child from Mei-Xing?"

"I—that is, Rose wrote that she and the others thought it was a possibility and they took a lot of precautions . . ." Kari's words trailed off.

Matthew nodded and smiled. Kari was again struck by the kindheartedness in his eyes.

"Kari, on April 12, 1911, Rose took little Shan-Rose and her infant grandson Edmund for a walk in a park near Palmer House. She took her journal and her Bible with her. That is where she wrote the last entry in the journal you found."

"Oh!" Kari imagined Rose penning that last entry and smiled.

Matthew did not return her smile. "Kari, Rose was accompanied by two very reliable and experienced bodyguards. Nevertheless, men hired by Fang-Hua attacked them in broad daylight as they left the park. The two guards were shot and killed. Fang-Hua's men also shot Rose."

"No! No, they didn't!" Kari was horrified and looked to Søren to deny it—only for him to nod his head. "But she didn't *die*, did she? She died years later, right?"

"Yes; that's right. She survived the shooting. But . . . the men Fang-Hua hired . . ."

"They took Shan-Rose?" Kari was confused.

"No, Kari," Matthew whispered. "They took Edmund."

Kari felt the blood in her body—like a crashing wave of icy water—rush to her feet. "They took *Edmund*?"

Matthew looked at the floor. "It was a mistake, Kari. The men had been told that Mei-Xing had given birth to a baby boy. When they saw *two* babies in the pram—a girl and a boy—they didn't look closely at them or think. They simply took the boy."

"But . . . but they got him back, didn't they? Joy got her baby back, didn't she?" The horror of it engulfed Kari's heart.

*Poor Joy! O Lord, why did she have to suffer so many heartaches?*

She realized that Matthew had not answered her. "Matthew? They found Edmund, didn't they?" Her question was no more than a strangled croak. "Didn't they?"

Instead of responding, Matthew asked, "Did Rose write in her journal about a man named Dean Morgan, Kari?"

"I . . . she mentioned him. He . . . wasn't he the man who owned the . . . houses of evil in Corinth? The journal starts the day after he was arrested. But then later he and Su-Chong escaped together from the jail in Denver?"

"That's right. What you might not know is that, although older than Su-Chong, Dean Morgan grew up with Su-Chong in Seattle. He was well acquainted with Su-Chong's mother, Fang-Hua Chen."

The images in Kari's head were spinning, colliding. "And so . . ."

"And so Fang-Hua sent *Morgan* to steal Mei-Xing's child for her."

"She sent Morgan. And so . . . he mistakenly took Edmund?"

"His men did, yes. What Grandma may also not have written in her journal is how much Dean Morgan hated our mother, Joy."

Kari stared at nothing and said nothing. The stillness and tension in the room seemed to grow.

Matthew cleared his throat again. "Our father, Edmund O'Dell, was a Pinkerton man and conducted most of the investigation into Edmund's abduction. Morgan hated Dad as well as Mother. He hated Dad because Dad had helped Mother close down the houses in Corinth.

"We know Morgan was the one who took Edmund because he left a note for Dad. The last line of Morgan's note read, 'Sorry about taking the wrong child, O'Dell.'"

"But if it was a mistake—"

"It was a mistake, but he decided to keep Edmund because . . . because it was the most painful way to punish Mother . . . and Dad."

"They never . . . they never found Edmund . . . ?" Kari thought her heart would break, so hard did it clench in her chest. *They never found him?*"

Matthew sensed that he was losing Kari to her emotions. "Kari, if you can, please stay with us. I have more to say."

She nodded, but he could see how distracted she was.

"Mother and Dad never gave up looking for Edmund, Kari. No one in the families did—the Thoresens, the O'Dells, the Carmichaels, and the Liángs. Rose, Mother, and Dad, Isaac and Breona Carmichael, Mei-Xing and Yao Liáng—and many friends—vowed that they would never give up.

"And we, their children, have never given up. Our families made a pact before God, you see: We bound ourselves in a solemn pledge to never stop searching for Edmund and to never stop trusting that God would restore him to us, whether in this life or the next. Our families vowed that we would hold to our faith in the Lord—to the firm belief that wherever Edmund was, until he returned to us, *God had him and would keep him safe.*"

Matthew grew emotional as he spoke so Jacob placed a calming hand on his shoulder and stepped in to continue the narration. "Mother married Dad in 1915 and our family grew—first Matthew, then me, then Luke and, last of all, Roseanne. We grew up knowing we had a brother named Edmund and that someday our great God would bring him back to us.

"Mother said that her father, Jan Thoresen, had a saying while she was growing up. He told her that, 'In God, the lost are found.'

"Those words became our family's catch phrase—our motto: Lost Are Found. We have used that phrase to remind ourselves that God *will* return Edmund to us—even if it is not until heaven."

"*Lost Are Found*," Kari murmured. "All those signs. That's what they were really about?"

Jacob nodded. "Later Mother founded the organization she named 'Lost Are Found' to help locate the missing children of other families. But to *our* families? To us 'Lost Are Found' only ever meant one thing: In God the lost *are* found. *He* had Edmund and would return him to us one day."

Kari sighed, grieving with him. "But you never found Edmund. And he would be older than any of you now."

"No, we didn't find him," Matthew choked. "But we found his daughter."

Kari blinked, not understanding him. She realized that most of the people in the room were sniffling. Ilsa was openly sobbing.

"What are you talking about?" she whispered.

"The journal," Matthew answered, his voice cracking. "That day in the park, Grandma put her Bible and her journal under the blanket that covered Shan-Rose and Edmund. Afterwards, after Fang-Hua's men had taken Edmund, her journal was missing. Her *Bible* was there, but the blanket and *her journal* were gone.

"It was thought that when the kidnappers picked up Edmund that they inadvertently wrapped the journal into the blanket at the same time. All these years, we have wondered what became of it—and we have hoped that wherever it was, it would someday lead Edmund back to us."

Kari jumped up. "Wha-what are you saying?" she demanded. "What are you saying?" but Matthew could not respond.

Alannah answered for him. "Kari, Dean Morgan hired a wet nurse to care for Shan-Rose while they took her to Fang-Hua. Instead, Morgan and the wet nurse took *Edmund* and left Denver and were never seen again. Morgan took Rose's journal with him."

Owen stood. "Miss Kari? Once Morgan reached New Orleans, he had three birth certificates forged: one for himself, one for the wet nurse, and one for Edmund." Owen turned. "Clover?"

Clover climbed to his feet next to Owen and, holding onto his arm, said, "Kari, Detective Carmichael here came to New Orleans last week. She showed me old pictures of Dean Morgan. I am possibly the only person still alive who could identify him. And Kari, I can say, categorically: Dean Morgan and Peter Granger were one and the same person."

Alannah continued, "We know now that Peter Granger was Dean Morgan, and we know that Alicia Granger was the wet nurse.

"Which means," she added softly, "that your father, Michael Granger, was Edmund Thoresen Michaels."

Kari was still standing, staring at the floor. Matthew got out of his chair and went to her. He grasped her gently by the arms. "We didn't find our brother Edmund, Kari, but we found his daughter. *You*, Kari, are Edmund Michael's daughter. Grant and Joy Michaels are your grandparents. Rose Thoresen is *your great-grandmother*. And I am your uncle, Kari."

*Rose was my great-grandmother?* Kari swallowed. Hard.

Tears running down his face, Matthew placed a kiss on her forehead. "God is faithful: The lost are finally found.

"Welcome home, KariAnn Thoresen Michaels."

# CHAPTER 24

Søren stood near Kari as the others in the room gathered around her. All of them were careful and gentle for her sake, but one by one they touched her and murmured their welcomes.

First, Matthew and Linda, followed by Jacob and Luke and their wives, embraced her. "You are our niece, Kari," Jacob rasped, his voice rough with emotion. "I am your Uncle Jacob. We have been looking for you for a long, long time."

"You are so much like Mama, Kari!" Luke added. "Tall, strong, beautiful—" He broke down and could not finish.

Then Clover and Lorene gathered her in their arms. "We only found out last week," Clover whispered, "and knowing how difficult this revelation would be for you, we wanted to be here to assure you that it was true and to help you through the shock."

Lorene embraced Kari, her familiar scent welcoming and soothing Kari. "Thank you," Kari whispered.

Owen gave her hand a gentle squeeze. Kari nodded her thanks.

*Oh, Rose! You are my great-grandmother? Oh, Rose! But how your words, the words of your journal, called to me, called to my heart! Across all these miles and all these years, God used them to call me to you? To my family? To himself?*

A relief, a hope, an indescribable joy was bubbling within her, etching away at the years and years of loneliness—aching, unrelenting loneliness. Every fresh realization washed her with healing oil.

*Joy and Grant! You are my grandparents? And Daddy! You were their precious baby boy? How they loved you! How they must have longed for you!*

Alannah hugged her and kissed her on the cheek. "We are cousins, Kari. Think of that! You are my cousin!"

*Cousin! I've never had a cousin. I've never had anyone . . . and now? I am not alone?* Kari couldn't answer Alannah; she clung to her and they sobbed on each others' shoulders. Kari could only repeat silently, *I am not alone! I am not alone!*

And then Alannah giggled and Kari, hiccupping, looked up and their eyes met. Joy bubbled up in Kari until it mixed with her tears and sobs and she laughed aloud.

"We're cousins, Alannah? Truly?"

"Truly." Alannah accepted a tissue from Ilsa and wiped her nose, laughing again. "From the moment you just *showed up* at the door to Palmer House with Rose's journal in your hand—asking if Shan-Rose were Mei-Xing Li!—Kari, your appearance has rocked us—*all of us*—to our cores!"

"Really?" Reality was gripping Kari, making her wobbly.

"Poor Uncle Quan!" Alannah laughed and Kari's uncles joined in. "If you could have heard him trying to repeat all that Shan-Rose told him on the phone the evening after you appeared! The uproar! The astonishment! The hope! The joy! And *so* many questions!"

Matthew chimed in. "Quan had to repeat himself three times when he called us. I-I just could not get my mind wrapped around it."

"And trying to keep it all in?" Alannah laughed. "You have *no* idea how hard the last two weeks have been!"

"You think it's been hard for you?" Søren demanded. "Ilsa and I have been waltzing around this secret for more than a week! Reciting Thoresen history to Kari, always leaving out Edmund's kidnapping, always skirting the elephant in the room."

He took Kari's hand. "Kari, I wanted to tell you so badly, but your uncles insisted that they be the ones to tell you. I almost gave in once, but Ilsa about had a fit and—"

"I did not!" Ilsa shot back.

Everyone gathered in the room responded with good-natured amusement.

"Yes you did, Ilsa. Your disapproving glare practically drilled holes in my head one evening, and don't you deny it!"

More laughter followed and Ilsa blushed.

"Kari, it was only right to honor your uncles' wishes, but I need you to understand that I did not like keeping you in the dark." Søren concluded, squeezing her hand.

Matthew shook his head. "And when Alannah went to New Orleans and confirmed everything? Well, we went to our knees in thanksgiving, all of us. The whole of our four families are praising God, Kari, and they are on their way here. They will be here tomorrow, and we are going to rejoice together!"

Alannah smiled and hugged Kari again. "Oh, Kari! God is so good!"

"They are all coming here?" Kari whispered.

"To meet you," Matthew confirmed.

Kari sank into a chair. Abruptly, it was all too much. *I'm not used to being so . . . happy,* she realized.

"Let's give Kari a little room to breathe, shall we?" Søren suggested, noting how pale Kari had gone.

Ilsa nodded and started herding their guests toward the kitchen. "I have coffee and dessert if anyone is interested?" A few moved in that direction; others remained in the room talking amongst themselves but giving Kari the space Søren had requested.

Kari stared straight ahead, replaying the revelations of the last half hour, trying to grasp and hold the many threads of them.

*Edmund was kidnapped; Daddy is Edmund.* Then she recalled Matthew saying, *Rose was also shot.*

*Oh, Rose!* Kari's heart clenched.

*They took Shan-Rose?*

*No, Kari.*

*They took Edmund.*

She ached over those three words and pondered their implications. *They took Daddy away from Joy and Grant. They took him and Grant died . . . without seeing his baby boy again before he died? Oh, Grant! Oh, Joy. I am so sorry.*

*And they lied to Daddy about who his parents were. Peter Granger and Alicia Granger lied to him—about everything. Daddy's whole life was a lie!*

Kari's musings turned toward the trunk in the garage's attic and how thrilled she had been to find it filled with Alicia Granger's beautiful gowns and handbags.

*But she wasn't Alicia Granger. She was a stranger with a false name! Not my grandmother!* she realized. *Not Daddy's mother at all.*

*Lies.*

*They stole Daddy from his family. They stole his life.*

*They stole my life, too. They stole my family and my heritage from Daddy and from me.*

*Not Peter Granger, but Dean Morgan.*

The very name of *Morgan* fanned emotions she did not recognize.

*Sorry about taking the wrong child, O'Dell . . .*

Matthew's voice . . . *He decided to keep Edmund because . . . because it was the most painful way to punish Mother and Dad.*

Dean Morgan. Peter Granger.

Demanding thoughts began to jitter about in her head: *Dean Morgan took Joy's baby boy! He took my father from his real parents! That evil, evil man stole my father's life!*

*. . . He decided to keep Edmund because it was the most painful way to punish Mother and Dad.*

*Dean Morgan. Peter Granger.*

Anger toward Dean Morgan was kindling within her.

*That evil beast!*

Her chest tightened as her emotions rose.

*Dean Morgan. Peter Granger.*

Fury toward the man who had posed as her father's uncle uncoiled in her chest and found an ember of wrath flickering there. Her rage grew.

Kari felt a primal urge—*a visceral need*—to strike at this man, this *Dean Morgan*, this *Peter Granger*.

Oh, she wanted to hurt him! No—she wanted to *destroy* him. Her fingers curled until the nails bit into the palms of her hands.

Then Kari could not catch her breath. She leapt out of the chair and swayed, already unsteady on her feet. Lights sparkled around the edges of her vision. The room began to blur.

"Kari?" Søren stared at her with concern but she could not answer. "Kari, are you all right?"

Owen shouldered his way toward Kari as her body began to slump. "Sit her back down. It's a panic attack. Just sit her down here until it passes. That's right."

Søren did as Owen directed and watched helplessly as Kari struggled to breathe and could not, as she gasped and panted until her eyes fluttered and closed. "You've seen this before?"

"Once."

"Me, too," he realized.

Linda ran to fetch a wet cloth.

"It was too much, Matthew," Luke accused. "Too much for anyone!"

"No." Søren's single word was quiet but forceful. "She is stronger than you think. And she had to be told. I'm tired of hiding the truth from her."

"I agree." Alannah took the cold, wet cloth from Linda and laid it on Kari's forehead. "We are Kari's family. She has been longing for us her whole life. This is just a reaction; she will get past it."

Kari's chest rose and fell convulsively and then she began to come around. "Wha—what happened?"

Owen knelt beside her chair. "You had an anxiety attack, Kari. You'll be right as rain soon."

"But . . . everything they said?"

"Take as much time as you need to think it through. Don't rush. It's all good news—nothing to worry over."

Søren and Ilsa motioned the rest of them into the kitchen and after a while Kari could distinguish the sounds of chairs scraping and plates rattling, Ilsa serving her guests coffee and dessert.

As the weakness left her, Kari finished muddling through what Matthew and the others had told her and tried to focus on Owen's encouragement: *It's all good news—nothing to worry over.*

Her brows furrowed. *Is he right? Is it all good news?*

Again Matthew's words tumbled through her mind. *Grant and Joy Michaels were your grandparents. Rose Thoresen was your great-grandmother.*

Could it really all be true?

Someone was coming back into the living room.

Søren sat across from her in the chair Matthew had used. "How are you feeling, Kari?"

"I'll be all right soon."

"You gave us all a fright."

Kari stared into his blue Thoresen eyes. *Wait . . . his eyes are like mine,* she realized. *I have Thoresen eyes?*

"It's a bit much to take in," she whispered.

"I did want to tell you sooner . . . but Matthew felt he should be the one."

"I know," Kari leaned her head against the back of the chair and closed her eyes. "I still can't believe that Daddy was Joy and Grant's son!"

They sat together in silence for a long time.


Kari arose the next morning later than she'd grown accustomed to and found the farm bustling with activity. She entered the kitchen, surprised to find it empty of people—but filled with good smells.

The counters were crowded with stacks of plates, syrup decanters, bowls of stewed cinnamon apples, saucers of butter and jam, and platters of freshly cut fruit. She opened the oven door and saw pans of potatoes, scrambled eggs, muffins, and pancakes warming there.

*What in the world . . .* Her first cup of coffee in hand, Kari wandered out the back door onto the kitchen porch.

The lawn and pasture below the house were being transformed.

A large white tent, similar to those used for weddings, was going up. At least ten men were hard at work as the three peaks of the tent rose.

Kari spied Søren and Lars unloading tables and chairs from a truck. Ilsa and Dalia were covering tables with cloths. The RVs in which the O'Dells had arrived were parked in a row in the pasture and two others—a camper and a trailer—had joined them.

Max ran up the back steps. "Are you up now?"

"I guess I am," Kari answered. "What is all this, anyway?"

"It's a family re-onion."

"Re-onion? You mean a reunion?"

"Yeah, a re-onion. Everybody's coming."

"Everybody? The whole Thoresen family?"

"Oh, more than just Thoresens. The O'Dells, the Carmichaels, the Liángs—the whole family." He glanced at her shyly. "They all want to meet you, Kari, 'cause you were lost and God founded you and brought you home."

*Home! God brought me home!* The import of Max's words struck a chord of joy in Kari's breast.

"Aunt Ilsa asked me to see if you were up and could help get breakfast out?"

"Of course." Kari set her empty coffee cup next to the sink and hefted a stack of plates. "Take those syrup jugs, will you, Max?"

As she walked down the sloping lawn to the tables, the eyes of many noticed and followed her. Ilsa, however, kept Kari running back and forth to the kitchen and she did not have to deal with meeting anyone until breakfast.

Then the floodgates opened. Ilsa made sure to stick close to Kari and make introductions. Kari grew used to receiving both a name and a relationship description but none of it seemed to stay in her head.

"Kari, this is Darren O'Dell, Matthew and Linda's grandson, and his wife Patsy."

"We're praising God for bringing you home, Kari. You are one of our family's miracles."

Smiles, hugs, handshakes, more hugs.

"Kari, may I introduce Bryce and Tess Carmichael and their children? Bryce is Sean Carmichael's son—Alannah's brother."

"We've heard so much about you, Kari. Welcome to the family. You are an answer to prayer."

More smiles and hugs.

"Kari, these are our Omaha Thoresen cousins, Arnie Thoresen's grandchildren . . ."

The next hour was both wonderful and overwhelming for Kari as many more people arrived and queued up to meet her.

After Kari had greeted An-Shing and Fen-Bai, Ilsa said, "Kari, this is our good friend, Sunny Richards."

"Yes; I know Sunny. I need to drive in and have you make me another one of your fantastic sodas! How are you? How has business been?"

"I think the more important question is, how are you, Kari? Your head must be ready to explode!"

Kari laughed and it felt good. "You know, Sunny, that's not far off the mark."

"Well, I've been praying for you. Ever since Mixxie called me and since we met."

"I really thank you, Sunny. It's quite an adjustment—will continue to be an adjustment, I think. Speaking of Mixxie, is she coming?"

Ilsa answered for Sunny. "I believe she will arrive this morning with Quan and Shan-Rose."

"Shan-Rose is coming?" Kari was delighted.

"That reminds me. Would you mind very much letting Shan-Rose have your room? It will be just for tonight. We have another room upstairs, but she cannot climb stairs as you know. Mixxie will take care of her in your room, if that is all right."

"It is absolutely all right," Kari replied. "I will be so happy to see her!"

After breakfast Kari managed to escape for a while. She cleared her things out of her bedroom and moved them to the little room upstairs next to Ilsa's. She put fresh linens on her bed for Shan-Rose and straightened the bathroom.

When she was done, she crept to the screened-in back porch. She just wanted to be alone for a bit. From the porch she could observe quietly as more people arrived and greeted each other. Those who came brought more food, lawn chairs, and laughter. The pasture now boasted eleven RVs of various sizes. Someone played a guitar and the sounds of singing floated up to Kari.

As the sun grew warmer, the adults gravitated to the tent. The sides were rolled up or tied back, and large fans kept cool air circulating inside. A horde of children, Max included, ran up and down the lawn, involved in loud games and general running amok.

*They are having such fun,* Kari mused, watching the children. *They take their many brothers and sisters and cousins for granted. They don't know what it's like not to have family.*

Kari watched it all from her solitary perch on the porch. Each time she recalled the fresh news that this was *her* family, she felt the same stab of awe, of shock.

*All of these people,* she sighed. *All of these people are my family. My heritage.* It was more than she could handle.

*Oh, Rose! I had no idea of the consequences, the commotion, finding your journal would stir up!*

"Doing okay?" Søren plopped down next to her on the cushioned bench. He was hot, and perspiration dripped from his face. He tilted his head back, letting a stream of ice water run down his throat.

"Yes. It's wonderful."

"But a bit much, huh?"

She nodded. "I think my face is going to crack if I smile one more time."

He looked at her then and cupped her chin in his hand, making a show of critically examining first one side of her face and then the other. "Doesn't look cracked to me . . ."

Their eyes met and Søren asked a silent question. Kari blinked and looked down.

"No, please . . . I'm not ready for anything like that, Søren," Kari whispered. "I-I've made so many bad choices. I don't want *you* to be another one. Your friendship means so much to me but I . . . I want to give all my devotion to my new love for God. For now."

"I understand," he croaked. "Sorry."

"Please don't let this ruin everything," Kari added. "I couldn't bear it."

"I will respect your wishes, Kari," Søren said quietly. After an awkward pause, he added, a tiny smile tugging at his mouth. "But it's okay, you know. We being cousins and all."

Kari laughed, and the tension eased. "Kissing cousins? Wow. I hadn't thought of that," she admitted. "Cousins! But-but that means—"

"We aren't *that* close of cousins," Søren growled. "You have Rose and Jan's blood flowing in your veins; I have Jan's but *not* Rose's. We're only half cousins—and several times removed at that.

"So you've thought about it, have you?" Kari answered, arching her brows.

"Uh, well, I guess . . . maybe."

"Oh?" Kari challenged him.

"Yeah, well . . . we can talk about that later. In the meantime . . . friends?"

Kari sighed, relieved. "Yes. Please."

Without further words, they got up and rejoined the others in the yard below.

More relatives and close friends arrived that morning, including Quan, who brought Shan-Rose and Mixxie. Kari's meeting with Shan-Rose was precious. The tiny old woman held Kari's face in her hands and kissed her on both cheeks. "Edmund's daughter! Joy and Grant's granddaughter!" she sobbed. "Kari, you are more precious to me than gold. Thank you for finding your way home to us."

Mixxie glanced at Kari and then away. She said nothing. No defiance or anger flared in her dark, black-lined eyes. It was as though the air had gone out of the girl, leaving her deflated and flat.

"You know Mixxie better than I do—what is wrong with her?" Kari asked Sunny.

"Wrong? I would rather say 'right,'" Sunny sighed. "She's having to face reality, having to face some things that she had given up faith in. It's making her confront the condition of her own heart. She will, I hope, make some right choices soon."

Kari turned her head to look for Mixxie, curious about the girl. She was taken aback to find that Mixxie was looking toward her.

What was disturbing to Kari was the sadness she found etched on Mixxie's face.

Kari managed to interact with all the strangers who were now—without any prior notice or emotional preparation—*her family.*

*I cannot believe I belong here, to all these people,* Kari rejoiced in wonder. She gave what she could of herself to the crush of strangers smiling and welcoming her into its bosom.

It was exhilarating.

It was healing.

*It was exhausting.*

After a few hours she had to take a break from it all. She walked alone down the lawn into the apple trees and, without planning to, found herself wandering up the knoll to the little graveyard.

She placed her hand on the wrought iron gate. *This is the Thoresen family cemetery. My family's cemetery. My family!*

The gate opened under her hand and she stepped inside. No longer a stranger, no longer an outsider, she walked among the graves with new eyes.

*Jan and Elli! Kristen. Karl and Amalie. Søren and Meg. Children and grandchildren; nephews, nieces, cousins. All mine. My family. My heritage.*

"My prairie heritage," she breathed. Suddenly she couldn't get to Rose and Joy's graves fast enough. She skirted around the plots and reached the back where Rose, Joy, and Edmund O'Dell's simple resting places were.

"Rose!" Kari murmured. "How can it be that you are my great-grandmother? Somehow God, our *awesome God*, used your words to draw me here. And Joy! You are my *real* grandmother—my daddy's *real* mother."

She fell to her knees between Rose and Joy's graves, tears streaming from her eyes. She didn't try to stem the flood; instead, she accepted it and welcomed its cleansing, healing release.

"*My* prairie heritage," she wept. "I read what you wrote about your prairie heritage, Rose, and I longed for it! How I longed for it! I longed to be yours and to have you wrap your arms around me! And now . . . your heritage is mine, too! My *family* prayed me home! All my life they have been praying and believing that our God would bring Edmund home and now . . . he has . . . through me."

Kari stretched herself out between the two graves and laid her forehead on the grass. "O Lord! she prayed, "I see now that you never forgot daddy. He came to know you even though he never knew the truth about his parents. Now their faith is answered; now he is with them in heaven!

"And you kept your hand on *me* all those long, lonely years. At just the right time, you moved to lead me here—to lead me home. O Lord! Your ways are past finding out. How can I ever thank you?"

There, lying between the soft mounds of Rose and Joy's graves, Kari's sobs finished. Quite naturally, she slipped into a peaceful sleep.

The morning and afternoon of food, games, and conversation were to transition to a song fest and then an evening barbecue. Refreshed and somehow settled, Kari rejoined the family throng.

During the lull before the afternoon drew toward evening, Kari caught Matthew and asked for a moment of his time. "Uncle Matthew?"

As awkward as calling him "uncle" felt, Kari was warming to the idea. The sweetness in his eyes drew her to him.

"Yes, Kari?"

"I-I have something to tell you, to give to you."

"All right." They walked away from the others and strolled side-by-side toward the little orchard.

Kari held tightly to the cloth bag as she brought it out from behind her back. "I want to tell you thank you, first of all, for allowing me to keep Rose's journal."

He nodded. "That little book has been God's chosen tool for many good things, don't you agree?"

"So many good things! Most of all, Rose's words led me to Jesus."

They stopped and Matthew slipped his arm around her shoulders and gave her a quick squeeze. "To hear that my brother Edmund was a follower of Christ—and that now *you* are—is a very large answered prayer, indeed. I was confident in faith that I would see him in heaven someday. Now I am confident in fact."

"Did you know how angry I was when Clover first told me Daddy was a Christian?" Kari whispered. "I had no idea that God was using Daddy's faith in the Savior to draw *me* to Jesus."

"We rarely see the hand of our great God when he is at work, but later? Later we can clearly make out how marvelous his plans and provisions are."

Matthew stopped walking. "But my dear, before we go any further, I have something to give *you*."

"But . . . you have already . . ." Kari didn't know what to say.

Matthew patted her cheek. "Dear Kari. I'll bet you don't know that after Edmund was taken—after Grandma Rose's journal disappeared—that she started another journal?"

"No." Kari could hardly breathe. "I didn't know. She wrote another journal?"

"Her journals fill three more volumes, to be exact. My brothers and I have discussed this and we are in agreement. They should have gone to Joy's eldest son and his family, so we want you to have them, to be their keeper for posterity."

He smiled at the look on Kari's face. "We brought them with us to compare their handwriting to that in the journal you found, but we didn't find it necessary to do so. After all, you are the image of our mother, just cast in gold and honey instead of sun-ripened wheat."

Kari swallowed. The thought of reading more of Rose's journals was the most enticing of gifts she could imagine. "I would be honored to keep them for the family."

"Good, then! That is settled. Now, what was it you wanted to give me?"

"Well," Kari answered quietly, "when I found the journal, I also found something else."

"Oh?" Matthew's look was expectant.

"I found a letter addressed to Joy."

Matthew's brows shot up. "A letter to Mother? From whom? From Edmund?"

"That's the thing—I don't know. I didn't open the letter, and the envelope does not say who it is from, but . . . I don't think it could be from Daddy. It was placed in the trunk with the journal in 1957 and Daddy had left New Orleans years before . . . although he did not die until 1958."

She fingered the edges of the envelope through the bag. "I didn't know who the letter was written to at first because the writing on the envelope cannot be seen by the naked eye. Owen and I took it to a friend who was able to make the writing visible for a few minutes."

She looked at the cloth bag she held with both hands. "Owen's friend put some chemicals on it and we were able to see that the front of the envelope read 'Joy Thoresen Michaels.' That was quite clear. The back, however, was harder to read. Some of the letters were scratched and the ink was smeared. I am certain, however, that it reads, 'Joy Michaels, Personal and Confidential.'"

"You are quite strong and persistent, Kari," Matthew praised her. "I see some of Mother's spirit in you—in how you were determined to find out more about Rose and how you searched for and found your way to Palmer House."

Kari glowed with pleasure. "Thank you, Uncle Matthew. That is so sweet."

She drew the letter out of the bag. "Because the letter was personal and confidential, I left it sealed. Now that I've found you all . . . well, it seems to me that you, Uncle Jacob, and Uncle Luke should have it."

Matthew's hand trembled as he took the letter. "Thank you, Kari. the Lord bless you for your kindness to us."

Kari enjoyed the singing: It was loud, fun, and unabashed, with lots of traditional songs thrown in followed by hymns and choruses. She was sorry when it ended and when the barbecue dinner was over.

Many of the attendees began to pack up and leave then, heading to their homes either in or around the community or headed to hotel reservations down the interstate on their way to their respective towns and cities. A crew began taking down the tent and hauling away the tables and chairs.

However, not everyone was leaving after the day's festivities. A smaller family group planned to remain and have a Sunday service on the lawn the following morning: the O'Dell brothers; a few Liángs, including Quan, Mixxie, and Shan-Rose; and Alannah and her father. Lars and Dalia Thoresen had offered to house Clover, Lorene, and Owen, so they would be joining them for morning worship, too.

Then, unexpectedly, Matthew and his brothers called them together, the smaller group staying over. "Before we retire for the night, I'm asking if you would gather once more. I have something to read to you."

His manner was solemn, and Kari deduced that he and his brothers had read the letter she had given him.

Kari shivered in nervous anticipation as the grassy area below Søren and Ilsa's little orchard filled. Family members sat on lawn chairs arranged in two rows in a semicircle. Those who could sit on the grass did so, leaving the chairs to those who could not.

It would not be dark for another hour but the heat of the day was, at last, lifting. Kari plopped down on the grass, slipped off her sandals, and ran her bare feet through the lush grass, relishing its coolness.

She nodded and smiled at Matthew, Jacob, and Luke and their families; Lars and Dalia and their brood; Sean and Alannah; Shan-Rose, Quan, and Mixxie; and Clover, Lorene, and Owen. They were no longer strangers; she trusted and loved them all. Well, with perhaps the exception of Mixxie.

*But I am willing to love her, Lord,* Kari realized. *I hope you will make a way for us to love each other.*

Søren placed a chair in front of the assembled group and gestured to Matthew to sit there. Søren pointed to three chairs at the outside of the semicircle where Ilsa already sat and wordlessly asked Kari to join them. As she left her spot on the grass, Max, cross-legged, front and center, grinned and waved to them.

Kari smiled and waved back and then took a deep breath. She had not been able to stop thinking about the letter addressed to Joy. *What did Matthew read in that letter that caused him to call us together this evening—and with such solemn insistence?*

"Welcome, everyone. Let's get started, shall we?" Søren called. The assembled group turned its attention to him.

Søren looked at Kari. "You have already met our cousin Kari. You have heard her story. What you might not know is that when Kari found Rose Thoresen's journal, she also found a sealed envelope with it. That envelope was addressed to Joy Thoresen Michaels."

Excited murmurs floated across the lawn.

Søren looked to Matthew. "Matthew, Kari gave that envelope to you, as Joy's eldest living son, to open and to share its contents with your brothers."

"Yes, Søren. Jacob, Luke, and I opened and read the letter this afternoon. I felt that it was imperative for the family to hear what it says. Jacob and Luke agreed. If I may have your quiet attention, I will try to read it loud enough for all to hear."

Matthew slid the letter from the envelope and unfolded it. He perused the first lines again and then began to read.

*Dear Mrs. Michaels,*

*I have attempted, in one fashion or another, to begin this letter many times over the past twenty years. The truth is, I was not ready to write it until now—at least not in the manner it should be written.*

*I have taken pains **not** to follow your life. The years have flown by, and I don't know if you are still alive. However, I felt that if I were to see your death notice in the papers, I would have lost, forever, the opportunity to speak what **must** be spoken.*

*Writing these words in a letter is a coward's way—a panacea for my own benefit. I acknowledge this, acknowledge that I am a coward, and acknowledge that I have waited far too long. Death, however, waits for no man; it is now stalking me. It is drawing near, and I can no longer put off saying what is required of me.*

*I stole from you what I can only believe was the most precious thing in your life: I stole your baby son, Edmund.*

The gathering, as one, sighed. There was no doubt now as to the writer of the letter Matthew was reading. Kari listened in stunned silence.

*I had never loved anyone other than myself before I took your child. I had spent my life to that point in selfish and vain ambition. Then, in a few weeks—mere months—I learned what it is to love, as I gave my heart to your son.*

*It was by loving him that I learned how precious he had to have been to you.*

*My love for little Michael—for that is what we named him—grew as he grew. He was the only thing in my life that was good and whole* and pure. My life and purpose were bound up in his life by cords of such love that they tie me to him even now.

I must now confess that, as he grew to be a man, I erred grievously in my dealings with him. I attempted to control him and force him into a mold of my choosing, a mold he could not bear. That is when I lost him.

Mrs. Michaels, it was by losing him that I experienced the agony you felt when you lost him.

For the first time in my life, I experienced regret. And more.

In the years following Michael's departure I raged against his defiance. I raged against the friends who had turned him to his faith and away from me. I raged against the universe that caused me to care so deeply for him—and then snatched him away. I raged at everyone and everything. Except myself.

I simmered in my pain for years. I ached in my loneliness. I sought relief in pleasure. Year after year I grew more debauched, more corrupt in my lusts.

Still, I would not acknowledge that my suffering was the just recompense for what I had done to you. Back when I took him, you were my enemy and I wanted not to kill you but to mortally wound you.

But, in truth, with the instrument of your wounding, I killed myself.

After many more years, I ceased my useless ranting and raging. I acknowledged that the hand of God himself must be against me.

Yet, isn't to acknowledge God's **hand**, also to acknowledge his **existence**? And if God exists, then what? It is a slippery slope to acknowledge God's existence and continue to defy him. Can a mere mortal defy the God of creation and remain unscathed, untaught, untouched?

A few years ago as I wrestled with these thoughts, I was on my way to assuage my sorrow in more drink and illicit pleasure. As I went on my way toward the outskirts of town, a crowd drew my attention to a large tent meeting.

I cannot say why I was drawn, for I have never darkened the door of a church that I did not view with disgust and I have never heard a message on God that I did not revile—yet drawn I was.

That evening, bankrupt in the core of my being, I stood in the crush of thousands and I heard a man from the platform within the tent shout these words: "God is a good God and the devil is a bad devil!"

I was struck with this one clear and indisputable truth: I have aligned my life with the devil and I am as evil as he.

Kari gasped, as did others listening. Matthew took the moment to pause and sip on his iced tea before he resumed.

*I could not escape this truth! Rather, it increased in certainty, my long-dead conscience awaking and adding these facts:*

*I have murdered men in cold blood—I am a murderer.*

*I have deflowered and debased young women for profit—I am a man most vile.*

*I have hated, stolen, cheated, and lied—I am altogether without honor, vindication, or excuse.*

***I am evil.***

*From that moment I could not escape the crushing finality of this truth: I am an enemy of God and he will judge me.*

*I could no longer sleep. I could not eat. I roamed my home finding no peace, no rest, no reprieve. I knew my end was coming and when it did, I would—**most justly**—burn in hell.*

*Then came a day of reckoning, when God spoke to me. "Surrender," he said. "Surrender to the Savior and be saved."*

Kari could not believe what her ears were hearing. She made no conscious decision to stand, but she found herself on her feet, moaning, "*No! No!* Jesus spoke those words to *me!* No—he would *not* forgive this man, *this evil, evil man* who stole my father's life and stole my family from me!"

The compassionate eyes of those present—*her family*—turned on her. Some nodded, understanding her outburst, her anger, her denial. A few wept and grieved with her.

She stood, shaking and repeating the word, "no" to herself and to anyone who would listen.

It was Søren who spoke, just to her, but for the rest to hear, too. "God will have mercy on whom he will have mercy, Kari. It would not be mercy if any of us deserved it."

"But . . ." Kari's voice trailed off and she could only weep.

Søren tugged her into his arms and pressed her to his chest. "Let's let Matthew finish, Kari, shall we?"

He signaled Matthew to continue reading. Kari stopped struggling and dropped her head to Søren's shoulder. Matthew wiped his own eyes before he could begin again.

*I wrestled with God for many weeks, for how could a just God forgive* ***me**, a murderer, a rapist, a kidnapper, the most vile of creatures? It was **not just**! It was blasphemous.*

*Still, he would not leave me. He spoke to me again and again, saying these words:* **Behold, I stand at the door and knock. Only you can open the door. Open and find me.**

The strength left Kari's body and she slid from Søren's arms to her knees. *No! It can't be true!*

Then Matthew finished reading the letter, his voice choked with emotion:

*I don't know why, but that day the love of God drew me to him and the blood of Christ cleansed me of my evil. I am not worthy! I am the worst of all men.*

*As death approaches I am no longer afraid of what is on the other side, but I am afraid of meeting you there, in God's kingdom, before I have pleaded for and implored your forgiveness. That I do with these words.*

*Mrs. Michaels, I beg your forgiveness. With every regret of my wretched life, I beg your forgiveness, if only because of the mercy of Christ.*

*Your enemy, whom you know as*
*Dean Morgan*

Most of the family members listening were openly sobbing now, and Kari, stunned into stillness, could hear prayers and even thanksgiving amid the weeping. Matthew, too, was crying, his eyes red with tears. When he was able to speak, he called for their attention once more.

"All our lives we have equated the name of Dean Morgan with the most unspeakable evil. For us, his name has been synonymous with the devil's. That must all change now. *We* must change now."

He wiped his face, his voice breaking again. "Whom God has made clean, we must receive as a brother."

Slowly heads nodded and Kari was astonished to hear more than a few 'amens' answer Matthew. Their acceptance seemed so easily bought, and their acquiescence angered her.

*How can they? How can they forgive and simply "receive" this man on the strength of his own words?* She stood up, clenching her hands into fists.

*Not me. No. I will never forgive him.*

Her back rigid and her eyes straight ahead, she brushed off Søren's hand on her arm. She stalked away toward the house.

And in her heart, she allowed a great, hard rock to settle.

༺ ✴ ༻

# CHAPTER 25

Breakfast on Sunday, with so many of the family having departed, was much more relaxed. The more intimate-sized group sat in chairs in a circle on the lawn, eating, chatting, and laughing comfortably— all except Kari.

Kari was conspicuously absent. She refused to speak to Søren or Ilsa and she avoided the others. With a cup of coffee in hand, she cloistered herself on the screened back porch, keeping herself apart from the others, stoking the seething fires of her anger.

Occasionally she saw someone look toward the porch as though searching for her. *I don't care,* she told herself. But she did care. Along with the anger she felt an ache, as though she had cut off what was dearest to her.

*But how could God forgive Dean Morgan? And how can my family just forgive and accept him? They didn't have to grow up without a family! They weren't the ones who suffered!*

Those thoughts twisted around and around in her head, cinching her anger tighter, widening the divide between her and the others.

It was from the porch that she noticed the black vehicles crawling up the drive toward the farmhouse.

*What now?* she sighed. *Who else could possibly show up? I am sick to death of all of this.*

She didn't know why their approach seemed so ominous, but it did. She saw those on the lawn watching the cars, too. The sounds of children playing and laughing and the chatter of conversations ceased. All eyes were on the approaching automobiles—a sleek black limousine sandwiched between two black Suburbans.

The vehicles drew abreast of the lawn. Before the motorcade had come to a complete stop, the doors of the two Suburbans opened and four men in dark suits stepped out. They surrounded the limo, their heads turning, their eyes scanning the area as though checking for danger.

The skin on Kari's arms crawled. Everything about the manner of the men intimidated her. The four of them had glossy black hair and wore dark glasses. That was all Kari could *see* of them—but her insides were set on edge.

Kari watched Søren leave his conversation on the grass and walk to meet the visitors. When the four men focused their attention on Søren, Kari became afraid for him.

She forgot her anger. *O Lord, please don't let anything bad happen to this good man,* she prayed. *I don't care how much of a pig-headed, stubborn Norwegian-Irishman he is—please don't let anything bad happen to him!*

One of the men blocked Søren's path and placed his hand on Søren's chest. It cheered Kari a little that Søren easily stood several inches over the man! Søren glanced at the hand and back to the man's face. Kari could see him speaking, but she could not hear.

She was relieved when the man nodded and removed his hand. He jutted his chin at two of his companions; they opened the back door of the limousine.

A dark and slender individual stepped from the car. He buttoned his suit coat and glanced around. Even from a distance, Kari could feel something emanating from him. Arrogance? Authority? Danger? She didn't know. Under his bodyguards' watchful eyes, he walked up to Søren and spoke to him.

Kari saw Søren's hand reach for his neck as though to rub it in frustration—or consternation?—she couldn't tell which. As quickly as he lifted it, though, he pulled it back to his side as though resisting the impulse. A moment later he beckoned to Sean and Alannah Carmichael, who hustled over. At a word from Søren, Sean turned to fetch Quan and An-Shing Liáng.

The conversation grew more animated, with Quan taking the lead in the exchange with the man. At one point the slender man stared up the slope to the house and Kari shrank down, hoping he couldn't see her through the screen's mesh. More conversation ensued and then it seemed to Kari that some agreement had been reached.

Quan and An-Shing bowed to the slender man before directing him, closely followed by his bodyguards, toward the front entrance of the house, the one that led to the living room. Søren said something to Sean, who nodded and walked off at a brisk pace. Kari saw him approach the O'Dell brothers.

*My uncles!* she reminded herself for about the hundredth time. The remainder of her anger dissipated, and she felt something akin to a fierce protectiveness grip her. Sean spoke to the O'Dell brothers, who rose and, after some close conversation, followed him.

Kari got a very bad feeling when Søren and Alannah both looked up to where she was sitting and started her way. Their faces were solemn.

They entered the kitchen and then the back porch, and Søren reached his hand toward her. "Kari."

She let him lift her to her feet and spoke to him for the first time that day. "Who are those people? Who is that creepy little man?"

He shook his head. "You wouldn't believe it if I told you."

Alannah looked at Kari, her expression carefully blank. "He wants to talk to us. To you."

"No, thank you. I don't think so." Kari removed her hand from Søren's. "I don't know him. Whatever it is, you deal with it. I've had enough unwelcome surprises."

Søren pressed his lips together and Kari could tell he was reluctant to push her. "I understand why you are . . . angry, Kari, but . . . I think what this man has to say is important. And what he needs to say, he needs to say to you."

"To me?"

"Yes."

Alannah nodded her agreement.

Kari sighed.

When Kari entered the living room with Søren and Alannah, she was relieved to see that the man's bodyguards were not present. Then she noticed their shadows through the window curtains where they had remained on guard outside. Her uncles and Ilsa and Quan were waiting for her, though.

The man who had arrived in the limo stood up as she entered. She turned her attention to him, able then to see his features clearly.

*Why, he's Chinese,* she realized. *And he did not leave* all *his scary men outside.* One of the bodyguards stood post behind the man's shoulder.

"Ms. Hillyer?" The man's enunciation was perfect, cultured—the obvious product of pricey schools, perhaps even European ones.

Before anything else could happen, the front door opened. An-Shing entered with Shan-Rose leaning on his arm. Mixxie slipped in behind them. No one spoke as An-Shing took the time necessary to seat Shan-Rose and make her comfortable. Kari noticed how pale Shan-Rose appeared.

"Ms. Hillyer?" The man asked again.

"Uncle Quan?" Unconsciously, Kari edged toward Quan.

Quan's expression was impassive, guarded perhaps. "Kari, may I present Mr. Wei Tao . . . *Chen.*"

"Chen?" Kari's eyes skidded back to the man's face. "Chen? Are you . . ." Her question trailed off.

"Yes." He nodded to her. "I am Wei Tao Chen, the grandson of Wei Lin Chen."

Mixxie uttered a low gasp, and Kari swung around to make sure Shan-Rose was all right. Shan-Rose, although seated, was leaning on An-Shing. She appeared dazed.

"I have her, Kari," An-Shing assured her.

Kari swung back. "Why are you here, Mr. Chen?"

He nodded again and smiled, but Kari doubted the smile's sincerity. The hair on the back of her neck was prickling.

"My family has long had . . . a connection, both personal and business, with the Li family of Seattle. However, the Li family has never, shall we say, allowed us to forget our family's role in the, uh, *unfortunate events* of the past. I speak of the abduction of the infant, Edmund Michaels and, uh, other things."

"Twist your tail, do they?" Kari sneered. She didn't understand why she seethed with anger, but she did, and she did not much care if she let it show.

Chen examined her, his eyes narrowing. "Yes, that is a colorful description of our relationship. The Lis have made a point of never allowing us Chens to forget our family's role in those, er, *events*."

He smiled again, that expression not reaching his eyes. "Only the day before yesterday a Li family representative informed us that the *daughter* of Edmund Michaels had, at long last, been found."

Kari didn't answer him. She thought he was making an attempt to be pleasant, but her newly embittered heart had only disdain for the Chens.

Kari saw that he noticed. How could he not?

The smile faded from Chen's face at her insult, replaced by a hardness around his mouth. His eyes glittered as he studied Kari.

"I would very much request the privilege of speaking with you on my family's behalf. Perhaps we could be seated?" His polite words did not mask his condescension.

Kari shrugged and looked at Quan, who nodded. "Very well," Kari answered. She took the seat Quan offered her.

When they were seated, Chen said, "Ms. Hillyer, I am the emissary of my family. As I said earlier, the Chen family has been connected with the Li family for many years, by friendship and by business. However, the relationship between our families has, for many decades now, been strained . . . by past deeds."

"You are the *emissary* of the Chen family," Kari repeated.

"Yes."

Kari saw speculative expressions around the room but she ignored them. "If I understand correctly, it was *your family* who arranged the abduction of Edmund Michaels. *My father*." No one could mistake the slur in her tone.

Wei Tao Chen inclined his head, his eyes glittering again. "Yes. That is so. When the Li family learned that the daughter of Edmund Michaels had returned to Denver, word spread quickly. That is why I was dispatched and am here."

He smiled, that same false smile Kari already disliked. "The Li family has challenged the Chen family to make right the wrong that was committed against the Michaels. I was dispatched yesterday to bring a message to you."

Kari kept staring at him, and he at her. It was obvious to Kari that while Chen was tasked with this duty, he considered it beneath him: It was, in essence, an unpleasant obligation.

He made a small gesture with his hand. "As the emissary of my family, I have been sent to express our sincere apologies for the actions of one *individual*, a Fang-Hua Chen, who was the first wife of my grandfather, Wei Lin Chen." He spoke her name with distaste.

"We are related then," a weary voice floated from across the room.

Wei Tao glanced up, surprised. "I beg your pardon?"

Shan-Rose lifted her hand and Chen focused on her. "My name is Shan-Rose Liáng. My mother was Mei-Xing Li."

Wei Tao paled. "So. Su-Chong Chen was your father?"

"His blood flows in my veins but he was never my father," Shan-Rose corrected gently. "Yaochuan Min Liáng was my father."

"Yes; I take your point." Chen swallowed. "Then as you said, we are related. Half second cousins. My father is from Wei Lin Chen's second marriage. And you . . . you were the child Fang-Hua intended to abduct rather than Edmund Michaels."

He pondered those facts a moment longer, sober in his thoughts. "I am sorry. I beg your indulgence for my distraction. My task is quite simple, really."

With a sigh he firmed his mouth to complete the distasteful duty. He stood and took a small lacquered box from the man standing beside his chair. He approached Kari, stopping several feet from her. He bowed low.

"Ms. Hillyer, as the emissary of my family and before you and before these witnesses, I formally beg your forgiveness for the gross misconduct of Fang-Hua Chen. Her actions were and remain a disgrace to our family, even these many years later.

"My father, Wei Long Chen, and the entire Chen family apologize for her behavior. We cannot make up for the grave injustice done to your father and to you. However, we send a gift, and humbly implore that you accept it as a token of our very great regret."

Still bowing, he extended the box to Kari. Kari didn't know what to do. The bitterness simmering in her heart toward Dean Morgan seemed ample enough to cover the Chens, too. The moment dragged on and Kari did not move to accept the box from Chen.

At the last possible second, Quan stepped forward and took it. "Mr. Chen, the family of Joy Thoresen Michaels and Mei-Xing Li accept your apology and this gift. Thank you for coming all this way to right this wrong."

Chen bowed again. "We, my family and I, thank you." He glanced again at Kari and his eyes shied away from the hard reception they found there.

"I must also say . . ." he walked to where Shan-Rose was seated, "our family has watched you from afar, Miss Liáng, for many years. We know of your selfless life."

He stumbled a little in his speech. "We had seen and marked your mother's work with, er, fallen women . . . and your work also, following in her footsteps."

He added, "I will take this opportunity to extend our family's—*your* family's—apology to you for your mother's sake. We did her great, great wrong and yet . . . she lived a remarkable life of service to others. She . . . and you . . . have won our respect and honor."

For all this man's previous arrogance, Kari heard sincerity in his apology and thought she detected a tiny crack in his voice as he bowed before Shan-Rose and remained bent over, his face toward the floor.

Shan-Rose, leaning on An-Shing, struggled to her feet. Mixxie held one arm steady while An-Shing held the other.

Kari watched Shan-Rose place her tiny, faded hand on Chen's head. "Young man, I accept your apology. More than that, I willingly, joyfully forgive you from my heart in the name of my Savior Jesus."

Kari's gut twisted. *How can she forgive him that easily? For all the years of grief and pain suffered by so many?* In her mind's eye Kari was recounting the many crimes Fang-Hua and Su-Chong Chen had committed against Mei-Xing and how she had suffered at the hands of the Chen family.

And yet . . . Shan-Rose, who knew every sordid detail of her mother's suffering, freely forgave the young, arrogant man before her? No recrimination? No demand for justice? Only forgiveness, freely offered?

She saw the look on Mixxie's face. It was probably the same look that was on her own: revulsion and disbelief. And then Mixxie turned toward Kari, a question in her jaded expression.

A challenge.

Discomfited, Kari frowned and looked away. *What does she expect from me? Just to forget all the evil this family has caused? Just like that?*

Kari glanced again at Shan-Rose, so frail but serene. At peace.

Kari stared at the carpet, wondering at Shan-Rose's compassion. Questioning her own bitterness, so newly spawned.

*If Shan-Rose freely forgives this man and his family, should I hold resentment against him and them?* she wondered. *If she shows him grace, what gives me the right to . . . hate him? And how can I hold a grievance toward Dean Morgan, a man long dead, a man who threw himself on the mercy of God . . . in just the same way I did?*

A small, choked sound jerked their attention back to Shan-Rose and Wei Tao Chen. Shan-Rose was bent over Wei Tao Chen, caressing his face, whispering to him. Wei Tao trembled under Shan-Rose's touch but remained bowed, his face toward the floor.

"Dear, dear boy, I pardon you and set you free from your burden of shame. Please know that because Jesus has forgiven me, I now forgive you. I declare this offense paid for in full by the sacrifice of Jesus on the cross. I beg you to surrender your life to Jesus and allow him to cleanse your soul. And I send you away to your family with our peace and blessing."

Kari's lips parted as she sensed the power of God on Shan-Rose. Wei Tao's trembling increased. "I-I thank you, great and honorable Auntie; from the bottom of my heart, I thank you. I-I will go home . . . and seek this Jesus as you say."

"But there is no need to wait, dear one. He is here . . . right here, right now."

And then Kari saw tears—large spatters of tears—fall from Chen's downturned face to the floor. A sob escaped him—the sound of a rending heart—and Kari felt the walls of bitterness she had erected begin to crumble.

*O God! O God! What have I done!* Kari cried in her heart. The crushing revelation of her own sin swept over her.

She gasped and clutched her stomach with both hands. Sinking to her knees, she cried out, "O Lord, I am *so sorry*! Please forgive my hard, bitter heart! Please have mercy on me and on this man, O God!"

The redeeming power of the Holy Spirit rained down in the room—like fine mist it enveloped and washed over them. Søren dropped to his knees near Kari, praying aloud. Others did the same.

Kari was caught in her own intimate encounter with her God, forgiving Dean Morgan and the Chens, extending to them the same grace God was pouring on her.

She did not see Wei Tao collapse to his knees or Shan-Rose and An-Shing praying with him. She did not see Quan and Matthew approach Wei Tao's bodyguard and, kneeling with him, pray over him. She did not see Mixxie slide from her chair to the floor in broken disbelief and Alannah reach her hand out to grasp hers.

Kari saw nothing—nothing except her own flaws in comparison to the perfect, righteous face of God. With his face before her, she confessed her sins aloud:

"Lord, I freely forgive Peter Granger, this same Dean Morgan who stole my father. I forgive him and all he did, Lord," she groaned, "for now I see how much of a sinner in need of forgiveness I am! I set aside my anger and hate, Lord God! I lay them down and I forgive Peter Granger.

"I forgive Fang-Hua and her family. I forgive them all and I release them, Lord. I let them go.

"In Jesus' name, I let them go."

# $C$HAPTER 26

It was hours later. The Chens were gone and the family had dispersed. Cleanup and afternoon chores were done. As the sun sank in the west, Kari and Søren sat alone on the screened-in back porch. They sat cross-legged on the cushioned bench facing each other.

Kari was still teary. "I can't believe how ugly my heart became when I allowed unforgiveness in," she confided to Søren, wiping her eyes. "At the drop of a hat. So easily! And after all the Lord has done for me!"

Søren nodded, understanding. "The enemy of our souls is very crafty, Kari. Offense and unforgiveness are his primary tricks. His goal is to divide us from the Lord and from other Christians. You aren't the first to have been snared in this way."

"It seems like I have so much to learn," she murmured.

"You do, but you will grow if you press in to the Lord. The Bible tells us to 'guard our hearts above all things.' That's your lesson for today. In the meantime . . . you are here, with your family who loves you . . ."

He went silent then, thinking. "What will you do now? Now that you know who you really are, Kari?"

"I-I'm not sure yet."

"You said you had inherited a house in New Orleans?"

"Peter Granger's house. *Dean Morgan's* house! I don't know if I'll ever be comfortable living there, now that I know the truth."

"It's just a house, Kari. And your dad did grow up there."

"Yes." She fidgeted a little. "But I've been thinking that I might . . . build another house."

"Oh? Just like that? 'Build another house.'"

"Um, well . . ."

"Well, what?" He leaned back and sought out her eyes. "What are you not telling me, Kari?"

"Well, I *might* have just bought some land . . . near here, er, the other day. Um, when I borrowed your car to take a check to Jeff for fixing my Caddy."

His brows arched. "Just up and bought some land. Near here. Do tell!"

She started to smile. "How about I show, instead?" She grasped his sleeve and tugged. "Come with me."

As she led him out the back door and down the steps, Max ran out from the barn. "Where are you going? Can I come with you?"

Kari ruffled his strawberry blonde hair. "As far as I'm concerned, you can come with me anytime." Max grinned and grabbed her hand.

Kari led Max and Søren out into the pasture, past the barn. She faced the glorious reds and purples where the sun was disappearing in the western sky and stared across the pastures, across the creek, to the little, falling-down house shadowed in the hollow of the bluff that rose behind it.

"I asked your realtor not to tell you," she whispered. "I told her that I wanted to do it."

"My realtor? Not tell me what?" Søren frowned. "What are you saying?"

She turned toward him, the last of the dropping sun behind her catching the gold in her brown hair and setting it afire. "Søren, *I bought Rose's land.* I bought my great-grandmother's homestead. So, it *will* stay in the family."

"You. Bought it."

She nodded, her smile growing. "Cash on the barrelhead. No dickering. Asking price." She put her head to one side. "You Thoresens *really* drive a hard bargain."

Max's mouth hung open and he frowned, not understanding the adult conversation flowing back and forth over his head. His father ran his hand across his neck and over his head, standing his close-cropped blonde-and-red hair on end.

"You bought Rose's land. You have that kind of money?" Søren squinted as he half-asked, half-demanded.

A chuckle rippled low in her throat. Grinning now, she tossed her head. "Oh, yes; I do. And I think I'll build a little house for myself on Rose's land, my own, *my very own home,* and live over there a while."

"You'll live there."

"Not all the time. Maybe part of the year. Summers possibly— summers in New Orleans are miserable, you know."

Her smile was a little sad. "I have a life and a lot of responsibility waiting for me back in NOLA. I can't ignore it and pretend it will go away. The learning curve will be steep but I have to stop running from it and start becoming the woman God felt could handle all of . . . well, all that is waiting for me there."

Max gripped her hand tighter. "But I don't want you to go, Kari."

She pressed the boy to her side. "I promise I'll be back. You are my family—my real, honest-to-goodness family. How could I ever stay away?"

Kari stared up at Søren, including him in what she said next. "So. So when I build my little summer house and come to stay in it over *there*, I'll look over *here*, the way Rose used to before she and Jan married. I'll pray and study the Bible and *grow*. And I'll let the Lord do whatever it is he's going to do."

She turned her head toward the apple orchard, toward the Thoresen's cemetery. "And I'm thinking about the rest of my family, those whose final resting places are not here . . . where they should be."

"Your parents?" Søren understood immediately.

"Yes. And Grant, my grandfather. I don't know how difficult it would be, but . . . I would really like it if they could be buried here, with their family. Do you think that is foolish of me?"

He followed her gaze. "No, not foolish. I think it fitting that Edmund should, at last, come home and that he should have his real name restored to him. You know the cemetery as it now stands has room for only a few more?"

"Yes. I've thought of that."

"I can't imagine anyone in the family denying Grant, Edmund, and Edmund's bride the last plots inside the fence . . . but it is a big decision, Kari. Why don't you pray about it?"

"Thank you, Søren; I will pray about it. I know their spirits are in heaven, but it would comfort me to see Daddy's grave near his mother's and his father's."

She gazed back across the creek at the picturesque hollow carved into the bluff, trying to see it as Rose had first seen it and fallen in love with it. "I have said this many times in my life, but I've never had a home of my own, you know. Never had a family."

"You've always had a home and you've always had a family," Søren reached his arm around her and squeezed her once. "You just didn't know your way here—until now. God himself has shown you the way."

"Yes, he has. I still can't believe *how* he has, but he has. And I'm so glad, Søren! So very glad."

Søren shoved his hands into his pockets, a gesture now familiar to Kari. "You know that we are glad, too, don't you? So I want you to know: whatever comes of . . . the future, I make you a promise, *KariAnn Thoresen Michaels.*

"I promise that you will never be alone in this world again, never without family, never without friends. I promise I will always be your friend."

"Always?"

"*Ja*, Kari. *Ve er venner*. Forever."

Max threw his arms about Kari and echoed, "Friends always!"

Kari fell asleep that night comforted by a peace her understanding could not fathom. She slept deeply until, in the dark, early hours before dawn, she began to dream.

In the dream she stood on the road that ran east from Søren's farm, out onto the prairie. From far down that road she spied the dust of travelers coming toward her. They walked, some together, some singly, all with their eyes on her.

Then she saw her mother and father. Their faces radiant and joyous, they stretched their arms toward her.

*Mommy! Daddy!*

Daddy reached her first and she could even smell the familiar scent of his cologne on his collar before they touched.

Always, at this point in her nightmares, before his arms reached her, she would awake, filled with that unseen dread she knew only as *The Black*—the dense curtain that hid something vital she could never grasp or recall, something she struggled to remember but could not, the thing that terrified and grieved her so deeply.

But this time . . . this time Daddy's arms curled around her, and she sank onto his shoulder. She was again six years old and he was comforting and holding her.

In her sleep Kari wept in exquisite joy. She clung to his neck, burying her face in the scratchy hollow below his jaw.

*Daddy!* Kari felt she could not get enough of his strength, his warmth, his love. She would never let him go. And she would never need to face *The Black* again.

But she was wrong. The old nightmare began to intrude.

It was dark—so dark! She was on the side of a black, moonless highway. Daddy and Mommy had put her far away from the narrow shoulder of the road, far from the faint outline of their car, broken down on the edge of the highway.

"Wait here where it's safe," Daddy had said. "Watch over them for us." He had hugged her before he and Mommy went back to the car to try to fix it.

Kari had stayed close by her charges—just as Daddy had asked.

Until the blinding lights of the semi tractor and trailer swept down on her parents and carried them away.

In her dream, Kari lay curled into a ball in the dirt and weeds, shrieking, crying, pushing the sight from her mind. With her eyes squeezed shut, she clung to Daddy's neck, clung as hard as she could, blocking out the horror. Blocking out everything. Everything.

Then strong hands pulled at her, trying to pull her away from Daddy.

"No!" Kari protested. In her dream she clung harder and squeezed her eyes shut.

"Kari," Daddy whispered. "Open your eyes."

He wanted her to look? Look at *The Black*?

"No, Daddy! I don't want to!" *No! I don't want to, Daddy!*

Daddy's mouth breathed in her ear; his voice grew insistent. "Please, Kari. Open your eyes."

"No, no! I can't!" Kari squirmed and burrowed deeper into his shoulder.

*"Kari! Open your eyes!"*

Kari's eyes flew open. Unseen hands ripped her from the comfort of Daddy's arms where she had, *in her mind*, hidden from the horror she had witnessed.

She looked around. She was no longer near the side of the highway in the dark. She was in a room, a brightly lit room, struggling, trying to reach—

Those same unseen hands restrained her, but for the first time she could see what she strained *toward*: A man bending to pick up a tiny girl with curly brown pigtails; a woman holding an infant in her arms.

The man spoke to the person gripping Kari, holding her back. "We do want this little girl and the baby boy, but I'm afraid, well, we don't want *her*," the man insisted, thrusting his chin toward Kari, "She's too old and likely too set in her ways. We don't want her."

"Don't worry; it won't be a problem," the faceless woman restraining her declared. "She's been catatonic since we picked her up, night before last. Hasn't said a word until now, in fact. We'll send her into foster care. She's so traumatized she likely won't remember a thing."

"What about their family? Won't someone come looking for them?"

The woman laughed, sounding confident. "Nope. We found the father's address book. The only emergency contact was some church denominational headquarters back east. We called them. Turns out the Grangers were *missionaries* and have been out of the country for years. The woman from the church headquarters said that neither of the parents had any family."

She temporized. "Well, the woman we talked to said that the man *did* have an uncle but that they had no record of his name or where he lived. Apparently, Mr. Granger and his uncle were not close. Hadn't been in contact for years. The situation is perfect, really."

"But what if someone from that church calls back, asking more questions?"

"Oh, we've already sent them a letter. Thanked them for their help; told them we'd located the uncle and that he had made provisions for the burial and the children."

"What about the police?" the man demanded.

"Stop worrying. I have an arrangement with the officers at the scene; I will pay them, too. They will 'neglect' to put the two smaller children into their reports. They will only mention *her*."

"Yeah. We don't want *her*," the man frowned, "but what if she talks?"

"She won't talk." The woman shook Kari and twisted her arm. "You hear me, little miss? You aren't going to remember any of this, got it? If you tell anyone about this, I'll make you wish you hadn't been born."

She slapped the side of Kari's head with her palm and jerked on her arm when Kari cringed and whimpered. Kari tried to pull away but the woman yanked her close. She leaned into Kari's face.

"Look at me!" the woman hissed.

Kari stared, terrified, into the woman's face. She gagged on the woman's cheap cologne infused with cigarette smoke and noted her hard eyes and harder mouth and the plastic tag pinned below her collar . . .

"That nice man and woman are going to give your sister and brother a good home. But if you *ever* mention your sister or brother to anyone—*if you ever say their names*—well, very bad things will happen to them. Do you hear me? In fact, if you ever even *think* about your sister or brother again, I will know it, and I will have that man and woman *throw your sister and brother in a river to drown*."

She shook Kari. "Nod if you understand."

Kari, a deep, dark tunnel opening before her, somehow nodded. Then the tunnel swallowed her and the darkness was spilling over her, filling her mouth and eyes with thick sand until she was choking and retching . . . until consciousness began to fade.

The woman turned back to the man, "See? She won't say a word. Now give me the money."

Kari struggled up from the dark tunnel and tried to scream, "No! You can't take them away! You can't take them!"

They ignored her. Did they even hear her? Or was she screaming her protests only in her own mind? She tried to open her mouth but the dark—*The Black*—flooded in.

"No!" Kari struggled against the sand clogging her throat and managed to croak again, "No!"

And then she *was* screaming. "No! You can't take my sister and brother!"

Kari's shrieks woke the house. A frantic Max thundered down the stairs and reached her locked door first; Søren was right behind him.

"Break it, Papa! Some 'un's hurting Kari!" the terrified boy shouted.

Søren's shoulder popped the flimsy lock and he spilled into the room; Kari was sitting up in bed, still shrieking. Max, scared nearly out of his skin, fell to his knees sobbing—something he would vigorously deny later on—as Ilsa arrived at Kari's door.

Wide-eyed, Ilsa watched Søren sit on the bed and wrap his arms around Kari. He held her, rocked her, and repeated her name. "Kari! Kari, it's all right. Kari, it's just a bad dream. Kari!"

Kari's screams dwindled and she relaxed into Søren's embrace. Instead of shrieking, she babbled.

"I saw, Søren, I saw! Daddy made me look and I saw *The Black!* I saw them!"

Ilsa sat on the edge of the bed facing Søren and took Kari's hands. "You had a bad dream, Kari. You are safe. We have you."

"Yes, Kari. It was just a bad dream," Søren repeated. Max crept up onto the bed and put both his hands on Kari's arm.

"Please be all right, Kari," he sobbed. "Please be all right!"

Kari made an attempt to calm herself, conscious of Max's young, impressionable heart. She shuddered and took a gulping breath. "But, Søren, Ilsa, it wasn't just a dream. I remembered!"

"Remembered what?"

"I remember what happened after they told me Daddy and Mommy were dead! The police took us somewhere and there was a woman. And then a man and a woman, a couple. They-they said, "We don't want *her*! But we want the little girl and the baby!""

It was so clear in her mind now—so very clear. Kari made herself breathe slowly. "Søren. Ilsa. They took them."

"Took who, Kari?"

"They took my little sister and baby brother," Kari whispered.

Søren and Ilsa exchanged confounded looks.

Hours and many cups of coffee later, Kari remained adamant and critical of herself. "All these years! I forgot them all these years! *How could I?*"

At last Søren believed her. "Kari, you were a child. You watched your parents die—you were traumatized. It's not your fault."

"But—"

"Listen, Kari. If someone took your brother and sister, then we'll find them. We will start an investigation."

"I remember . . . seeing some sort of tag on the woman's coat. A name tag. *Marge* something. It started with an 'S.' *Marge S.*"

Søren touched Kari's face. "All right, then. Owen found you; we'll have him start looking for this woman, this *Marge S.* She had to be a social worker, right?

"And we'll get that guy you used in Albuquerque—what was his name? Anthony something? He's an investigator, too, yes? If this woman was a social worker the year your parents died, there can't be many with the name of Marge, can there? And there would have to be a record of your brother and sister's adoption the same year somewhere in New Mexico, right? We will find it."

"But what if we don't find them, Søren? I have forgotten them all these years! What has become of my little sister and baby brother?"

"Do you recall their names, Kari?"

Kari blinked and her brows drew down. "Funny you should ask. I have forgotten them all these years, but . . . but it feels like their names *should be* right on the tip of my—oh! Sammie! My baby brother's name is Samuel, but we called him Sammie!"

"And your sister?"

Kari nodded. "I think . . . Elaine! Yes; Elaine and Samuel. How could I have forgotten?"

"Kari," Ilsa said quietly, "They aren't babies any longer. You said your sister was three and you were six? She would be, what? Thirty-five, now? Your little brother would be thirty-two? They aren't children anymore. They aren't in immediate danger."

Kari considered what Ilsa had said. "I-I know you're right. But I'm having trouble seeing them . . . grown."

She thought a moment longer. "And now that I remember them, it means I am not the sole heir of Peter Granger—his estate does not belong exclusively to me."

Kari turned to Søren. "I had already been praying about using my inheritance for God's glory. I still intend to do that with my portion, but now Clover and his firm will need to make provision for Elaine and Samuel in the probate, too."

"Those are their names? Elaine and Samuel?" Ilsa asked.

"Yes," Kari whispered. "Sammie was only a baby."

Søren nodded. "Kari, your homecoming is the answer to decades—*generations*—of prayer and trust that the 'lost are found.' But maybe . . . maybe we should take a wider view."

Ilsa, Max, and Kari looked to Søren to explain.

"Maybe you are the first-fruits of our family's faith, Kari."

He took her hand and set his jaw in determination. "You are the first to be found, but the others are coming. Until then, we trust the Lord—and we never stop searching. Because *we know* that in God the lost are found."

## THE END

Read an excerpt from the glorious conclusion of
**A Prairie Heritage**

# ALL GOD'S PROMISES

An Excerpt from

# ALL GOD'S PROMISES

## AUGUST 5, 1991

The screen door slapped closed behind her as Kari ran down the porch steps. She crossed the farmyard, paused near the pump, and drained the last of the coffee from the mug she held.

In the hour before dawn, Kari had helped Max feed and milk the cows and goats, feed the chickens and gather their eggs, and muck out the stalls. Now morning chores in the barn and outbuildings were done, and she had a few minutes to herself before Ilsa called them to breakfast.

The sun was cresting the horizon at her back; its heat warmed Kari's shoulders, warning of the scorching day ahead. Showers had pummeled the ground the night before, leaving mud and puddles in their wake, but the glowing ball of fire rising in the sky east of them was already wicking the moisture from the earth, shrouding the rain-soaked fields in mist.

Kari's gaze fastened on a point unseen, west, across the misty pasture.

*It's all right,* she thought. *The haze will burn off quickly.*

Besides, she knew the way by heart.

With wisps swirling around her boots, Kari strode down the slope, away from the house and far down the pasture, until she reached her destination.

Kari had made a habit of spending this precious part of each morning the same way—standing on the bank of the stream that separated Søren's farm from the abandoned homestead on the other side.

She found her usual vantage point. The creek bank was strewn with wild poppies. Their long stems lifted sleepy crimson heads to greet the rising sun; their furled buds peeked above the mist that swirled across the ground and about Kari's feet.

Kari often sat among the poppies in the late afternoon, but not this morning, not while the soaked earth was surrendering its moisture. Instead, she stood on the bank of the stream and peered across its dancing water to the other side. Through the mist, she spied the shape of the little house that, these many generations later, was still standing, although near to falling down.

*The remains of Rose's house,* she thought. *Rose and Jan's home. Where they raised their daughter, Joy.*

*Joy.*

*Joy, my grandmother.*

*My* real *grandmother.*

Those three words still stunned her. With shaking fingers, Kari wiped cobwebs from her eyes and wished the empty mug she clutched in her other hand still held steaming coffee.

"Must have more coffee," she muttered. A moment later she added, "Actually, what I really must have is more of you, Lord."

Of the many revelations of the last three weeks, finding Jesus had been the best. The most . . .

Earthshaking.

Life-changing.

Awe-inspiring.

*Finding Jesus has changed everything!*

She snorted under her breath. *Actually, he found me, 'cause I sure wasn't looking for* him!

And then the chuckle caught in her throat and became a sob. *O Jesus! I am so glad you found me! When I think of the intricate thread you spun to guide me to you, your hand is evident.*

*It is nothing short of a miracle.*

A miracle?

Yes, a miracle.

And the precious land across the creek was hers now. Rose and Jan's falling-down house was hers now.

*Someday I will build a house near theirs and spend part of my life looking from the other side of this creek.*

That idea boggled her mind, too.

*So much has changed.*

Too many aspects of Kari's life had changed in such a short period of time, and she struggled daily to process it all.

Only four months ago, Kari had been nursing the wounds of her husband's betrayal and their subsequent divorce. The divorce, finalized in January, had required her to sell their home in Albuquerque and split the proceeds with David, the man who was now her ex-husband. But Kari had nowhere to go after the house sold.

She had been flat broke, without a job or the prospect of one. She had been balancing on the sharp edge of desperation.

*I didn't even have enough money to rent an apartment until the sale closed and paid out. And the proceeds from the sale of the house, once they paid out? That money would have kept me for a mere six months.*

And then a letter had arrived. A letter from *Brunell & Brunell, Attorneys at Law*, New Orleans. The words still burned in Kari's memories.

*. . . If you are KariAnn Alicia Hillyer, born in 1952 to Michael D. Granger and Bethany M. Granger, and legally adopted by William and Eleanor Friedman in 1961, would you kindly contact our offices at your earliest convenience?*

*Brunell & Brunell has been managing Mr. Peter Granger's estate for many years now and we are most anxious to settle it.*

*Cordially,*

*C. Beauregard Brunell, Managing Partner*

*Brunell & Brunell, Attorneys at Law*

Kari stared with unseeing eyes into the distance. The memory of the disdain she'd felt as she read that letter remained with her, strong and vivid.

*This has to be a joke or a scam*, she had reasoned. *I mean, what kind of nut names their child 'C. Beauregard,' for heaven's sake?*

But it had been no joke. It had not been a scam.

The man named in the letter as Peter Granger had left the sum of his earthly possessions to his estranged nephew, Michael Granger. Apparently the breach between Peter Granger and his nephew, which occurred when Michael was in his early twenties, had been deep—so deep that uncle and nephew had never spoken again.

Years after their parting, however, Peter Granger had regretted his actions and had sought to be reconciled to Michael. Although Peter had spent large sums on private detectives, the investigators had been unable to locate Michael. Peter Granger had died in 1964, leaving all he possessed to his nephew—or, should his nephew have died, to his nephew's offspring.

As the attorneys of Brunell & Brunell had explained to Kari, this Michael Granger had been *her father*. That meant that she, Kari, was the sole heir to Peter Granger's estate.

Why had it taken so long for the attorneys to find her?

Kari sighed and rehearsed the details. Again.

Kari's father and mother had died on the shoulder of a New Mexico highway when a truck crashed into their disabled car. The year had been 1958, and Kari had been six years old.

Unable to locate any relatives to take custody of Kari, the State of New Mexico had placed her into the foster care system. Later she had been adopted by Nell and Bill Friedman. Even later, Kari had married David Hillyer. Their seven-year marriage had ended when David announced he was leaving Kari.

It wasn't until this past January, when The Albuquerque Journal published Kari's divorce decree, that Brunell & Brunell's in-house sleuth had, at last, located the heir to the Granger estate.

And so, in a matter of days, Kari's situation had been dramatically, irrevocably altered. Kari had inherited Peter Granger's home in New Orleans and the entirety of his estate—an estate so large that its size, at first revelation, had bewildered and terrified her.

"It still terrifies me."

Kari shuddered. Her grip on the cold, empty coffee mug tightened. "O Jesus, please help me to make peace with all these changes."

The size of the Granger estate was not the only change Kari was adjusting to. No, it had been only the beginning, for then, mere days later, Kari had discovered a journal—the journal of one *Rose Thoresen*.

Kari had been acquainting herself with Peter Granger's sizable house. After she had explored every room on both floors and in the attic, she had decided to see what secrets the old detached garage held.

To Kari's immense delight, the garage had housed a classic, candy-apple-red Cadillac Coupe de Ville—securely covered and mounted on blocks. Under its wraps, the car was in like-new condition.

According to the attorneys of Brunell & Brunell, Peter Granger had bought the car off the showroom floor in 1959 when he was 87 years old. However, because of his advancing years, he had not driven it much.

When their client passed away in 1964, his attorneys had found the car in a neglected state, its tires flat and ruined. They hired a specialty company to remove the car's wheels, set the chassis on blocks, drain the car's fluids, and secure a custom-fit cover over it.

After Kari discovered the vehicle, her attorneys had the Caddy towed to a classic car restoration company. When the company delivered the restored, ready-to-drive Coupe de Ville to Kari, she had been thrilled.

4

*Classic Caddy!*

But as much as Kari loved the Caddy, the vehicle had not been the garage's most meaningful treasure. In the attic above the garage, Kari had found an old trunk filled with her grandmother Alicia's evening gowns—beautiful relics of the 1910s and 20s. Kari had lifted each dress from the trunk with love and care, exclaiming over their exquisite beading and lace work.

But under those gowns? At the bottom of the trunk, concealed by boxed hats, shoes, and handbags, and tied up in a diaphanous silk scarf, Kari had found a small cedar box. The box was locked; glued about its girth was a paper seal with the year "1957" scrawled across the paper in a shaking hand.

The date on the seal had puzzled Kari, for Alicia Granger, whose belongings filled the trunk, had died in 1927. Everything in the trunk—with the exception of the cedar box—predated the sealed box *by three decades.*

Someone had hidden the little cedar box away. Someone had, quite intentionally, placed the box where it would not easily be found.

Kari had searched for and discovered the tiny key that fit the lock on the cedar box—it was glued to the underside of the trunk's lid. Once she had unlocked the box, she found a velvet bag. In the bag were two items: a sealed envelope and a small red volume, its binding faded and cracked with age.

The ink on the envelope had faded over time; nevertheless, Kari was reluctant to break its seal until she knew to whom the envelope had been addressed.

The book, however, was not sealed. The inscription inside the brittle cover read:

*Rose Thoresen*
*My Journal*

The journal's opening date was April 25, 1909.

Eighty-two years ago!

Although Kari had no idea who this Rose Thoresen had been or why her journal should be at the bottom of Kari's grandmother's trunk, the account recorded in the little book became the most precious, most important portion of Kari's inheritance.

"O Rose!" Kari moaned as her fevered mind traced the details of the last three weeks.

*Because of you, my life has changed.*

Kari had devoured the words penned in Rose's own hand. What Rose had written during a two-year period had set Kari's heart afire. But when Rose's account ended abruptly on April 12, 1911, Kari could not relinquish the woman or her words.

She longed to know more about this Rose Thoresen: What had become of her? How had her journal ended up in Peter Granger's attic, buried beneath Alicia Granger's clothing? And what of Palmer House, the home in Denver Rose had described with such passion? What had become of the girls who had lived there?

. . . And what of the God Rose loved and served?

Kari had to find answers to the questions that burned within her.

Less than four weeks ago, armed with the scant few clues the journal provided, Kari had left New Orleans en route to Denver in search of the mysterious Rose Thoresen. Rose's journal had led Kari to . . . *such grace!*

Rose's journal had led Kari to Palmer House and the elderly woman who still lived there and could personally speak of Rose Thoresen.

Rose's journal had led to the revelation of a heartbreaking event of decades gone by, an event that had defined the families it touched.

It had led to the faith-filled prayers of generations.

It had led to the infant boy who was lost—and to his daughter *who was found.*

And it had led her to Jesus!

*I found you, Lord. I found you! Because of Rose's journal, I found you, and I found the truth about myself. I found my real family—three uncles and a gazillion cousins and dear friends.*

*You stripped away decades of deceit, Lord. You showed yourself to be faithful to those who trusted in you, but . . .*

*But I still have so many unanswered questions.*

*Questions like, who am I really? I am not KariAnn Hillyer, not KariAnn Friedman. I am not even KariAnn Granger.*

*Peter Granger was not my great-uncle. Alicia Granger was not Peter Granger's sister-in-law, was not my father's mother, was not my grandmother.*

*They tell me my father's real name was not Michael Granger but Edmund Thoresen Michaels, and that he was stolen from his parents, Joy and Grant Michaels.*

*They tell me that my real name is KariAnn Thoresen Michaels.*

*But who is that person? Who is Kari Michaels?* Kari wondered again.

She shuddered. *I am drowning in change; I am mired in uncertainties.*

Kari stirred from her deep reverie. She blinked and sucked in deep, reviving breaths. Her reflections always ended here—frozen. Stuck at this place of unanswered questions and concerns.

The concerns were not only for herself, either, because the startling revelations of the past week had unlocked another door, the door to Kari's earliest childhood remembrances.

For her entire life, a mental fog had imprisoned Kari's memories—particularly her recall of the night her parents had died. Now, like the morning haze that surrounded her on this creek bank, that fog was lifting away under the intense light of truth.

Her lost memories were returning.

Kari sighed. *It is almost too much, Lord. Too much—and yet not enough.*

As far back as Kari could remember, she had suffered nightmares and debilitating anxiety attacks.

The attacks came on her whenever she dreamed of or tried to recall her parents, whenever she sought to remember their touch, their voices, or even their faces. Or if she thought about the night they died.

For when she dreamed or thought of them, *The Black*—a dark, terrifying curtain—would engulf and smother her. Once she was caught in the grip of a full-on panic attack, the episode usually ended in Kari losing consciousness.

To avoid these attacks, Kari had taught herself not to think of her mother or father. She had learned not to think or speak of the night they perished.

But eight nights ago, *The Black* had lost its hold over her.

Eight nights ago, Kari had been dreaming of her father—his comforting voice, the familiar smell of his suit, the scratchy roughness of his cheek on hers. As usually happened, the precious moments were interrupted and Kari was soon caught in the suffocating clutches of another nightmare featuring *The Black*.

This time, though, her father had *not* disappeared. He had encouraged her to fight the dark curtain.

"Kari," Daddy had whispered. "Open your eyes."

He wanted her to look? Look at *The Black*?

"No, Daddy! I don't want to!" *No! I don't want to, Daddy!*

Daddy's mouth breathed in her ear; his voice grew insistent. "Please, Kari. Open your eyes."

"No, no! I can't!" Kari had squirmed and burrowed deeper into his shoulder.

Her father had been insistent.

*"Kari! Open your eyes!"*

Inside the dream, Kari had opened her eyes—and she had remembered.

She had remembered the truck hitting her parents and their disabled car on the side of the road. She had remembered the sirens and flashing lights, the police coming and finding her.

She had been unresponsive to them. For hours, perhaps days, activity had swirled around her, but she had been locked in her own body, unspeaking, unmoving.

"Catatonic," she'd heard a woman say from a far distance. "She won't talk."

That same woman had assured the man and woman holding a little girl and an infant that Kari would not present a problem—except that Kari had woken then, screaming, "No! You can't take them away! You can't take them!"

The woman had shaken Kari and twisted her arm. "You hear me, little miss? You aren't going to remember any of this, got it? If you tell anyone about this, I'll make you wish you hadn't been born."

She had slapped the side of Kari's head with her palm and jerked on her arm when Kari cringed and whimpered. Kari had tried to pull away but the woman had yanked her close.

"That nice man and woman are going to give your sister and brother a good home. But if you *ever* mention your sister or brother to anyone—*if you ever say their names*—well, very bad things will happen to them. Do you hear me? In fact, if you ever even *think* about your sister or brother again, I will know it, and I will have that man and woman *throw your sister and brother in a river to drown."*

That was Kari's first encounter with *The Black*. The darkness had spilled over her, had filled her mouth and eyes with the choking sensation of thick sand, and had stolen the very breath from her body—until consciousness had faded.

But in the dream eight nights ago, Kari had, after thirty-three years, remembered. Now that she saw what lay behind the curtain, *The Black* would never again hold her in its death grip.

*I remember my little sister and baby brother now.*

For the umpteenth time she berated herself. *How could I have forgotten them? How could I have not remembered them all these years? How could I?*

She frowned. *And where are they? Who took them? Where are they now?*

*O Lord, I'm so grateful to be free of The Black! I am so grateful that you are restoring my memories of Sammie and Elaine. So grateful for everything.*

She took a slow, deep breath. "But it is time. Time to start looking for them."

ॐ ❀ ॐ

**End of Excerpt**

# About the Author

Vikki Kestell's passion for people and their stories is evident in her readers' affection for her characters and unusual plotlines. Two often-repeated sentiments are, "I feel like I know these people," and, "I'm right there, in the book, experiencing what the characters experience."

Vikki holds a Ph.D. in Organizational Learning and Instructional Technologies. She left a career of twenty-plus years in government, academia, and corporate life to pursue writing full time. "Writing is the best job ever," she admits, "and the most demanding."

Also an accomplished speaker and teacher, Vikki and her husband Conrad Smith make their home in Albuquerque, New Mexico.

To keep abreast of new book releases, sign up for Vikki's newsletter on her website, **http://www.vikkikestell.com**, find her on Facebook at **http://www.facebook.com/TheWritingOfVikkiKestell**, or follow her on BookBub, **https://www.bookbub.com/authors/vikki-kestell**.

Faith-Filled
Fiction™

Made in the USA
Columbia, SC
31 July 2017